T5-AGT-441

A Garland Series

THE BALLAD OPERA

A Collection of 171 Original
Texts of Musical Plays
Printed in Photo-Facsimile
in 28 Volumes

Volume III

HARLOTS, RAKES, AND BAWDS

Selected and Arranged by
Walter H. Rubsamen

Garland Publishing, Inc., New York & London

1974

Library of Congress Cataloging in Publication Data

Rubsamen, Walter Howard, 1911-1973, comp.
Harlots, rakes, and bawds.

(The Ballad opera, v. 3)
Facsims.
CONTENTS: Cooke, T. Love and revenge; or, The vintner outwitted; an opera. 1729.--Odell, T. The patron; or, The statesman's opera. [1729]--Colonel Split-Tail; a new opera. 1730. [etc.]
1. Ballad operas--To 1800--Librettos. I. Title. II. Series.
ML48.B18 v. 3   782.8'1'208s [782.8'1'208]   74-4445
ISBN 0-8240-0902-9

Printed in the United States of America

Contents

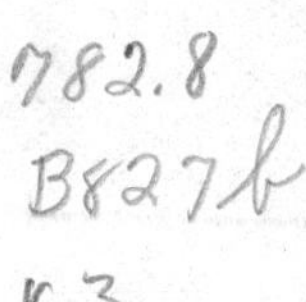

Love and Revenge

Bibliographical note:
This facsimile has been made from a copy in the
Clark Library
University of California at Los Angeles

LOVE *and* REVENGE;

OR, THE

VINTNER *Outwitted*:

AN

OPERA;

As Acted at the

NEW THEATRE

IN THE

HAY-MARKET.

LONDON:

Printed for *J. Clark* under the *Royal Exchange* in *Cornhill*; *T. Worral* at the *Judge's Head* near the *Temple-Exchange Coffee-House* in *Fleet-street*; *J. Jackson* near St. *James's* House; and Sold by *J. Roberts* in *Warwick-Lane*.

(*Price. One Shilling*)

1729

Persons of the DRAMA.

Heartfree, *Father to* Charlot, *and Uncle to* Louisa.	*Mr*. Wells.
Rovewell, *in Love with* Bellamira.	*Mr*. Mullart.
Trueman, *in Love with* Charlot.	*Mr*. Lacey.
Brainworm, *a Cheat*.	*Mr*. Fielding.
Mulligrub, *a Vintner*.	*Mr*. Stoppelaer.
Shameless, *a Felon*.	*Mr*. Dove.
2d *Felon*.	*Mr*. Hicks.
3d *Felon*.	*Mr*. Cross.
Brush, Rovewell's *Man*.	*Mr*. Wells.
Simon, *a Barber's Boy*.	*Mr*. Hicks.

A Fiddler, a Drawer, Constable, Watchmen, *&c*.

WOMEN.

Bellamira, *a Courtezan*.	*Mrs*. Mullart.
Charlot, *in Love with* Trueman.	*Mrs*. Clarke.
Louisa, *in Love with* Rovewell.	*Miss*. Wood.
Mother Pearce, *a Bawd*.	*Mr*. Reynolds.
Mrs. Mulligrub, *the Vintner's Wife*.	*Mrs*. Nokes.

Scene *LONDON*.

TO THE

Right Honourable

THE

Lady *ROMNEY*,

THIS

OPERA

Is most humbly Dedicated

by her Ladyship's

Most obedient

and devoted

humble Servants

The Company of Comedians in the

HAY-MARKET.

PROLOGUE

Spoke by Mr. Fielding.

As routed Squadrons quit the hostile Field,
O'erpowr'd by Numbers, yet too brave to yield,
Their Troops they rally, and their Loss supply,
Once more resolv'd the Fate of War to try;
So from successless Toils our Heads we raise,
Studious to please, and proud to aim at Praise;
Your Smiles alone can animate the Stage,
Inspire with comic Mirth or tragic Rage;
New Life we breathe, when crown'd with your Ap-
And glory to pursue so just a Cause: (plause,
Honour commands, and we obey the Call;
And if we fall, 'tis no Disgrace to fall;
In great Attempts alone true Merit lies;
He well deserves in Fight who bravely dies.
No envious Motives shall our Labours stain;
By no mean Arts we wou'd our Glory gain;
Unenvy'd we behold each rival Stage,
And with them happy in a grateful Age;
Wheree'er the Muse and her Attendants dwell,
Still may they flourish as they merit well.
* *From Scenes of old our present Tale we draw,*
And make with Joy your Taste alone our Law;
We dare not on the comic Scene rely,
Till to the sprightly Song for Aid we fly;
Henceforth we may, if thus we gain your Praise,
Improve your Pleasures, and our Merits raise.

---

* The first Play that was wrote on this Plan, was by one *Marston*; it was alter'd by Mr. *Christopher Bullock*, almost 100 Years after; and on the same Plan put into the Form in which it now is.

LOVE and REVENGE;

OR,

The VINTNER *outwitted.*

ACT I. SCENE I.

Rovewell *and* Brush.

Brush. AY, good Sir, consider what you are doing; can a Man of Sense find any Excuse for falling downright in Love with a common Woman? Alass! he regards me not—pray, Sir, hear me—

SONG I. Peggy grieves me.

Rove. *Give me, Heaven, the Power to range,*
And rifle every Flower,
Thro' all the sweet Delights of Change,
And lose no joyful Hour.
The Nymph who, lavish of her Charms,
To more than one gives Fire,
Has Raptures left to bless these Arms,
And gratify Desire.

Why are Prostitutes such odious Things? *Bellamira's* beautiful as the most chast; can Custom

 spoil

ſpoil what Nature made ſo good? if ſo, the Birds and Beaſts are happier far than Man, in whom an inborn Heat is held no Sin.

Bruſh. Good lack! good lack! what a ſtrange Thing it is to ſee a Man in a Dream with his Eyes wide open! I beg, Sir, you will hear me a little, and not let your Paſſion run away with your Reaſon; 'tis want of Philoſophy makes Men fall in Love at all; but nothing leſs than Want of common Senſe could ſuffer a Man to grow paſſionately fond of a Whore, as you, Sir, know *Bellamira* is, you know ſhe has been kept by your intimate Friend *Trueman*, and now left and deſpiſed by him.

Rove. Impudent Raſcal! ceaſe your Impertinence.

Bruſh. You may call my Love what you pleaſe, Sir, but I muſt, and will be your Friend; I cannot be dumb, and ſee you run headlong into your Ruin, as moſt certainly you do, while you indulge this dangerous Paſſion for ſuch a vile Woman.

Rove. Very good! Have you done I pray?

Bruſh. Read your Hiſtories, Sir; ſtudy your Philoſophers; examine your Poets; and you'll ſee how full their Writings are of the wicked Examples of lewd Women. Oh, Sir, they are the moſt giddy, uncertain Motions under the Heavens, and he is happieſt, who has leaſt to do with them.

SONG II. Trumpet Minuet.

Would you paſs all your Moments in Health and in Joy,
Let a Friend and a Bottle thoſe Moments employ;
The Nights which you give to your Friend and the Glaſs
Are free from the Stings that attend the falſe Laſs.

Rove. I would fain know how thou cam'ſt by all this Wiſdom and Experience.

Bruſh. I have juſt enough to make me beware of that ſubtle Sex. Women, Sir, do Things beyond

yond any Man's Underſtanding, they give you cauſe to love them to day, and Reaſon to hate them to morrow, they pleaſe you this Minute, and torment you the next; and, in ſhort, Sir, if you'll excuſe a Proverb, brought out of the Kitchen, they'll give you Roaſt-Meat, and beat you with the Spit.

Rove. I know not by what ſtrange Fate I am hurried on, but I muſt enjoy her, be the Conſequence what it will.

SONG III. Young *Feſton*'s Minuet.

Thro' every purple Vein
Her Charms like Magick run
I glory in my Pain
And yield to be undone,
A thouſand glowing Loves
Lie wanton in her Eyes,
While from each Part,
With thrilling Smart
A pointed Arrow flies.

[Goes out.]

Bruſh. Undone indeed, poor Gentleman, good Counſel is but thrown away upon him. O Cupid! Cupid! how unſearchable are thy Myſteries?

[*Goes out.*]

II. SCENE *Changes.*

Trueman *and* Mulligrub.

True. How now, *Mulligrub*, thou ſeem'ſt in great Diſorder.

Mull. And have Reaſon to be ſo, Sir.

True. Why what's the Matter.

Mull. I have been in queſt of that Rogue of all

all Rogues *Brainworm*, but to no Purpoſe— O, Sir, he has play'd me ſuch a Prank lately—

True. Prithee what was it?

Mull. Why, Sir, he brings a fine Lady with him to my Houſe one Night, whom he told me he had juſt married, and that ſhe was a great Fortune; upon which, you may think I grew extremely civil: A Supper was beſpoke, which was upon the Table in a Trice; then he draws out a Bill of twenty Pounds, and deſired me to let him have the Money for it, the Goldſmith living too far to ſend to at that time of Night; I very readily, like an Aſs as I was, comply'd with his Requeſt, took the Bill, and withdrew.

True. Very good, pray go on.

Mull. Then comes up a blind Harper, and cries, Do you lack any Muſick? he cries play, the Drawer is nodded out, who obeys to be ſure, beleiving he would be private with the Gentlewoman, and 'tis for *Flaſh*'s Intereſt, you know, Sir, to wink at ſuch Things.

SONG IV. Young *Damon* once the happy Swain.

The God of Wealth is painted blind,
A Satyr on the human Mind,
None from the Cenſure's free:
When he commands we all obey,
And to the Night convert the Day,
And neither hear nor ſee.

True. Well this was but right and civil; but what happen'd afterwards.

Mull. Having eat his Supper, and perceiving no one in the Room but the blind Harper, whoſe Eyes Heaven had ſhut from beholding Iniquity, he packs up my Plate, and with that and his Whore, decently conveys himſelf out of the Window: The poor Harper plays on, wiſhes the empty Diſhes good Stomachs, and plays on ſtill; the Drawer returns, cries do you call, Sir? but out,

and

and alas! the Birds were flown, Sir, flown; Laments were rais'd——

True. Which did not pierce the Heavens.

Mull. Flash bawls, my Wife Skriems, I heard the Noise, and thunder'd, the Boys flew like Lightning, and all was in an Uproar; my Plate being gone, and the Thief after it, I bethought myself of my Bill, and ran with all speed to the Goldsmith's, to receive the Money; but now comes the worst part of the Story, the Bill prov'd forg'd, I was seiz'd, *Brainworm* ran away, my Word would not be taken, I was found guilty of Forgery, lost my Reputation, and was put in the Pillory for being cheated, which you'll own was hard, Sir.

True. And is it impossible to find this Rogue *Brainworm* again?

Mull. He walks invisible, Sir, you may as soon find Truth in a Gamester; Sincerity in a Lawyer; or Humility in a Priest. He changes his Dress and his Lodgings as often as a Whore does her Name and her Lovers. But I hope I shall one Day have the Pleasure of seeing the Rogue hang'd in Hemp of his own beating. And so, Master, your humble Servant. [*goes out.*]

True. This is a most agreeable piece of Justice. This Vintner is a Knave, who has cunning enough to cheat all who put Faith in him, and Wit enough to avoid the Punishment of his own Crimes, but, by the Malignity of his Fate, is ever suffering for other Men's Roguery, and no Body pities him.

SONG. V. Says Roger to Moll.

When Sharpers are bit,
We're pleas'd with the Wit
Of those who the Plunder share.
The Law we pass by,
Bid the Judge shut his Eye,

Reprizals

Reprizals for Justice declare,
To cheat the Deceiver is fair.

Ha, here comes the ambo-dexterous Knave.

Brainworm enters.

So Mr. *Brainworm*, you are in great haste, upon a hot Scent, I suppose; what Darling of Fortune are you going to run down?

Brain. Fye, Mr. *Trueman*, you should not judge so hard.

True. The Accusation of *Robin Mulligrub*, the Vintner, concerning the forg'd Bill, will give your Acquaintance just Cause to suspect you.

Brain. Sir, there is not a greater Rogue in the whole Company of Vintners, and *They are a numerous Body.*

True. His being a Knave is no Proof of your Innocence, you shou'd have appear'd in Court and disprov'd his scandalous Accusation.

Brain. The Rogue knew I could not confront him in the Court, having a swinging Action out against me, so took the Advantage of my Misfortunes, and thought to vindicate his own Reputation by aspersing mine. The Villain keeps an Estate of 200 Pounds a Year from me, which my Father mortgag'd to him for a thousand Pounds; and now he would rob me of my good Character.

True. Which you have been a Stranger to these twelve Months at least. Come, come, your scandalous Practices, your Tricks and Cheats are pretty well known, consider you have but few Friends, little Reputation, and less Money; and if you should be taken hold on by the Law, and convicted, you'll hardly escape its Punishment.

Brain. As you say, Sir, being poor, I shall have but little Hopes. Few Men indeed suffer for Dishonesty, but for Poverty many: the greatest

greateſt Part of Mankind being Rogues within or without the Law, the little Thieves are hang'd for the ſecurity of the Great.

SONG. VI. Have ye ſeen Battledore Play?

Have ye ſeen Weſtminſter-hall,
Where the Lawyers ſhould meet to do Right Sir?
Or have ye noted the Stock-Jobbers bawl,
Where, in Exchange-Alley,
They cheat the World daily,
As Knavery were all their Delight Sir?
The firſt 'mong themſelves your Chattles divide,
And ſteal whole Eſtates with the Law on their Side,
And as to the others,
They'll trick their own Brothers,
Their Fathers or Mothers,
But who does attempt Sir,
Their Crimes to admoniſh?
While poor Rogues you puniſh
For Trifles, and tuck up in Hemp Sir.

Take my Word, Sir, there are greater Rogues ride in their own Coaches, than any that walk on Foot.

True. I wonder a Man of your Underſtanding and Education can deſcend to ſuch an infamous way of living. Have you no Friend that——

Brain. When I had Money, Sir, I had many Profeſſors; but Neceſſity is the Touch-ſtone of Friendſhip, which is but a Shadow that attends the Sunſhine of our Proſperity, that once over clouded with adverſe Fortune the other ſtrait becomes inviſible.

SONG. VII. Young Jemmy.

When in my Chariot debonair
I flutter'd in the Ring,
What Flower was half ſo ſweet or fair
Or who like me cou'd ſing.

But lo! the sudden turn of Fate,
I flutter now no more,
The Love of all is turn'd to Hate,
None ever prais'd the Poor.

True. I am well assur'd of your Misfortunes, but if you endeavour to maintain a good Reputation, you stand fair for Preferment, you are well qualify'd for a Place, and have Merit enough to countenance your Pretensions.

Brain. With Submission, Sir, I find you have studied Books more than Men, you know what should give a Man Pretensions to Preferment, but are ignorant of what does. Alass! Sir, Virtue is of little Use, for he who has the most Money, is now the worthiest Man, no Matter by what Means he obtains it.

True. You are very satyrical, but I have always made one Observation, that the greatest Knaves are the most severe Judges, they view all Mankind in the false Mirror of their own Actions, and when they can't defend their Villanies, think to extenuate them by pleading the Example of their Betters.

SONG VIII. The Twitcher.

So scarcely you meet
Any Drab in the Street
But tells you with impudent Face, Sir
If her Manners you blame,
She counts it no Shame,
To do what is done by her Grace, Sir,
To do, &c.

Brain, Ay, Sir, if Example could justify Actions, there would be no Theives in the World, Possession would then be the only Right, Children might turn their Fathers out of Doors, Servants their Masters; Perjury, Rebellion, and Blasphemy, would all become lawful; I could say more

more, Sir, but great Men's Vices muſt be ſacred ——where *Scandalum Magnatum* is puniſh'd with ſuch Severity, and Money an Argument to prove Black White, poor Men dare not ſpeak the Truth of their Betters.

True. I own few Men have the Senſe to bear honeſt Satyr as they ought.

Brain. Sir, give me leave to recommend this ſmall Treatiſe to your Peruſal, 'tis call'd, *beware of a Knave*; 'tis a Deſcription of Mankind, written originally in *Spaniſh*, by an excellent Maſter in the thriving Art of *Chicane*.

True. What ſhould I do with it? Think'ſt thou I am ſo baſe to ſtudy ſuch vile Arts, or ſo indigent to practice them?

Brain. I mean no Reflection, Sir, on your Honour or Fortune; but in theſe cozening Times, it is more neceſſary to ſtudy other Men than our ſelves; 'tis proper to know falſe Dice, tho' a Man ſcorns to make uſe of them; ah, Sir, there's many a Man, that you may think honeſter than my ſelf, would, if Opportunity ſerved, look in your Face, and pick your Pocket.

SONG IX. In the Fields in Froſt and Snow.

Lend the Knave a watchful Eye,
Who to act his Part, Sir,
Talks of nought but Honeſty,
To diſguiſe his Heart, Sir,
Full of Flams
Lies and Shams
All he meets
Tricks and cheats
Your Care defeats
Looks upon you with a Smile
And your Pocket picks the while.

[Picks his Pocket.]

The Times, Sir, are alter'd, Intereſt is now the Spring of all Actions, and for a Man to ſeek Preferment

ferment with nothing but a good Reputation, would be as fruitless, as to sue for an Estate in *Forma Pauperis*.

True. I wish it were otherwise — however the worst of Times can't make an Impression on true Virtue, for that's a Rock, which stands immoveable in the most violent Storms of Fortune; there is somewhat for you, and all I have about me, faith, at present: Be honest, and I shall be proud to serve you. [*Goes out.*]

Brain. A good civil Fellow! I pickt his Pocket, and he, generously rewards my Ingenuity: Be honest, ha, ha, ha, I thank you, Sir, no, I love no such starving Virtue, I should be proud to serve you! I despise a Life dependant on others Courtesy: There are Fools enough in the World for witty Men to strike their Fortunes out of, and he only deserves to live, who has the Art to extract Gold out of Lead. [*Goes out.*]

III SCENE *Changes*.

Mother Pearce *and* Bellamira.

M. Pearce. Good, honey Daughter, do not indulge thy Passion thus: You hear *Trueman* is to be married, true; he has abus'd you, right; he has cast you off, ay; he will leave you to the wide World, what then? tho' blue and white, black and green, forsake you, may not red and yellow entertain you? Is there but one Colour in the Rainbow?

Bell. Cease your sententious Nonsense, let me go loose as the Winds, when mad, when raging Mad, 'twas you that first seduc'd me, besieged my Heart with Tales of *Trueman*, repeated all his Charms, and made my Virtue fade like Flowers with too much Heat, which when you saw, you let him know how small my Strength, and how he best might Conquer; and he, lovely Tyrant,

Tyrant, found it true, and never ceaſed till he had vanquiſh'd all; leave me, thou that haſt brought my Soul and Body to Nothing.

M. Pearce. To Nothing! I'll be ſworn I have brought you to all the Things I could, how can you belie my Induſtry thus? I have made as much of you as a Woman of any Conſcience could, I help'd you to no ill Chapman, Miſtreſs, none of your ſwaggering Blades, that Sin *gratis*, and bully a Woman into Compliance; none of your Lawyers Clerks, your pitiful Half Crown Sinners; but wealthy Citizens, that cou'd pay for their Paſtime.

Bell. I'll be revenged, nothing but dire Revenge ſhall appeaſe my Rage. Nor Fear, nor Shame, ſhall check my daring Spirit.

SONG X.

What Pow'r can Woman's Heart reſtrain
When Love has got poſſeſſion there?
Virtue and Reaſon plead in vain
To keep us from the tempting Snare:
All Laws both human and divine
We Sacrifice at Cupid's *Shrine.*

Oh! how can I bear the Thoughts of his paying thoſe Vows to another Miſtreſs, which are due to me alone? and which he has breath'd ſo oft in Kiſſes on my Boſom? Falſe Traitor! tell me why didſt thou praiſe this Monſter to me?

M. Pearce. I did praiſe him, I confeſs I did praiſe him; I ſaid he was a Fool, an Unthrift; a true Whore-Maſter, a conſtant Drab-keeper. I did praiſe him; but what, the Wind is turn'd, the Puppy's grown wiſe on a ſudden: But will not his Friend *Rovewell* go down with you? he is wealthy, an almoſt out of his Wits for Love of thee. Then he is a fine Gentleman, and a ſtrong one too, or I have no skill; he has a Leg like a Poſt, a Brow like a Bull, and a Noſe of goodly Expectation. *Bell.*

Bell. I hate *Rovewell* for his Friend's ſake, and could murder all who know him; I cannot live without the perjur'd *Trueman*, nor ſhall he live to boaſt his Infidelity. O! I could curſe the happy *Charlot*, whoſe Charms have robb'd me of his Heart.

Rovewell *Enters.*

Rove. What clouded in Grief, fair *Bellamira?* in ſuch a Sorrow ſat the Queen of Love, when in the Woods ſhe mourn'd her young *Adonis* dead.. Light of my Soul! my Heart's ſublimeſt Joy, why doſt thou weep? why like diſtilling Roſes waſte, diſſolving thus thy Beauties in a Dew?

Bell. Oh! 'tis not in the Power of Eloquence to eaſe my tortur'd Heart, talk not of Love, 'tis talking of my Ruin. I can no more give Credit to your deluding Sex, whoſe Pride is to deceive.

Rove. Condemn not all our Sex, for the Inconſtancy of one: Indeed I cannot play the Hippocrite, and court thy Beauties like one, whoſe Love hangs only on his looſe Tongue.

Bell. Juſt ſo he talk'd, and I, fond Fool, beleiv'd, and tired him out with Love: But you are all falſe, inconſtant, faithleſs Tyrants, and Betrayers even in that very Moment that ye gain us.

Rove. Come, come, you muſt conſent, this Body ſure was form'd for Love's ſweet Exerciſe. Oh! how ſhe fires my Soul! [*Embracing her.*]

M. Pearce. Ah! ah! ah! cunning Gipſy! how ſhe works him up by Degrees! well, if I had bred her of my own Body, ſhe could not have been more like me —— ſee, ſee, how prettily ſhe manages him, her Eyes bid him come on, and her Hands keep him off: The beſt Way in the World to ſhut up his Underſtanding and open his Purſe.

SONG XI. Abbot of Canterbury.

The Damſel who deals in the Buſineſs of Love
To its Pleaſures ſhould only by Intereſt move,

Should

Should check her strong Passions her Wishes disguise,
And what her Heart longs for, deny with her Eyes.

Bell. This Man, whom I abhor, through all my Rage I see has Passion for me; raise it, ye Powers, 'till it becomes so high, to be employ'd a fatal Instrument in my Revenge [*aside*] Nay, pray Sir, leave the neglected.

Rove. Can such Beauty be neglected? Oh! happy, happy *Trueman*, who uncontroll'd may range o'er such a Field of Love!

M. Pearce. Ay, there was a Rapture for you! that's ten Pieces more in our Way, if she is Rhetoric Proof, and don't consent too soon.

Bell. Oh, my poor forsaken Heart!

M. Pearce. Ay, marry, that Sigh was artfully flung in.

Rove. Alass! *Bellamira*, why dost thou waste those precious Drops in Memory of a false ungrateful Man? Sorrow will fade the rosey Tincture of thy Cheeks, and blast thy springing Beauties; he saw thee not who left thee, such Charms could not be seen and slighted; uplift thy Eyes, and see in me a Man, who doats upon thee. Oh, I am all Faith and Constancy.

M. Pearce. So, now she should begin to dissolve a little, there's an Art in all Trades; in ours the Difficulty is to know when to come on, and when to stand off; the Man's Passion is now at the Top; and Things cannot long stand at the Top. It is an old Observation I have made, that when the Pot boils over, it cools itself: But then all the Fat's in the Fire. Ay! that is not as it should be —— she should encourage him a little, or the hot Fit will be over, and he'll degenerate into cool Reason again.

Rove. My Love grows high, and rages in me like a Storm, believe my Vows; but you have been deceiv'd that way already; therefore thou dear, thou lovely, injur'd Fair one, credit my plain

plain Sincerity, I will be grateful in what Way you pleafe. Take me to your Embraces.

Bell. Do you then believe me fuch a Creature, that have no Senfe, but Appetite, the brutal Part of Love? I am not yet abandon'd to fuch Wretchednefs.

Rove. Forgive me, who too haftily run o'er what ought to have been faid of my vaft Paffion.

Bell. Think on the Sin.

Rove. 'Tis none, but a vile Impofition on the Law of Nature, contriv'd by cunning avaricious Fathers, to ftop the rapid Tide of generous Love, and tye it down to fordid Intereft: Defire is a Law, fet down by Nature's Counfel, and not to be difputed.

M. Pearce. Ah, Marry, there's Logick! there's an Argument to encourage Trading in our way. If I had not left my Pocket-Book and Pencil at Church laft Sabbath-Day, I would have taken it down in Short-hand.

Bell. Think how you'll fuffer in your Reputation.

Rov. No Matter what the Fools of Form fhall fay, I love to pleafe my felf and not the World, I chufe not with others Reafon but my own, which points out you as my fupreameft Good. Dull Cuftoms I defpife, I'll follow Nature's Laws; Beauty was made for Ufe, it gives Defire, Defire is natural, and what is natural cannot be a Sin.

M. Pearce. An excellent Doctor of Fornication, I vow, and argues learnedly for its Practice.

Bell. Well, I will confent —— fhall I?

M. Pearce. Ay, that's prettily acted to the Life, the Girl has nickt her Cue.

Bell. Shall I, or can I, truft again? oh Fool! how natural 'tis for Women to believe! will you not forfake me then?

Rove. Oh, no, my Love fhall ftill increafe, ftill grow upon Enjoyment; upon thy Lips I fwear, by this, and this, and all the thrilling

Joys

Joys to come, not Time it ſelf ſhall leſſen my Affection.

M. Pearce. So, ſo, the Articles are ſign'd, I'll leave them to exchange Preliminaries by themſelves. [*Goes out.*]

Bell. Can you believe this Heart, that has been uſed ſo ill already, can truſt to feeble Vows? will you be bravely kind? and as a Proof of your avow'd Affection reſolve upon a Deed, would ſhake a Soul that is not fix'd in Love.

Rove. If within my Power, ſuppoſe it done.

SONG XIII. Love leads to Battle.

Thro' Scenes of Battle Love may command me,
I to his Service devote my Days;
Nor Fire, nor Sword, nor Seas ſhall withſtand me,
What Love commands my fond Heart obeys.

Bell. Oh! *Rovewell!*

Rove. My Life! my Love!

Bell. Thou haſt ſtolen into my Heart—indeed I do not love *Trueman.*

Rove. Then I am happy.

Bell. Nay, I hate him.

Rove. You make me bleſt.

Bell. I wiſh he were not your Friend, for I hate him, by this Kiſs I do.

Rove. I love to feel ſuch Oaths, ſwear again.

Bell. Oh *Rovewell!* I have made a Vow..

Rove. What Vow, my Charmer?

Bell. I dare not tell —— endeavour to forget me, as I muſt all Mankind. [*Going.*]

Rove. Stay —— rack me not thus with thy unkind Delay.

Bell. As long as *Trueman* lives, I muſt not, cannot, dare not love.

Rove. Then he muſt die——

Bell. Would I was any Thing, ſo he was dead.

Rove. Will you be mine when he is dead?

Bell. Will I! yes, by my Hopes of dear Revenge I will, and only yours, inviolably yours.

Rove. Why then he dies, his Doom is fixt as Fate.

Bell. Now I am ſure you love me.

Rove. Beyond Expreſſion, no Words can tell the Tranſport of my Heart. Oh, let me claſp thee in my deſiring Arms.

Bell. *Rovewell*, forbear, while *Trueman* lives you cannot take Poſſeſſion of my Love; and of his Death this Token I require: He has a Ring, dear to him as his Breath, a Pledge of Love from his fair *Charlot*; I have often try'd, with cunning Art, to get it from him, but even in the ſofteſt Hours of Love, when I thought his Heart was mine by his proteſting Tongue; he ſtill refus'd me, ſwearing his Life and that muſt part together——now bring but this Ring, and you ſhall ask nothing I'll deny.

Rove. What kill a Man! my Friend too? let me not think of it——Reaſon avaunt——Love now commands my Heart. Madam, farewel, I'll give a fatal Proof, how well I love. [*Goes out.*]

Bell. Miſchief ſucceed, my Heart ſwells high with Vengeance; the Friend will kill his Friend, him that ſurvives I'll hang; then the Ring! that gives Malice larger Scope — Oh! the Joy 'twill be to torture *Charlot*'s Heart, the Hatred which proceeds from Love neglected, out-does the moſt inveterate Malice, and thus,

The baſe, the perjur'd Race of Men ſhall ſee
How injur'd Woman can reſent in me.

[*Goes out.*]

IV SCENE *Changes*,

Heartfree *and* Trueman.

Heart. Sir, I am very well ſatisfy'd, you need not make any Apology, if my Daughter likes you as well for a Husband, as I do for a Son-in-Law, you ſhall be happy as you pleaſe to think yourſelf.

True. I am only ſorry for *Charlot*'s Sake, that my Fortune is not equal to my Love.

Heart,

Heart. Look you, Sir, if my Daughter likes your Perſon, the Smallneſs of your Fortune ſhall not be a Bar to your Pretenſions. Underſtanding is better than Land I ſay, and I had much rather marry my Daughter to a Man that wants Money, than to Money that wants a Man.

True. Sir, this is a Bleſſing——

Heart. That's as it proves, look you, young Fellow, no ſet Speeches, the Girl has an Inclination for you, I believe, by what I have heard and ſeen, and if you can have Love enough to make one another happy, I'll endeavour to preſerve it by a good Fortune.

True. If I can make my Way to *Charlot*'s Heart I ſhall be the happieſt of Mankind.

Heart. If a good Word of mine will do thee any Service, thou ſhalt not want it, for I like thee, and think thee a proper Match for my Daughter. I am for an Agreement of Years and Hearts in Marriage; I am not ſo old to forget I was once young, I would not have her Hand given in one Place, when her Heart is in another. But, young Man, here have been Tears ſhed upon your Account, but that's *entre nous*, here was a naughty Woman of your Acquaintance Yeſterday with my Daughter, I wiſh you have done honourably with that Creature.

True. Sir, ſhe is the vileſt of her Sex, I confeſs I have had an Affair with her, and now I have broke it off, ſhe purſues me with implacable Hatred.

Heart. Well, well, we have all had our Follies, every one muſt have his Time of Probation, you'll know the Value of a vertuous Woman the better: But I'm inform'd your Friend *Rovewell* is grown paſſionately fond of her.

True. Even to Madneſs, I never knew a Man of Senſe ſo beſotted.

Heart. *Rovewell* has not acted like a Man of Honour to my Niece *Louiſa*, his Love to that Creature has robb'd him of his good Manners as well

well as his Senſe, or he might have made ſome tolerable Excuſe for his Neglect of the Girl.

True. Tho' *Rovewell* is, at preſent, bewitch'd by this pernicious Woman, yet I dare ſay he is a Man of ſo much Honour, that he will acquit himſelf to your Satisfaction.

Heart. Your Pardon, Sir, I do not think ſo, I know how to reſent an Injury——but here comes my Daughter.

Charlot *Enters.*

Good morrow, Child, here is an Acquaintance of yours has been asking me to accept of him for a Son-in-Law: I won't put you to the Bluſh by asking if you like him, tho' that's a Kind of Tell-Tale Look, my Dear, and if I have not forgot the Language of the Eyes, I can tell how your Heart beats.

Char. Lord, Sir, this is ſo ſurprizing.

Heart. Pſha! Pſha! what you have not dreamt of a Husband to Night, I warrant; well, well, *Charlot*, without more ado, Child, if you have any Love to diſpoſe of, here's your Chapman, and if you can give him your Heart, I'll give him my Conſent, and a Coral for your firſt Boy. Up to her, young Fellow, and cut a Caper into her Heart. Be but impudent enough, and I'll warrant Succeſs.

SONG XIII. Three Sheep-ſkins.

If of a Woman's Heart you would ſecure you.
Be briskly bold, and ſtorm her Fort with Fury
Be not tame,
Nor think of Shame,
For then ſhe can't endure ye.

Odd methinks I long to ſee them a-bed together, well, I'll leave open the Door of Opportunity, and Cupid ſpeed ye. [*Goes out*]

True. This, Charlot, is a Happineſs beyond our Expectation.

Char. Now am I ſorry my Father has given his Conſent.

True.

True. How, Madam, are you ſorry for it?

Char. Yes, for methinks I don't like you half ſo well, there's a Pleaſure in overcoming Difficulties, and I ſhould ſtrangely like to be run away with.

True. This is all Romance, when ſhall be the happy Day, my Charmer?

Char. Ay, now 'tis my Charmer, I wiſh Marriage don't make me your Tormentor. I have obſerv'd among ſeveral of my Acquaintance, that a very few Months have chang'd the moſt violent Raptures into a cold Indifference.

SONG. XIV. Princeſs Royal.

I.

When to the Bed
Of Love we're led
To yield our Virgin Pride,
What Oaths are ſwore
They'll love us more
Than all the World beſide.

II.

But when away
No longer they
The Marriage Promiſe keep
But love each Fair
Too much to bear
And leave their Wives to weep.

Enter a Servant.

Ser. Sir, Mr. *Rovewell* is below, and deſires to ſpeak with you immediately about important Buſineſs.

True. I'll wait upon him; you'll excuſe me, Madam; but in the mean time, conſider, now we have ſecur'd your Father's Conſent, I ſhall think every Hour an Age, till the happy Moment is fix'd.

SONG XV. No more invade me. 1ſt. Part.

No more, my Treaſure,
Delay our Pleaſure,
Oh give me Poſſeſſion of thy Charms.

Char

Char. *Then all is over,*
The kneeling Lover
Turns to a Tyrant, whilst in these Arms.
True. *Fair one believe me,*
Char. *You will deceive me,*
And when possess'd of, will slight these Charms.
True. *No one can slight such heavenly Charms.*

End of the first Act.

ACT. II.

Trueman and *Rovewell.*

True. So, my Friend, what News from Babylon? How does the Woman of Sin?

Rove. O Trueman! sure Nature never before produc'd so damn'd a Devil.

True. Which way does the Wind sit now?

Rove. I have escap'd falling into the worst of Mischiefs; I have been tempted to thy Death, and in my Heat of Passion, inflam'd with wild Desire, and robb'd of Reason, by her bewitching Charms, have vow'd to kill thee.

True. What is the rampant Strumpet grown mad for the Loss of her Man? now do you consider, *Rovewell*, what you might have done, urg'd by your Love, and her inveterate Malice? then think betimes, and let this drive her from your Heart. How can'st thou neglect the profer'd Love of fair *Louisa*, and court the lewd Embraces of so vile a Creature?

Rove. I must pity poor *Louisa*; but oh, my Friend, that Creature, vile as she is, has got into my Heart, and Reason cannot drive her thence, You have a Ring?

True. Which she would have.

Rove. Ay, and thy Heart too, and as a Proof that I have kill'd you, she commanded me to bring that

that Ring, which ſhe was well aſſur'd you would not part from but with Life, for which Deed, and only which, I may poſſeſs her Love.

True, And then you vow'd to kill your Friend?

Rove. My Paſſion, not I, for when my Reaſon interpos'd, I could not bear to look upon myſelf; I am almoſt mad to think I doat upon a Body, whoſe Soul, I know to be ſo foul; oh! that I could maſter my impatient Appetite!

True. You may, you can, call Reaſon to your Aid and ſtifle this Low, and ſenſual Fire.

Rove. Oh! no, my Friend, there is no Reaſon in Deſire, I fear, I ſhall be urg'd to act ſome Deed, whoſe Name is hideous: I dare not truſt myſelf.

True. No.

Rove. It is my Fate, I muſt enjoy her.

True. You ſhall, here take this Ring, ſhew it that fair Devil, it will confirm her in the Belief that I am kill'd, and my Abſence at the ſame time will put it out of Diſpute.

Rove. But if it be given out that you are ſlain, and that by me, I ſhall be ſeiz'd, where ſhall I find you?

True. At Burniſhe's, the Goldſmith, I dare truſt him with the Deſign.

Rove. Pardon me, my Friend, every Man has his Follies, eſpecially the Lover.

SONG XVI. The Play of Love.

Oh God of Love, what human Art
Can ward againſt thy fatal Dart?
To what hard Fate are Lovers bound!
Since nought can cure
What we endure,
But the fair Pow'r that gave the Wound.

[*goes out*]

True. Now Repentance, the Fool's Whip o'ertake thee, I'll be a Friend to thee, but not to thy Vice, no Goldſmith ſhall ſee me, I'll make thee know and feel thy Errors in the ſevereſt Senſe.

[*Goes out.*]

II SCENE

II. SCENE *Changes.*

Brainworn *Enters.*

Brain. The Devil take all Dice; I wiſh I could forbear touching a Box while I live; for what I get by the Follies of other Men, I loſe by my own. The Silver Tankard which I ſtole from *Mulligrub* (as great a Rogue as myſelf) I ſold for five and twenty Pounds, and loſt it in two Hours at Hazard I have now but one ſolitary Shilling left. Heigh ho! —— let's ſee, ſomething may be made of this Barber's Boy perhaps.

Simon *Enters.*

So, my Lad, where art thou going?

Sim. To ſhave Mr. *Mulligrub*, Sir.

Brain. Oh! that's well, I was juſt going to your Maſter's.

Sim. To my Father's you mean, Sir.

Brain. Ay, right, thy Father's thou art a pretty Boy; I have heard my Friend *Mulligrub* commend thee much.

Sim. He is my Godfather, Sir.

Brain. Yes, he told me ſo, and your Name is—

Sim. Simon Smack, Sir.

Brain. A wiſe Boy, well, Simon, I was juſt going to thy Father's to borrow an Apron, a Baſon and Razors to ſhave Mr. *Mulligrub* in a Frolick; but now I've met thee, I'll take thine.

Sim. O dear! Sir, what do you mean?

Brain. No harm, my Lad, only a Frolick. Here's Six-pence for thee, thou ſhalt find thy Things at thy Godfather's if you come back in half an Hour.

Sim. 'Tis very well Sir, I thank you. [*Goes out.*]

Brain. This is lucky enough, *Mulligrub* is ſo near ſighted that he can't diſcover me thro' my Diſguiſe, and if I can fix my Birdlime Fingers on any thing that's moveable, I'm ſure my Conſcience will not fly in my Face. I take more Pleaſure in cheating that Rogue than any Body I know; and if I don't ſhave him now, I ſhall ſay my Wit and my Razors are both very blunt.

SONG

SONG XVII. Hey boys up go we.

Thus his Foes in each Shape,
Old Proteus *defy'd;*
Now a Bull, now an Ape,
His Godſhip bely'd.

Thus I cheat Foe or Friend,
Before their own Eyes;
Firſt I anſwer my End,
Then ſhift my Diſguiſe. [*Goes out.*

SCENE III. *Changes.*

Mulligrub *and his* Wife.

Wife. 'Tis right, I aſſure you, juſt two and forty Pounds. [*She lays a Bag on the Table.*

Mull. Well, I'll ſend home the Punch-Bowl; then I muſt go and taſte ſome Wines, which are juſt landed; but I ſhall come home to Supper.

Wife. Truly, Husband, I begin to diſlike this Vocation of ours; what ſignifies mincing the matter, you know we do cheat moſt abominably, and truly it goes againſt my Conſcience.

Mull. Hold your peace, Woman, what have we to do with Conſcience? Don't we keep a Tavern? 'Tis time enough to talk of that when we have got an Eſtate. Go, go, mind your Buſineſs; ſcore falſe, with a vengeance.

SONG XVIII. Old *Orpheus* tickled, *&c.*

Oh never let Conſcience interfere,
While we are getting Money, my Dear;
Be all your Care to cheat and to pleaſe;
When we are rich, we'll repent at eaſe.
With a Twinkum, twankum, twang.

Go, go, I ſay, and take my Advice with you.

Wife *sings.*] SONG XIX. *Same Tune.*

I'll warrant you, Spouse, I'll play my Part,
Since Cheating, you say, must be my Art;
My Conscience I'll quiet, never fear,
And when we're rich, we'll repent, my Dear.
With a Twinkum, twankum, &c. [*Goes out.*

Brainworm *enters like a Barber.*

Mull. How, now, who are you?

Brain. Your Barber, Mr. *Smack*'s Journeyman, at your Service.

Mull. Pray, what's your Name?

Brain. *Timothy Truth.*

Mull. A very good Name; but where's my God-son? he us'd to shave me.

Brain. *Simon*'s gone to shave Parson *Grub*, the Curate, and my Master fear'd you might be in haste, and therefore sent me——Will you be pleas'd to sit down, Sir? [Brain. *puts the Cloth about him.*

Mull. How long have you been a Barber?

Brain. About a Year, Sir.

Mull. Then you did not serve your Time to one?

Brain. No, Sir, but I am willing to do any thing for an honest Livelihood: A wagging Hand, you know, gets the Penny. [*Making a Lather.*

Mull. An ingenious Fellow!

Brain. Yes, Sir, I have nothing else to trust to.

Mull. What was you bred to?

Brain. The Sea, Sir.

Mull. What made you leave the Sea?

Brain. Ill Luck, Sir.

Mull. What was it?

Brain. If the Devil forsakes me now, I'm undone. [*Aside.*] In my first Voyage, Sir, we met with three *Algerine* Pyrates, which we made all the Sail from we could; but being deep laden, we found it impossible to escape them, and having heard so much of the Barbarity of those People, I chose rather to trust to the Mercy of the Waves, than become their

Pri-

Prisoner; I therefore prevailed with our Cooper to put me in a Barrel, with six Biskets, then cork me up, and throw me overboard.

Mull. And how didst thou escape at last?

Brain. Merely by Providence, Sir. I sail'd about upon the Sea twelve days, and had nothing to live on but the Biskets——Hold up your Head, Sir.

Mull. Twelve days! O Pox! that could not be, *Tim.*

Brain. 'Tis true as I'm an honest Man—At last I was cast on Shore, and thinking any Fate better than starving, I struck out the Bung, and putting my Head out for a little fresh Air, found I was on *Greenland.*

Mull. On *Greenland, Tim?* How did you know you was on *Greenland?* Was you ever there before?

Brain. The Devil confound that Question—— [*Aside*] O, Sir, by a white Fox, a Creature that was never seen in any other Country; it came galloping down to the Sea-side, and I, at his approach, pull'd my Head into the Barrel again.

Mull. A white Fox! how big was this white Fox?

Brain. Somewhat bigger than a large *Flanders* Mare. So, as I was saying, he came to the Barrel, and smelling whereabout I was, roar'd like a Lion; but as Providence would have it, in that very Moment a Fly stung his Buttocks, he turn'd round to rub himself against the Barrel; his Tail lying over the Bung-hole, I clap'd hold of it with both Hands; the Fox frighten'd gallop'd as if the Devil was at his Tail, and dragg'd the Barrel, with me in it, over Hedge and Ditch, for three and twenty Miles together; at last he jump'd into a Wood, and running full speed between two Trees, which stood close together, stav'd the Barrel to pieces; away ran the Fox, and out came I.

Mull. O! *Tim*, this muſt be a Gun, *Tim.*

Brain. Every Word true, or I wiſh I may never ſhave any more. So, Sir, I travell'd to the Port, where I met an *Engliſh* Veſſel, and thence I came home in her.—Shut your Eyes, Sir, or my Ball will make them ſmart.

Mull. I find you have been a great Traveller. Was you ever in the Popiſh Countries?

Brain. In moſt parts of *Italy*, Sir, and am acquainted with all the Monaſteries. O Lord, Sir, my Travels would make a large Hiſtory of curious Knowledge. I have been in *Finland*, where I have ſeen Ships ſwift ſailing againſt the Wind; where the Men can ſhoot Weſtward, and kill the Game that flies behind them Eaſtward——Take Time by the Forelock, ſays the Wiſeman—I muſt leave the Vintner in the Suds.

[*He takes the Bag off the Table, and goes out.*

Mull. O! Pox, theſe muſt be damn'd Lyes, *Tim*——Come, make haſte tho'. I can't but laugh, Ha, ha, ha, when I think what a Bed-roll of Lyes thou haſt told off hand, with thy Barrel, thy white Fox, thy Horſe-ſhoe, and *Finlanders.* Thou doeſt not take me for ſuch an Aſs to believe all this, ſure? Why don't you ſhave me? Why *Timothy*, I ſhall be blind with winking——*Tim*—[*ſpitting*]—why *Tim*—[*ſpitting*] O Lord, my Mind miſgives me. [*Feels on the Table.*] Why Wife, Wife—O! the Devil, my Money is gone——Why Wife, Wife!

Wife *enters.*

Wife. What's the Matter with you, Mr. *Mulligrub*, that you make ſuch a noiſe?

Mull. Where's the Barber?

Wife. He's gone, are you not trim'd?

Mull. Trim'd! yes I am trim'd with a vengeance. Did you take the Money off the Table?

Wife. Not I, as I'm an honeſt Woman.

Mull.

Mull. O Lord! I have wink'd to ſome purpoſe now. Why the Devil could not you ſtay in the Room, while I was ſhaving, you are never in the way when you may do a Man any good.

SONG XX. Red Houſe.

When Women are wanted they'll not come near us,
And when we are moſt ſad, the leaſt they can chear us;
How much we miſtake in purſuit of our Pleaſure!
We graſp at our Torment, and think we've a Treaſure.

Wife. *Unhappy is the Marriage State;*
A Race of Sorrow is her Life,
Whoſe Spouſe in each hard Turn of Fate,
Lays all the Blame upon his Wife.

[Mulligrub *goes out.*

Wife. Go thy ways for a ſnarling, couzening Cuckold. This Fellow's Humours grow intolerable to me: When we were firſt married, he thought nothing too good for me, and now he is ever finding fault; he pretends to be jealous, and I'll take care it ſhan't be without Cauſe. 'Twill be but Juſtice; for I know he has been falſe to me, with my own Maid too.

SONG XXI. Young *Philoret.*

The youthful Pair
Their Pleaſures ſhare,
Nor think they'll e'er be ſated;
But when we're wed
All Joys are fled,
If Spouſe grows jealous-pated:

If once to her
He does prefer
Some Trull for Nymph divine,
No Wife's to blame,
Who does that ſame,
And pays him in his Coin.
And pays him, &c. [*Goes out.*

SCENE III. *Changes.*

Mother Pearce, Bellamira, *and* Brainworm.

Bell. Oh! Impudence, am I reduced ſo low to be ſollicited by thee?

Brain. By me! why, *Bellamira*, not by me? Here's that which makes me equal with the beſt; Honour and Love are both deriv'd from this. [*Shews a Purſe.*] 'Tis the Baſis of all Friendſhip, and I'm ſure the moſt prevailing Argument with your Sex.

SONG XXII. Young *Bacchus* when merry, *&c.*

1. *Come haſten together*
Bright Men of the Feather,
Of the Sword, the Tupee, or the Pen;
In your ſev'ral Parts,
Diſplay all your Arts,
Which e'er made Women Captives to Men.

2. *Behold here a Bribe,*
Out-does all your Tribe,
Shall the Sex of their Coyneſs defeat;
This glittering Snare
Shall lead all the Fair
From St. James's, *to bleſs'd* Lombard-ſtreet.

M. *Pearce.* By my Conſcience, what he ſays is right, and the wiſer we for knowing what to prize. What ſignifies a Title? 'Tis but an empty Sound, and Sound is but Air, and a Woman can't live upon Air. And what is Honour but the Workmanſhip of Opinion? Marry, there is no thriving in this World if you prefer any thing to Money.

Brain. Right, Mother *Pearce*, you ſpeak like an Oracle, 'tis the grand Mover of all things.

M. *Pearce.* Ay, by my troth is it, and the Quinteſſence of Virtue too. No Diſgrace is like Poverty; for if you obſerve, none but poor Harlots are call'd Whores; get but Money, and you are above Scandal; you may go to Church without bluſhing;

blushing; nay, upon my Honesty, you are company for the Parson of the Parish. I remember a pretty Couplet written by an old Bard, to this purpose,

O London! *say what Shame thy Town reproaches,*
Poor Whores are whipt, and rich ones ride in Coaches.

Brain. Right, the first beat Hemp in *Bridewell*, and the later drink Tea with the Justices.

Bell. Cease your hellish Doctrine.

Brain. Come, *Bellamira*, whatever you may think of me, I was once a Gentleman, though poor, depriv'd of all; I have a Heart that pants to venture on when Beauty calls; and this small Stock, which my own Industry has got, I must employ in the dear Cause.

M. *Pearce.* Take it, *Bel*, I have an Apothecary's Bill to pay.

Bell. Hell take you, and that together.

SONG XXIII. When bright *Aurelia.*

All Dignities in Church and State
May yield to pow'rful Gold;
But, such the wise Decrees of Fate,
The Love of Sexes, and the Hate,
Are neither bought or sold.

Cease your Importunities, you Witch, you Destroyer of my Peace.

M. *Pearce.* O! bless me, was ever such an uncharitable Creature? Go, you would be asham'd to use a Woman of my Years thus, if you had any Grace. Have you forgot how kind I have been to you, Hussy? Did I not take you from the Waggon, a poor, ignorant, aukward, Country Girl, with nothing but an old Stuff-Gown to thy Back? And instead of making thee a Servant, did I not put thee into a goodly Condition, give thee fine Clothes, and bring thee into the best Company? Well, well, the Sin of Ingratitude is worse than the Sin of Witchcraft. Where do you think of going when you die, for using me at this rate? [*Crying.*]

[*Crying.*] Have I not help'd you to Culls of all Nations, and am I thus rewarded? Well, *Betty Pearce*, go thy ways, thy kind Heart will bring thee to the Hospital.

Brain. Take this small Tribute of my conquer'd Heart, I may in time increase it.

Bell. Base, servile Wretch! who liv'st by Noise and Riot, can'st thou believe, that after *Trueman's* Love, I will receive a Villain to my Arms?

Brain. These Insults are unjust for proffer'd Love. All that I have I offer, my Heart and Gold; and if the first's despis'd, the last may plead.

Bell. Take no advantage o'er my slighted Charms; for though that prejur'd Man, false *Trueman's* gone, I yet have Beauty that may awe the Man whose Looks would make thee tremble: and dare you stand my Power?

Brain. I dare, and am resolv'd upon a Conquest. [*Seizes her.*

Bell. Sirrah, desist, nor tempt too far my Rage. [*Goes out.*

Brain. I will not leave you so.

When Love commands, we must pursue the Chace;
None but the Resolute obtain the Race.

[*Goes out.*

M. *Peace.* Go thy ways for a cunning Knave. I am no Judge of a Man if he succeeds not: He has what will debauch half our Sex, Money and Impudence.

Trueman *enters disguis'd.*

What would you have, Sir? would you have aught with me?—— A proper handsome Fellow!——but ill dress'd. [*Aside.*

True. Madam, I am a decay'd Gentleman.

M. *Pearce.* Alas! you can be nothing worse.

True. This is a Recommendation of me to you, whom I would gladly serve.—[*Gives her a Letter.*] How one Baud will impose upon another! They are like Lawyers in the way of Business, give them but a Fee, and they'll go through thick and thin. Mother *Frowzey* has here recommended me for a Stallion,

Stallion, in order to anſwer my Deſign on *Rovewell.* [*Aſide.*

M. *Pearce.* Well, Siſter *Frowzey* gives you a goodly Character, you are obliged to her.——And ſo am I; this Fellow will pleaſe the Counteſs of *Skimmington* admirably, and my Lady *Night-and-Day*, and the *Alderman's* Wife out of the City, and, by my troth, he'll ſerve my own turn.—I like his Symmetry, he is well built; my Blood is not ſo cold as to make me paſt Pleaſure. Well, I vow he is a portly Fellow.

[*Bellamira within.* Help! help! undone, O help!

True. Ha! Is my Service ſo ſoon demanded?

[*Draws his Sword, and goes in.*

M. *Pearce.* Surely the Rogue is raviſhing her.

[Trueman *drags in* Brainworm, Bellamira *follows.*

True. Dog!

Bell. Hold, do not kill the Villain; 'tis enough that you have ſaved me from his Miſchief.

True. Tho' he deſerves a ſeverer Fate, I will obey you. Be gone, baſe Scoundrel. [*Kicks* Brainworm *out.*] What a wretched thing's a Whore, that every Raſcal dares approach with Love! [*Aſide.*

Bell. Pray, Sir, who are you to whom I am ſo much obliged?

True. One that would gladly ſerve you.

Bell. Thou haſt a brave Soul, I'm ſure. I will endeavour to prefer you; in the mean time make this your home.

M. *Pearce.* Shall any have admittance?

[*Knocking without.*

Bell. Only the perjur'd *Trueman's* Friend.

[*M.* Pearce *goes out.*

You may retire, and wait my farther Pleaſure.

True. I will. Now, *Rovewell*, ſhall I witneſs to thy Weakneſs. [*Goes out.*

Rovewell *enters.*

Rove. Now, my fair Miſtreſs, Soul of my Deſires,
I come with all the Spoils of conquering Love,
And lay them, with myſelf, at thy dear Feet.

The Bar to all my Happineſs is dead;
And here's the Witneſs of my Victory.
[*Shews the Ring.*

SONG XXIV. Whilſt I gaze on *Chloe* trembling.

What in Life is worth deſiring,
If the Fair we ſeek's unkind!
See me at thy Feet expiring,
To each other Object blind.

Drive me to the hardeſt Trial,
To the fartheſt India *ſend:*
Command, be ſure of no Denial,
Though it is to ſlay my Friend.

What, not a Smile when *Trueman* is no more?
Bell. Is *Trueman* dead? O! thou inhuman Friend,
Who took the ſpecious Title to betray!
O! Juſtice, can you let this Traitor live,
That has ſo baſely us'd the Name of Friend?
Since *Trueman*'s gone, Life has no Charms to me.
Rove. Surprizing! Shall I ſay he is not dead?
Bell. Not dead! and haſt thou, Wretch, deceiv'd my Hopes?
And is not *Trueman* dead? oh, what is Man?
Did'ſt thou not ſwear, and beg, to give me Proof
Of thy falſe Paſſion? And I ask'd but one,
And that thou haſt deny'd me. From my Sight,
Or thou ſhalt feel what my Revenge can act.
Rove. Calm that dear angry Brow, and tell me, Love,
What Anſwer beſt can pleaſe.
Bell. Preſumptuous Man!
How dar'ſt thou trifle thus with my Commands?
Rove. Since I am fated to offend, my Love,
I will not ſtain my Paſſion with a Lye.
I have, my Fair, obey'd thy ſtrict Commands,
And *Trueman* now is number'd with the Dead.
Bell. And may'ſt thou ſoon be number'd with the Damn'd;
For thou haſt kill'd all that my Soul could love.

SONG

SONG XXV. One Evening as I lay.

1. *If my Belov'd is dead,*
All Joy on Earth farewel;
Henceforth I'll lay my Head
In ſome far lonely Cell.

2. *Welcome the mournful Shade,*
And Deſarts, where I'll ſtray;
I'll to the gloomy Glade,
And weep my Life away.

Rove. This is an ill Reward for all my Love;
Ingratitude like this ſhall cure my Heart. [*Going.*
Bell. I muſt not let him go till I'm reveng'd.
O *Trueman*, I ne'er knew how much I lov'd,
How much I priz'd thee, till this fatal Hour. [*Aſide.*
Stay, I relent; O ſtay! and give my Heart
The ſoft Indulgence of a Moment's Grief,
For him I once ſo lov'd.
Rove. Forget him now,
He groſly wrong'd you, and who wrong'd ſuch Charms,
Ought to be puniſh'd with no leſs than Death:
I made your Cauſe my own, and ſtab'd my Friend,
And for my Service wait the dear Reward.
Bell. One Hour I ask to moderate my Woes
For him who lately was ſo dear to me.
Rove. Still on that Subject!
Bell. Thou art ſtain'd with Blood,
I cannot yet receive you to my Arms;
But grant the Hour I ask, and I'm your own.
Rove. Do not deceive me, Fair-one.
Bell. No, by Heaven!
I will reward thee—as thy Guilt deſerves. [*Aſide.*
Rove. Here, keep this Ring, and every Moment
I count, in Abſence, a long Year of Love. [think

SONG XXVII. *Tweed*-ſide.

1. *Farewel to all Joy for a while,*
Here I leave my fond Heart in your Power.
O! bleſs my Return with a Smile,
An Age ſhall I count the long Hour.

2. *From thee a sad Exile I go,*
By my Hopes, my fond Hopes kept alive;
While absent my Sorrows shall flow,
When we meet, all my Pleasures revive. [Goes out.

Bell. Thou credulous, vain, treacherous Fool, farewel.
Now shall my Soul indulge her great Revenge:
This Ring instructs me how to act, I'll go,
And frame to *Charlot* such a dreadful Tale,
As thro' her Ear shall stab her to the Heart.
And when this faithless *Rovewell* shall return,
I'll be prepar'd for him. Who waits without?

Trueman *enters.*

True. What a Devil this Woman is! [*Aside.*

Bell. Call a Coach this minute; and attend me.

True. Where-ever you command. How Love, and how Revenge possess her Soul? [*Aside.*

[*They go out.*

SCENE IV. *The Street.*

Brainworm *alone.*

I think it is the Fate of Men of my Vocation to apply what we extract from Fools, to the Use of some insolent Whore, who maintains her Paramour at our Expence. I, who am so excellent a Master in all the subtile Arts of Circumvention, am not proof against the Insinuation of Beauty. A kind of Witchcraft is in *Bellamira*'s Face, that makes me her Bubble whether I will or no.

Enter Mulligrub, *and the Goldsmith's Apprentice with a Silver Punch-Bowl.*

Mul. Be sure you take particular care of it; deliver it to my Wife's own hands. My Head runs plaguily on that Rogue *Brainworm*, who is able to cheat the Devil; if ever I catch him, I'll play the Devil with him.

[Mulligrub *and Apprentice go off separately.*

Brain. The Fox grows fat when he's cursed: I'll have you closer yet, Friend *Mulligrub*, my Mouth waters after your Punch-bowl. If I was to bite a poor Poet, a penurious Parson, who, for want of Learning, has but one good Meal in a Week, it would be a Sin; but to wring the Withers of this base Jumbler of Elements, is meritorious. I will draw a Lot for the Punch-bowl, without the Fear of a Halter before my Eyes. [*Goes out.*

SCENE V. *Changes.*

Heartfree, Charlot *and* Louisa.

Heart. I know you love him, *Charlot*; Dissimulation therefore is needless. I give you my Consent, and once more tell you, I can never approve of any Man for your Husband whom you dislike your self.

Char. Sir, I know not how to requite your Goodness, but by an entire Submission to your Will.

Heart. What says my little Volatile, ha? Well thou sha'not gnaw the Sheets for want of better Employment. I'll take care that you shall not lead Apes in Hell.

Lou. Indeed, Sir, you ought to provide me a Husband as soon as you can; for when my Cousin's dispos'd of, I shan't care to lie alone.

SONG XXVII. The *Jamaica.*

When Maids alone
Must make their Moan,
To Grief their Friends betray 'em;
They spend the Nights
In fear of Sprites,
Without the Power to lay 'em.

A Servant enters.

Serv. Sir, here's a Lady desires to speak with you.

Heart. Wait upon her in. 'Tis well my Age guards my Heart against the Power of Beauty: I once could not hear of the Approach of a Lady without sending my Heart half-way to meet her.

Enter

Enter Bellamira *and* Trueman *disguised.*

Is your Business with me, fair Lady?

Bel. I cannot tell, Sir, till I know your Name. Are you Father to the fair *Charlot Heartfree?*

Heart. I am, fair Witness; and this is the Maid you name.

Bel. My Time's but short, and what I have to say must be with speed. Madam, you had a Lover once, young *Trueman.*

Char. Had! good Heaven; I hope, and have.

Bel. No, *Rovewell* has basely kill'd him.

Char. O! miserable *Charlot!* [*She faints.*

Heart. Look to my Daughter.

Bel. Madam, lock up, this Concern he merits not; Pity brought me here to undeceive you. His Vows and Soul were mine, entirely mine.

Lou. This must be Malice sure.

Bel. Madam, do you know this Ring? he gave it me in triumph o'er your Love.

Char. Sure all Mankind is false.

SONG XXVIII. Send back my long stray'd Eyes.

How hard thy Fate, unhappy Maid!
By Vows of Love too soon betray'd.
Men court our Charms and then they fly:
They leave despis'd
What once they priz'd,
And view unmov'd th' enchanting Eye.

I cannot blame his Passion for so much Beauty as appears in you; but he should not have sported with my Misfortunes; at least I deserv'd his Pity. Help me, for I grow faint.

Heart. Lead her in, and be careful of her.

[Charlot *and* Louisa *go out.*

True. Come, Patience, to my aid; till I have seen how far this Woman will extend her Fury. [*Aside.*

Heart. Confess'd, Madam, and to you? on what Acquaintance pray?

Bel.

Bel. He lov'd me, and, ſeeing no Poſſibility of gaining me while *Trueman* liv'd, murder'd his Rival, and vaunted of his Villany to me. If you will go where I'll conduct you, you ſhall hear him confeſs it again to me.

Heart. Madam, I'll loſe no Time, but follow you, we'll take ſome Officers with us; and if *Rovewell* is ſuch a Villain, he ſhall feel the utmoſt Rigour of the Law. [*They go out.*

SCENE VI. *Changes.*

Enter Mrs. Mulligrub *and the Apprentice with the Bowl. She ſpeaks as the Boy goes out.*

Wife. Well, *Jarvis*, remember me to your Maſter and Miſtreſs, and tell them I acknowledge the Receit of the Bowl.

Brainworm *enters, dreſs'd like a Gold-ſmith's Apprentice, with a Jowl of Salmon in a Diſh.*

Brain. A fair Hour to you, Miſtreſs.

Wife. A handſome Compliment, I'll write it down. I'm ſure it deſerves a good Return. A beautiful Thought to you, Sir!

Brain. Your Husband, and my Maſter, Mr. *Burniſh*, have ſent you a Jowl of Salmon, and they intend to be with you ſoon, with my Miſtreſs and Maſter *Billy* to ſeaſon the Bowl; which your Husband deſires you to ſend back, to have the Two firſt Letters of your two Names engrav'd on it, which were forgot before, and they'll bring it with them.

Wife. Has he ſent no Token?

Brain. That he was in the Suds this Morning?

Wife. That's a ſad, but a true Token. Here take it, and tell them, I ſhall expect their Company impatiently. [Brainworm *goes with the Bowl*] *Flaſh*! why *Flaſh*!

Flaſh. Coming, Madam, coming.

Wife. Come quickly, ſpread the Table, lay Napkins, and perfume the Room a little; for this profane ſane Tobacco is very offenſive. Well, this Mr. *Burniſh* is one of the beſt Gallants I ever had, for he is always ſending me a nice Bit, and is very reſpectful to my Husband.

SONG XXIX. Health to *Betty*.

If you would gain the Wife, Sir,
Whom you love as your Life, Sir;
Do all you can
To pleaſe the Man,
'Tis one Way to the Wife, Sir.

Mulligrub *enters.*

Mul. Well, *Robin Mulligrub*, be not diſcourag'd; Things will go well at laſt.

Wife. I'm glad you're come, Husband. Where are they?

Mul. How now! how now! a Treat going forward! Who treats, *Peg*, who treats?

Wife. Prithee, leave fooling. Are they come?

Mul. Come! Who come?

Wife. Lord, how ſtrange you ſeem!

Mul. Strange! how ſtrange? Is the Woman mad?

Wife. I ſay, ſtrange! You don't know who ſent me a Jowl of Salmon, and ſaid they'd come to Supper; do you?

Mul. Ha! Salmon! Peace, not I; the Meſſenger has miſtook the Houſe. Let us eat it before it is enquir'd for. Come, come, Vinegar, quickly, *Flaſh.*—I ſhall have good Luck.—I never taſted Salmon that reliſh'd better.—Well, 'tis delightful to eat at another Man's Coſt.

Wife. Ay, Mr. *Burniſh* is a civil Man.

Mul. Mr. *Burniſh!*

Wife. Yes, did not he, or you, or both, ſend the Salmon?

Mul. No, I ſay, no. [*Eats faſt.*

Wife. By Mr. *Burniſh*'s Man?

Mul. I ſay no.

Wife. Did no body ſend Word, that he and his Wife,

Wife, and their Son *Billy* would come to ſup here?

Mul. No, no, no. [*Eats faſter.*

Wife. And ſeaſon my Punch-bowl?

Mul. Ha! Bowl! [*Lays down his Knife and Fork.*

Wife. And did not I ſend the Bowl back, according to your Order?

Mul. Ha! back! [*Starts up.*

Wife. Was not the Token you ſent, that you were in the Suds in the Morning?

Mul. And is the Bowl gone? Is it delivered? departed? defunct? ha!

Wife. Deliver'd! yes, ſure, it is deliver'd; and who can blame me?

Mul. I will never ſay my Prayers again: and is the Bowl gone?

SONG XXX. *Joan* ſtoop'd down.

Mul. *Thou Plague of my Life——*
Wife. *Thou Husband!*
Mul. *Thou Wife!*
Was I, O! was I unmarry'd,
I'd never be ty'd.
Wife. *The Name of a Bride*
I'd ſhun, ſince thus I've miſcarry'd.

Mul. Look to my Houſe, for it is haunted ſure with evil Spirits. Hear me, thou Plague, thou Woman! Thou Wife; if I have not my Bowl again, I will ſend thee to the Devil: I'll go to the Conjurer, and he ſhall raiſe his Maſter. Death and Hell! [*Goes out.*

Wife. Bleſs me, what frightful Words are theſe! I hope he is but drunk. [*Goes out.*

SCENE VII. *Changes.*

Brainworm *enters.*

Brain. Sure the Devil is about extraordinary Buſineſs. *Rovewel* is committed to *Newgate* for the Murder of his Friend *Trueman*; and *Bellamira* who betray'd him, is ſent with good Mother *Pearce*, to keep him Company: ſo if I ſhould happen to rattle my Darbies ſoon, I ſhan't want Company. Ha! here comes a Fellow that ſeems to have Money in his Pocket.

A Fidler enters with a Cloak on. Brainworm *knocks him down.*

Fid. O! O! O!

Brain. [*ſearching his Pockets*] The Devil has ſent me a fine Prize, a poor Fidler; I took him for a Gentleman: but ſince I'm diſappointed, I'll have a Cloak for my Knavery. [*Takes the Cloak and goes out.*

Fid. The Rogue has made a ſoft Place in my Head. Stop Thief, Stop Thief. [*Runs out.*

Mulligrub *enters, and meets* Brainworm *in the Cloak.*

Mul. That muſt be my Arch-Rogue *Brainworm.* [*ſeizes him.*] Have I caught you at laſt! I'll make an Example of you, Sirrah. [Brainworm *ſlips away, and leaves the Cloak with* Mulligrub.] The Dog has given me the Slip; but I have a good Cloak, which will go a little way to repair my Loſſes.

Enter Fidler, Conſtable *and* Watch-men.

Fid. Stop Thief, ſtop Thief. Here's the Rogue, Mr. *Conſtable*, with my Cloak on his Back.

Conſt. Seize him.

Mul. What's the Matter, Gentlemen? for God's ſake.

Conſt. You may as well hold your tongue, the Cloak on your Back convicts you.

Mul. Why, ſure the Fellow's a Fool.

Fid. No, no, he's no Fool, he's a Conſtable: and that's my Cloak, which you ſtole from me, and I'll ſwear it.

Conſt. Come, come, bring him along.

Mul. This damn'd Rogue *Brainworm*, is certainly my evil Genius. I may happen to be hang'd for his Roguery; and that would be hard.

Conſt. Come, Sir, no Words; you dare not reſiſt.

SONG

SONG XXXI. March in *Scipio.*

Mul. *I am prepar'd,*
To the Round-house I'll go;
I ne'er will be dar'd
By any saucy Foe.
If to Newgate *I'm sent*
I'll behave like a Man:
To be hang'd I'm content,
If my Race is quite ran.

Follow, follow, brave Boys,
He that loses his Life
Is remov'd from the Noise
Of a termagant Wife.

Chorus *of* Fid. Watch *and* Constable.

Follow, follow, brave Boys,
He that loses his Life
Is remov'd from the Noise
Of a termagant Wife.

ACT III.

Enter Charlot *and* Louisa.

Char WHY, dear *Louisa*, should it be a Crime to die, when Life becomes a Torment to us?

Lou. Prithee leave these melancholy Thoughts; 'S Life, pine for one Man! why, Girl, consider thou art young, and hast Beauty enough to attract half the Fops in Town.

Char. Oh! thou art happy; would I could be so unconcern'd, or had even a brutal Temper that could resist these violent Emotions of Grief or Joy.

Lou. Call you that brutal? now methinks 'tis great, to have a Soul that can withstand the Shocks of Fortune, and is not liable to be made ridiculous by Mirth or Sorrow: But I must confess I'm griev'd for *Rovewel*; for you know I love him; yet not so much as to whine and die for him: I feel his Misfortune as a Friend, not as a Lover.

Char. Oh *Louisa!* thou talk'st like one whose Heart ne'er felt the Symptoms of a gen'rous Passion; in real Love there cannot be so much Indifference. Yet when I consider *Trueman* was false, methinks I should not die.

Lou. My Dear, I do not believe he was false, by what my Uncle has told me; for this Woman was a Mistress, whom he has long since cast off, and what has happen'd was by her Contrivance to be reveng'd on him, or put you in Despair. Nay, I believe *Trueman* is not dead; nor can I think *Rovewel* could be so base upon any account to kill him, much less on this, which would be a Blot on both his Understanding and his Honour: therefore be pacify'd, you have not slept to-night, lie on this Couch, and I'll sing to you.

SONG XXXII. Piu benigna.

Sleep, Oh! Sleep, thou kind Composer
Of the Lover's tortur'd Breast,
With thy gentle Touch dispose her
To the Sweets of balmy Rest.
Let no hideous Dreams affright her,
Let no direful Forms annoy,
Send soft Visions to delight her,
Give at least Ideal Joy.

Char. I cannot sleep, alas! I'm tasteless grown, there is no Musick but in Sighs. [*Faints.*

Lou. Help, help, she faints.

Trueman *enters.*

True. By your Leave, sweet Creatures.

Lou. Uncivil Sir, who are you?

True. One that brings Comfort: ha! my Love dying! Stand by, I have a Cordial in my Voice.

Lou. *Trueman* alive! What Miracle is this?

Char.

Char. Ha! *Trueman!* or does my Senſe deceive me? Sure I'm in Heaven, and he an Angel there.

True. I ſcarce could wiſh it yet. No, we have an Age to come in Love, e'er we arrive at that.

Char. Oh! I ſhall die with Joy; forgive my Tranſport, 'tis the Effect of a ſincere and honeſt Paſſion, which I can conceal no longer.

True. Call back thy Blood into thy pale Cheeks, thou Miracle of thy Sex! By all that's good, I never was unjuſt; that Woman, that beauteous Sinner, whom you ſaw, ſeduced my growing Virtue; but you muſt forgive the Errors of my Youth.

Char. I do, and think of them no more.

True. How I adore thy Goodneſs! Hereafter I'll tell thee all my Life; but now my Time is ſhort, and I muſt yet remain in this Diſguiſe, to accompliſh my honeſt Deſign on *Rovewell*, for he ſhall ſuffer to the laſt Degree, for leaving thee, *Louiſa*, for another.

Lou. And has he been ſo wicked?

True. Yes, but is now reclaim'd: I'll return the Penitent to your Arms again.

Lou. Why, in good Faith, Couſin that muſt be, I do love the Fugitive, that's certain; and, if my Uncle pleaſes, will run the Hazard of taking him *for better for worſe.*

Heartfree *enters.*

Heart. Oh! my Girls, I'm ſorry to be the Meſſenger of ſuch ill News, poor *Rovewell* is condemn'd.

Lou. I thought you ſaid he would produce *Trueman* at the Goldſmith's.

Heart. I did ſo, but the Goldſmith denied his ſeeing him; ſo his own former Confeſſion hangs him: *Rovewell*, *Bellamira*, and that Mother of all Miſchief, the Bawd, were found guilty of the Murder: however, I'll uſe all the Intereſt I have, to procure *Rovewell* a Pardon.

Lou.

Lou. Then, pray Sir, ſollicit this Gentleman.

Heart. Ha! *Trueman* alive! may I believe my Eyes?

True. You may.

Heart. O kiſs me, kiſs me. But how? which way? when? what? where?—I am ſo tranſported; ſure I am in a Dream all this while: well, I'll go back to *Newgate* again and wake my ſelf. But this Surprize had like to have made me forget to tell you our Neighbour *Mulligrub* the Vintner is condemn'd too, for a Robbery.

True. How! *Mulligrub* for Robbery? Was it prov'd upon him?

Heart. By a poor dirty Fellow; but he ſwore point-blank againſt him. 'Tis certain a Cloak was ſtolen; that Cloak was taken upon *Mulligrub*'s Back; the Juſtice of Peace was drunk that committed him; the Judges ſevere and in haſte; the Jury unbrib'd and hungry; and ſo the Knave was caſt: but, to hear his Wiſhes! his Curſes! his Prayers! and his ill-tim'd Zeal! by my Troth they would have made a Comedy. But come, let us all to *Newgate* with Expedition, and releaſe the poor Gentleman from his dreadful Contemplations of Death and the Gallows.

All. With all our Hearts. [*They go out.*

SCENE II. *The Outſide of* Newgate.

Priſoners begging.

Jack. Pray remember the poor Priſoners! Cloſe, cloſe, a Double-dabber in the Condemn'd-hold, and Change for a Tiſſey: Pray remember the poor Priſoners.

Shameleſs. D——n you for a Son of a Whore, how ſneakingly do you beg!—Remember the Poor, you ſniveling Bitch. Is that a Voice to dive to the Bottom of a Uſurer's Pocket, and fetch out his Money in ſpite of his harden'd Heart? Stand by you Dog, and let me come to the Grate.

Jack. Ah, dear Mr. *Shameleſs!* Methinks we ſhould

ſhould have but little Stomach to beg, who are to be hang'd within theſe three Hours.

Shame. Why then, you whining Cur, we have more need to beg, that we may drink at parting. Stand by, and obſerve me, with what an audible Voice I'll move Compaſſion——Chriſtians, pity the poor Priſoners of this loathſome Dungeon, and it will be reſtor'd to you ten-fold; drop your Bounty into this little Box, the only Support, Relief and Comfort of twenty poor wretched Souls. Noble Sir, remember the poor Priſoners.

Heartfree *enters, gives Money, and goes in.*

Heaven reward your Chriſtian Charity, and reſtore it to you ſeventy-fold.

Trueman, Charlot, *and* Louiſa *enter, they put Money into the Box, and go in.*

Ha! Ladies alighted! Moſt beautiful Ladies, diſpenſe your noble Charity among twenty miſerable Wretches oppreſſed with Hunger and Cold, merciful and fair, pity the Miſeries of unfortunate young Men, whoſe few ſhort Hours of Life ſhall be all employ'd in Prayers for our noble Benefactors—Oh, remember the Poor. Ha! 'tis Gold, by this Light! So now a ſhort Life and a merry one; we'll have it all in Drink, Boys, and when the Hour comes, die like Heroes, ſing the Pſalm merrily, and then—be hang'd till we're ſober.

[*They go from the Grate.*

SCENE III *a Chamber in* Newgate.

Rovewel *and* Heartfree *enter.*

Rove. No, Sir, I do not bluſh, nor are my Cheeks grown pale, tho' I'm condemned to die this ignominious Death.

Heart. No kind of Death is ſo, but from the Cauſe of it.

Rove. Which I well know is none: but are there no Hopes of a Reprieve?

Heart.

Heart. Not the least.

Rove. Upon my Honour, Sir, *Trueman* is safe, I have already satisfy'd you, how I came to say what I did of his Death, to that false Fair-one. Sure some Lethargy has seiz'd him, that he appears not, he could not else be thus unkind. I'm sure 'twou'd grieve you, Sir, to see me die, and after find me innocent.

Heart. By the Mass and so it would; but to put you out of all these hanging Apprehensions, know *Trueman* is alive, and if you won't take my Word, here he comes to tell you so himself.

Trueman, Charlot, *and* Louisa *enter.*

Rove. Ha! my dear *Trueman*, have you been kind to me?

Tru. I was resolv'd to make you suffer for your Follies, and now I have, I hope you will forgive what's pass'd.

Rove. Ha! *Louisa* too! which way must I look?

Lou. Nay, do not hide your Face, or turn away. I'm very glad to know where a Maid may find you, when she has need of you: and tho' you may think these Chains easier than those of Matrimony, yet like a malicious Woman I am for proposing a Change. What say you? Dare you venture, or had you rather say, Drive away Carman, and sing the penitential Psalm at the Gallows?

Rove. Can you accept this Criminal in Chains?

Lou. The sooner for that Reason, with my Uncle's Leave, for I shall have a hank upon you, when you're insolent, and can upbraid you with the Place from whence I had you.

Tru. He cannot but commend your Passion for him.

Rove. I'm asham'd to be so much obliged.

Char. Nay, leave the Shame to her, since she is resolv'd to be so extravagant. 'Twas but yesterday she thought you deserv'd to be hanged for your Infidelity, and o'my Conscience, to-day she could marry you under the Gallows: but 'tis the

Frailty of the Sex to be so easy, and that makes you Fellows think so lightly of us.

SONG XXXIII. The Mansel.

Women in Joy or Woe
Are to Extremes inclining,
This Day our Sorrows flow,
In weeping, sobbing, whining.
To-morrow finds us gay,
Endeavouring to be pleasing,
But take us either way,
In Joy or Woe we're teasing.

Rove. You're too severe upon your own Sex, Madam. There is nothing this Lady can do but must be pleasing.

Lou. Not even when I offer Matrimony to you: Then here's my Hand upon it.

Rove. Thou art all heavenly, and I am thine for ever. Farewel all youthful Follies, I have been wild and roving in my Time; long tost on the dangerous Ocean of loose Desires, but am now resolv'd to rest contented with a virtuous Love.

SONG XXXIV. Bartholomew-Fair.

The Sailor thus, of every wanton Wind the Sport,
When Billows are roaring,
His Fortune deploring,
Looks out for Port;
And when his kind Stars have safely brought him to the Shore,
He then resolves to trust the Seas no more.

Louisa *sings.* SONG XXXV. Same Tune.

But being out of Danger once, his Fears subside;
Of Land he grows weary,
Nor longer will tarry,
Whate'er betide,
But hoisting Sail he makes away before the Wind,
Nor ever thinks on aught he leaves behind.

So, Mr. *Rovewel*, I fear 'twill be with you; you have been ſo much us'd to roam from Place to Place, that you can never confine yourſelf to one Station——but however I'm reſolved to take my Chance.

Rove. You are ſo generous 'twill be impoſſible for me ever to think of diſobliging you. And, now, Sir, I muſt ſue to you for Pardon. [*To* Heartfree.

Heart. No, Sir, I muſt have my Revenge on you, and ſince you have eſcap'd the Hangman, you ſhall be noos'd by the Prieſt.

Lou. Hanging and marrying, you ſee, go by Deſtiny.

Heart. I'll have the Sentence put in Execution immediately; the Ordinary ſhall do the Buſineſs, he can bring a Man to Repentance as ſoon as any one of his Function; come, we'll go down, and ſee what ſort of Figure my Neighbour *Mulligrub* makes under his Misfortunes, and releaſe the two wicked Women, and in the mean time I'll ſend to Doctors-Commons for a conjugal Warrant, and commit you both to the Cuſtody of *Hymen*.

[*They all go out.*

SCENE IV. *The Lodge of* Newgate.

Keeper *calls.*

Bring out the Priſoners that are order'd for Execution.

Enter Bellamira, *Mother* Pearce, Shameleſs, Harry, Jack, Tom, Mulligrub, *and others.* *Mrs.* Mulligrub, *and a Friend of one of the Priſoners.*

Shame. So, Mother *Occupy*, you are preparing for your Journey, you are equipt with a Noſegay, and a Prayer-Book? What do you weep for, the Sins of your Youth, or the Fear of a Halter? Now if you had kept within the Bounds of your own Trade, Fornication and Adultery, and not proceeded to Murder, you had not been fatigu'd, in your old Age, with a Journey from *Newgate* to *Tyburn*.

M. *Pearce.*

M. *Pearce.* Well, well, if I am to be hang'd I can't help it; but my Comfort is, I ſhall die a good Proteſtant, and a High-Church Woman.

Mull. O Lord, little did I think of coming to this untimely Death.

Shame. Come, prithee leave whining, a Pox on thee for a Chicken-hearted Son of a Whore, you are enough to make us all Cowards. I think it's a great Mercy you are to be hang'd in ſo good Company.

Mull. O dear! how can you talk ſo, and are juſt going to leave the World?

Harry. Will no kind Chriſtian give one a Draught of Drink, I'm almoſt choak'd?

Shame. Have but a little Patience, and you'll be quite choak'd. Why, what haſt thou loſt thy Courage too, *Tom*, what do'ſt cry for?

Tom. I don't cry ſo much becauſe I'm going to be hang'd, but to think I have no Money to buy me a Coffin.

Shame. Never trouble thyſelf about that; my fond, fooliſh Father has ſent me a Coffin, but faith I have bit the old Prig, and ſold my Body to the Surgeons: ſo I'll equip thee with my Carrion-Box.

Tom. Thank you kindly, I wiſh I could do the ſame for you.

A Boy enters with Drink.

Shame. Come, come, here's ſome Liquor, booze about, we have not long to live, let's make the moſt of our Time.

SONG XXXVI.

Since Life is at beſt but a Cheat,
An empty chimerical Bubble,
The Prig who would truly be great,
Will ſooneſt get rid of its Trouble.
Then to thee, my Buff, let us quaff,
Who next to the Nubbing-Poſt trudges,
At Pimps that ſurvive him may laugh,
And ſhew his bare Meg to the Judges.
Tol, lol, dee.

[Tom *sings.*] *Then bid we farewel to the Wit,*
To-day puts an End to our Sorrow,
The Cull well deserves to be bit,
Who builds his fond Hopes on to-morrow.
What have we now longer to fear,
We're got to the length of our Tether:
We'll knock off our Darbies and Care,
And merrily morris together.
Tol, lol, dol, dee.

Friend. Well *Tommy*, I am sorry I can't stay to see the last of you, but I wish you a good Journey.

Shame. Thank you, thank you, *Bob*, I wish you the same with all my heart; but do you hear, remember my kind Love to my Brother *Sam*, and be sure tell him I die like a Cock, damn'd hard——
Tol, lol, de, dol.

Enter Keeper.

Keep. Here's good News for the two Women; the Gentleman, who was thought to have been murder'd, is found at last, and perfectly well.

M. *Pearce.* Ha! then I'm a Woman again, Heaven be thanked. *Bellamira*, I hope no body has taken our House, it stood rarely well for Business.

Mull. What, is there no hope of a Reprieve for me?

Keep. None at all; but here's a good Man come to prepare you for t'other World.

Mull. A-lack-a-day! then I'm in a bad way indeed.

Enter Brainworm *disguis'd like a Presbyterian Parson,* Heartfree, Trueman, Rovewel, Charlot *and* Louisa.

Brain. Friend, I have been acquainted with thy Misfortunes, from thy pious Pastor, Master *Zachariah Thumpit*, who, lying on a sick Bed himself, hath sent me to give thee some spiritual Advice, and be, as it were, a Staff to thee in the grea Leap thou art going to take, as it were, thou knowest not whither.

Tru.

Tru. Bellamira, 'twas Madneſs in thee to ſuppoſe thou could'ſt enſlave me for ever; you muſt now quit all Hopes of me; but as I think thou art in thyſelf ſomething nobler than moſt of thy Profeſſion, howe'er thy Love to me had plung'd thee in ſuch wicked Deſigns, which Providence has prevented, if you think you can forgo your former Courſe of Living, I will provide for you in a decent manner.

Bell. Such Generoſity muſt conquer every Breaſt that has any Spark left in it of Gratitude, or Shame. I am too ſenſible of my paſt ill Conduct, and the Wickedneſs my Love urg'd me to; but hope my future Penitence will make me deſerve your Pardon and your Pity.

Mrs. *Mull.* Indeed, my Dear, this is a very comfortable Man.

Mul. He is ſo; but, pray Mr. *Zeal*, leave my Soul a little to itſelf, and let me have ſome of your Counſel concerning my Body; I owe Mr. *Burniſh* the Goldſmith forty Pounds, and ſuppoſe he ſhould be ſo unneighbourly now to ſet a Serjeant on my Back, as I am going to Execution.

Brain. Ah! trouble not thyſelf with tranſitory Things, but have an Eye to the main Chance.

[*Picks his Pocket.*

Tru. Obſerve, *Rovewell*, that Rogue of a Parſon is picking *Mulligrub*'s Pocket.

Rove. Have patience, we'll detect him preſently.

Brain. Your Shoulders are in no danger,—but for your Neck,—*Plinius Secundus*, or *Marcus Tullius Cicero*, or ſomebody, ſayeth, that a threefold Cord is not eaſily broken.

Mull. A very learned Man!—Well, I am not the firſt honeſt Man that has been hang'd, and I hope in Heaven I ſhall not be the laſt.

Mrs. *Mull.* Ah, Husband! I little thought to have ſeen this Day; had you been hang'd deſervedly, it wou'd never have vex'd me, for many an innocent Man has been hang'd deſervedly: but

but to be cast away for nothing! oh! oh! oh!

Brain. Moderate thy Grief, good Woman, thou wilt shortly be a Widow, and I will come and comfort thee.

Mrs. *Mull.* You shall be welcome by Night or by Day. But pray, Husband, are we to find the Halter, or they?

Mull. Thou simple Woman, how can'st thou ask such a Question? they, they, to be sure.

Mrs. *Mull.* I could not tell, and so brought one with me, for fear of the worst. Thou hast been a dear Husband to me, *Robin*, and I was not willing you shou'd want any thing I could help you to.

Mull. Thank you kindly, dear *Peg*.

Mrs. *Mull.* I bespoke it of our Neighbour *Thong* the Collar-maker, and gave him strict Charge to make it strong enough; and he assured me, he cou'd not make a better, if it was for his own Wife.

Mull. I'm beholden to all my Friends, who are so ready to serve me at this time.

Mrs. *Mull.* Oh, my poor, dear Husband! I can't bear the loss of you; wou'd I was to be hang'd in your stead.

Mull. Ah, my Dear, I wish you was with all my heart, that would be a Mercy indeed. Well, I here make Confession of all my Sins.—If I owe any Man any thing, I heartily forgive him; and if any Man owes me any thing, I desire he may pay my Wife.

Brain. Very good.

Mull. Here, *Peg*, are the Writings of that Rogue *Brainworm*'s Estate, who has brought me to this untimely End, dear Writings to me! take care of them.

Brain. Ha! my Writings! now for a lucky Stratagem to retrieve those, and I'm a Man again. [*Aside.*

Mull. And now, my Dear, take leave of thy honest Husband.

Mrs. *Mull.* No, and pleaſe the Lord, I'll not leave you now, I'll ſee you hang'd firſt.

SONG XXXVII. Let the Soldiers rejoice.

With my Love can I part?
Oh! 'twill break my fond Heart,
To behold thy ſweet Neck in a Halter.

Mull. *If the Fates wou'd ſo pleaſe,*
Now to give my Spouſe eaſe,
I my Neck for thy Neck moſt gladly wou'd alter.

Brain. But Brother, you muſt have been a Broacher of prophane Veſſels, you have made us drunk with the Juice of the Whore of *Babylon*, for whereas good Ale, Cyder, and Perry, were the true Antient *Britiſh* and *Trojan* Liquors, you have brought in Popery, *French* and *Spaniſh* Wines, to the ſubverting, ſtaggering, and overthrowing of many a good Proteſtant Subject.

[*Picks Mrs.* Mulligrub'*s Pocket.*

Tru. Ha! Mr. Hypocrite, have we caught you? *Mulligrub*, he has pick'd thine, and thy Wife's Pocket.

Rove. By this Light 'tis *Brainworm!*

Brain. Dear Sir, endeavour to ſave my Life, and I'll tell all.

Mull. Oh! Rogue, Rogue, wou'd you have been ſo wicked to have taken away my Life?

Brain. Why, really, Sir, to tell the plain Truth, I believe I ſhou'd have let you been hang'd before I had told of myſelf: but conſider 'tis you who have brought me to the Condition of hanging or ſtarving.

Keeper *enters.*

Keep. Mr. *Mulligrub*, here is a Pardon come down for you.

Mull. Heaven be thanked. Now, Rogue, I think I have you upon the Hip.

Tru. Come *Mulligrub*, this good News ſhould ſtop all Reſentment. 'Twou'd be pity to hang the

the poor Fellow. Consider, he was born a Gentleman, and his Dishonesty was partly owing to your Knavery; whilst you unjustly kept his Estate from him, the Fellow must eat some how or other.

Mull. Well, I won't prosecute the Rogue now, though he will certainly be hang'd at last.

Brain. I thank you, Sir, but I'll make you a false Prophet if possible. Desperate Diseases must have desperate Cures; I'll e'en marry, and see if that will save me from the Gallows.

Mull. Say you so, why then to turn you honest, and make you amends for the Injustice I have done you, I'll give you my Daughter for a Wife, and a Thousand Pounds to maintain her. 'Tis best to compound with the Knave, or he'll rob me of as much as her Fortune comes to, and I shall have the Girl to keep still.

Brain. What, lovely *Nancy!* a delicious Girl, and kisses lusciously; I accept your Proposal, Sir.

Mull. Then here's the Mortgage of thy Estate to bind the Bargain. I'll leave off Trade, and set thee up in my House: Thy Reputation is good enough for a Vintner, if not, I'll get thee chose a Common-Council-Man; and when you are once got into the Herd, your former Roguery will soon be forgot.

Keeper *enters.*

Keep. Sir, the Licence is come, and the Ordinary waits for you.

Heart. Come, young Fellows, take your Girls by their Hands, and lead them to Execution.

[*Exeunt.*

A GRAND CHORUS.

FINIS.

The Patron

Bibliographical note:
This facsimile has been made from a copy in the British Museum
[82.b.1.(2.)]

THE PATRON:

OR,

The *Statesman's* Opera,

Of Two ACTS,

As 'tis Acted by the

Company of Comedians

AT THE

New Theatre in the *Hay-Market.*

By Mr. *ODELL.*

Let the gall'd Jade winch, our Withers are unwrung. Hamlet.

To which is added the Musick to each Song.

Dedicated to the Right Honourable the

Earl of *SUNDERLAND*

LONDON:

Printed by *W. Pearson*, for JOHN CLARKE at the *Bible* under the Royal Exchange *Cornhill.* *Price* 1 *s.*

TO THE

Right Honourable

THE

Earl of *Sunderland*.

MY LORD,

Y *Obligations to your* Great Father (*the late Earl of* Sunderland) *being Many and Singular, will, I hope, plead ſome Excuſe for me, whoſe greateſt Misfortune, next the Loſs of* my late Lord, *is that of being unknown to Your Lordſhip.*

That Great Miniſter, *who never encourag'd Idle Sollicitations, and whoſe Ear was alwaies* open

open to Merit, *even of the lowest Degree, as soon as inform'd of some small unrewarded Services of Mine, became my* Patron, *and obtain'd His late Majesty's Order for Two hundred Pounds to be paid me Yearly, till otherwise provided for; and that Bounty, during the two last Years of his Important Life, I had the Honour of receiving from his own Hands, but lost it at his Death, and with it all future Hopes of Preferment.*

I must own, my Lord, *(without regarding the common Strain of Dedications) the Impulse I have of expatiating on the* Profound Skill, Publick Spirit, *and* Incorruptible Integrity *of my* Illustrious Patron, *as well as to enumerate those shining* Qualities *which adorn Your Lordship, and which presage us all we can possibly expect, even from a* Nobleman *descended from the most Renowned* Captain, *and the most Intrepid* Statesman. *But as I am conscious I cannot add any thing to a* Name *already consecrated to Endless Fame, so likewise I chuse not to Interrupt Your Lordship in the Exercise of your own Virtues, nor sully for want of Skill, those Excellencies I mean to illustrate.*

As for the Opera *I now humbly dedicate to Your Lordship, I shall only observe this,* That *the sham-*

sham-Patron, its chief Character, and from which it takes its Name, is drawn corrupt, vicious, and unsincere; and serves only as a Foil, to illustrate the Virtues of the real Patron; and those that have yet seen it agree, the Contrast is no where exactly good, but with the late Earl of Sunderland. *And, that such I intended it, my own Conscience bears me witness; and likewise, that I indulge my Gratitude sufficiently in publishing of it at a time when some abandon'd Hirelings have in vain attempted to defame a Character held Sacred by all True Lovers of their* KING *and* Country.

My Lord, *suffer me to entreat your Pardon and Protection, and to profess my self with greatest Zeal,*

My Lord,

Your Lordship's

most Dutiful,

and most Obedient

humble Servant,

Tho. Odell.

Dramatis Personæ.

MEN.

Lord *Falcon*, a Minister of State, Patron to *Merit*, ———	Mr. *Hulet*.
Sir *Jolly Glee*, Friend to Lord *Falcon*, in love with Mrs. *Rhubarb* ———	Mr. *Giffard*.
Merit, a Gentleman undone by depending on Lord *Falcon* ———	Mr. *Reynolds*.
Stout, a Friend to *Merit*, —	Mr. *Gillow*.
Pointer, a Pimp to Lord *Falcon*	Mr. *Pearce*.

WOMAN.

Peggy Lure, A Woman of the Town, a pretended Wife to *Merit*	Mrs. *Nokes*.

ACT

ACT I. SCENE I.

Scene Merit's *Lodging.* *Enter* Merit *and* Lure, *singing to the Tune of* The Country Farmer.

AS Virtue from hence was banisht long since, And fools have the
Fortune of rising; That Craft shou'd prevail where Merit must
fail I think 'tis no longer surprising. Could a good Conscience
like vi--ci--ous Nonsence succeed 'twould raise One's be--haviour,
But who in their Senses, would form such Pre—ten—ces,
Whilst Wretches ri—ot in Fa--vour.

Merit. [*giving a Conditional Note.*] There's the Last Stake, my Dear, play it wisely; for on this Cast depends our future Happiness or Misery.

Lure. Ne'er fear it, Love; if the Deceit is n't too honest for the Occasion, I'll warrant ye Success.

Merit. The Hook's lusciously baited, I'm sure; and if you angle with Caution, I'll answer for a Bite: You'll see when to strike, I'll trust ye.

Lure. Indeed you may, I cannot mistake my Duty any more than my Interest. Adieu *Tom.* (*kissing*) *Exit* Lure.

Merit. Fare thee well: I'll hope for Success however; if we fail, I am but where I was, the most Unfortunate Wretch in the Universe.

Enter Stout.

Stout. Faith I think so. But hark ye *Tom!* Is your Patron gone to the Devil yet? Gad, I curs'd him last Night at the *Rose* with half a dozen Friends o' yours, till we were all hoarse to hear how he had us'd ye.

Merit. No *Sam,* not yet I believe; but, lest he should loyter by the way, and ruin any more of his Friends by his fine Speeches, I've sent the Devil to him this Morning I can tell ye.

Stout. Ha, my Friend! But how got you Bravo's in *London?* Thou'rt not o'th' Blood o' the *Feltons* thy self *Tom.*

Merit. No, *Sam:* The Devil I sent is a soft, luscious, alluring Devil, —— my Wife, Sir.

Stout. Your Wife, Sir! Oons, that's the Devil indeed, in your Circumstances: I did n't know thee hadst a Wife, *Tom.*

Merit. Yes; God help me.

Stout. Nay, hereafter you have Hopes, I confess, if your Wife be not wanting t'ye; an' let me tell ye, you've sent her to a very likely Person to assist her in't.

Merit. I've given her Leave, *Sam,* to Jilt him, if such a Wile can be of any Use to us.

Stout. Believe me, *Tom,* I shou'd n't suffer a Wife to engage in a Project of that kind on any Pretence, lest from such a License she take Occasion to Jilt her Husband too.

Merit. I have but little to fear, *Sam,* as I take it.

Stout. Not much, I confess. But, prithee *Tom,* what did the Caitiff say to thee? How did he put thee off?

Merit. He told me I was again too late; That he'd dispos'd o'the Place I ask'd for, to one *Purchase,* who was recommended by an Interest he cou'd by no means withstand.

Stout. His Name, I shou'd ha' thought, had been sufficient.

Merit. I told him, 'twas odd he shou'd give Places to Strangers, and suffer his Friends to perish for want of 'em. He reply'd, He did nothing without Reason, and wish'd he could find the Opportunities o' providing for all his Friends, but the Difficulties were in-

insurmountable; and as I could bear him witness how many Years he had endeavour'd it to no purpose, so now he was convinc'd that he never cou'd; and therefore the kindest thing he cou'd say to 'em was, to bid 'em not expect it; and as I was, on account of my Services, his greatest Favourite, so he began with me first.

Stout. Perfidious Monster! Was there ever such a Friend? May his Insolence spirit up his Dependants to *De-Witt* him, and his stupendious Fall be remember'd with Horror. *Tom*, I'm your Friend, and tho' this *Falcon* soars so high, I've a Gun will reach him; I'll lend it thee, shoot the Dog. ———

Merit. I thank ye, *Sam*; but your Zeal's too hot for my present Purpose, *Cupid* has lent me his Bow already, and with that I hope to take a sufficient Revenge, without exposing my self.

Sings to the Tune of Hey Boys, up go we, &c.

Stout. I'm glad you're so merry, tho' I can't see any great reason you have for it.

Merit. Hang it, *Sam*, I'll not despair while I've any Chance left: Will ye walk in the Park?

Stout. Aye, any thing, so you'll allow me to curse your Patron.

Merit. Aye, with all my Heart; I'll joyn with ye, *Sam.*

[*Exeunt.*

SCENE *at Lord* Falcon's; *discovers a Levée, his Lordship dispatching those attending.*

First Attendant. My Lord, 'tis Seven long Years I've waited a Vacancy.

Ld Falcon. Sir, I can't help that, I can't knock People o'th' Head to make a Vacancy for ye.

2d Attendant. My Lord, my Merit as well as Recommendation I should think ———

Ld Falcon. What, Sir? Merit's a meer Drug, Sir; the Market's o'erstockt with it: But my Lord *Worthy*'s Recommendation I shall always regard.

3d Attendant. My Lady *Hush* begs your Lordship will remember her Zeal to serve you, and take some Notice of the Bearer of this. (*giving a Letter.*)

Ld Falcon. (*putting up the Letter*) Give my Service to her Ladyship, and tell her I'll be sure to obey all her Commands.

4th Attendant. My Lord, Mrs. *Sweetlips* begs you'll take Notice of me.

Ld Falcon. Tell her I'll call on her, to consult what can be done for ye.

——— (*turning to the others*) Sir, I'll be sure to take Care of you ——— Sir, you may rest satisfied ——— Sir, call on me next Week ——— Sir, I've set you down for the first Vacancy ——— &c. [*Exeunt.*

Falcon solus, *sings to the Tune of* The Ordnance on board.

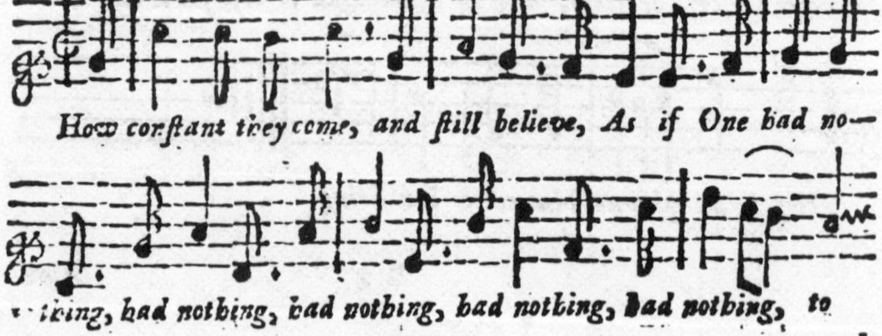

-thing, had nothing, had nothing, had nothing, had nothing, to

do

Enter a Servant.

Serv. My Lord, there's one Mrs. *Merit* without, desires to speak with your Lordship.

Ld *Falcon.* An' you cou'd n't tell her I was gone out, or busie, or any thing. — I have n't been teaz'd an' plagu'd enough a'ready I warrant.

Serv. I did, my Lord, but she saw the others coming from you, an' is resolv'd to wait your coming out, if she is n't admitted.

Falcon. Curse on't! What's her Name *Merit* say ye? sure *Tom Merit* has n't got a Wife to plague me too.

Serv. Yes, my Lord, she says she's Mr. *Merit*'s Wife; she's very handsome, and won't be said Nay.

Falcon. She ought not, if she's handsome; shew her in, (*exit Servant*) if I like her, I'll not be said Nay neither.

Enter

Enter Lure *as Mrs.* Merit.

By St. *Hamon* ſhe's an Angel. (*aſide*) Madam, your moſt devoted Servant, (*ſalutes her*) Pray what Command have you to honour me withal?

Lure. (*weeping*) I come only to reproach you. Nothing but your unheard-of Cruelty to my Husband cou'd have given me the Courage to come near ye: His Services have deſerv'd a better Fate, and your repeated Promiſes, had you either Honour or Gratitude, wou'd ha' been thought worth performing too; but to diſcard him in ſo vile a manner! ———

Falcon. Dear Lady, (*drawing near*) cou'd you be ſenſible how much I intereſt my ſelf in your Happineſs, you'd entertain kinder Sentiments of me; we muſt have a better Underſtanding of each other: Well, hang me if I thought *Merit* cou'd ha' choſe ſo well, I muſt compliment the Rogue when I ſee him next.

Lure. Not on his Choice of a Patron, I hope: he cou'd n't ha' choſe a worſe I'm ſure.

Falcon. Dear Charmer, be not thus ſatyrical: Had I known Mr. *Merit* had ſo fine a Lady, I had provided for him long e're this: Your Worth both the *Indies* cannot purchaſe. Oons, ſhe's an Angel. (*aſide.*)

Lure. For his own ſake he might have expected it; I come but to upbraid ye, and let ye ſee another Wretch your falſe Friendſhip has made ſuch, for I expect no real Advantage from it.

Falcon. No, but indeed you ſhall, Charmer, (*ſeizing her Hand*) I'll yet provide for him, only eſteem it for Your ſake that I do it, for I cannot poſſibly live out of your good Graces. How long have ye been married, Madam?

Lure. (*weeping*) Too long, my Lord, by Five long Years, ſince I'm ruin'd by't, tho' I've the beſt Husband living; for by his Attachment, and your fine Pretences, we've ſpent a very handſome Fortune together; and now, by your baſe Treatment, have the honour to underſtand we've nothing left us to truſt to.

Falcon. (*handing her again*) Dear Creature, don't grieve thus; I'm really a Couvert, and, thro' your Interceſſion, will certainly provide for *Merit:* Only be You kind, an' command any thing.

Lure. (*ſhrieking*) Oh, hideous! Have you not already ruin'd us? An' wou'd ye deſtroy our domeſtick Peace? It is n't enough then that my Spouſe has danc'd Attendance ſo many Years to no Purpoſe, unleſs his Wife be diſhonour'd too! I'm aſtoniſh'd a Man o' your Caſt does not ſend ſome body to murder him likewiſe, and ſo compleat your Cruelty; or, perhaps you think it beſt he ſhould live to underſtand his Miſery.

Falcon. All this is but raiſing the Price, ſhe knows I'm able to purchaſe, an' by St. *Machavel* I'll have her. (*aſide.*) Dear Charmer,

mer, have a little Patience: Hear me a Word, I'll now convince ye of my Love. The Place your Husband ask'd for Yesterday shall still be his: 'Tis true, I've given it to one *Purchase*, but I'll make it worth his while to consent to have his Name erac'd out of the Patent, and *Merit* shall be inserted in its stead; only meet me according to Directions, and I'll this Day give it into your Possession.

Lure. Or, in Fact, you'll give me the Trouble of exposing my self for a Fiction, and so have the Power of reproaching Mr. *Merit* with his Wife's Levity: You want to finish his Destruction.

Falcon. Nay, this is astonishing, Madam: Did you never hear you was handsome? Don't distrust your own Power thus; but I'll soon put it out of Dispute: Pray accept these, (*offering a Purse and a Dagger*) the Purse is yours for meeting me only, an' if I fail performing Conditions with you, let the Dagger be mine. (*turning the Point to's Breast.*) Upon my Life I'll then put the Patent into your Hands, only promise to be mine, and I'll trust your Generosity for the rest.

Lure. (*putting 'em back*) Mr. *Merit* will think it strange indeed I should succeed thus, when he with all his Services cou'd n't. I must refuse ye.

Falcon. Dear Angel! his Blind shall be, that I have heartily repented of my Unkindness to him, and the moment you came was sending my Servant to tell him so, who shall be order'd to vouch it. (*offering 'em again.*)

Sings to the Tune of Why Soldiers, why, &c.

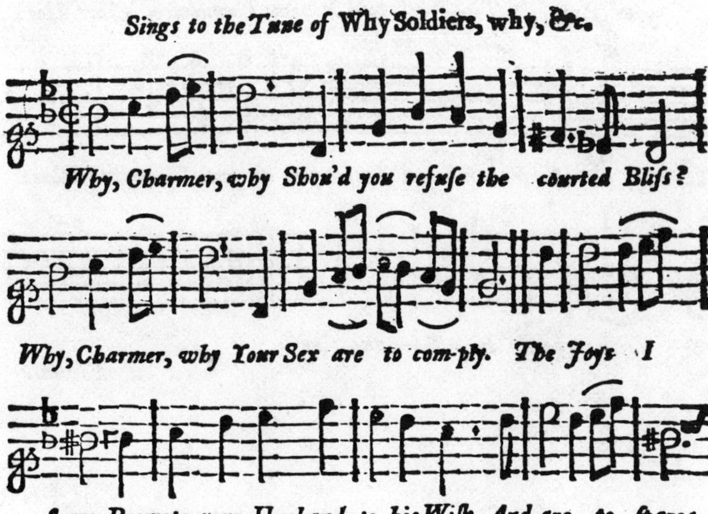

Then

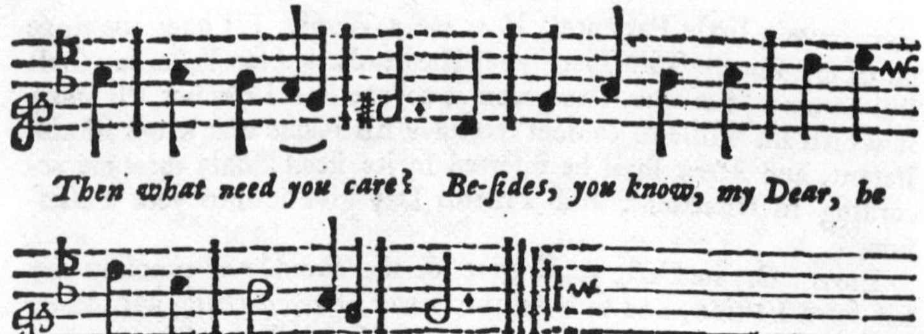

will Have Neighbours Fare.

Lure (*accepting the Purse and Dagger*) *sings to the Tune of* A lovely Lass to a Fryar came.

Exeunt.

SCENE

SCENE *the Park.*

Merit *and* Stout *walking.*

Merit. Dear *Sam,* prithee don't reproach me thus; I'm ruin'd, and now claim your Pity.

Stout. Pity! Heaven knows I pity thee, and will do any thing to serve thee too; but I'm distracted, *Tom,* to see thee thus. A Man o' Sense, of Service, and a Gentleman too, us'd thus! Curse on the Trifler. Does n't he daily prefer such as hate him, because necessary to his Pleasure, and turn a starving those that have render'd him useful and laudable Services? Are not his select Friends a Sett of the sorriest Scoundrels, such Vermin as a Man of Sense or Honour wou'd blush to be seen withal?

Merit. Indeed they're a sorry Pack, but such he chuses to unbend himself with.

Stout. Unbend himself, quoth-a! What, then he's only warp'd into the Figure of a Statesman. A real Great Man thinks the Conversation of Men o' Sense necessary to raise himself by to a Standard of Real Greatness, and has often recourse to 'em, as your Foplings to their Glasses to adjust their Dresses by. But he has a vile Character, his Person I'm a Stranger to.

Merit. I wish I'd been so too: But yonder he comes, if your Curiosity tempts ye to look at him; my Abhorrence forbids me, lest I forget where I am, and that he's a ———

Stout. Prithee which is he, *Tom?*

Merit. In that Chair yonder, but I'll avoid him. (*going.*)

(Stout *runs to see him,* Falcon *lets down his Glass, and says,*)

Falcon. Sir, I'll be sure to take Care of you. (*going on.*)

Stout. Take Care o' me! What the Devil does he mean?

Merit. Ha, ha, ha, ha.

Stout. Take Care o' me? Sure 'tis n't Treason to look at this Lord o' yours; a ———

Merit. Ha, ha, ha, ha; No, *Sam*; but he takes you for one o' those he has promis'd to provide for; ha, ha, ha, ha.

Stout. Oh Pox! Is it that? I thought I must ha' gone to the *Gatehouse* for't. What, then I'm to have a Place, I warrant, because I star'd at a Lord: Very pretty truly. But the worst on't is, that such as promise without good Reason, will break 'em without much Scruple; so that I'm not at all lifted up about it.

Merit. His Promises are fatal Snares to his Friends: I wish he'd promise his Enemies only; he'd be more secure too than in promoting them as he does.

Stout. He fears his Foes, and therefore enables 'em to hurt him by giving them Power: His Friends he thinks he's sure of, and therefore neglects 'em.

Merit. Fear and Falshood are indeed the main Springs of all his Politicks: Tho' an honest Brave Man is above the little Tricks commonly call'd *Policy*, Cowards only can lye, and Fools deceive: Such Talents, however fitting a Sharper or a Pimp, are very unbecoming a Gentleman, and much more a Statesman.

Stout *sings to the Tune of* Ye Nymphs and Sylvian Gods, &c.

Merit. *Sam,* be so good to turn up that Walk a little; I see one coming that I'd gladly talk with alone for two or three Minutes.

Stout. (*looking*) Your Wife, I guess; but 'tis an odd time with her, Joy; so I'll leave ye. *Exit* Stout.

Enter Lure.

Merit. Well, my dear Life, I long to know my Fate, an' yet fear to ask it: How say ye?

Lure. (*kissing him*) I know you're big with Expectation, Dear: Suppose I shou'd tell ye now ———

Merit. Nay, prithee Girl, don't trifle wi' me: Am I happy or miserable?

Lure. Now hang me, *Tom,* if I cou'd n't find i' my Heart to put on the Woman for half an Hour, an' plague ye with Uncertainties: But come, you're too honest an' open your self, I'll put ye out o' your Pain. Here, my Dear, (*pulling out a Dagger and Purse*) see these, an' then judge of my Success.

Merit. *Peggy,* you shew me Wonders, pray unriddle 'em to me.

Lure. This Purse of 100 Pieces is to convince me of his sincere Intentions of giving you the Patent Place he refus'd you Yesterday: He's now gone to have the Name of *Purchase* erac'd, and yours inserted in its stead. I'm to see him in half an Hour at a certain Place, when he'll give it into my possession; and in case o' failure, this Dagger is given me to revenge the Affront withal.

Merit. What do I see? What do I hear? My better Angel, (*embracing her*) I must alwaies love thee; and tho' I'm acquainted with his am'rous Vein, 'tis even cruel to ask what he expects from thee for all this.

Lure. Gen'rous *Merit,* I'll not keep thee in the Dark as to that neither. He has Hopes, I confess, of being very free with me; but I've so manag'd it with him, that even that too is left to my Gen'rosity. I'll deal with him, *Tom,* ne'er fear me.

Merit. I'll trust thee, Love; my Honour can never suffer by thee, I'm sure. You're going to meet him now, I suppose.

Lure. This Moment, Child, tho' a little before the Time; for it becomes me to wait our good Fortune thee know'st. Adieu.

Exit Lure *singing to the Tune of* The Old-Man's Wish.

Shall the Thieves watch all Night, and the Bailiffs all Day,

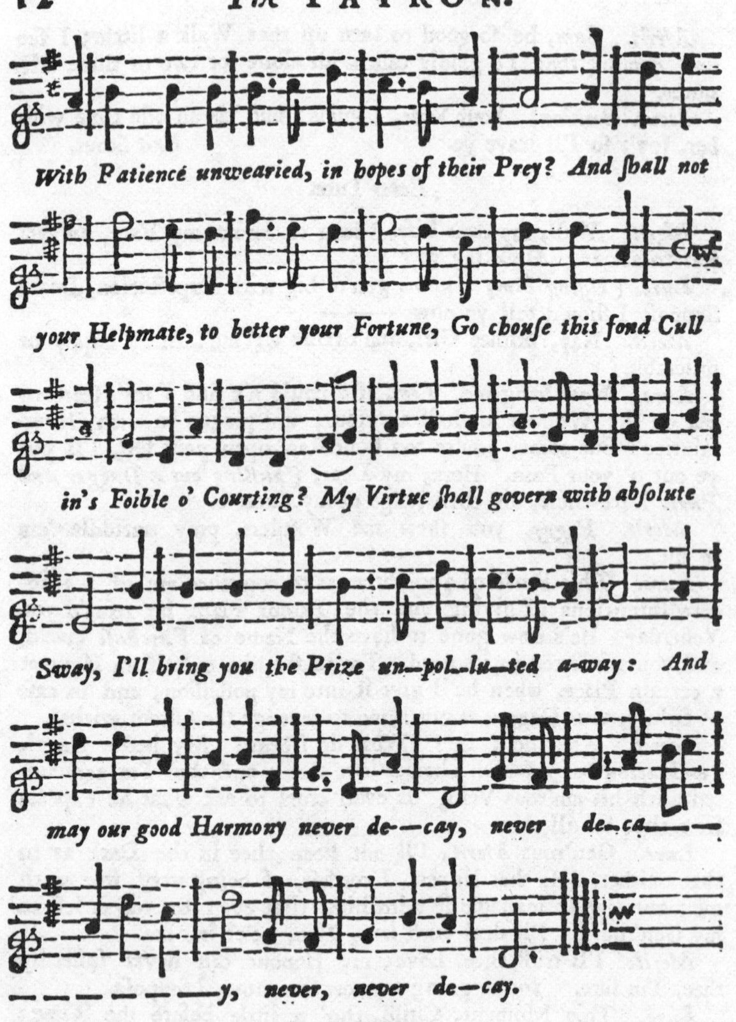

Re-enter Stout.

Merit. Come wish me Joy, Friend; my Wife gives me Reasons to hope.

Stout. Aye, an' to fear too, I shou'd think, that have a Wife so handsome. His Lordship likes her then? Hey?

Merit. Yes, yes; I believ'd he wou'd like her: But what think ye if I shou'd have a Patent to-day for what he refus'd me yesterday?

Stout.

Stout. Why, that your Wife has ſtuck at nothing to ſerve ye: Was I your Herald, *Tom*, I'd give ye the Stagg's Head for your Creſt. You'll pay dear enough for your Promotion i' faith.

Merit. Why thou'rt a very Infidel, *Sam*: D'ye think I cannot truſt my Wife?

Stout. Yes faith, with any body, I'll ſay that for thee: Not that I've any Perſonal Objection to thy Wife, but think that no Wife is to be truſted in ſuch Circumſtances, with ſuch Allurements too, as that Wretch will certainly offer who has already ruin'd your Fortunes.

Merit. I thank thy Friendſhip, *Sam*; but to what purpoſe ſhou'd I ſuſpect the Wife I can truſt, and call in imaginary Evils, that have but too many real ones already?

[*Sings to the Tune of* Love's a Dream of mighty Treaſure.

[Exeunt.

Sir

Sir Jolly Glee *and* Pointer *meeting.*

Pointer. Sir *Jolly Glee*, your moſt Obedient; I did n't imagine I ſhou'd ſee you but at your Lodgings, and was going thither: I hope you lik'd the Lady you've left ſo ſoon.

Glee. Dear *Pointer*, lik'd her, ſay ye? Who cou'd do otherwiſe? She's *Elizium*, ——— Ah *Paul!* ſuch a Night! ſo wrapt! ſo tranſported! that Fleſh and Blood cou'd n't bear it any longer.

Pointer. I'm glad, Sir *Jolly*, you'd no other Reaſon for parting.

Glee. No, only that Love and Deſire had wound up my Spirits high as the Chain of Nature cou'd reach, and it became neceſſary I ſhou'd quit the Extaſies of the Night for the ſeaſonable Recruits of the Day.

Pointer. The Bottle, Sir *Jolly*, is ſov'raign in ſuch a Caſe; but you're ſatisfied now that ſhe's Mrs. *Rhubarb*, the Lady you fell in love with at the Play-houſe.

Glee. Yes, *Paul*; your Directions had ſatisfied me o' that before, or I'd ne'er parted with my Money ſo freely. I ſaw her in an Undreſs behind her Father's Counter, reaching ſome Things ſhe wanted; and, after that, drinking Tea in the back Shop.

Pointer. Pray how did you diſpoſe o' your ſelf, Sir *Jolly*, the while? I had forgot to tell you I had an Acquaintance liv'd over the Way.

Glee. No matter; I walk'd by the Door for near an Hour, making my Remarks to my own Satisfaction. She'as promis'd to dreſs to-day in the Cloaths I gave her, and wear the Watch and Equipage.

Pointer. I commend her, faith; they're extreamly fine.

Glee. Aye, had they been all, I'd been well off; but Two thouſand Pounds is a monſtrous Price for One Year's Enjoyment.

Pointer. But then you're to conſider, Sir *Jolly*, that ſhe's a Woman of Fortune; her Father can give her Five thouſand Pounds at leaſt; ſo that her Reputation's worth more than the Trifle you mention; And had n't her Inclination been equal to yours, let me tell ye, Sir, you'd ne'er have had her on any Conſideration.

Glee. You have not paid the whole Sum, *Paul.*

Pointer. No, only the Five hundred Pounds, Sir *Jolly*, in hand; the other Fifteen hundred Pounds I ſhall, by Agreement, pay her to-morrow Morning; they're the Terms you depoſited it upon.

Glee. True; but hark ye, *Paul:* Cou'd n't I contrive to ſave the reſt? You ſhan't pay it yet at leaſt.

Pointer. Indeed I muſt, Sir *Jolly*; I'm bound in Honour; Such a Trick wou'd ruin me with the Ladies for ever.

Glee.

Glee. Cou'd I ha' ravish'd now, what a mass of Money had been sav'd!

Pointer. Yes indeed, but you my Lord, and Colonel *Fitz-Devil*, have done too many of those things a'ready; shou'd either of ye attempt it again, the Mobb will tear ye to pieces.

Glee. Well, since there's no Relief, I must e'en kiss it out, *Paul*: I'd fain ha' sav'd the Fifteen hundred however.

Pointer. 'Tis impossible, (*aside*) for that comes to me.

Glee. *Paul*, good by t'ye: Shall I see ye at Lord *Falcon*'s by and by? [*Exit* Glee.

Pointer. Sir *Jolly*, your Servant; I shall certainly be there.

[*Sings to the Tune of* We Dragoons lead merry Lives.

Pimping is the Trade best thrives, fal de ral, &c.
Sale of Maidens, and of Wives, fal de ral, &c.
Brings us Profit, gives Pretence,
More than Virtue, Wit, or Sence,
And may sometimes raise one up to Posts of Honour.

ACT

ACT II.

SCENE, *an Apartment, with a Couch.*

[*Lord* Falcon *and* Lure *coming forward Hand in Hand.*]

Falcon. WELL, my Dear, you see I have kept my Word.

Lure. I hope too I have answer'd your Expectation, my Lord.

Falcon. Yes, my transporting Angel, Possession has given me such Pleasures! such exquisite Pleasures! that Imagination never form'd an Idea of. You must alwaies be mine.

Lure. It must be with Caution then; my Honour must not be suspected, lest my domestick Quiet be destroy'd: This Place of Four hundred Pounds a Year will plentifully furnish us all the Necessaries of Life, and 'twill be too prodigal to throw away the Enjoyment on't.

Falcon. This Place, Dear, is but an Earnest of my Love, and thy Honour will alwaies be safe. The Mistress of this House will be glad o' your Acquaintance, she's supported by my Bounty.

Lure. She tells me, she's an Officer's Widow.

Falcon. She passes for such, but her Husband never was in the Army: He cou'd exercise his Knife and Fork very well, and dy'd at the Siege of a Venison-Pasty, I'm told; but no matter, she has Reputation enough to secure thine, an' I shall alwaies esteem thy Honour as sacred as *Magna Charta.* Shall I see thee again tomorrow?

Lure. Not till the Day following, my Lord; I shall then go abroad to buy a few Necessaries, and will take that Opportunity of meeting you here.

Falcon. Delicious Creature! (*pulling out's Pocket-book*) accept this small Bill to buy 'em withal, 'tis a Hundred Pounds only, a meer Trifle to the Woman I love. But I'm on the Rack, Child, to think I must wait so long e're I see thee: May I then promise my self a full Feast of Love?

Lure. (*kissing him*) You may, my Lord: But stay, (*returning his Dagger*) pray take this back again, as you're a Man of Honour, I shall alwaies act on the Defensive.

Falcon.

Falcon. Ha, ha, ha, ha, dear Angel! (*kissing*) But lest I faint, Love, with fasting so long, I have thought to come and wish *Merit* Joy to-Night of his Patent; I'll bring a Friend or two to drink a Bottle of his Wine tell him, an' in case he has a Friend likewise, so much the better; we'll be merry, ——— an' wise too, I promise ye.

Lure. I hope so: What time may we expect your Lordship?

Falcon. About Eight. You told him I'd repented of my Cruelty to him, and was sending to let him know as much when you came?

Lure. I did, my Lord; an' can assure ye he believ'd it too.

Falcon. Ha, ha, ha, ha! I'm well acquainted with his Credulity, an' have exercis'd it too, but no matter, he had then been only serviceable to me in Elections, or so, ——— an Article I seldom regard when over; but now he's useful to my Pleasures, and shall have an ample Reward.

Sings to the Tune of Go build me a House in the Moor.

Let Sots that can serve
Court-Virtue and starve,
And still dance Attendance, and wait;
My Pleasures I prize,
And those that will rise
Must Pimp if they mean to be great, brave Boys;
Must Pimp, &c.

Lure. I'm pleas'd, my Lord, at the Share I've had in this happy Turn o' Mr. *Merit*'s good Fortune, 'twill insure me his Affection however.

Falcon. Ay, Jewel, he's a Brute else: But I know honest *Tom*, he'l now be as fond o' thee as I am, allowing for the Deference of

Spouſe and Spark; but he ne'er eſteem'd thee before, or I had heard o' ſuch a Treaſure; an' not, that he'ad ſpent all, an' had nothing left to recommend him to any-body.

Lure. Ha, ha, ha! He did n't think of me in ſuch a way, my Lord.

Falcon. Amazing Stupidity! Not think of thee? Oons, hadſt thou been mine, I had thought o' nothing elſe: Why, in Publick Buſineſs thee hadſt alwaies been uppermoſt, and (tho' a pleaſing Miſtake) a *Billet-deux* o' Thine might ha' been ſent to a Foreign Potentate inſtead of a State-Letter.

Lure. You're extreamly gallant, my Lord; but you wou'd n't let the Honour of your Office ſuffer for ſuch a Trifle.

Falcon. What if it had? Better any thing (nay, every thing) ſuffer, than the Miſtreſs of my Soul ſhou'd be forgot.. The Honour o' my Office, quoth-a.

Sings to the Tune of Come, be jolly, fill your Glaſſes.

Falcon.

Falcon. Dear Life, (*kissing*) you'll remember me to *Tom.*

Lure. I'll be sure to obey all your Lordship's Commands.

Falcon. (*kissing again*) Matchless Treasure! adieu.

Exeunt.

SCENE, *Lord* Falcon's; *present Sir* Jolly Glee *and* Pointer.

Glee. His Lordship sends for us only to make us wait: I think these Great Men imagine one has nothing else to do.

Pointer. He'll not be long, his Servant tells me.

Glee. If Pleasure falls in his Way, one can't answer for him; the Ladies must be attended.

Pointer. His Lordship has n't any such Affair on's Hand to-day that I know of.

Glee. Then, I suppose, he has none; for he does nothing without ye.

Pointer. He has too much Business to help himself.

Glee. And too much State to engage in the sweetest part of an Amour, the Courtship.

Pointer. 'Tis a Drudgery to us that Procure only.

Glee. You've the Pleasure of being well rewarded for't; you do nothing o' Freecost, *Paul*; or you might help one to a Cast-off o' my Lord's.

Pointer. Oh, Sir *Jolly!* you're provided for already, for one Twelvemonth, Mrs. *Rhubarb*, ——

Glee. Ay, *Paul*, at a hellish rate —— Two thousand Pounds: 'Tis well there's a Heaven in those Arms, or I'd been devilishly bit.

Pointer. Ay, those Arms, Sir *Jolly!* Did you ever see such? Then those Eyes! those Cheeks! those Lips! those Teeth! those Breasts! Then such a Neck! such a Hand! such a Leg! such a Foot! Gad, I'm quite out o' Breath with describing her Beauties; What must You be then that enjoy 'em, Sir *Jolly?*

Glee. Why, intranc'd, *Paul*, what d'ye think? Not but the Jade's a little awkard, I must tell ye.

Pointer. A little at first it may be, Sir *Jolly*; but now she comes to be mouth'd, and set upon her Haunches, she'll soon grow more tractable.

Glee. Rot ye, *Paul*, you talk like a rough Rider: Don't ye want to compleat the Breaking of her, hey?

Pointer. No, by the lard, Sir; I want no more to caress the Woman I praise, than a Jockey does to mount the Horse he means to part with; 'Tis my Business to set 'em off, Sir *Jolly*.

[Pointer *sings to the Tune of* To see the Troopers all come home.]

That Pimp's in a piteous Condition
Who gives up his Gain for his Love;
And he's but a dull Politician
Whom Merit or Mercy can move.
The Wise think their Profit their Pleasure,
All Things by Self-Int'rest they measure,
And, when they mount, will ride like Mules
Your easy, honest, human Fools,
And tickle 'em out of their Treasure.

(*a knocking at the Door.*) But here comes my Lord.

Enter Lord Falcon.

Falcon. Sir *Jolly Glee*, your humble Servant, (*embracing*) I'm sorry I made you wait thus; but, immortal Love! such an Affair you'l pardon me, I know, when you hear it.

Glee. Not a Lady sure: *Paul* said, your Lordship had n't any such Affair in hand to-day that he knew of, and therefore I concluded you had none.

Falcon. He knew of! No, no, *Paul* ne'er knew of any thing like this; he has no Correspondence worth encouraging.

(*Both.*) No!

Falcon.

Falcon. No, no, he'l wait ye a Country-Waggon at the *White Bear* above (*pointing*) indeed, and help one to a clumsy Jade made vicious by ill breaking; or a discarded Chamber-maid, that has been the Hack of a whole Family; *Paul* flies no higher; I've had Twelve Gross of such from him.

Glee. Nay, my Lord, he sets nobler Game to my Knowledge.

Pointer. Pray, my Lord, remember the Banker's Wife.

Falcon. Damn her, I shall ne'er forget her, a saucy clumsy Cit, I had such Drudgery on't.

Pointer. But the Woman o' Quality last Week; here's a Letter from her to your Lordship. (*giving a Letter.*)

Falcon. Oh! she wrapt in Woollen only, according to Act of Parliament: I wonder I shou'd forget her indeed.

Pointer. Mrs. *Frisky*, my Lord, what think ye of her?

Falcon. A young skittish Thing, that shou'd ha' been train'd Three Months e're a Man o' Quality shou'd undergo the Toil of her. In short, *Paul*, I'll now consent to your going abroad, since I can help my self so deliciously.

Glee. *Paul* go abroad, my Lord! I hope you don't cast him off.

Falcon. No, no, Sir *Jolly*; *Paul* goes in a good Character; 'tis what he'as long sollicited.

Glee. I shall rejoice in *Paul*'s Advancement, my Lord, who has provided for me so lusciously; for I have had a Lady of his procuring, and a Miracle too, notwithstanding you run him down thus.

Falcon. Not to compare with mine, Sir *Jolly*, I'll be sworn.

Glee. Because mine's incomparable, my Lord, either in Beauty, Wit, or good Humour. She was a Virgin last Night too.

Falcon. Ha, ha, ha, poor Sir *Jolly*! I really pity you; a fine Woman, and the First Time, like Fox-hunting, is more Toil than Pleasure. Mine's a married Woman, I confess, but of unsully'd Reputation, and incomparable Beauty.

Pointer. My Lord, I'll lay you Odds on Sir *Jolly*'s Mistress.

Falcon. D'ye tell me so, Pimp? Why had n't I her then?

Pointer. Nay, my Lord, Sir *Jolly*'s did n't want for Price.

Falcon. What then, ye Sot? Did ever I refuse a Price? I'm as able to purchase as Sir *Jolly*, I hope: But you need not think of going abroad, Sir, now. However, to convince ye both of your Mistakes, I shew her t'ye: I'm to drink a Bottle to-night with her Husband.

Glee. The Husband won't look awry at us, I hope.

Falcon. No, I've sufficiently oblig'd him already; I've sent him a Patent by his Wife to-day for a Place of Four hundred Pounds a Year, and therefore may expect a Welcome to a Bottle at Night with a Friend or two.

Poin-

Pointer. Pray, my Lord, whose Wife is't has Power to please thus after you've had her?

Falcon. Tom Merit's.

Both. *Merit*'s! Is he married then?

Pointer. Gad, if I had known he'ad a Wife so handsome, I had been more complaisant to him.

Falcon. You know nothing that conduces to Pleasure; to sit with thee is Drudgery: I've had her to-day, but no Words on't, the Lady's Honour is not to be soil'd.

Glee. (*aside*) No, I'll be sworn, after you've handl'd it so freely: (*aloud*) But your Lordship can't boast much of your Thrift neither, Four hundred Pounds a Year's a pretty good Price.

Falcon. A publick Gratuity for a private Favour, my Way of doing Business, Sir *Jolly*; but the Husband has Worth, and the Wife's inestimable. Will ye go, Sir *Jolly*? The Time's come, and my Coach waits ye.

Glee. I must go first and make an Excuse to my Charmer, but will be with you in half an hour. I know Mr. *Merit*'s.

Falcon. Be sure ye come, Sir *Jolly*, for I long to shew you my Treasure, and don't half enjoy her till my Friends know my Happiness.

Sings to the Tune of, Of all the simple things we do, &c.

Prize,

Prize, And all the World envies our State?

Glee. But neither the Lady nor her Husband will have much Reason to thank your Lordship for making so free with their Reputations.

Falcon. Ha, ha, ha, hee! Dear Sir *Jolly*, you make me laugh. Prithee haven't I made their Fortunes? And what the Devil ha' they to do with Reputation? Your poor Dogs indeed pretend to live by it, an' poorly, Heaven knows, not having Stock enough to get a Living by; but for the Rich, they're absolutely above it. We'll go, *Paul*; you'll be sure to come, Sir *Jolly*.

Glee. I'll certainly wait on you, my Lord.

Exeunt.

SCENE, Merit's *Lodgings*.

(Merit *and* Lure *meeting*.)

Merit. Come, my dear Life, Isn't that the Instrument of my Preservation? (*pointing to the Patent.*)

Lure. Ay, my Dear (*kissing*) here's Life, and it comforts; take it into thy possession, and long may'st thou live to enjoy it.

(*giving it.*)

Merit. (*opening it*) Verily the same, and to You 'tis I owe my future Happiness, Dear Angel! (*embracing*) kind Preserver! a Helpmate indeed! I'm amaz'd, *Peggy*, and yet 'twou'd be ungenerous to enquire into thy Conduct in this Affair.

Lure. Generous *Merit*, I'll save you the Trouble, by assuring you, that I've preserv'd my Character entire; your Honour, Child, has n't suffer'd in the least.

Merit. (*kissing*) I must believe thee, Dear; thee wast alwaies consistent.

Sings to the Tune of Whilst the Town's brim-full of Folly.

What

What tho' Wilely Po—li—ticians Men be——
—guile of all Conditions, And their self-ish Ends disguise?
Beau—ty Magick has will charm'em, Of their boasted
Arts dis—arm'em; Love-ly Woman's on—ly Wise.
Beauty Magick has will charm'em, Of their boasted Arts
disarm'em; Lovely Woman's on—ly Wi——————
—————se, Love—ly Woman's on-ly Wise.

Enter

(*Enter* Stout.)

Come, *Sam*, now give us Joy; my Wife has brought me the Patent, and will take it ill if ſhe has n't a Kiſs on this Occaſion.

Stout. (*ſalutes her*) I heartily wiſh ye Joy, both of your Marriage and the Place: 'Tis Four hundred Pounds a Year; Is n't it?

Merit. Yes, *Sam*, a *quantum ſuff*. I bleſs my Stars, my Spouſe too has preſerv'd her Honour.

Stout. The Lady has indeed done Wonders, at which I heartily rejoyce.

Lure. My Lord bid me tell ye, Child, that he intends to come to-night, with a Friend or two, to give you Joy, and drink a Bottle o'your Wine: If you have a Friend likewiſe, 'tis ſo much the better, he ſays: The Deſign is, to be merry.

Merit. His Lordſhip has provided his Welcome: *Sam*, I claim your Company on this Occaſion.

Stout. Rot him, you cou'd n't ask a greater Proof of my Friendſhip, than to ſit an Hour in ſuch Company; however, for thy ſake, *Tom*, I'll try to be civil.

Merit. Ay, prithee *Sam* don't ſhew any Reſentment, let's be merry however.

Sings to the Tune of, Of all Comforts I miſcarry'd, &c.

I can

I can hate him, yet forbear him,
For thy sake this Night I'll spare him:
Attendance was thy Curse, no Doubt on't;
'Tis happy thou'rt deliver'd out on't.
Merit. *Come, kind Friend, no more let's grieve,*
No more the Monster shall deceive;
Friendly Fate forbids our Fears,
Gen'rous Wine shall drown our Cares.
Stout. *Pox, let him rot, let his Name be forgot,*
For it is n't one good Deed can give him Fame:
May his Ruin be closely pursuing,
And he overtaken, be cover'd with Shame.
May his Ruin, &c.

Exit Lure.

Enter Lord Falcon *and* Pointer.

Merit. My good Lord *Falcon*, I'm your very humble Servant, many Thanks for my good Fortune: Mr. *Pointer*, I'm yours.

Falcon. I come, honest *Tom*, to rejoyce with thee, and assure thee I have done it with a friendly Heart. (*shaking Hands*)

Merit. I thank your Lordship, 'tis a generous Action, and will (I hope) redound to your Honour.

Falcon. I come likewise to give thee Joy o' thy Marriage, *Tom*, I was a Stranger to it till now: I have given thy Wife Joy already. Thou hast an excellent Choice i'faith.

Merit. Every way, my Lord, my Wife regards my Honour, and my Patron his Promises.

Pointer. I heartily wish you Joy, Mr. *Merit*.

Merit. I thank ye, Sir. My Lord, here's Mr. *Stout*, a good Friend of mine, thinks himself oblig'd likewise on my account. (*presenting* Stout)

Falcon. Sir, your humble Servant; I'm so well pleas'd with serving our Friend *Merit*, that I'm sorry I did it not sooner.

Stout.

Stout. My Lord, I'm heartily glad you've done it now, *Better late than never*; for a Good Man was never much nearer being lost, nor more critically sav'd.

Falcon. Sir, I had certainly distinguish'd him e're this time, but am so pester'd with Swarms of Suitors, that I had almost dropt him in the Crowd; but a little Leisure and Reflection had this Morning brought me to a Resolution of providing for him, even just as his Lady came to upbraid me for my Neglect, and was that Minute sending my Servant to let him know it. Where's Mrs. *Merit*?

Merit. But in the next Room, she'll be here in a Minute, my Lord.

(Falcon, Merit, *and* Stout *seem talking together.*)

Pointer. (*aside*) Rot it, this Day's Work undoes me, if she appears as charming now as in the Morning; and I cou'd e'en hang my self for not knowing o' this Woman, seeing her Husband every Day at my Lord's; but then, seeing him coldly us'd, I like a Puppy must shun his acquaintance: Had it come thro' my Hands, it had been the making of us both; but, as 'tis, infallibly ruins me, unless Sir *Jolly* shou'd come; and I can prevail with him to disparage her to his Lordship; he never was accus'd of Constancy that I remember.

Enter Lure.

Falcon *to* Merit *sings, to the Tune of* See, see, my *Seraphina* comes, *&c.*

[*Exit* Merit.

Pointer. (*aſide*) Oons! Is this the Rarity? I don't need, Sir *Jolly*, to help diſparage her, I can do it effectually my ſelf, and hope, by his ſtaying, he'll not come at all; he'll ruin me another Way if he does.

Falcon. Madam, your moſt devoted. (*ſalutes her*)

Lure. My Lord, your Servant. Sir, I'm yours. (*to* Pointer)

Pointer. Your Servant, Madam, (*ſalutes her*) Why was n't I in this Secret pray? (*aſide*)

Lure. (*aſide*) Becauſe 'twas your Intereſt to betray it, Sir; but mum ————

Enter Sir Jolly Glee.

Pointer. Oons, he's come; now, dear Impudence, protect me, or I'm undone.

Glee. My Lord, your humble Servant: Your Servant. (*to the others*) [*Aſide to* Pointer] I'gad, ſhe's elop'd, *Paul*; but, being dreſs'd in my Livery, I fancy I ſhall ſee her again e're it be long.

Pointer. Yes, Sir *Jolly*, (*aſide*) too ſoon, (*aloud*) no queſtion on't.

Glee. Pray where's Mr. *Merit* and his Lady?

Falcon. That's his Lady, Sir *Jolly*, (*pointing to* Lure) Mr. *Merit*'s hard by.

Glee. (*ſaluting her*) Madam, your moſt devoted, I hope Mr. *Merit*'s well. (*ſtill looking at her*)

Lure. Your humble Servant, Sir, at your Service. (*turning away*)

Falcon. (to Glee) There's an Angel, Sir *Jolly*! Did n't I tell ye? There's an Air, and a Grace! (*Sir* Jolly *ſtill looking*)

Start. (*aſide*) Damn him, he's in Raptures; my Friend has a ſweet time on't.

Falcon.

Falcon. Why, you're amaz'd, Sir *Jolly*.
(*striking him on the Shoulder*)

Glee. I have Reason, my Lord: How's this, *Paul*? What's Mr. *Merit* married to Mrs. *Rhubarb*?

Pointer. Ha, ha, ha! No, no, Sir *Jolly*; this isn't Mrs. *Rhubarb*, tho' somewhat like her: This Lady has been married to Mr. *Merit* these Five Years, I'm told. This isn't she you fell in love with at the Play, Sir *Jolly*.

Glee. No! may be not, Sir; but I'll be sworn she's the same you pass'd upon me for that Lady; the same too that I saw at Mr. *Rhubarb*'s yesterday Morning in an Undress.

Pointer. Pray, Sir *Jolly*, look again; Mrs. *Rhubarb* is taller than this Lady, younger too, and, if I may be so free, a good deal handsomer.

Falcon. Ha, ha, ha, ha! What d'ye mean, Sir *Jolly*? Every like isn't the same: Doesn't *Paul* tell ye, that your Lady is younger, taller, nay, even handsomer, tho' that, I think, is impossible? Pray contain your self, Mr. *Merit* will be here presently, to convince you of your Mistake: Ha, ha, ha!

Glee. Softly, my Lord; I've too many Reasons to assure me I'm right: First, the Lady's now in my Livery; those (*pointing*) are the very Clothes I sent her by *Paul*: Can you deny it pray?

Pointer. I do indeed, Sir *Jolly*: I own the Pattern to be like, but not exactly the same.

Glee. Then there's the Watch and Equipage I'll swear to; (*taking up the Watch*) Here's *Grigg* the Maker.

[*All*] Ha, ha, ha! that's a fine Proof truly.

Glee. But then my Picture: I hope no-body will perswade me that this isn't my Picture.

Pointer. Not in the least like you, Sir *Jolly*; 'tis Mr. *Merit*'s Picture: I'll be judg'd by my Lord else.

Falcon. (*looking*) Nay, faith, the Picture is like; but for the Lady, I'm sure she's not the same you mean, Sir *Jolly*.

Glee. Pray what say ye, Madam, to all this? Did not You and I bless each other last Night, on certain Conditions? And was not you to be mine for a Twelvemonth, ha?

Stout. Sir, you're a Stranger to me, but one thing I'll tell ye, that my Friend wou'dn't spare ye his Wife on any Conditions, not for a Night, much less for a Twelvemonth, were ye better than you are.

Glee. Sir, you're a Stranger to me too, but, in spite of you, your Friend, and the Devil himself, I will say it again, that this Woman was mine last Night, and had contracted to cohabit with me a Year, as Mrs. *Rhubarb*, Daughter to an eminent Druggist in the City, on certain Conditions, one of which were, To have Five

hundred

hundred Pounds in hand; which was paid her yesterday by *Paul Pointer*; I have her Receipt in my Pocket, I'm sure.

Enter Merit.

[*All*] Ha, ha, ha, ha!

Falcon. Dear *Tom Merit*, set us right: Sir *Jolly Glee* has mistaken thy Wife for a Lady that gave him her Company at a Lodging of his last Night, and won't be perswaded out on't.

Stout. Yes truly, and that she was to cohabit with him for Twelve Months as his Harlot: Will you take this o' your Wife, *Tom*?

Merit. Ay, any thing, *Sam*; she has oblig'd me so highly that I can't in Honour take any Exceptions to her Conduct.

Stout. What the plague, *Tom*, not take Exceptions at a Charge of this nature! You're fit to be yoak'd i'faith, your Horns won't choak ye. Were my Wife so aspers'd, I'd ———

Merit. Wife! now ye say something, *Sam*.

Stout. Why, is n't she your Wife then?

Merit. Yes, Sir, under proper Restrictions *pro tempore*, to have and let go at pleasure; not *To Have and to Hold*, I'd have you to think.

Falcon. What, *Tom*, is n't she your real Wife then?

Merit. Only in the same sence, my Lord, as she has been yours, Sir *Jolly*'s, and any-bodyes else that has Occasion for her. *Peggy*'s very communicative, let me tell ye: Honest *Pegg*!

(*chucking her Chin*)

Falcon. Oons! am I bit too? I took her for your real Wife.

Merit. I know you did, I understand you; but I've only the Patent you see, but half the Favour you design'd me, yet I'm a moderate Man, reasonable in my Desires, and content my self without the Horns, you find. Ha, ha, ha, ha!

(*All*) Ha, ha, ha, ha! a good Joke faith.

Falcon. Damn ye all. (*All*) Ha, ha, ha!

Stout. But hark ye, *Tom*; Are you sure, amongst all these Mistakes, that you've really got the Patent at last?

Merit. Yes faith, here it is. (*shewing it*)

Sings to the Tune of Gamiorum.

My

My Lord, becauſe he lik'd my Wife,
Condeſcended to better my Fortune,
And, thank him, gave me this for Life
To excuſe him the Trouble of Courting.
Fal de ral, &c.

II.

But ſhe's no Wife, my Honour's ſafe,
Yet 'twou'd be ungrateful to ſlight her,
Tho' Winners are allow'd to laugh,
Since by her 'tis I've bit the Biter.
Fal de ral, &c.

Falcon. Well, Sir *Jolly*, you're my Companion in Ridicule however.

Glee. But you're nothing out o' Pocket, my Lord; Mr. *Merit* has deſerv'd the Publick Favour you've done him, but that Villain (*to* Pointer) has now Fifteen hundred Pounds in his Hands, beſides the Five already paid to no purpoſe.

Lure. An unconſcionable Pimp! I knew nothing of the Fifteen hundred, I have only a poor Five, which I'm very willing to deſerve at your hands, Sir *Jolly*.

Glee. Phoo pox, you're a Sham, don't prate to me thus.

Lure. Sir, I ſcorn your Words; ask my Lord, pray, whether I'm a Sham or no; I ſcorn to ſham it with any-body, I muſt tell ye.

Stout. The Ladies have it, You were both bewitch'd lately in *Leiceſter-fields*; and I think you're worſe, to purchaſe at ſuch Rates what neither of you can poſſeſs: You'd better return to your Di-

verſions

versions in *Greenwich*-Park, than foil your selves thus at Chamber-Practice.

Glee. Come, Mr. *Pimp*, have ye your Pocket-book about ye? (*shaking his Cane at* Pointer) Pray refund the Fifteen hundred Pounds immediately; the other Five I shall expect by to-morrow Night: I've nothing to do with the Woman.

Pointer. Yes, Sir, (*giving Bills*) here 'tis, but you can't blame me, I was impos'd on; she assur'd me she was Mrs. *Rhubarb*.

Glee. Sir, your Excuses do you no Service; you undertook upon your own Knowledge, and as you're worth the Five hundred, I'm very easie about it, only suffer me to give a Receipt for this in the mean time. (*kicking him out*)

Falcon. Sir *Jolly*, let's go, we only stay to be laugh'd at: There's one (*pointing to* Stout) can be merry enough at such Mistakes in his Betters.

Stout. I allow none my Betters but such as have more Sence or Virtue than my self; and if at any time I give way to Wealth or Power without 'em, 'tis as I do it to a Chimney-sweeper, lest they harm me. Betters, quoth-a! None are better that aren't honester. For your part, my Lord, you have dealt long enough with Pimps and Scoundrels, to think there's Credit in being innocently deceiv'd by a Man of Sence.

Falcon. I never dealt with you, Sir, however; that's one Comfort.

Stout. No! why you promis'd to take Care of me this Morning in the Park; and, having no Pretensions, I thought I stood fair. You seldom provide for such as have really serv'd ye.

Sings to the Tune of The Old Wife she sent to the Miller her Daughter.

Most

Most Courtiers will promise a Place to provide you,
But from that same Promise your Undoing date;
Attendance for Nothing will likely betide you,
If you can't condescend as a Tool to be great;
A Vacancy find, Sir, is ever the Tone,
And all the Day long
This, this is the Song,
Depend on't, Dear Sir, your Business is done.

II.

But sooner or later we come to our Senses,
And their poor shuffling Arts are thorowly seen;
They ne'er by Evasions can make Recompences,
Or think, 'cause in Power, prov'd Vices to screen:
In spight of their Grandeur, the Tricksters are known,
And all the Day long
This should be the Song,
We hope that your Business will quickly be done.

Falcon. I'll promise now, Sir, to take Care of you in another manner; the State has too much of my Service to suffer this from you.

Stout. I'm glad you threaten, because you alwaies break your Word. But, prithee, what has the State to do with thy Vices? Did the Service require you to neglect *Merit*, or dishonour his suppos'd Wife? Sorry Trifler! I despise ye; such Statesmen will make any State ridiculous. Had I been abus'd like my Friend *Merit*, I shou'dn't have had Leisure to concert such a Scheme of Revenge, but had

Falcon. Oh, the Assassin! Bear witness Gentlemen.

Glee. My Lord, I have a Gentleman's Memory.

Merit. So have I, my Lord; I never remember any thing out of Company.

Falcon. Curse on ye both, what a Conspiracy is here lost now for want of Evidence!

Merit. Come *Peggy*, I owe you a Hundred Pounds on Conditions now happily executed; give me up my Note, and here's a Bank-Bill of a Hundred Pounds for you.

(*exchanging Notes.*)

Lure. I thank ye, Sir; your Hundred, my Lord's Two, and Sir *Jolly*'s Five, makes me a Fortune of Eight hundred Pounds; a good Week's Work, let me tell ye.

Glee. But *Paul*, I fancy, Madam, will make you refund the Five hundred he paid you on my Account.

Lure. I defie him, when I can get a Prisoner in the *Fleet* to marry me for Five Pieces, and acquit me in Law, was it for Five thousand Pounds.

Merit. Well, Sir *Jolly*, I see no great Hurt, tho' the Pimp pay the Five hundred out of his own Pocket, cou'd we reconcile his Lordship and Mr. *Stout* to each other. I shou'd be glad you'd give me your Company in the next Room, I've a Supper and a Bottle o' good Wine waits your Acceptance there.

Glee. With all my Heart, Mr. *Merit*; I'm glad Things are no worse, every one will rejoyce in your good Fortune that knows you. Come, my Lord and Mr. *Stout*, we'll accept of Mr. *Merit*'s Offer. (*putting their Hands together.*)

Sings to the Tune of, Lay aside the Reap-hook, &c.

Lay

Lay aside your Anger, let's be Friends,
And be easie, easie, easie, easie,
Easie whilst we stay:
'Tis certain ev'ry Man has private Ends,
Tho' Pleasure, Gain, or Honour
Make us differ in the Way.

Then let's not envy Others, but pursue,
Each in his Course, with all his Strength
And Skill, his darling Game:
For, were the Tables turn'd, the Worst we do,
Ev'n those which most bespatter us,
Themselves wou'd do the same.

Exeunt omnes.

THE

THE EPILOGUE,

Spoke by LURE.

HEre ends the Dream, no longer Merit's *Wife*;
Poor Pegg *returns to lead her wonted Life,*
Where, free to range, (secur'd by Native Right)
Thro' all the various Scenes of soft Delight:
Tho' but a Day, I stood the sober Joke,
My Neck's e'en gall'd with this same Nuptial Yoke.
What then must be the Case of real Wives?
They lead, no Doubt on't, strange delicious Lives.
Cage'd up like Squirrels, the same Rounds they ring,
And all their Pastime's but the self-same thing.
Not but the Wise will take their Times to stray,
And drop their Friends their Favours by the Way;

But

But then the Clogg, while it excites Desire,
Restrains the Joy, and quells the raging Fire.
To me, 'tis true, when Merit's *Wife in jest,*
'Twas some Relief to seem to Horn his Crest;
And such Intrigues who wou'dn't be pursuing,
When 'twas to save one's own Good Man from Ruin?

Gentiles,
You see a Statesman, *for his Ends,*
Can sometimes, tho' it's late, reward his Friends;
But to o'er-reach him is a Case, it's true,
You Men think strange, with Us 'tis nothing new,
For Women born to Rule are Politicians too.

FINIS.

BOOKS printed for, and sold by JOHN CLARKE *at the* Bible *under the Royal Exchange in* Cornhill.

THE Smugglers, a Farce. *Price* 1 *s.*
The Works of Mr *Farquhar*, 2 vol. 12° *Pr.* 5 *s.*
The Works of Mr. *Cibber*, 2 vol. 4*to*. *Pr.* 1 *l.* 10 *s.*
Scarron's Works, 2 vol. 5 *s.*
The Adventures of *Proteus*; being a Sett of new Novels, in 3 parts, 8*vo*. *Pr.* 5 *s.* 6 *d.*
The Jealous Husband, a Novel, 8*vo*. *Pr.* 1 *s.*
Bulstrode's Essays on 21 different Subjects, 8*vo*. *Pr.* 4 *s.*
Misson's Travels, 4 vol. 8*vo*. *Pr.* 1 *l.*
History of *Virginia*, 8*vo*. *Pr.* 4 *s.*
——— *Guinea*, 8*vo*. *Pr.* 5 *s.*
Gordon's Geographical Grammar, 5 *s.*
As you find it, a Comedy, 4*to*. 1 *s.* 6 *d.*
The Governor of *Cyprus*, a Tragedy, 1 *s.* 6 *d.*
The Fate of *Capua*, a Tragedy, 1 *s.* 6 *d.*
The Grove; or, Lovers Paradise, an Opera, 1 *s.* 6 *d.*
Lady's Last Shift, 1 s. 6 *d.*
Love and a Bottle, 1 s. 6 *d.*
Liberty asserted, a Tragedy, 1 s. 6 *d.*
Love at a Venture, 1 s. 6 *d.*
Love's a Jest, a Comedy, 1 s. 6 *d.*
Pyrrhus King of *Epyrus*, a Tragedy, 1 s. 6 *d.*
Perolla and *Izadora*, a Tragedy, 1 s. 6 *d.*
Phædra and *Hippolitus*, a Tragedy, 1 s. 6 *d.*
Sir *Harry Wildair*, a Comedy, 1 s. 6 *d.*
Titus and *Beronice*, a Tragedy, 1 s. 6 *d.*
Ulysses, a Tragedy, 1 s. 6 *d.*
Voluntiers; or, Stockjobbers, a Comedy, 1 s. 6 *d.*
Constant Couple, a Comedy, 1 s. 6 *d.*
String's Voyages to *Africa*, &c. 7 s. 6 *d.*

Ra-

Books printed for J. Clarke.

Raleigh's Voyages round the World, *Price* 4 s.
Boyer's Dictionary, Fr. and Engl. 7 s. 6 *d.*
Essay on the Nature, Use, and Abuse of Tea; by a Physician, 1 s.
History of the five *Indian* Nations, 2 s.
The Present State of *Great Britain* and *Ireland*; with the best Account of the King's Dominions in *Germany*, 6 s.
St. *Augustine*'s Meditations; English'd by Dr. *Stanhope*, 4 s. 6 *d.*
Sale of *Dunkirk* to the *French*, 1 s. 6 *d.*
Poems on several Occasions; with *Anna Buloigne* to K. *Henry* VIII, an Epistle, 1 s.
Quarles Emblems, 12°, 3 s. 6 *d.*
Rochefoucault's Moral Maxims, 2 s.
Sydenham's Method of curing all Diseases, 12°, 2 s.
Annals of *Corn. Tacitus*, 12°, 10 s.
Vassor's History of *Lewis* XIII. 10 s.
A Collection of the best Novels, 6 vols. 15 s.
Cassandra, a Romance, 5 vols. 12 s. 6 *d.*
The History of the *Saracens*, 2 vols. 8*vo*. 9 s.
Bradley's Universal Calendar of Gardening, 2 s.

Colonel Split-Tail

Bibliographical note:
This facsimile has been made from a copy in the
Henry E. Huntington Library

Colonel *SPLIT-TAIL.*

A NEW

OPERA

As it was Acted at *Verſailles.*

Tranſlated into *ENGLISH* by Monſieur De *DUX.*

—— *Tutum me copia fecit.* Ovid. Met. L. VI

LONDON:

Printed for T. *WARNER*, at the *Black-Boy*, in *Pater-Noſter-Row*, 1730. Price 6 *d.*

PROLOGUE.

P*Ardon Stupidity, the Author craves,*
Apparent Faults, Forgiveness from the Brave.
A criticising Audience damns a Play,
Fortune assist they mayn't be here to Day.
From Box to Pit, and Galleries all round,
Eccho with Claps, 'tis an harmonious Sound.
Kind Fortune grant a Smile from ev'ry Sect,
The Poet charm'd, the Actors do their best.
Sence stick them to the Wall is here presented,
Virtue betrayed, the Colonel's blanketed.
Bawds, Cullies, and Whores, together have combin'd,
To make Examples of all human Kind.
May Virtue reign, and Vice be still subdu'd,
Pernicious Luxury, may it be withstood.
Each Couple Raptures sign with mutual Bliss,
With foulded Arms enjoys each others Kiss.
The World, when honest, Goodness will abound,
United Minds, I wish they may be found.
Each Person strives for his Sovereign's Peace,
Contented Mind is a continual Feast.

Dramatis Personæ.

Colonel SPLIT-TAIL

Jack Playwell - - - } *Two Gamesters.*
Tom Hazard - - - - }

Billy Pleasewell - - }
Tom Bully - - - - } *Three Bullies.*
Anthony Cleverfinger }

Gentlemen Procurers *to the Colonel.*

	Mutes.
Innkeeper,	Harlequin,
Highwayman,	Punch,
Housebreaker,	Scaramouch,
Blowing Doctor,	Satyrs *and* Death, *&c.*
Constable,	
Informer,	

WOMEN.

Bawd,	Sally,
Two Whores,	Innkeeper's Daughter.

Colonel *SPLIT-TAIL.*

A NEW OPERA.

ACT I.

SCENE *a Coffee-House.*

Enter Bawd *and* Two Whores.

Bawd.

HE's ſo inſatiable in his Amours, a perfect Humouriſt in his Savage Diſpoſition, that the Seraglio of *Drury* are quite ſurfeited, and I am e'en tired with my Vocation.

1ſt Wh. Such a Man,

2d Wh. Ought to paſture in *Romney-Marſh*, for the better Eaſement of the fair Sex.

Enter

Enter Sally.

Sally. Ladies your Servant, I ſhall die with Laughter, to think how the Innkeeper has been out-witted.

Bawd. What's the diverting Object ?

1ſt Wh. No doubt Coll. *Split-tail* is the Theme ; —— Nay, out with it.

A SONG *by Sally.*

I.

AN Innkeeper bold, as I ſhall unfold,
Kept beautiful Damſels to wait ;
A Colonel of late, 'twas his good Fate,
With one of thoſe Girls to be great.

II.

The Purchaſe was made, and ſhe was miſlaid,
Bliſs of Pleaſures with Nuptial Embraces.
My Dear I can't bear, ſuch a monſt'rous Share,
Take your Money without more Entreaties.

III.

He trebl'd the Sum, which was nineteen and one,
Such Trifles he ne'er gave before,
The ſecond Attack made the Bed to crack,
I believe it for a Son of a Whore.

IV.

IV.

He swore, Damn his Blood, that he was then
robb'd
By his Landlord's vile Bitch of a Maid,
Of Britches and Money, and she of her Honey,
Such Virtue was ne'er so betray'd.

V.

The Girl, out of Fear, to save Credit most dear,
Returned the Sum to one Farthing;
The Innkeeper her Master, for Fear of a Disaster
Lost twenty times that Sum by her Bargain,
ha ha ha ha

Bawd. A true Emblem of Villainy, the Coll. promised me 50 Pieces, which happen'd to be Copper Plate —— proved all Half-pence, for procuring beautiful *Sally*, declar'd it was Money enough as Times went.

Sally. I'll blanket the dear Soul.

Bawd. Every kind Girl has her Favourite Man; their Assistance is requisite.

Sally. The Scrub —— he's a perfect Antidote against Lechery; — and for debauching of me I'll ——

1st Wh. Take his Money first.

2d. Whore.

2d. Whore. In my Opinion, Coach Hire and Whores-Hire ought to be paid beforehand, especially by Bites and Gamesters of the Town.

Sally. Here comes my favourite *Billy* —— the Air of so agreeable a Soul I must adore.

Enter Billy Pleasewell *and Sings,*

I'VE rov'd and I've rang'd o'er the Town,
But now my true Heart I've found,
The Pleasure pursuing has turn'd my own Ruin,
Fair Sally *thou gave the Death Wound.*

Sally *Answers.*

SInce Cupid *has engag'd both our Hearts,*
A Silken Band, and ties us both fast,
No Love shall be wanting that I'm possess'd in,
My dear Soul I'll die e'er I part.
[They embrace each other.

Bawd. Nausious Love without Money, is like a beautiful Man without a prevailing Argument.

1st. Whore. Here comes my *Tom Bully*; he's a charming Fellow for Woman; Who can chuse but love him.

2d Whore.

2d Whore. And my Beauty, *Anthony Clever-finger.*

Enter Tom Bully *and* Anthony Clever-finger *drunk.*

Tom B. Zouns the Coast is clear —— hey, Bitches, no Culls —— turn out.

1st Whore. Our Husbands have caught a Fox.

2d Whore. Our Fellows are as fond of Money as a Courtier of a Pension.

A CATCH *by* Anthony Cleverfinger.

OF all the Cheats in the Town,
A Sharper, a Thief, or a Bum,
It's proper to mix a Whore in betwixt,
Your Money they ne'er will return.

First Whore.

SInce Pelf is a Thing you adore,
Take it —— for a Son of a Whore;
In Process of Time Jack Catch will confine,
And pay thee off all thy old Score.

Sally. Here comes the Hell-fire Colonel, with two more of his sinking Culls with him: Since our Husbands are by, be sure, Gentle-

men,

men, when I cry out, come to my Affiftance —— I'll tofs him with a Pox to him; bring one of the largeft Blakets to your Affiftance, begon. [*Exeunt three Bullies.*

Bawd. Now Proftitutes, every Girl to her Poft.

Enter Colonel, Jack Playwell, Tom Hazard.

Col. Ouns Man every one to his Bird; and for the Diverfion of the whole Company, I'll give you a polite Catch, and a very Authentick one.

I'LL *fing you a Song of late,*
By my Sol Mon 'twas that Girle's Fate
To facrifice her All for nothing at all,
For her Money of me fhe muft wait, ha ha ha

Jack Pl. Colonel you are known amongft the Harlots.

Tom H. One of his own making —— beft known to his moft Noble Honour.

Bawd. Colonel confider an unfortunate Girl that once facrificed all that was moft dear to your Honour, is now become a Sacrifice — and an Object of Pity.

Col. The Bitch —— not a Grigg, by *Jupiter*, however, make a Guinea Bowl of Punch; clap

clap in a dozen Glasses of Jellics ——— Mrs. *Flirt* may want *Rosin.*

Sally. Tortur'd ---- rack'd ! ---- I am impatient for Revenge [*Aside.*

Playwell. A Captivated entangled by a Harlot ——— admits of Room ;

Hazard. Especially his own bringing up. My Friend, 'tis Time to be gone.

Playwell. Come, Girls, we'll away to the *Bagnio* ——— Colonel, your Servant ; we'll meet you to Morrow, precisely, at eleven, at *Sebastin*'s Gaming-Table.

[*Exeunt* Playwell, Hazard, *and two Whores.*

Bawd. On my Reputation, Colonel, this Cowl deserves Five Pieces ——— but not Brass.

Col. Face, as you have been an Old Procurer in the Practice of Domesticks, suitable to my vitious Inclinations, take the Money in solid Gold, begon for New Ware, for I am quite surfeited with two Amours with one Woman ; 'tis properly the Work of Porters ; we fine Gentlemen know better.

Bawd. As I'm a Woman of Honour, I must kneeds own, 'tis only bite the Biter. [*Aside.*

Bawd *sings.* [*Aside.*

FIVE *Guineas to one the Col'nel's undone;*
Sally *the fair, with a politick Air,*
Blankets the Col'nel into a Despair.

Exit Bawd.

Sally cries out Murder! Murder!

Enter Bullies *with a Blanket*; Harlequin, Blowing Doctor, Punch, Death *with an Hour-Glass.*

Bullies. Thou Villain —— What Business have you with a Nobleman's Wife well known?

Sally. Because I would not yield, he was going to kill me.

1st B. In with him.

2d B. Colonel your Money —— or you're a gone Man.

[*A Dance by* Harlequin, &c. *round the Col. Death looking on.*

Col. Take Money and Britches, all all all.

[*Strips off his Britches, then they toss him in the Blanket.*

Sally. I'll accept of it as Part of Payment, dear Colonel; a corporal Punishment to you is very requisite, 'tis only for the Good of your Understanding —— March you Bitch.

[*Death*

[*Death descends, the Colonel ascends in a Chair three Yards in Heighth, without his Britches, by Harlequin's Magick Art.*

Enter Satyrs, they dance, one with an Hour-Glass in one Hand, with this Inscription,

Time's almost spent.

With a Dart in the other, with this Inscription,

This Dart shall pierce Thee to the Heart.
[*Exeunt Satyrs.*

Blow. D. Since those Outlandish, Black Monsters are gone down with the Colonel, O poor Soul! How dismal he looks! ---Whoring is a crying Evil, it sends Mankind certainly to the Devil, especially when Maids are often civil. Seignior *Harlequino, &c.* assist me in my Opperation, and with this Machine Bellows I'll blow out all his Iniquity.

They assist him, and he blows.

By Gad he's lighter by a hundred Weight: away with him, away with him, the Col. is not used to walk; take up the Body, March. [*Exeunt Omnes* in Ttriumph.

END *of* ACT. I.

ACT II.

SCENE *the Masquerade Table standing; Gamesters on one Side.*

Enter Bawd, Sally, Innkeeper's Daughter, *Two* Whores, Colonel, Gentleman Procurer, Innkeeper, Highwayman, Housebreaker.

Bawd Sings.

THIS Humour's a politick Invention,
Where Whores and Rogues meet for Diversion,
Then Girls of Debonere, be not in Despair,
We'll settle the Sins of the Nation.

The Colonel slips a Billetdeux *in* Sally's *Hands, imagining her to be a Woman of Quality.*

Sally

Sally Reads.

AT once my Eyes beheld your lovely Charms,
Unguarded Passions yielded to my Arms;
Transported Pleasure, intermix'd with Pain,
Languishing, dying, ye Gods! 'tis very plain:
Conquer'd, surrender'd Captive to your Power,
Pity me not, 'egad I'll die this Hour.
[Goes to stab himself.

Sally. Hold! ('tis the Colonel, how gouty he's grown. *Aside.*) a thousand Gold Finches; then trust to a Woman of Honour; a mere Trifle in a Gentleman's Pocket.

Col. Take them all.

Sally. What Britches and all, ha ha. [*Aside.* Well then, since you're a Man of Honour, meet me at the *Crown* in an Hour. —— and then I'm a Devil: Poor Soul, this is worse than tossing in a Blanket. [*Aside.*

Col. Thou Angel, I'll not fail, your Servant. I'll to the Hazard Table.

Sally. Sings.

OF all the Debauchees in the Town,
Such Creatures as these will be known.

Bawd.

Bawd. Your Money, my Dear, you know I am Old Care.

Sally. Take it all all. [*Exit* Sally.

Gent. P. That muſt be the Innkeeper's Daughter, by the *Briſtol* Stone on the Hook —— the Gallows muſt be my Portion without procuring a freſh Bit for the Colonel —— Impudence protect me by this Diſguiſe; Who knows but I'm a Man of the Firſt Rank? [*Aſide.* —— Thou Charmer, I'm inſpired beyond Though I want Words to expreſs my Love! thou Charmer, I do adore you!

Bawd. Does your Honour ſpeak to me?

Gent. P. Love, that conquering Paſſion, has captivated my very Soul; thou Angel of a Woman, pity a wounded Heart! I ſhall expire without a favourable Acceptance.

Bawd. Not for the World; but can you love a Perſon you never ſaw before, even in Diſguiſe.

Gent. Pr. 'Tis the Faſhion at thoſe Places, thou Charmer of my Soul.

Bawd. Perſons of my Rank may as well be out of the World, as not to follow the Quality End of the Town.

Gent. P. As a Proof of my tender Love, accept of this Diamond Ring, and trifling Preſent of 100 Guineas; then, O ye Gods!

[*She takes the Preſent.*

Bawd.

Bawd. Your Will be done.—— 'Tis Time for me to be gone. *Exit Laughing. Aside.*

Gent. P. I'll change my Habits with my Master; Madam won't know the Difference: Get 500 *l.* for procuring a Maid; then run away with an *English* Fortune; I think I am a clever Fellow. *Aside.* —— Madam, I will wait on you in a Minute; (*turns and starts*) Oh Ruin'd, Plunder'd, Robb'd! ah, what bit in my Old Age!

SONG.

SUCH Raptures of Bliss ne'er before,
Caught a Fox, a Bawd, and a Whore;
The Pleasures of Wooing turns often one's Ruin,
Such Bites I ne'er saw before.

Egad I'll rally once more; Courage is a sufficient Armour for a Soldier.

Speaks to the Innkeeper's Daughter.

Thou Jewel, I've lost my Diamond, but now I have found her. My Dear lend me 50 Pieces, I'll try my Fortune at the Gaming-Table: As I am a Man of Honour, I'll return the Obligation.

She gives him a Rowl of 50 Counters.

Innk. D. How can I deny ſo clever a Fellow? Here, take them and try thy Fortune.

Gent. P. My Angel, you have ſaved me from eternal Ruination; Adieu, my Charmer, for a Moment. Come, Gentlemen, Seven the Main for 50 Pieces.

High. and *Houſeb.* Having no leſs Sum than a Bill of 5000 *l.* we'll anſwer it on Honour.

Houſeb. Duce Ace, fairly loſt.

Highw. Let us divide the Spoil.

Houſeb. With all my Heart.

Innk. Out of nothing remains nothing; out of 2000 *l.* of my Looſings Colonel *Splittail* has bit me of every Grigg; doubt not, I ſhall find him the ſame Man; as for you two Gentlemen, you may divide your fifty Counters, and tell me the intrinſick Value of each Man's Share?

Highw. and *Houſeb.* Thou villainous Rogue, Do you come here to bite Gentlemen? Give us Counters for ſolid Gold?

Enter Conſtable and Informer.

Conſt. Pray don't diſpute about your Honeſty; here's a Search Warrant for robbing the Mail of a Note of 5000 *l.* unmaſk Villains.

Inf. We have them as round as a Jugler's Box; thoſe are the Men (the Innkeeper, the Colonel,

Colonel, and Gentleman Procurer excluded) however, ſince there is an Act of Parliament againſt Gaming, away with them. *Exeunt.*

A SONG *by the Innkeeper's Daughter.*

I.

THE *Maſquerade's a pleaſant Place,*
Where Rogues together combine, Sir,
In Domeſtick Arts, and Deeds of the Dark,
They're Abomination to all Mankind, Sir.

II.

There's Sally *the fair, the Bawd in her Care,*
Often roars on bad Times like Thunder,
Becauſe her Bullies of late, 'tis their hard Fate,
Not getting the fair Girl no more Plunder.

III.

I'll be hang'd for the ſame, if they arn't all to blame,
If it don't turn to the Great Colonel's Shame,
Then a Warning to all true Lovers of the ſame,
Since Redcoats they are in Faſhion.
[*Exeunt Omnes.*

SCENE *changes.*

Enter the Blowing Doctor, Harlequin, Punch, Scaramouch, *haling the Colonel in.*

Blow. D. The black Beauty has certainly forgot himſelf; if Seignior Harliquino, *&c.* had not ſtood your Friend, Colonel, the Family of ſad Dogs in *Newgate* wou'd have tore you to Pieces like wild Horſes: As for your Comrades they are gone to *Exchequer-Court*; peradventure, in Time, you may meet them in the Nocturnal Regions.

Col. Forgive me this Time, and I'll I'll I'll

Blow. D. One Blaſt, then to Confeſſion.

They all aſſiſt to blow the Colonel.

Col. Imprimis, *For Sins committed* - - Dr.

To a Girl's Virtue at an Inn - *Bilk'd them.*

To a Juſtice of the Peace's Daughter - Dr.

To a Lawyer's Daughter in my Chariot - Dr.

Ditto - Ditto - Ditto - Ditto - Ditto - Ditto

Eaſt - Weſt - North - aud South, ſpar'd None.

Now

Now for *Hazard.*

To Nicodemus *the Banker, a Warm Sum.*

Ditto the Innkeeper; that's a mere Milk Score, 2000 *l.*

Do. Heirs just come to their Estates 100000 *l.*

Ditto - Ditto - Ditto, &c. o' my Conscience!

Blow. D. Hazard with a Pox to it——in the Memory of Man it will never be blotted out.

——*Fate will pursue,*
Eternity shocks your Soul, youll' bid the World adieu.

Death ascends with a Dart in one Hand, and an Hour-Glass in the other, just out, with this Inscription,

In a Minute you'll take a Leap in the Dark.

The Satyrs ascends; they all dance, interwoven with the Colonel; the Hour-Glass being out, Death gives the fatal Stroke. The Satyrs and Colonel descends, with Thunder and Lightning.

EPI-

EPILOGUE.

*F*Ortunes 's a Gift deceives the most sublime,
Tortures the Mind if not vanquish'd in Time,
This dismal Spectacle has been in View,
A perfect Counterfeit and Sinner too,
What Shepperd *did refuse he then did do.*
Storm Forts, pawn Dies, was artful bastinado'd,
Witness the Cinder Maid he was afraid of.
Dom the Mon, quoth he, I made a good Night,
My Virgin was ---- my Friend will not fight,
Get all the Money, I wish you good Night.
For why should we make two Wants of one,
At the worst of Times we are but undone.

FINIS.

The Female Parson

Bibliographical note:
This facsimile has been made from a copy in the British Museum
(161.h.15.)

THE FEMALE PARSON:

OR,

BEAU in the SUDDS.

AN

OPERA.

As it is Acted at the

NEW THEATRE in the *Hay-Market*.

Dulce est desipere in loco. Hor. Od. 12. Lib. 4.

By Mr. *CHARLES COFFEY*, Author of the BEGGARS WEDDING.

LONDON:

Printed for LAWTON GILLIVER, over-against St. *Dunstan's* Church; and FRAN. COGAN, at the *Middle-Temple Gate*, in *Fleet-street*. MDCC XXX.

[Price One Shilling.]

TO THE

RIGHT HONOURABLE

WILLIAM,

Earl of *INCHIQUIN*,

Baron of *Burren*, Member of Parliament for *New Windſor*, in the County of *Berks*, and Knight of the Moſt Hon. Order of the BATH.

My *LORD*,

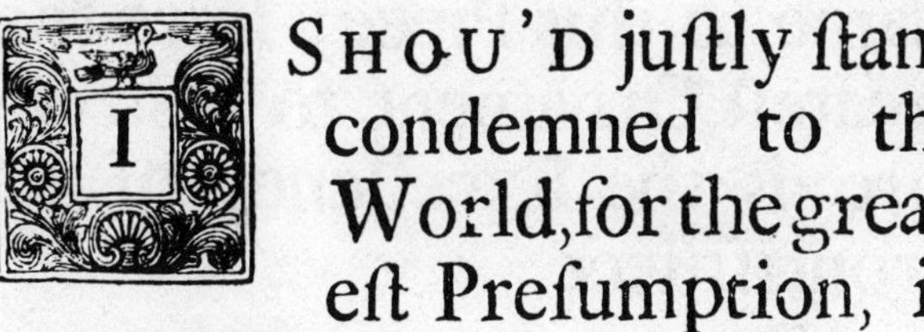

I SHOU'D juſtly ſtand condemned to the World, for the greateſt Preſumption, in addreſſing your Lordſhip after

ter this Manner, eſpecially when I have the Misfortune of being an entire Stranger, did not your Lordſhip's diſtinguiſh'd Virtues in ſome Meaſure plead my Excuſe; for where ſhou'd a deſolate and an Orphan Muſe fly for Protection, but to the Generous and the Brave?

How far this is eminently conſpicuous in your Lordſhip, I leave to your general Character to illuſtrate; which was the only Motive that induc'd me to prefix your Lordſhip's Name to this Piece; ſince the greateſt Ornament to a Structure is the Excellency of its Frontiſpiece.

As the many ſhining Virtues and Heroick Actions of your noble and ancient Family are univerſally known, and already tranſmitted to Poſterity, it wou'd be eſteem'd the Height of Flattery to expatiate any further upon them; but whilſt I am carefully avoiding to offend by Adulation, I am fallen into the Snares of Vanity, when I beg Leave to acknowledge it my greateſt Felicity, to have receiv'd my firſt Breath and Education in a Country which is proud to boaſt the Honour of your Lordſhip's Nativity.

If the following Sheets have the good Fortune to amuſe a

ſerious

ſerious Thought, or divert a tedious Minute, I have attain'd the Summit of my Ambition; and if they are thought worthy the leaſt Merit to entitle them to your Favour and Acceptance, your Lordſhip may then ſay, you have made one Perſon perfectly happy, who will with Pleaſure and Gratitude ever profeſs himſelf,

My LORD,

Your Lordſhip's

Moſt Humble,

Moſt Dutiful,

And ſincerely devoted Servant,

CHAR. COFFEY.

THE

PROLOGUE.

Spoken by MODELY.

LADIES, your most Obsequious —— you must know
That, Demme, I am call'd a Modern Beau;
A Thing so much in Fashion —— tho', by Gad,
Some are such horrid Dags —— you'd think 'em mad.
But I, who split me, just am out of Limbo,
With Snuff-Box, powder'd Wig, and Arms a-kimbo,
Cane, Ruffles, Sword-Knot, Burdash, Hat and Feather,
Perfumes, fine Essence, brought from Lard know whither;
Can with a thousand wanton soft Grimaces,
Steal all your Hearts, by Gad, before your Faces.
These are my Weapons, Ladies, —— take my Word,
Upon my Soul, I hate to draw my Sword:
The Devil take me, —— 'tis an odious Sight
To see a finish'd Beau —— lug out to fight,
When, rat me, he had rather bid good Night.
Ladies, Gad's Curse, let each one guard her Heart,
For when I come just now to play my Part,
Demme, —— each am'rous Glance shall prove —— a fatal Dart.

Persons

Perſons of the DRAMA.

MEN.

Sir *Quibble Quibus*,	An old debauch'd Juſtice of the Peace.
Captain *Noble*,	An Officer in Love with Lady *Quibus*.
Modely,	A Beau extremely Foppiſh.
Standiſh,	Clerk to the Juſtice.
Comick,	An intriguing Fellow, Servant to the Captain.
Tom.	Servant to *Quibus*.

WOMEN.

Lady *Quibus*.	Marry'd to *Quibus* unwillingly, loves *Noble*
Miſs *Lure*.	A Jilt of the Town, kept by the Juſtice.
Pinner.	Maid and Confidant to Lady *Quibus*.
Garniſh, *Darby*,	Bravo's, Creatures to Miſs *Lure*.
Conſtables.	

SCENE London.

THE FEMALE PARSON: OR, BEAU in the SUDDS.

ACT I. SCENE I.

The *Captain*'s Lodgings near St. *James*'s.

Enter Noble *dressing, and* Comick *combing his Wigg.*

AIR I. Vain Belinda.

CAPT.

CUPID, *gentle God of Love,*
To my Hopes propitious prove;
Lead me kindly to her Arms,
Where reside immortal Charms:
Then with most exstatick Bliss,
Mingling Souls in ev'ry kiss.
In Embrace intranc'd I'll lie,
Till the Gods with Envy die.

Capt.

Capt. *Comick!*

Com. Sir,

Capt. What's o' Clock, my Watch is down?

Com. About five by the Day, Sir, but eight or nine by our Journey.

Capt. Well —— These Country Quarters are the Devil, that's certain; for if a Man's Inclination tends to Variety, a Trip to *London* is absolutely necessary; and to me the Fatigue of Riding is equal to that of Recruiting, did not the living Hopes of future Pleasure allay the present Pain —— *Comick*, have you brought every Thing from the Inn, and taken Care of your Horses?

Com. I have, Sir—— The poor Beasts are always my immediate Care, your Honour my next, and lastly——your most obedient humble Servant, Sir.

Capt. Still at your old Cant, Sirrah? —— but to my Business—— You know before we left our last Quarters, Sir *Quibble* mov'd his to *London*, with his young Lady, my *quondam* Mistress, which depriv'd me of the Opportunity of carrying on my Amour with her, and is the only Loadstone that now attracts me hither; therefore, you Rogue, as you have Wit and Conduct sufficient to manage an Intrigue, exert your native Impudence, and now do me a Piece of Service; you must put on a Disguise, which I leave to your own Contrivance, and if you want any Necessaries, you know where to have a Supply.

Com. True, Sir —— I have hitherto been pretty successful for you, and doubt not, but by the Help of this pregnant Brain of mine, I shall prove so for the future.

Capt. First then, you must convey this Letter to my Lady *Quibus* herself, or to her Maid *Pinner*; but beware of that old, testy, jealous-pated Fool the Justice, for he watches her and all her Actions as close, as two encamp'd Armies do the Motions of each other.

AIR

AIR II. Hark how the Trumpet calls to Battle.

Love like the Trumpet still calls forth to Battle,
And is the Prelude to amorous Prattle;
In Love as in War a fair Town we assail,
And Stratagem must, when our Force can't prevail:
The Soldier destroying,
The Lover enjoying,
Thus Art both employing,
To conquer ne'er fail.

Com. Enough, Sir; leave the rest to me——indeed, Sir, I have often wonder'd that one so young, so charming and so gay, shou'd tie herself to such an old sapless Crabtree.

Capt. 'Tis wonderful—— but fly, execute your Message, and if you can, prevail upon *Pinner* for your self, she's a pretty Tit, you Rogue, and will recompence your Trouble.

Com. Yes, Sir, the Jade is young and tolerably handsome, but then, Sir, she's most consumedly proud; a plague on her nice Stomach, nothing less than a fat Parson, or a Town Beau will down with her; but if I don't nick her——I'll say no more.

Capt. Begone, Sirrah, and return ſpeedily; in the mean Time I'll take a Turn or two in the Park.

[*Exit.*

Com. Sir, I'm gone in an Inſtant —— but hold gentle Maſter of mine; I don't ſee any Reaſon why you ſhou'd engroſs all the Love and Muſick to your ſelf; egad, I'll put in for my Share I can tell you; and ſince you're in the merry Vein, give me Leave in my Turn, to ſing a Song too.

AIR III. Once I lov'd a charming Creature.

Why ſhould none indulge their Paſſions,
But the Great in Maſquerade?
Love deſcends like other Faſhions,
And becomes a ſervile Trade;
Then for her down, down derry derry,
Then for her down, hey derry down. [*Exit.*

SCENE II. The Mall.

Enter Modely *and Miſs* Lure *turning affectedly from him.*

Miſs. Sir, I beg the Privilege of the Place, I wou'd be alone.

Mod. Split me, Madam, if you wou'd, you can't be alone.

Miſs.

Miss. No, Sir! —— that's very ſtrange methinks— your Reaſon, Sir?

Mod. Demme, Madam, I'll affirm it, for go where you will, you ſtill have my Heart in your Company, Madam, tol, lol, lol, *&c.*

Miss. Your Heart, Sir? Ha, ha, ha! —— I don't know that ever I ſaw you before, Sir.

Enter Captain Noble *at a Diſtance.*

Capt. So —— I ſee ſtill that Gallantry in the Gentlemen is as eſſential a Qualification, as Cocquetry in the Ladies, and generally much more advantageous— Now for the Eſperites and Belles of the Town; This is the Beaumonde, where half the Intrigues of the City are carry'd on —— What the Devil have we got here? *Don Quixot* making Love to his *Dulcinea!*— Romantick enough, faith; I'll obſerve them a little— [*Walks aſide.*

Miss. You'l pardon me, Sir, if I can't conceive your Meaning; but you learn'd Gentlemen generally ſpeak in Riddles.

Mod. O la! Madam, we Gentlemen never trouble our Heads with Learning at all; we ſtudy nothing but the Faſhions, and the Art of making Love *en paſſant* —— Learning in Gentlemen is pedantick, Madam, and wou'd ſeem as prepoſterous in us Beaus, as Virtue in a fine Woman —— but, rat me, Madam, you ſhall not only have my Heart, but my individual Perſon into the Bargain.

AIR

AIR IV. Sweet's the little thing.

I adore thee, charming Creature,
And to please won'd pawn my Soul;
Beauty sits in ev'ry Feature,
And thy Eyes in Magick rowl:
I adore thee, charming Creature,
And to please won'd pawn my Soul.

Capt. Ha, ha, ha! Inimitable Coxcomb——[*Aside.*

Miss. Indeed, Sir, I don't understand you; I fear you misconstrue this Freedom I allow you, if so, I'll leave you, Sir. [*Going.*

Mod. Demme, by no Means, Madam; by Gad, I never in the least misconstrue any Ladies Freedom with me——Devil take me, Madam, you may use your humble Servant as you please [*Bowing*]. But, Madam, the Walks begin to fill, and 'tis Time for Persons of Distinction to withdraw; we'll first laugh at these rude Animals that approach, and then I'll wait upon you to your Ladyship's Lodgings.

Miss. My Lodgings! What do you mean Sir—— I never suffer any Person to see me to my Lodgings I assure you; if you think otherwise, you are mistaken, Sir.

Mod. But, Madam, I am a Gentleman, and an elder Brother just come to my Estate, therefore no such despicable Person, Madam; besides, if your Ladyship

dyſhip ſhou'd at any Time happen to be out of Caſh, I can furniſh you with any ready Money you may have Occaſion for.

Miſs. [*A good Hint, I muſt improve it.*] Well Sir, you are ſuch a pretty humour'd Gentleman, and inſinuate your ſelf into one's good Opinion with ſo genteel an Air, that I can deny you nothing in my Power —— but firſt —— O la —— I ſwear I have forgot my Watch to Day —— here, *Jack*, run to my Cabinet —— what no Servant neither —— undone. ——

Mod. No Trouble, rat me, Madam —— I have one at your Ladyſhip's Service —— 'tis *Tompion*'s, goes perfectly true, and thus humbly courts your Acceptance, Madam.

Miſs. O Sir, you have the moſt obliging way of preſenting a Gift, that ——

Mod. No Ceremony, Demme, Madam —— obſerve that red Coat yonder; how he looks —— ha, ha, ha!

Miſs. Ha, ha, ha! Poor Creature! Some caſhier'd Cadet, I'll engage, that has not eat a good Meal this Fortnight, yet walks here with as much Aſſurance, as if he were in full Pay.

Mod. Cadet ſay you, ſimple Shamaroon —— Devil take me, I nauſeate this Kind of half Gentlemen —— you ſhall ſee, Madam, if he comes this Way, I'll affront him to his Face, and if he dares reſent it, kick him afterwards.

Miſs. Ha, ha! That I confeſs wou'd be worth ſeeing.

Capt. (Will you ſo *Puffpaſte*, have at you then).

[*Advances ſinging.*

Madam, I'm your moſt obedient ——

[*Ruſhes between them, and puſhes* Modely *down.*

Miſs. (A good pretty Fellow o'my Conſcience) Do you know me, Sir?

Capt. Only your Occupation, my Dear.

Miſs. Sir, you are rude.

Capt.

Capt. But not miſtaken, Madam.

Mod. Very fine upon my Soul —— he, he, he! The Gentleman is merry, Madam, and ſo, ſplit me, he's heartily welcome —— he, he, he!

Capt. Another Word, Puppy, and I'll ſpoil your Faſhion. Are you for a Pinch Madam.

[*Offers his Box.*

Miſs. I ſeldom take any, Sir.

Mod. Right *Orangeree*, I preſume Sir. ——

Capt. At your Service, to clear your Eyes, Sir.

[*He offers to take a Pinch, the* Captain *blows it in his Face.*]

Mod. Zauns my Eyes —— Death and the Devil— is not this an Affront, Madam? [*Whiſpers.*

Miſs. Truly, Sir, I think ſo, and to your Face too, I hope you will not kick him into the Bargain (Cowardly Fop).

Mod. Sir, the Lady ſays this is an Affront, and ſo, Demme, Sir, I draw to vindicate her Honour, Sir.

[*Draws.*

Capt. 'Sdeath, you *Powderpuff*, do you prate ——

[*Draws.*

Miſs. Sir, is this Behaviour before a Lady — (pray Heaven he beats him well).

Mod. Odſo, Madam, Devil take me, I beg your Ladyſhip's Pardon —— Sir, it was not out of any Malice prepens'd to your Perſon —— So, Sir, I am yours again —— I wou'd not diſoblige the Lady for the Univerſe —— you may put up as I do, for I hate to quarrel mortally, that's all, Sir, ha, ha, ha!

Capt. You are below my Reſentment, Scoundrel, but for this Lady's Satisfaction, as well as an Example to all Cowards, I will not draw in Vain.

[*Exit beating him off.*

Miſs. Ha, ha, ha! ſince ye are for Blows, adieu gentle Mr. *Milkſop*, and you good Mr. *Bully Bluff*— however they ſay 'tis an ill Wind that blows no Body Good, witneſs my Gold Watch.

AIR

AIR V. When first I saw my *Nancie*'s Face.

Who can our Female Arts withstand,
We Wits as well as Fools command?
And like our ancient Mother Eve,
We charm them first and then deceive. [*Exit.*

SCENE III. Sir *Quibble*'s House.

Enter Lady Quibus *and* Pinner.

Lady Qui. Pinner, what Day of the Month is this?

Pin. The Tenth, Madam.

Lady. Right, the very Day the Captain promiss'd to be in Town; I wish he be come —— O Matrimony, Matrimony! What a Poison art thou to their Joys, whom thou bind'st unequally together! If thy uncomfortable Yoke sits no easier on others, than upon me, Heaven help my whole Sex, say I.

Pin. Marry and Amen with all my Heart.

Lady My Grief is insupportable, but it shall not be of much longer Continuance, for I'm resolv'd, that if the Captain's Passion for me be virtuous, the Moment he makes the welcome Declaration, I'll disengage my self from Sir *Quibble*, and throw my self at once into his Arms, for you know, *Pinner*, it lies in my Power.

Pin. I do, Madam; nor can I blame your Ladyship's Resolution; for the Usage you daily receive from my Master, almost frightens me from the very Thoughts of Matrimony.

Lady. True; but I expected a better Kind of Treatment here than in the Country, where my only Pleasure was twice a Year to travel ten or twelve dirty Miles to a beggarly Market-Town, where they held a pompous Show, call'd a Fair; and where all our Diversion was to see a preposterous Rout of People guzzle fat Ale; and behold a Parcel of unintelligent Beings Jig it about to the nauseous Discord of a droning Bagpipe. And now I am come here, I am cloister'd up from the Park, the Play, the Opera, and in short from all the Recreations the Town affords.

AIR VI. Happy the youthful Swain.

Happy the Virgin State,
Where blissful Freedom reigns,
Void of Restraints that wait
On Wedlock's weighty Chains:
What greater Curse can be
Entail'd on Womankind,
Than to wed Misery,
Compell'd against their Mind.

Pin. But I remember when your Ladyship return'd from the Boarding School here to the Country; I have

have often heard you praiſe the harmleſs Pleaſures of a Country Life, and the innocent Simplicity of the rural Nymphs that enjoy'd it; which brings into my Memory an old Saying, that the Mind of a Woman is like a Weather-cock, fickle and inconſtant, and ſubject to veer about with every Blaſt of Wind.

Lady. I own I have ſaid ſo, but I was juſt then return'd home free and at Liberty from the ſevere Reſtraint impos'd upon me by a peeviſh ſuperannuated Governant; who being herſelf paſt the Senſe of any Pleaſure, did not conceive our youthful Imaginations were ſuſceptible of any, and hated as much to have us out of her Sight, as an old jealous Husband does his young Wife —— but come, *Pinner* ſince you intereſt your ſelf ſo much in my Affairs, 'tis but reaſonable I ſhou'd enquire about yours: How do you and *Standiſh* go on now?

Pin. As we ſhou'd, Madam; for I never had the leaſt Inclination to him in my Life; he ſeems to be a brisk, airy, witty Fellow —— but hang it —— I don't know —— I hate any thing that ſavours of Servitude; I muſt ſay ſo much, and I believe your Ladyſhip knows the ſame, that I am of a more refin'd Taſte than thoſe of my Station generally are, and therefore cannot down with a Servant.

AIR VII. Fair *Iris* and her Swain.

Let other Maids in vain
Take up with ev'ry He;
I'm for a youthful Swain
Of Wealth and high Degree;
Fine Equipage and Furniture,
And Servants at my call;
Then in my Coach I'll flaunt to Church,
And play my fill at dear Quadrille,
And shine at ev'ry Ball.

[*Knocking at the Door.*

Lady. Run to the Door, *Pinner.* [*Exit* Pin. Who in the Name of Wonder can this be that thunders ſo at the Door?

Re-enter Pinner *with* Comick, *in Diſguiſe.*

Deliver me, what uncouth Creature is this!

Pin. What now, Fellow, what does the Booby want?

Com. Ubbubboo, ſhee dat now, Boobys your ſhelf agra; I have Buſineſs upon ma——phoo——Mad ——Madam, Madam *Quibus.*

Lady. I am the Perſon, Friend, what wou'd you have?

Com. Saave you Miſhtreſs, my Maiſhter ſends his Shervice and this Paper upon you.

Lady.

Lady. For me, Friend? you are miſtaken ſure, I know you not; what is your Maſter's Name?

Com. By my Shoul, my ſhelf did forgot his Naam, indeed——ſtay——ay——'tis Captain *Noble*, I tink.

Lady. (To my wiſh) very well, Friend; ſtay 'till I give you an Anſwer. Here, *Tom*.

Enter Tom.

Tom. Does your Ladyſhip call, Madam?

Lady. Bring this honeſt Fellow a Tankard of Beer, and be ſure make much of him. [*Exit*.

Tom. In a Moment, Madam. [*Exit*.

Pin. How long have you liv'd with the Captain, Friend?

Com. Fet I never reckon'd, but 'tis as long as he live wid me, Joy.

Pin. What is become of his old Servant *Comick?*

Com. Ara he iſh dead, upon my Shoul.

Pin. Mr. *Comick* dead! you joke ſure?

Com. Fet aroon 'tis a true Jokes——plaague upon you now, phy did you put my Mind upon him? fen I tink upon his Goodneſs, it maaks the Cry come upon my Eyes indeed.

Pin. Poor *Comick!* how did the Captain take his Death; did he ſeem concern'd?

Com. Ara Joy, he went wid him to the Graav, and dat you know was a great Honour.

Pin. Can you tell what Diſtemper he dy'd of?

Com. By my Shoul, 'cauſe Death was upon him Joy, but my Maiſhter ſaid it was Love for one Miſtreſs *Pinner Clearſtarch*.

Pin. (Kind Fool!) dy'd for Love ſay you? now as I hope to live, I am ſorry I had not the Pleaſure of ſeeing him expire, that I might triumph in his Downfall, for, I confeſs, there is a ſecret Satisfaction in having a Booby-Lover die for one.

Com. (The Devil take your Pride, you Jade).

Pin. Did he die worth any thing, or leave any Legacies behind him?

Com. Ay fet did he, plaague upon his Kindnefs, (now to tickle her Vanity) he leave that Mifhtrefs *Pinner* twenty Pound to buy her Mourning.

Pin. Generous Man! now could I almoft pity him; but prithee in whofe Hands did he leave the Money?

Com. (O thou grand Devil of thy Sex) why fere do you tink agra? but wid de Prieft of de Parifh, wid whome he leave twenty Pound more to pray his Soul out of Purgatory.

Pin. Purgatory! did he die a Papift?

Com. No, Joy, he die a Fool, by my Shoul.

Pin. But can you tell how this Money may be had?

Com. Ay, by my Gofhip's Hand, can I; dat ifh if you will be after feeing me well.

Pin. What do require?

Com. Your Heart agra, and I will give you mine into de Bargain, indeed.

Pin. (Saucy Muck-worm) well as foon as I receive the Money, you fhall not complain of my Love; but firft what is your Name?

Com. My Naame, aroon; well, by my Fader's Shoul I will be after telling you den——My Naame is *Donell O Donell Mac Coghlan*, I was bred and born'd in the County of *Fermanagh*, and all my Pofterity before me, Joy.

Re-enter Tom *with a Tankard*

Tom. Come, Friend, here's to you, and my Lady's Health.

Com. By my Shoul, I wou'd pledge it an if it was Water; come fhedurt agra. [*drinks.*

Ububboo, ara Chrifte faave you, Joy, 'tis moft braave Beer, by St. *Patrick*, it maaks my own Heart glad indeed.

Pin.

Pin. Since you like it ſo well, you had better take the t'other Draught.

Com. Bleſs your ſweet Faace, Joy, and ſo I will, and den I will ſhing you a merry Song. [*drinks.*

Tom. O, by all means, it muſt be diverting.

Pin. Eſpecially if it be an *Iriſh* Tune: Come, away with it.

Com. By my Shoul it is, Joy, and a *Connaught* Tune too——hem——hem——.

Pin. You had better drink once more to clear your Pipes.

Com. Fet, I believe ſo too. [*drinks*] Now for it ——Hem——.

AIR

AIR. VIII. Plarakanarorka.

Plarakanarorka, *let all Men remember,*
The like was ne'er known, nor never ſhall be;
Six ſcore and forty Cows, Sheep were ſlaughter'd,
And all for to make us a Feaſt in one Day:
Pails full of Bulcaun we drank out of Meddars;
When we riſed next Morning we had a brave Sport;
Our Pipes they were broked, our Door was unlocked,
Our Breeches were ſtoled, they picked our Pocket;
Our Mantles and Kerchers, and Caps they were gone,
Teara where are the Folk, let joy go with them;
Come change up your Tunes on the Harp to our pleaſing,
And fill up the Meddars, bring a Box of good Sneezing.

Re-

Re-enter Lady Quibus *with a Letter.*

Lady. Here, Friend, give this Letter to your Master, run, it requires Haste.

Com. I will——but I must taak my leave of Mishtress *Sheele* first——come——ara, by my Shoul, my Mouth is clean indeed.

Pin. Faugh——stand of, you ugly Beast. [*Exit.*

Com. Ugly Beast your shelf——ara come up indeed——Deel taake your Mannersh——by your leave Mishtress, Madam. [*Exit.*

Lady. This is the most accomplish'd *Irish* Clown I ever saw; I wonder where my dear Captain got him; but certainly he knows his faithful Simplicity well enough to send him of an Errand of such Importance; *Pinner* and he have had a long Dialogue; I'll in and know all.

AIR 9. Geminiani's Minuet.

As in a Storm at dead of Night,
Th' impatient Sailor waits for Day,
That welcome Beams of chearful Light,
May chace his gloomy Fears away;
So now, ye Minutes, swiftly move,
And to my Wishes bring my Love. [Exit.

ACT II. SCENE I.

Sir Quibble Quibus's.

Enter Sir Quibble Solus.

WOONS, what the Devil had I to do to marry, cou'd I not have liv'd ſingly upon my Neighbours, but I muſt embarraſs my ſelf with a Wife, in the Devil's Name? and ſuch a Wife never had Man——Why, a pox, ſhe denies me the Privilege of my Marriage-Bed, yet I can't uſe open Violence; I ſhou'd be hooted at by the whole Neighbourhood ——d'ſheart, it makes me mad to think on't——. Let me ſee——how long have I been marry'd—— 'tis now about three Months, and Impotence ſeize me, if I know whether ſhe be Man or Woman, but by the heaving of her Breaſts, and Softneſs of her Lips——what can a Man do in this Caſe——If I wench in private, the World will blame me publickly——and yet Nature muſt have its uſual Courſe——why then, before Gad, I will keep a Miſs, inſpite of the World and the Devil——here *Standiſh.*

Enter Standiſh.

Stand. Does your Worſhip call?

Sir *Qui.* Have you diſmiſs'd that bauling Creature?

Stand. I have wrote her Mittimus, Sir; why, Sir, the poor Whore cou'd not make up Half-a-crown, were ſhe to be hang'd for it.

Sir *Qui.* No, not one Half-crown!——a poor Whore indeed.

Stand.

Stand. All ſhe cou'd muſter upon Earth, was but a Shilling in Half-pence, and for t'other Sixpence, and a Moveable for the Remainder, ſhe might have gone free till next time; but it cou'd not be had, ſo I e'en ſent her a packing.

Sir *Qui.* ——Ay, ay, let her go——tho' ſhe was a good likely Huſſy, *Standiſh.*

Stand. She was indeed, Sir, a clever cleanly Girl, and very young too, ſhe cry'd heartily, and ſaid, only you went away ſo ſoon, ſhe expected to have work'd out her Deliverance with your Worſhip.

Sir *Qui.* Did ſhe ſo? poor Jade——well you and I will talk more on't at my Return; my Occaſions now call me abroad, if you have any more Warrants ſign'd, 'tis well; if not, ſign them your ſelf, in my Name, till you ſee me; and be ſure, good *Standiſh*, have an Eye over your Lady, do you hear? [*Exit.*

Stand. So this old Rogue is like the Dog in the Manger, he'll neither eat himſelf, nor let thoſe that can; but faith, poor Lady, I pity her, and ſhe may e'en go where ſhe will for me. But now for my Amour with Mrs. *Pinner*; if this new ſerenading Song, which I was laſt Night to have ſung under her Window, don't touch her, I wonder at it——let me ſee——O here it is——.

AIR. O Caro Spene.

Rise charming Creature,
Fairest in Nature,
Suspend your blissful Dreams of Love;
Fly from your Slumbers,
Whilst softest Numbers,
Your gentle Breast with Transports move.

Sing forth the Charmer,
With Sweets alarm her,
Let trembling Notes inflame her Soul;
In dying Measures,
Convey such Pleasures,
That nought but Joys about her rowl.

Enter Pinner, *running across the Stage,*

Ha, pretty Miss, have I caught you! [*kisses her.*

Pin. You are extremely impudent, methinks.

Stand. And you are extremely charming, my Dear; but prithee, why so coy, Mrs. *Pinner*, do you really think I'll always be us'd in this Manner?

Pin. What Manner? ——forsooth indeed——.

Stand. Nothing my Dear, but here's a new Song, I made for you.

Pin. Psha! let me see it——.

[*takes it and puts it up carelesly.*

Stand. How well you kept your Appointment, last Night, you cunning Gypsey.

Pin.

Pin. What Appointment?—— the Fellow's mad ſure.

Stand. You forget, I ſuppoſe, you were to meet me in the Garden.

Pin. Inſufferable! I meet you in the Garden at Night! Impudence!—what can the Man mean!—

Stand. Only to make love to you, my Dear: I was to have whin'd and flatter'd; you to have been very angry, yet very kind; I eager and preſſing, you coy, but complying; in ſhort I was to have raviſh'd you with your own Conſent, and to have marry'd you the next Morning, that's all, my Dear.

Pin. Wickedneſs! How came all theſe Chimeras into your Skull?

Stand. Laſt Night I dreamt ſo, my Pet; and methought my Conſcience accus'd me of Indolence, in living ſo long under one Roof and not being better acquainted with you.

Pin. (I never lik'd the Fellow till this Moment) go, go, you are a ſly Devil.

Stand. And you are a bewitching Piece of Temptation.

Pin. Stand of, I will hear no more.

Stand. I'll ſwear but you ſhall.

AIR II. Once I lov'd a Laſs with a rowling Eye.

Prithee, why ſo coy
To the Man you prize?
Can you hide the Joy,
Brilliant in your Eyes?

Let

Let us hence, my Treasure,
To yon Bow'r of Bliss;
There with mutual Pleasure,
Will we toy and kiss.

Pin. Nay, then I should be finely holp'd up indeed——stay, stay, Chops, here my Song first——

AIR. III. O the bonny Shoemaker.

If you wou'd true Courage show,
And would fain with love win her,
Turn the Clerk into a Beau,
Then perhaps you'l move Pinner;
Move Pinner, *move* Pinner,
Then perhaps you'l move Pinner.

'Till then, thus I fly thee, Satan.

Stand. And thus I follow my Dear, witty *Proserpine.* [*Exeunt.*

SCENE II. *Miss* Lure's *Lodgings.*

Enter Sir Quibble *and Miss* Lure.

Sir *Qui.* And don't you love your own Chuckee, eh? kiss and tell, kiss and tell then.

Miss. What Reason have I given you to doubt it, Sir?

Sir *Qui.* None, none, my Dear, only kiss and Friends——ha, ha! I love to try you, Dearee, you look so prettily Innocent, that's all——ha, ha, ha!

Miss.

Miss. Indeed, my Dear, you are a great Wagg, and love to teaze one, so you do——but methinks, Sir, you are not so kind to me as formerly.

Sir *Qui.* Faith and Troth but I am, Chuckee, ah, you little sly Rogue you, that's to try me now——ha, ha,——fair Play, fair Play——come one Kiss will set all even again [*kissing*]. I never had so great a Mind to laugh and be merry in my Life; what says Lovee, shan't we be merry, eh?

Miss. With all my Heart, Sir, I love to see you sprightly and gay; I hate Melancholy.

Sir *Qui.* Sbud, and so do I;
And thus we'll live and laugh, and kiss and revel Night and Day;

Miss. We'll sport and toy, with Mirth and Joy, and love the Hours away.

Sir *Qui.* Ha, ha, ha! O, how I cou'd devour thee my Sweeting! when I am nigh thee, I am a new Man; the very Sight of this bewitching Face recruits my old Age with fresh Vigour; and I now fancy my self but sweet five and twenty again; nay, I am as light as a Cork, and sound as an Acorn—— 'ds Death I am all Life and Love, and long to lie basking in your Arms.

Miss. Hold, hold, Sir; methinks you go too far with your Mirth.

Sir *Qui.* Go, go, you witty little Wagtail, you trifle with my Passion——adod, I wish my Wife was dead this very Moment, for thy sake——come, come, you pretty Loiterer, let us in, let us in, I say, come——

Miss. But, Sir, you are grown very Niggardly of late, you did not use to be so Penurious to your own Lifee——I owe a deal of Money for Lodging, Cloaths, Coffee, Tea, and Servants Wages, and must have a little now——I must, Dearee——

Sir *Qui.* Peace, peace, my Sweeting; you shall have every thing if you will love nown Chuckee——

come in then, and you ſhall have a Purſe, come, you ſhall, I ſay.

Miſs. Well, Sir, ſince you will have it ſo, I obey.

AIR IV. Sweet *Nelly* my Heart's Delight.

My Humour's frank and free,
As Women ſtill ſhou'd be;
We Girls of Bliſs
Rove, toy and kiſs,
And with ev'ry Cull agree.
Let Prude and Coquet alike mourn their Fate,
'Till they are uſeleſs grown;
Whilſt we who dare
Thus venture fair,
Obtain our Share
Of Pence, and are
Sole Goddeſſes of the Town.

Sir *Qui.* Ah! my little Chuckee——come, come along. [*Exeunt.*

SCENE

SCENE III. *Sir* Quibble Quibus's.

Enter Captain Noble, *leading in Lady* Quibus.

Capt. Come, Madam, now no more Excuſes ſure, they only ſerve to blow the Fire up, which you, by vain Delays wou'd ſtrive to quench; come, come, you have fool'd too long, and only dally'd with my Paſſion.

Lady. As you're a Man endow'd with Reaſon and a generous Soul; O, Sir, reflect and be more kind.

Capt. Kind as thy Soul can wiſh, or as the loving Turtles coo together; but ſtill you croſs me, and deny thoſe Joys which brought me hither by your own Command: Why do we ſtay then? let us fly together, and mingle both our Souls in Exſtaſy of Love.

Lady. Thus low as Earth, I beg for Pity, Sir, [*kneels*] can ought, that bears the Image of a Man, thus wed with Luſt, and trample Virtue down? think, Sir, O think, and ſtain not thus your Honour.

Capt. (She mocks me ſure, and plays but with my Patience.) And is it come to this? is this the ſoft Reception I expected when you deſir'd I ſhould meet you here? and have I thus long ſpent my Hopes in vain, put of from time to time with trifling Scruples of that Bauble Virtue, the fooliſh Niceneſs of your artful Sex? Madam, I beg you will forbear to rack me thus.

Lady. True, Sir, I have receiv'd your frequent Viſits, but Witneſs Heaven for me of the Truth, if ought but Virtue ever fill'd my Soul. You know, Sir, I was marry'd againſt my Will; and tho' another did command my Perſon, you were the Object of my chaſte Affection. For your ungrateful ſake I have preſerv'd my ſelf unſpotted, and though a Wife, yet am a Virgin ſtill.

Capt. Ha, ha, ha! a pretty Story faith; perhaps, Madam, you may find Tools to believe you, but you are in the wrong, if you design to palm such idle Whims on me. 'Tis probable indeed, a Lady shou'd be three Months marry'd and never lose her Virginity, the only thing she marries to get rid of! no, no, Madam, I will not thus be baffled——ha ——she weeps——there must be more in this than yet I know.

Lady. These Tears are the Reward then of my constant Love, ungenerous!——Now hear me, and condemn your Infidelity—— When first my Father propos'd to match me off to *Quibus*, my Inclinations wholly were for you; and when he tore me from my Mother's Arms, I then resolv'd to play a Cheat that one Day might be serviceable to me. I caus'd my Maid *Pinner* to disguise herself, and as a Parson, marry us together; which she perform'd so well, it never was found out; and the Aversions I had to Sir *Quibble*, made me e'er since abstain from his Embraces, which has so much incens'd him, that now he hates me worse than I did him.

Capt. Amazement!——she has stung me to the Soul with just and merited Reproach; her Virtue, like her Beauty, is transcendant, and ne'er display'd its Lustre to these misty Eyes, 'till this auspicious Moment. Already I begin to feel the Symptoms of a pure and lasting Flame blaze round my Soul with irresistless Power [*Aside*]. And cou'd you, Madam, be thus wonderous kind, to one whose Baseness ne'er can claim a Hope of Pity, or Remission of his Crime; but if you can vouchsafe to look upon me, behold the suppliant Posture of a Convert, [*kneels*] who now abandons every vitious Thought to wrong what, next to Heaven, he adores; and since I have found a Jewel worth an Empire, permit me here to wear you in my Soul, repleat with Honour, Faith, and endless Love.

Lady. Ha! what do I hear! ſo ſudden and ſo bleſt a Reformation! [*Aſide*] Riſe, Sir, you over-pay me with your Penitence; you ſpeak a Nobleneſs that wants a Name, and I'm not able to requite you; but to repay, in part, your generous Kindneſs, I'll now propoſe a Means to make me yours. Know then, Sir *Quibble* keeps a vile Proſtitute, whom he adores, even to a degree of Madneſs; if you can come upon 'em, when together, the Fear and Shame of a Diſcovery, will make him readily conſent to give you up his Right in me, which, with the mock Parſon, will diſengage me from him.

Capt. Now, by this Light, I ne'er was truly happy 'till this Hour. My Tongue, my Eyes, my Soul, o'erflow with joy; how ſhall I requite this unexampled Goodneſs? Give me thy Hand, thy Lips, thy Heart; and here, O here thus let me dwell for ever. [*embracing*.

AIR V. If Powers above cou'd mind.

Were Jove's *imperial Crown*
To be poſſeſs'd by me;
I'd ſpurn the Bawble down,
Thus bleſt in charming thee.

Lady. *Were Gods themselves descending,*
And for my Love contending;
With Scorn I'd view,
Th' immortal Crew,
And quit 'em all for you.
Capt. *Were* Jove's *imperial Crown*
To be possess'd by me;
I'd spurn the Bawble down,
Thus blest in charming thee.

Lady. And still, to make me yet more welcome to you, my Brother dy'd a Month ago, and left me Heiress to a vast Estate, which by my Father's Death he then enjoy'd; and soon as kind Fortune makes me yours, you shall possess it all.

Capt. Inestimable Woman! Madam, your Dross is but contemptible, nor adds one Feature more to grace thy Beauty. By Heaven, I'd quit the *Indies* richest Mines, and the Extension of my great Ambition shou'd bound within the Circle of those Arms.

Lady. Matchless, glorious Honour! Now, Sir, as soon as with Convenience you can dispose of all Things to your Wish, command me, I am yours.

Capt. Yes, Madam, I'll begone, I die till I obtain you.

'Till then, farewel, my dearest, kindest Love,
My Diligence shall my Impatience prove.

Exeunt.

SCENE. IV. *The* Park.

Enter Comick *in a riding Habit.*

So, thus far have I been successful for my Master; now if I can but prove so for my self, I am happy. I have sent him wing'd with Love to his longing Mistress's Arms, and do hope, e'er long, to be even with him. I saw *Pinner* enter here just before me, and if this Habit and Scheme don't take, I'll never intrigue

intrigue again. The Girl has Money, and is worth looking after, had ſhe not the common Curſe of all Chamber-Maids, full upon her, Pride, Levity, and Ambition; but Mum —— yonder ſhe comes —— now, dear Impudence, aſſiſt me.

AIR VI. O, how ſweet's the Month of *May*.

O, how fine is a neat Diſguiſe,
Charming fine is a neat Diſguiſe;
When the gay Rover turns a true Lover,
And by Stratagem gains his Prize.

Enter Pinner.

Pin. Now is my Miſtreſs enjoying her Gallant at home, and my Maſter his Punk abroad; whilſt poor Peelgarlick is oblig'd to walk here alone, without one Fellow to make a Speech to me, except I take up with a Valet, or ſo: But my Ambition has always ſoar'd above ſuch Underlings. I have Youth and Beauty, as well as my Miſtreſs, and a pretty competent Fortune, but all without one Proſelite to their Charms. Well, —— before I will live thus, I'll e'en marry the firſt Thing that asks me the Queſtion. ha! what ſprightly Spark is that —— he comes this Way, and ſeems to obſerve me ——

AIR

AIR VII. The Groves the Plains.

O, Queen of Love,
Look from above,
Behold a solitary Maid;
Must I alone
Sigh thus and moan,
Without a Husband's kindly Aid! [*bis.*

Com. [*approaching*] Madam, I am most superlatively yours——

Pin. I profess, Sir, you have the Advantage of me.

Com. O, Madam, that's what I wou'd willingly have of your whole Sex; but you are no Stranger to me, Madam: I have been a long time a silent Admirer of your Beauty and extraordinary Merit. 'Tis strange you don't know me, Madam.

Pin. Not I, really, Sir, your Face and Person are entirely new to me.

Com. That is wonderful, very wonderful, by Gad, Madam. I have often had the Honour to see you at Court, and the Felicity of dancing with you, but more particularly at the last Ball.

Pin. (He certainly takes me for a Lady of Quality, he talks so like a fine Gentleman; I will not undeceive him) Very like, Sir, it may be so——but you must know, Sir, that we Ladies seldom remember next Morning what we did the Night before; it would be troublesome to carry perpetual Almanacks in our Heads.

Com.

Com. (Inimitable Vanity!) but ſure you muſt have heard of me, Madam; my Name is Sir *Theophilus No-land*, a Knight of *Welſh* Extraction, born in *France*, and educated in *London*. My Father is juſt dead, Madam, and has left me ſole Heir to two thouſand Pounds a Year, as good Land as any *in Nubibus*: I am now going to take Poſſeſſion of my Eſtate; and ſo, Madam, (excuſe this abrupt Propoſal) if you have any Inclination to a Coach and Six, a tripple Couple of Liveries at your Ladyſhip's Heels, and an Humble Servant into the Bargain, they are all at your Command, Madam.

Pin. (In the Name of Wonder, where will this end?) Indeed, Sir, you amaze me—you are pleaſed to be very facetious, I hope you are not in earneſt, Sir. (Wou'd I cou'd be ſure on't tho').

Com. Begad, but I am, Madam; I never was in jeſt with a Lady in all my Life. I know you to be one, Madam, whoſe Perfections deſerve a better Fortune—But, Madam, I have ſecretly languiſh'd for you a conſiderable Time, and never durſt venture my future Hopes 'till this lucky Turn of Fortune, which now renders me more worthy your Acceptance; therefore if any of theſe Conſiderations can prevail, Madam, now or never is the Moment to make me happy, for I am ſworn never to ask the Queſtion twice; 'tis a Sort of a poſitive Humour, Madam; and ſo I hope you will excuſe it.

Pin. As I live, Sir, this is very particular; I am confounded at your Generoſity.

Com. (The Poiſon works rarely.) No Apologies, Madam; if you like me, I am eternally bleſt; if not, I muſt be for ever miſerable.

Pin. But, Sir, I muſt beg Leave to be free with you; methinks yours is a ſingular Humour; for you know, Sir, ſhou'd a Woman's Inclinations diſpoſe her to condeſcend, our Sex's Modeſty diſallows us to comply at the firſt Addreſs; though I muſt own I think you a moſt accompliſh'd Gentleman, nor can

I be ungrateful; but I hope you'l grant me a little Time of Consideration.

Com. (She's mine, by Jupiter.) Considerations are dangerous, Madam; besides, Time is precious to me. Perhaps whilst I linger here, one of my Juniors may step in before me, and so whip me out of my Acres in a trice; for you know Possession is eleven Points of the Law; so that Delays are hazardous, very hazardous, Madam; therefore if you are for Matrimony, pardon my Brevity, take me now, or for ever hereafter —— [*going*].

Pin. (Come what will, I'll embrace the Offer.) Lord, Sir, I never saw so hasty a Gentleman in all my Days, you must certainly be good-humour'd; and though I blush to own it, your Generosity has engag'd me to surrender sooner than ordinary; but I hope you will excuse my Forwardness, since it is wholly out of Complaisance to you, that my Delays might not impede your Necessity of Travelling; and therefore, Sir, I give you my Hand, lead me where you please.

Com. Raptures and Transports! Now, my Dear, in me you shall find all the Happiness Wedlock can afford you: In order to which we'll instantly to a Parson, tie the Knot, and then ——— O Heavens and Earth ——

AIR

AIR VIII. Butter'd Pease.

Thus with Love and ſoft Delight,
We'll tread the Paths of Marriage, O.
Pin. *Joy ſhall crown each Day and Night,*
Exempt from all Miſcarriage, O.
Com. *You ſhall be my only Dear,*
And I'll prove your Honey, O.
Pin. *You ſhall undergo the Care,*
And I'll ſpend the Money, O. [*Exeunt.*

F ACT

ACT III. SCENE I.

Miſs *Lure*'s Lodgings.

Enter Miſs Lure *and* Modely.

Miſs. AND what then, Sir?

Mod. You know Captain *Noble*, I preſume, Madam?

Miſs. I have ſeen him, Sir.

Mod. Then, Madam, know he's as ſtrong as *Samſon*, and ſtout as *Hercules*; beſides, there is one that ſhall be nameleſs, which is—— your humble Servant and all that, Madam, as brave as he; and ſhou'd any Man but dare even to whiſper in my Preſence, that he is not as courageous as *Hector*, and bold as *Alexander*, Demme, I'd ram the Lie down his Throat with the Pummel of my Sword; but no Matter for that——

Miſs. But what's all this to me, Sir?

Mod. Wou'd you believe it, Madam? ſink me, I pepper'd two cowardly Bravoes laſt Night with both their Swords drawn againſt me at once.

Miſs. Wonderful indeed, Sir; but methinks your boaſted Courage was aſleep laſt Time you encounter'd the Captain, or you wou'd never have endur'd ſuch a Beating.

Mod. Look'ee there it is now, rat me—— ha, ha, ha! humorous enough faith. Why, Madam, I am very often paſſively active, and actively paſſive; that is, ſometimes I am pleas'd to give a beating, and at other Times to take one; Cowardice was only the predominant Paſſion that ſeiz'd me then, but now I am am as valiant as any Man, and by thy supernatural Charms I adore you.

AIR I. Whilst the Town's brim full of Folly.

Whilst your Eyes so full of Fire
Fill my Soul with soft Desire,
Who can bear their Influence?
All Mankind must needs adore you,
Gods themselves too fall before you,
Ev'ry Glance charms ev'ry Sense.

[Knocking at the Door.

Miss. O Lord, Sir, we are all undone —— 'tis my Husband, I saw him thro' the Glass —— what shall I do —— where will you go? —— I am ruin'd, inevitably ruin'd if he finds you.

Mod. Your Husband —— eh! —— Gad's Curse, what will become of me —— Demme, my Character will suffer eternally —— Oh! I shall be murder'd

 positively

positively —— I feel his Sword already, split me—— Madam, I'll run into an Oven, a Chimney, an Augre-hole, or any where to hide me from Disgrace —— for Gad's Sake thrust me in some where.

Miss. Then fly, Sir, be quick into that Closet, I'll lock you in, but don't so much as draw your Breath, least you be heard. [*Exit to the Door.*

Mod. The Devil take Wenching if this be the Case. [*Exit.*

Re-enter with Sir Quibble *singing.*

AIR II. There was an old Man, he liv'd in a Wood.

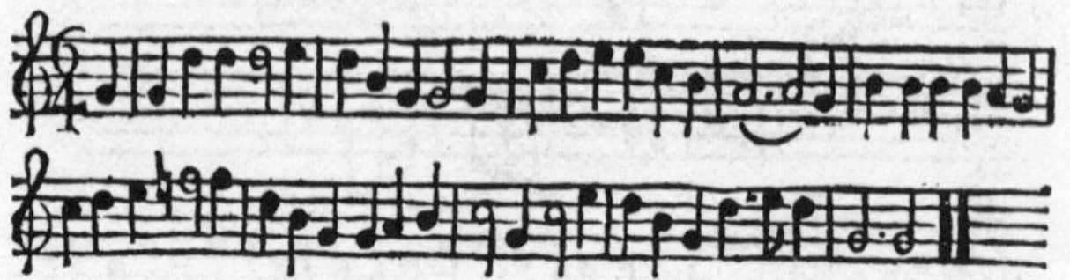

Thus laden I come to charm thee, my Dear,
And tho' I may seem somewhat old,
Here's what will delight thee still never fear,
A Purse of good yellow bright Gold,
Bright Gold, a Purse of good yellow bright Gold.

Ha, ha, ha! —— well my little Lovee, you see I have brought you more Money, an't I welcome?

Miss. Always to me, Sir, with, or without it —— but how much is there my nown Lifee?

Sir *Qui.* Just Twenty Pieces, Lifee, a great Deal of Money, and you shall give me a great Deal of Love for it, you little wonton Baggage you, eh—— [*Gives the Purse.*

Miss. That I will, Sir, as much as you please, for you know I am always ready to oblige you.

Sir *Qui.* That thou art Dearee, but come open this Door, Chuckee, let us in a little.

Miss. O by no Means, Sir, you cannot enter there. How came I to forget the Key in the Door? [*Aside.*

Sir

Sir *Qui.* Faith and Troth but I will, Lovee. [*opens it and ſtarts*] Bleſs my Eyes, a Man lock'd up here? —— who are you, Sir?

Mod. O Lard——what ſhall I ſay now?——Who am I, Sir, [*Advancing out of the Cloſet.*

Sir *Qui.* Stand of I ſay, [*retires*]. Ay, Sir, who are you?——I pay for theſe Lodgings, and have a Right to enquire.

Mod. (Egad who knows but he may be as great a Coward as my ſelf, I'll try him.) And ſo have I too, Sir; I am ſure I have paid dear for 'em within theſe two Hours——only a Watch worth Fifty Guineas, that's all, Sir, that's all.

Sir *Qui.* (An errant Coward I ſee, therefore I'll venture to bully him.) Blood, Sir, tell me none of your *Canterbury* Tales; I ſay, Sir, you're a Counterfeit, a Cheat——and if you don't quit the Chamber inſtantly, you ſhall pay dear for your Intruſion, you ſhall Friend. [*Couragious enough i' faith.*

Mod. ('Tis ſtrange we Cowards ſhou'd know each other by Inſtinct, the Fellow braves it ſo much, he dares not fight.) Demme, Sir, I am not us'd to ſuch Language, and in Return for your Menaces, if you do not this Moment depart, I'll make a Cullander of your Carcaſs in a Twinkling, ſink me ——

[*Bravely ſpoken, rat me.*

Sir *Qui.* (Now if the Fellow ſhou'd fight and deceive me after all, I were in a fine Condition truly; however I'll puſh it home.) Woons, Sir, I can't bear it any longer, therefore draw Sir.

[*Lays his Hand to his Sword.*

Miſs. O fie, Gentlemen, I hope you will not make a Diſturbance in my Lodgings. (Let them fight tho', ſay I, if they have but the Spirit.)

Mod. Draw, Sir? what do you mean Sir?——— (Bloody Dog, by *Jupiter* my Heart miſgives me.)

Sir *Qui.* Draw, Sir? ay Draw, Sir——d'sdeath, do you trifle with me? (Now I find I'm right.) [*Draws.*

Mod.

Mod. (Gad's Curſe, I am a dead Man, but I muſt fight cunningly.) Trifle with you, Sir? —— rat me, you ſhall ſee to the contrary, Sir——[*draws*] ſa, ſa, Sir——now have at you——

[*They both ſtand at a good Diſtance in a Poſture, ſtill retreating from each other.*

Enter Captain Noble *as drunk, ſinging.*

AIR III. A Damſel I'm told.

Capt. *Thus we live and we reign,*
Whilſt the Strength of Champaign
Makes our Lives with new Pleaſures run over;
'Tis the Bottle and Glaſs,
And a ſprightly free Laſs,
That heighten the Joys of a Rover, my Dear,
That heightenthe Joys of a Rover.

Thus, Madam, have I liv'd ſince I ſaw you; I have been toaſting your Ladyſhip's Health in ſparkling Bumpers of victorious Burgundy, till I am all Love and ſoft Deſire——ha——what have we here——*Neſtor* and *Achilles* at Sharps—— well done, my Heroes——Blood why don't ye fight?——

Sir *Qui.* Sir, I ſcorn to fight, to oblige any Man.

Mod. And I by Gad, Sir.

Cap. What not fight Scoundrels! ——— 'tis the Trade I profeſs, and love to encourage it in others—come—— come half a Dozen decent Thruſts, and then ———

Sir

Sir *Qui.* Sir, this Insolence won't pass upon me, Sir, and I will not fight. [*Puts up.*

Mod. Nor I neither, Demme——[*Putting up.*] fight!—— a pretty Jest, rat me——no, no, have a Care of that.

Cap. Nay then have at you both——I must oblige you to it, and you shall fight.

[*Beats* Quibus, *who runs behind* Modely.

Sir *Qui.* What do you mean, Sir?

[*Pushing* Modely *forwards*

Capt. O nothing at all, Sir——only to beat your Companion, that's all, upon my Word, Sir.

[*Beats* Modely, *who runs behind* Quibus.

Mod. This is beyond Forbearance, Sir.

Capt. Why don't ye fight then Puppies? Why don't ye fight. [*Still beating the foremost.*

Mod. Death, stand to him you Coward, stand to him.

Capt. Now good old *Letcher*, if you don't draw and fight him for calling you Coward, I'll bastinado you to some Purpose.

Sir *Qui.* Bloody minded Rogue!

Capt. And if you don't draw and defend your self Mr. *Powderpate*, I shall pink your Doublet for you.

Miss. This is rare Sport, I'll step out, and unseen observe the Diversion. [*Exit.*

Mod. Well, if I must, I must; but rat me I have no Stomach to it.

Capt. Fire and Furies, why don't ye begin?

Sir *Qui.* Come, Sir, we must fight, but do it gently if you expect any Mercy.

Mod. And do you take Care of me, or Death is your Doom.

Capt. Now he that spares the other shall have my Sword against him too. [*They fight aukwardly.*

Ha, ha, ha!—— well done, my Champions.

Sir *Qui.* Now who dares say that I am a Coward?

Mod. Or that I can't fight?

Capt. No Body, no Body, Gentlemen——you have fought it most heroically——and now, good Sir *Quibble* look me full in the Face, and tell me, if this publick Stew and a vile Prostitute are consistent with your Years and Gravity? Your Lady is young, handsome and virtuous; and to be found here is beyond Redress.

Sir *Qui*. (A Pox on his Morals; the Rogue has awaken'd my sleeping Conscience, and almost made me a Proselite to his Doctrine.) But pray, Mr. *Infallibility*, whence had you this Inspiration?

Capt. Look seriously on me, and my Face will tell you.

Mod. A fatal one, by *Jupiter*, to my Back and Shoulders: And now, egad, I think it adviseable to sneak off into this Closet again, to avoid another Battery. [*Exit*.

Sir *Qui*. O Ignominy! Captain *Noble*.

Capt. The very same faith, Sir.

Sir *Qui*. And art thou that formal Piece of Divinity, that has been preaching up Continence to me, when thou art thy self as very a Wag as ever made a Cuckold? Prithee was it kind to conceal your self so long?

Capt. Was it generous in you to give me Reason, Sir? for shame reflect on your Folly.

Sir *Qui*. I do, I do, *Captain*, and acknowledge my Crime——but come, no more on't, you shall go home and sup with me, but take no Notice on't to my Wife.

Capt. With all my Heart, I long to see her.

AIR

AIR IV. *Wooley* is gone to *France*.

I fly now on Wings of Desire,
Impatience shall hasten my Flight;
Her Presence new Joys will inspire,
And fill my fond Soul with Delight:
Farewel to the Wars then for ever;
If I but my Charmer obtain,
No Power on Earth shall us sever,
We'll mutually blest remain. [*Exeunt.*

Re-enter *Miss* Lure.

Miss. I am heartily glad that terrible Fellow is gone; now for my sweet-scented Spark, and since I mist my Revenge on the Captain, it shall all light on him. [*Aside.*] Sir, Sir, come forth, the Coast is clear.

Enter Modely.

Mod. Are you sure all is safe, Madam; may I get off in a whole Skin?

Miss. All is safe upon my Honour, Sir.

Mod. (That's but a slippery Oath, rat me.) Before Gad, Madam, I was never in such a Condition in my Days——the Sweat ran down my Face like Drops of Ambergrise, for Fear of that blustring Red-coat.

Miss. Indeed, Sir, I can't blame you; I'll swear he has almost frighted me out of my Wits.

Mod. Sink me, Madam, I am not safe whilst I stay here methinks——for Heavens Sake, shew me the Way out——I shan't recover my Complexion this Month, stupify me. [*Knocking at the Door.*

Devil take me, he's here again——now am I a dead Man, consume me.

Miss. O horrible! more ill luck, Sir——here are my two Brothers——besure do every thing I order you, or we are entirely ruin'd. [*Exit to the Door.*

Mod. O Fortune, Fortune!——by Gad thou art a Bitch.

Re-enter Miss Lure *with* Garnish *and* Darby.

Gar. Hey day! who have we got here——a Man lock'd up with my Sister?——

Dar. By these Hilts a Plot to debauch her——who are you, Sir——what do you here?——speak instantly or my Sword's in you Guts.

Mod. Sink me, I am gone——what the Devil shall I say?——Madam, Madam—— [*To her softly.*

Miss. O fie, Sirs, be more civil; this Gentleman is my Dancing-Master, and come to teach me.

Mod. Yes, Yes, Gentlemen, I am her Ladyship's Dancing-Master, rat me.

Gar. O Sir, we cry you Mercy.

Dar. (Indeed he looks like a moving Antick.)——But pray let us not disturb you, Sir.

Miss. By no Means; come, Sir, I have made my Honours, please to begin, Sir.

Mod. (Zauns, I don't know a Step, by Gad.) Yes, yes; pray mind me, Madam——tol, lol, lol, la——

[*Sings and leads her about in Confusion.*

Miss. Methinks, Sir, I don't much affect this odd Kind of Ruggadoon——I wou'd rather see you perform the new Passby alone; I shall have the better Opportunity to observe it.

Mod. Devil take me, Madam, I hope you will excuse me; my Joints are ſo ſtiff, that Demme, I can't move at all. [*Damn'd Jade.*

Gar. No Apologies, Sir; you move exceedingly.

Dar. Come, pray Sir, begin.

Miſs. Quick, quick, Sir, or we are diſcover'd.

Mod. I will, I will, Gentlemen; but rat me, I ſhall ſpoil it.—— [*Confound ye all.*

[*He dances foppiſhly.*

Miſs. Excellently fine, Sir.

Gar. The Gentlemen dances to Admiration; but it ſeems ſomewhat dull. My Siſter and we often dance the Hays together, and to my Mind, 'tis much the merrier.

Dar. Ay, ay, Brother, you ſay right; the Hays for my Money——let us dance it now; you'l make one Sir?

Mod. With all my Heart Gentlemen. (Bloody minded Rogues, they have a Deſign upon me).

They dance and ſhove Modely *about, at laſt they puſh him down.*

Miſs. O la, Sir——I fear you are hurt.

Mod. Not at all, Madam; Demme; 'twas only a falſe Step or ſo. [*I wiſh I was fairly out, that's all.*

Gar. The Gentleman dances ſo well, Siſter, he muſt needs be a Maſter of Muſick, and ſing to a Miracle.

Dar. Beyond Diſpute; pray, Sir, oblige us with a Song.

Miſs. That I can promiſe you he does, even to excel *Nicolini* himſelf.

Mod. O dear Madam——facetious pretty Gentlemen——you are all too obliging——however I muſt try to pleaſe you——hem——hem.——

AIR V. Ye Beaus of Pleaſure.

Thus gay and airy,
I dance like Fairy,
And ſing moſt rarely,
When e'er you call:
But now with Pleaſure,
Above all Meaſure,
I bid, with Leiſure,
Adieu to all.

And ſo your moſt obedient—— [*running out.*

Gar. Hold, hold, Maſter of mine——one Word or two more before we part.

Mod. I vow to Gad, Gentlemen, I have outſtay'd my Time, I am exquiſitely in haſte.

Dar. Well, but Sir, what do you think we have learn'd from all thoſe fine Accompliſhments of yours? that you are the only Perſon in the World we have ſingled out to be our Brother-in-Law.

Gar. Nay, Sir, my Siſter deſerves every thing you are Maſter of; and therefore reſolve this Moment to marry her.

Mod. But, Gentlemen, this is ſo ſurprizing——rat me, if ever I once thought of a Wife in all my Days.

Dar. What, not wed her, ſay you?——do you refuſe to marry the Quinteſcence of Beauty, Wit and Virtue——Zoons, ſuch another Syllable and I'll——

Gar. The Matter is abſolutely thus, Sir, take your Choice, Matrimony or Caſtration.

Mod.

Mod. They are both alike, by Gad——I cannot chuſe either.——(Once more Fortune thou art a Bitch.)

Gar. What, does he ſtand debating?——we'll ſoon bring him to a Reſolution.

Dar. Ay, ay, away with him, away with him, plump into the Sudds.

Mod. Madam, Gentlemen——Murder——Treaſon——Robbers—— [*They carry him off.*

Miſs. Ha, ha, ha! an excellent Contrivance——I muſt follow, and have my Share of the Diverſion, which may poſſibly turn to an Husband.

AIR VI. *Hendal's* Hornpipe.

Since Wedlock is a State in Life,
And ev'ry Maid wou'd be a Wife, [bis.
Let's all in this agree:
I'll do the beſt that e'er I can,
And marry when I meet the Man, [bis.
So cheat him who'd cheat me. [Exit.

SCENE II. *Sir* Quibble's.

Enter Lady Quibus *and* Pinner.

Lady. And are you ſure he's no Counterfeit, *Pinner?*

Pin. I wou'd not ſuſpect him for the World, Madam. His very Air and Mien ſpoke him a Gentleman.

Lady.

Lady. But have you any Aſſurance of his Fortune, for 'tis an Affair ſo ſudden and extraordinary, that I know not how to credit it.

Pin. Madam, he gave me ſuch evident Proofs of it, that I am throughly convinc'd all is true. He is now gone down to his Eſtate, and will be back in a Month, or perhaps ſooner than I imagine.

Lady. Well, I ſhou'd rejoyce at your good Fortune, were I not in ſome Doubt of the Truth on't; however, a little Time will diſcover all. You ſee Sir *Quibble* has brought the Captain home to Supper, and this Night my Deſign is to diſengage my ſelf; therefore that I may be every way ſatisfied, deſire *Standiſh* to take an Officer with him, and bring Miſs *Lure* hither immediately; and do you go into my Cloſet, and whip on the Parſon's Gown and Things that lie there, and be ready to appear when I call.

Pin. I fly, Madam; I love a Diſguiſe with all my Heart. [*Exit*.

Lady. Thus are all my fearful Doubts appeas'd, my daily Cares and nightly Thoughts blown over; I long ſuſpected the Virtue of his Paſſion, and all my Fears were leaſt I ſhou'd have loſt him; but now my Heart's convinc'd he truly loves me, and that my future Days ſhall ſmile upon me with ſucceſſive Pleaſure.

AIR

AIR VII. My Bony Jean.

Long have I been with Grief opprest,
Each Night o'erwhelm'd with Misery;
But now I shall lie down in rest,
And rise each Morn to Liberty:
Our Life is oft with Clouds o'ercast,
As are the brightest Summer's Days;
But when those Shadows all are past,
The Sun shoots forth enliv'ning Rays.

Enter Sir Quibble *and Captain* Noble.

Sir *Qui.* Madam, I have brought your old Friend Captain *Noble* to see you —— bid him welcome.

Lady. That I have done already, Sir, but now he's doubly welcome.

Capt. Madam, I can never repay your Goodness.

Sir *Qui.* The Devil—have you seen him before, and unknown to me —— then my Horns begin to sprout.

Lady. Yes, I have seen him, besides, 'twas I gave him Directions where to find you out.

Sir *Qui.* Fire and Furies! does she know it too——

Lady. Nay, ben't supriz'd, Sir, I have known it long, tho' I with-held Resentment, but now I can no longer bear it; and since we can't agree as Man and Wife, 'twere better much to part.

Sir

Sir *Qui.* Wou'd to Heaven we cou'd do it legally.

Capt. Then you are ſatisfied, Sir?

Sir *Qui.* With all my Soul.

Lady. Agreed; and for your further Satisfaction, the Parſon that marry'd us is now in the Houſe, and, if you pleaſe, the very ſame ſhall part us.

Sir *Qui.* Let him but enter, and I'll keep this as my Birth-Day as long as I live.

Lady. Then here he comes. [*Stamps.*

Enter Pinner *diſguiſed as a Parſon.*

Sir *Qui.* The very ſame, by *Jove* —— tol, lol, lol, —— welcome, welcome, my dear *Puzzletext*, if thou can'ſt but do thy Buſineſs effectually, I will ever adhere to thy Doctrine.

Pin. That I warrant you.

Capt. Now, Sir, you muſt know, this Couple are much diſſatisfy'd with their preſent Condition; and as you are the Parſon that join'd 'em, they alſo deſire you wou'd ſeparate them; that's all, Sir.

Pin. It ſhall be done in a Moment —— now join your Hands [*they take hold*] and thus I break aſunder.

[*Looſes them, opens the Gown, and diſcovers herſelf.*]

Sir *Qui.* Eh —— *Pinner*, the Parſon! —— O my lucky Stars —— why was I deceiv'd ſo long? —— thou dear kind Hypocrite, thus let me thank thee. [*Kiſſing her.*

AIR

AIR VIII. Jockey has gotten a Wife.

And now I am once more ſet free,
If ever again I do marry,
May Beaſts my Aſſociates be,
And what I deſign ſtill miſcarry:
I'll wanton and live as I pleaſe,
Still wallow each Night in good Nectar;
And ſtudy nought but my own eaſe,
Exempt from a damn'd Curtain-Lecture.

Enter Standiſh, *Officers, and Miſs* Lure.

Ha, —— *Standiſh*, how come this?

Stand. Her Ladyſhip can tell, Sir.

Lady. 'Twas by my Orders, that ſhe might be made a publick Example to all vile Proſtitutes, like herſelf; and I inſiſt that you ſend her this Moment to the proper Place of Confinement.

Sir *Qui.* Well, Madam, ſince you requeſt it —— away with her.

Miſs. Stand off, ye Villains, I will ſpeak to the dear Man —— I will not go ——

[*Runs and hangs upon Sir* Quibble.

Enter Modely, *all in Diſorder.*

Mod. So the Fates have deliver'd me at laſt —— what do I ſee —— Sir *Quibble* and my Tormentor in Embrace —— nay, then, by Gad, I have follow'd her hither in vain for Justice, since this is the Case.

Sir *Qui.* Help, help, she'll devour me, eat me alive —— help ——

Miss. Ha! my Husband that shou'd have been —— welcome ——

[*Quits* Quibble, *and runs to him, he draws upon her.*

Mod. Stand off, or, sink me, you are gone.

[*Stands a Posture.*

Miss. Nay, then I am deserted by all I see.

AIR IX. Gavot in *Otho.*

Mod. Celia's *Eyes have lost their Splendour,*
Whilst the pretty blushing red
That adorn'd her Cheeks is fled,
And those Looks, once soft and tender,
Now have lost their Influence.
What tho' late I did adore her,
I behold her fading Charms,
Free from trifling Love's Alarms,
And unmov'd can stand before her,
Once the fairest Excellence.

Hence

Hence I fly thee,
Come not nigh me,
All your Artifice is vain;
I will ne'er be trap'd again,
By your false Caressing:
Now I bid adieu to Woman,
Whilst a sparkling Glass at Night
Shall be all my dear Delight,
Since the Sex is grown so common,
Wine shall be my Blessing.

[*Exeunt* Const. *and* Miss.

Enter Comick *in his Riding Habit.*

Pin. Bless my Eyes! my Husband so soon return'd —— now I am happy ——

Com. I am your Ladyship's most Humble Servant— [*Discovers himself.*

Pin. O Heavens! Mr. *Comick*, whom I thought dead ——

Com. Don't be frighted, my Dear, the very same, and your Husband.

Pin. Confusion! all my Greatness come to this— lost and undone ——

Lady. Ha, ha, ha! Poor, *Pinner!* now my Prediction is come to pass.

Sir *Qui.* The Parson fob'd —— ha, ha, ha, —— I love a pretty Trick with all my Heart.

Com. Here Page, a Coach and Six for her Ladyship, —— ha, ha, I am even with you, Madam.

AIR X. The Clock has ſtruck I can't tell what.

Now we have both been in the wrong,
Let's make up Matters with a Song.
Pin. *And ſince Ambition was our Aim,*
We neither can each other blame.
Com. *Hence then, my Dear, both be ſincere,*
And jog thro' the Road of Marriage.
Pin. *Be you but true, as I to you,*
Fear not then the leaſt Miſcarriage.

Mod. The Devil take me, Humourous enough—— rat me, theſe Intrigues wou'd make a pretty Plot for a Comedy, where I not concern'd in the Buſineſs.

Lady. Now, Sir, you have given me a generous Proof of your Paſſion, and I feel my ſelf tranſported with Joy, when I think I am capable of making you this grateful Return of my Perſon, which together with my Fortune, now is wholly yours.

Capt. Kind Heaven, I thank thee——come, my deareſt Joy, let's haſte to perfect our eternal Bliſs; whilſt every gentle Breeze, ſweet as thy fragrant Breath, may diffuſe its balmy Sweets upon us as we paſs;

paſs; and when our blended Souls lie drown'd in mutual Pleaſure; propitious *Jove* himſelf ſhall ſmile upon us.

AIR XI. Do not ask me charming *Phillis*.

Thus like happy Turtles cooing,
All our Moments we'll employ:
Lady. *Ev'ry Pleaſure gayly wooing,*
'Till we taſte immortal Joy,
'Till we taſte immortal Joy.

Capt. Thus virtuous Woman ſweetens Life alone,
Salves all our Cares, and keeps Misfortunes down;
Gives us a Taſte of future Joys above,
When crown'd with bliſsful Harmony and Love.

F I N I S.

THE EPILOGUE.

Spoken by Miss LURE.

BEHOLD, I have escap'd with good Success;
Ye must protect me, Sirs,——ye can't do less;
See——how those Whore-son Dogs have maul'd my Dress.

Not one kind Spark——do all my Cause disown!
Is Pity now, as well as Money flown?
I'll swear ye're all most barb'rous Devils grown.

Can't poor Miss Lure, *with her accomplish'd Parts,*
Her tempting Smiles, her most engaging Arts,
Now soften one of your obdurate Hearts?

Well, to the middle Region I'll repair,
'Mong'st my own Sister-Misses, and take Share;
I'm sure to find some friendly Coxcomb there,

Who, now the Play is done, will take me hence,
And treat me fairly at his own Expence,
With Oisters, *Wine, and downright Impudence.*

But if my Project there shou'd chance to fail,
To some pert Skip I'll set my self to Sale,
And e'n take up with fulsome Cakes *and* Ale.

The Decoy

Bibliographical note:
This facsimile has been made from a copy in the University Library, Cambridge England (S721.d.70.26[8])

THE DECOY: AN OPERA.

As it is ACTED at the

NEW THEATRE IN GOODMAN's FIELDS.

Nil admirari prope res est una Numici,
Solaque quæ possit facere & servare beatum.
Horat. Epist. VI. Lib. 6.

LONDON:
Printed for, and Sold by. T. OSBORN, in *Gray's-Inn*.
MDCCXXXIII. Price 1s. 6d.

To the Right HONOURABLE

CHARLES Earl of *Tankerville*,

One of the Knights of the antient Order of the Thiſtle; one of his Majeſty's moſt Honourable Privy Council, and one of the Lords of the Bedchamber to his Royal Highneſs the Prince of *Wales*.

My LORD,

WHEN I conſider the Countenance your Lordſhip ſhew'd to the celebrated *Beggar's Opera*, I cannot but rejoice at my good Fortune to have this ſmall Piece of mine (ſo much inferior to that) reciev'd by ſo judicious a *Patron*: And as your Lordſhip has done me the Honour to accept of this my Dedication, I cou'd wiſh my ſelf capable of ſome poetical Logick to argue your Lordſhip into a good Opinion of it.

But I think, from the little Knowledge I have of your Lordſhip, and from the general Eſteem which every one (who is ſo fortunate as to have the Honour of being acquainted with you) has for you; I with great Confidence may flatter my

ſelf,

ſelf, that thoſe Rays of Goodneſs, which are ſo diffuſive in your Lordſhip, and which you ſo liberally beſtow upon all Mankind, muſt ſupport whatever you take under your Protection.

I have endeavour'd in this Piece to ſhew the *general Decoy* of Mankind, how Innocence is betray'd, and how ſoon Folly takes Place. I have attempted to ſhew what *Dupes* the Youths of this Age are made of, and what Traps are laid to enſnare young ignorant Girls, unacquainted with the Town. I have painted as much Diſtreſs as the Nature and Circumſtance of this Sort of Drama will allow of. I have expos'd the Vicious, and made them ſenſible of their Follies.

This is the Plan and Model I have built upon; and whether I have done Poetical Juſtice or not, I ſhall ſubmit to your Lordſhip's better Judgment.

But here I muſt be ſilent, leſt I ſhould attempt to give an Evidence to that, which all the World are already acquainted with; I ſhall only beg, therefore, to aſſure your Lordſhip, no one can have a greater Senſe of your juſt and due Merits, than he, who has the Honour to ſubſcribe himſelf,

My LORD,

Your Lordſhip's,

moſt oblig'd,

moſt obedient,

and moſt devoted humble Servant,

HENRY POTTER.

THE

INTRODUCTION.

Enter *Tragedy* and *Comedy.*

Trag. T*HE Task is difficult, I needs must own,*
To write a Tragedy, to please the Town. ——

Com. *Tragedy, my good Friend, will ne'er go down.*
Comedy's the Taste, — be it good or bad,
The Audienee come to laugh, — not to be sad.
Take my Advice, withdraw your Tragick Muse,
For when 'tis on the Stage — there's no Excuse.

Enter *Opera,* and slaps *Comedy* on the Shoulder.

Op. *Your Caution's good; I'd have you both agree,*
And leave the Bays entirely to me. ——
Not that I'm a Laureat, I'd have you know.—
I've only brought a little Sing-song Show.
A Thing you've seen; the Sketch is now in Print;—
To say the Truth, — there's little Meaning in't.

Trag. *Then why would you produce it on the Stage?*

Op. *To shew you 'tis the Fashion of the Age.*
Writing, you know, is grown a meer Disease,
And all that write, — sure were not born to please.

Com. *Sir, I've a Comedy that must be play'd.*

Trag. *And I a Tragedy: — Pray, who's afraid?*

Op. *Patience! here's Tragi-Comedy in one,*
And if you'll father it, — why, 'tis your own.
I here submit to th' Mercy of the Night,
Applaud, or Damn, — I'll think you in the right.

Dramatis

Dramatis Personæ.

Sir *Francis Firebriecks*, an old Fornicator.	Mr. *Lyon.*
Mr. *Xenodcchy*, a *Grecian* Merchant, and a great Admirer of the Ladies.	Mr. *Stoppelaer.*
Sir *Ralph Reformage.*	Mr. *Huddy.*
Justice *Hamper*, of the *Quorum.*	Mr. *Penketbman.*
Justice *Touchmore*, of the *Quorum.*	Mr. *Excell.*
Justice *Bridleman*, of the *Quorum.*	Mr. *Collet.*
Mr. *Lookout*, Clerk to the Justices.	Mr. *Rosco.*
Captain *Wou'dbe*, a Sharper.	Mr. *Bardin.*
Sir *Thomas Pairnails.*	Mr. *James.*
Squire *Spendthrift*, Nephew to Sir *Thomas.*	Mr. *Jenkins.*
Skinflint, Steward to Sir *Thomas.*	Mr. *Norris.*
Thomas Drivewell the Carrier.	Mr. *Norris.*

WOMEN.

Mrs. *Haverly.*	old Bawds.	Mr. *Hulett.*
Mrs. *Clarkwell*,	old Bawds.	Mr. *Pearce.*
Mrs. *Frisk*,	Women of the Town.	Mrs. *Williamson.*
Mrs. *Stroaker*	Women of the Town.	Mrs. *Haughton.*
Mrs. *Feelmore*,	Women of the Town.	Mrs. *Christian.*
Jenny Ogle	Country Girls.	Mrs. *Roberts.*
Harriette Shuffle	Country Girls.	Miss *Wherrit*
Sukey Slattern,	Country Girls.	Mrs. *Purden.*
Mary Licklips,	Country Girls.	Mrs. *Vallois.*
Diana Stepwell.	Country Girls.	Mrs. *Morgan.*
Betty Dropspue,	Maid to Mrs. *Haverly.*	Miss *Sandham.*

Constables, Watch, Servants, and Attendants, &c.

THE DECOY: AN OPERA.

ACT I.

SCENE I. *New Chamber.*

Mrs. *Haverly*'s Houſe. *Two Chairs.*

Enter Sir *Francis Firebriecks* and Mrs. *Haverly.*

Sir *Francis.*

LOOK ye, Mrs. *Haverly*, I muſt have new Women; and if you deceive me, I muſt go to another Market.

Mrs. *Haverly.* Sir *Francis*, you know that I have uſed you as well as any body could do; and have but a little Patience till *Tom Drivewell* comes in, and I'll engage you ſhall have freſh Goods.

AIR I. The Virgin Queen.

Mrs. Hav. *The Lasses that spin at the Wheel,*
Have Notions of seeing the Town,
And Girls that are willing to feel
The Sense of more Pleasures than one,
Will all haste away to the Goal,
And gratify their Ambition;
No one will refuse to enrol,
Where Money's the Instigation.

Mrs. *Hav.* I do assure you, Sir *Francis*, I had more bid me from a Lord at the other End of the Town for *Nanny Goodflesh*, than you gave me, by fifty Pounds; besides, — when you had done with her, you made your Money of her again in a very little Time, by recommending her to your Friends. — Therefore 'tis not generous for you to tell me you will go elsewhere for a fresh Supply.

Sir *Fran.* Nay, don't be angry, Mrs. *Haverly*; you know I always had a great Respect for you, and what I said was only to spur you on to Business.

Mrs. *Hav.* Sir, I know my Trade as well as any Woman in Town, and therefore want no Spur; — and you know I have at all Times given you the Refusal of my Ladies; — and tho' I say't, that shou'd not say't, I have as fine Goods as any Man can wish or desire.

Sir *Fran.* Why, 'tis true; — but when do you expect the Carrier to come in?

Mrs. *Hav.* To Night, Sir; — but Sir *Francis*, cou'd not you let me have ten Guineas upon Account.

Sir *Fran.* Ten Guineas! — Why really, Mrs. *Haverly*, I have not so much about me. — Let me see — There, — there's five, if that will do.

Mrs. *Hav.* Sir, I'll make shift with that for the present, and your Honour will owe me five more.

Sir *Fran.* Very well; — I understand you.

AIR

AIR II.

Sir. Fran. *The Man who indulges his Pleasure,*
Must not lay up Money as Treasure;
But e'en let it go,
For Service, you know,
And get it again at his Leisure.

Well, Mrs. *Haverly!* — you remember your Promise. — The first Interview, you know!

Mrs. *Hav.* Sir *Francis*, you'll always find me a Woman of Honour. [*Exit* Sir *Francis*.

Come, this is something towards equipping out *Dolly Spindle*, and White-Neck *Jenny* for the Masquerade; — and if the Devil's not in the Dice, they must get Business.

SCENE II.

Enter Mrs. Clarkwell.

Mrs. *Hav.* Your Servant, good Mrs. *Clarkwell.*

Mrs. *Clarkw.* Oh! Mrs. *Haverly*, have you got e'er a Dram? Oh! I shall faint.

Mrs. *Hav.* A Dram! Ay, I'll fetch you one in a Minute.

[*Runs out, and re-enters with a Bottle and Glass.*

They sit down.

Here, take it, and drink it off, if 'twere a Gallon. — But what's the Matter, Mrs. *Clarkwell?*

Mrs. *Clarkw.* Oh, I can't speak! give me another Sup, and I shall be able to tell you.

Mrs. *Hav.* Here! 'tis special Gin as ever was tasted. — So! how do you find yourself?

Mrs. *Clarkw.* Something better, Mrs. *Haverly.*

AIR III. In *Perseus* and *Andromeda.*

Mrs. Hav. *Oh, what comfort do we find,*
In a Glass of Liquor kind,
When the Spirits are sunk low,
When the Heart beats to and fro!
How it raises
Beyond Praises
To a gen'rous Pitch of Mind!
Makes the Ladies
Gay as Dazies,
Full of Love, and unconfin'd!

But what is the meaning, good Mrs. *Clarkwell*, of this sudden Disorder?

Mrs. *Clarkw.* Matter! these Cursed Reforming Justices have plaid the Devil with me, and that Rogue *Justice Touchmore* took the last Guinea from me, and then gave me and my poor Girls up, to be sacrific'd to that merciless Wretch Sir *Ralph.*

Mrs. *Hav.* Why truly, Mrs. *Clarkwell*, 'tis monstrous, that in a free Country, we industrious Women should be thus interrupted in our Vocations.

[*They rise.*

Mrs. *Clarkw.* Nay, 'tis a downright Shame, Mrs. *Haverly.* — It was not always so, let me tell you; and we too, who in the worst of Times, have been the chief Support to the Nation — Have we not promoted Trade? Have we not been Instrumental in the bringing up many a bold Soldier for his Majesty? And what not? — O! Mrs. *Haverly*, they do not deserve half what we have done for 'em. But in short, the World seems at an End, and so many bright Gentlemen, that we have been serviceable to, methinks might take our Case into Consideration, and bring it before the Parliament. — What think you of that, Mrs. *Haverly?*

AIR

AIR IV.

Mrs. Clarkw. *Then let us draw up a Petition,*
To relieve our ſad Souls from Deſpair,
Th' Indulgency of our good Nation,
May prove kind to Complaints from the Fair?
Mrs. Hav. *Oh, Siſter! Conſider the Senate;*
Let's be cautious in what we're about;
There's nothing but Wiſemen that's in it,
Who knows what their long Heads may turn out?

Mrs. *Clarkw.* Why 'tis true, Mrs. *Haverly*; but what muſt be done?

Mrs. *Hav.* Why, we muſt help one another.

Mrs. *Clarkw.* Alas! Mrs. *Haverly*, 'tis not in my Power at preſent to ſerve you in any Reſpect. And the Obligation I have already received, can only be repaid in the Acknowledgments of 'em.—— But you know, my Heart was always good; and when Times mend, you ſhall have the Renewal of my Friendſhip.

Mrs. *Hav.* I believe you to be a very honeſt Woman, and a good Chriſtian, Mrs. *Clarkwell*; and if it is in my Power to ſerve you, I will.

Mrs. *Clarkw.* Why then, Madam, give me leave to ask one other Favour of you.—I expect Squire *Spendthrift* this Afternoon; he's a good ſort of a Chap, and bleeds freely.——Now, as you know the Situation I am in, if you cou'd lend me a Couple of your Ladies, 'twill be of infinite Service to me.

Mrs. *Hav.* Why, I don't care to lend my Children out, as a great many of the Trade do, but I will do more than that for you. — You know the Hazard I run, and the Expence I am at. Now do you ſee, if you'll bring any Perſon of Reputation and Character to be bound for you, upon the Appraiſement of my Stock, I will take you in Partner.

Mrs.

Mrs. *Clarkw.* Dear Madam, You're very kind; but when a Woman's down, down with her, you know; and I profess, I don't know who to ask such a Favour of.

Mrs. *Hav.* Why then, I'll put you in a Way. *Black-ey'd Moll*, you know, marry'd your Brother-in-Law—What's his Name?—Mr. *Letgo* the Constable.—Suppose you was to tell him your Case; you know a few Guineas go a great way with him.

Mrs. *Clarkw.* 'Tis a lucky Thought indeed, Mrs. *Haverly*; 'twill certainly do; besides, 'tis making him our Friend at a dead Lift;— which, let me tell you, is no bad Thing.

AIR V. Moll Peatly.

Mrs. Clarkw. *The Merchant who fails in his Trade,*
No doubt but a Bankrupt must be;
So she that secures not her Blade,
Is full as precarious as he:
Then Fortune, I'll try thee once more;
My Sister in Partnership join,
In Love's Traffick my Stock restore,
And make up a Purse of good Coin.

Well! Good Mrs. *Haverly*, let me take my Leave of you; for surely you are one of the best of Women!—but who do I see? 'Tis *Thomas Drivewell* the Carrier; he brings a fresh Cargo to be sure.

Mrs. *Hav.* Why then, Mrs. *Clarkwell*, leave me; for I suppose he's coming to bring me Information that the Waggon's hard by.

Mrs. *Clarkw.* But what must I do about my *young Squire?*

Mrs. *Hav.* Why, bring him here. So, Madam, your Servant.

Mrs. *Clarkw.* Dear Madam, your most humble Servant. [*Exit* Mrs. *Clarkwell.*

SCENE

SCENE III.

Enter *Thomas Drivewell.*

Mrs. *Hav.* Your Servant, good Mr. *Drivewell.* Why, you're a pure Man to come in ſo early.—Well! what ſhall I give you?—What think you of a Dram of right *Iriſh Uſquebaugh* ſent me from *Ireland* for my own Drinking?

Tho. Driv. Nay, I'ze no Churl, you know, Mrs. *Haverly*, as to the matter of that; What you pleaſe'n.—The laſt time I were here, you ga' me a wounded good Dram, by the Maſs. I think it ſpic'd my Stomach for three Days afterwards.

Mrs. *Hav.* Why, that was a Water of my own making, Mr. *Drivewell*; and it has been much commended by People of Great Faſhion, let me tell you.—Then you ſhall have a Dram of that.——Here, *Betty!*

Enter *Betty Droſlepate.*

Bring a Glaſs of that Liquor from the Corner Cupboard next my Bed's Head: 'tis in a long-neck'd Bottle. [Exit *Betty Droſlepate.*

Well! what ſort of Goods have you?—Are they fit for a Gentleman's Service?

Tho. Driv. I know not, good Faith.—There are ſome pretty Girls enouf;—but you'll be beſt Judge, when you zee 'em.

Re-enter *Betty Droſlepate* with a Dram.

Mrs. *Hav.* There, drink it off. I'll engage 'twill make your Heart light.

Tho. Driv. Mieſtreſs, here's towards your good Health.

Mrs. *Hav.* Thank you, Mr. *Drivewell.*

Tho.

Tho. Driv. Why this is Neck an Brosia, as we caw it; it's main good indeed. — Well! an you're dispos'd to go to the Inn; belike *Robin*'s come by this time, for I left him at Stones-End.

Mrs. *Hov.* With all my Heart, Mr. *Drivewell.*

AIR VI. She wou'd not die a Maid.

Mrs. *Hov.* *Your Fate, my good Girls, now draws near;*
Your Virtue pray summons to your Aid:
Blame not the Stars that led you here;
'Tis Ungenerous them to upbraid.
But take my Advice as a Friend,
You'll not find me the worst of the Clan:
Feign, counterfeit well to the End;
'Tis your Interest alone to please Man.

[*Exeunt.*

SCENE IV. Changes.

Enter *Squire Spendthrift*, and Captain *Wou'dbe.*

Spend. Well, Captain! You see there's nothing certain under the Sun.

Capt. No, nor over it neither, in my Opinion.— *Omnium rerum vicissitudo.* — Sir, that's my Motto; and since every thing must have its Turn, why shou'd you be uneasy? — To-day is your's, — To-morrow's mine: — And the next Day may be some Body's else. —— Lard, Sir, the best Conjurer in the World can't tell how long his Wife or his Daughter will keep chaste. Then why shou'd you be uneasy at Mrs. *Feelmore*'s liking another Man? — Why they must have their Way, and will have it sooner or later. — Psha! Psha! There's nothing in it. —— Besides, you know, she never pretended to keep to any one Man.

Spend,

Spend. Why, that's true; — but cou'd not she a'gone off, in another manner, but to rob me.

Capt. Ha! Rob you!

Spend. Ay Sir, rob me. She's taken my Watch, seven Broad Pieces, and two Suits of Cloaths.

Capt. You amaze me, Sir. — This is a new Story. — [*Aside.*] Faith, I did not think the Girl had so much Wit. — But since that's the Case, I must assist you.

Spend. Which Way can you proceed to get 'em again without Prosecuting her? — for methinks I wou'd not have the Girl hang'd.

Capt. Hang'd! no, hang her, I wou'd not hurt her: — But you must know, I am intimately acquainted with Mr. *Lookout*, who is Clerk to three Justices of the Peace, — all my good Friends. — Now I'll take out a Warrant; and if we can light of her, we'll bind up the Minx to her good Behaviour; — whether we get your Things or not. — You know, they're Trifles to a Gentleman of an Estate like your Honour; and the Glory of bringing her to Repentance, is all that is required from a Person of your Rank.

Spend. That's right, Captain. And as you're a Man of Parts, and my Friend, I leave it entirely to you.

AIR VII. Altho' I am a Country Lass.

Then let us punish this bilking Jade,
Whose Study was to deceive me;
Sure no Man ever was thus betray'd;
I have doated on her Folly:
But now my Love is turn'd to Hate,
To Friendship true, I bid Adieu,
May she have Cause to curse her Fate!
Revenge is all, I have in view.

Capt. Sir, here's my Hand: — You ſhall have Juſtice done you. — There will be ſome little Expence attend it; but I will take Care and defray that, and place it to your Account.

Spend. Sir, You are very obliging, and I ſhall acknowledge it.

Capt. Sir, Your moſt Obedient. — You're a Man of Honour every Inch of you.

Spend. No Compliments, dear Captain. So your Servant. [Exit *Spendthrift*.

Captain Solus.

Come! this may be ſomething in my Way, if I play my Cards well.

AIR VIII.

Capt. *When his Brain's on the Rack,*
Then his Purſe I'll attack,
No Man ſure can think me to blame;
Is it not ſo with all?
Each one to his Call,
The Stateſmen all touch without Shame.
An Eſtate to a Fool
Makes him all the World's Tool,
Good Nature's abus'd by each Man;
Since that's here the Caſe,
Pray where's the Diſgrace,
To ſtrike at a Share if I can?

SCENE V.

Enter Mr. *Lookout*.

Capt. O Mr. *Lookout!* I was juſt going to your Office.

Mr. *Look.* What Services have you to command, Captain?

Capt. Why, you are to know, I am Privy Counſellor to a young Gentleman who is in Diſtreſs, and I ſhall make it worth your while to aſſiſt me.

Mr. *Look.* Sir, You know, you may at all times command your humble Servant. — But what is the Affair?

Capt. Why, Sir, there is a certain Lady of this Town, that the young Squire has kept for ſome time; and the other Night ſhe had a mind to change Hands, and make a Country Dance of it, and is gone off with Money and Goods to ſome Value.

Mr. *Look.* Pray, Sir, do I know her? What may be the Name ſhe goes by?

Capt. Sir, ſhe goes by the Name of Mrs. *Betty Feelmore.*

Mr. *Lookout.* Pray, was not ſhe intimate with Mrs. *Frisk* and Mrs. *Stroaker?*

Capt. The ſame, Sir.

Mr. *Look.* Why then the Affair is done. — I was laſt Night, at Mrs. *Frisk*'s Lodgings, when ſhe came in; — And I don't doubt but I can get my Information there, where ſhe is to be found.

Capt. At Mrs. *Frisk*'s Lodgings, ſaid you'

Look. Yes, Sir.

Capt. You're pretty intimate there I think. Pray have you any Acquaintance with Mrs. *Stroaker?*

Look. What! ſhe that was kept by the famous *Zenodocky*, the *Grecian* Merchant!

Capt. Ay, that's the Girl I mean.

Look. Know her! Why ſhe lodges with my Friend *Frisk.*

Capt. The Devil ſhe does.

Look. Pray why ſo curious, Captain?

Capt. Why, if we manage Things diſcreetly, there may be ſomething gain'd from that Quarter. — But more of that another time.

AIR IX.

Look. *A Town Justice's Clerk,*
Like a Cur that will bark,
Fetches out his Comrades together,
Then leaves 'em to squabble,
Surrounded with Rabble,
And fears no Approaches of Danger.
Bring me but the Money,
Your Warrant is ready,
Then do what you please with your Pris'ner;
I shall be satisfied;
You will be Gratified.
Capt. *Let's have it, and do not then loiter.*

Sir, to let you see that I am a Man of Honour, There — There's something for the present to Encourage you.

[*Takes Money out of his Purse, and gives him.*

Look. Why then, Captain, you shall find me diligent. — But pray, — is the Squire rich?

Capt. Rich! — Faith, I don't know how he is at present; but he had seven thousand Pounds a Year.

Look. Seven thousand a Year! — Doe's he play?

Capt. No, I can't say he does.

Look. Why then, how is it possible he can run out?

Capt. Whores and Hangers-on has plum'd him a little. — Why Sir, there's his Levee is worth any Man's while to see — There's, Imprimis, Doctor *Look-a-skew*, a *Welch* Parson, that can't read *English.* — He has the Care of his Soul. — Then there is Mother *Clarkwell*, the good Woman, — she has the Care of his Body. Signior *Violino primo* — an *Italian* Fidler — he has the Care of his Senses, and Monsieur *Tenez Vous droit*, a *French* Dancing Master, —— he is to set him upon his Haunches, and to learn him to make his *Exit* in a graceful Manner.

Lookout.

Look. Very good! and how long may he have been in Possession of this Estate?

Capt. Let me see. ——— Why, Sir, he and his Steward have had it between 'em two Years; and upon a Pinch, when-ever the 'Squire is out of Cash, (the honest Man having a great regard for his Master) will lend him a Brace of Thousands of his own Money, at five *per Cent.* only, paying one *per Cent.* Brokerage for the procuring of it.

Look. Is that customary, Captain?

Capt. Customary! — Ay, with Numbers that I could name. —— Why, half your fine Gentlemen in *England* are short-sighted, and obliged to make use of a Glass to see their most intimate Acquaintance. ——— Then how is it possible they should ever be able to look into Accounts? ——— And who so proper to assist them with Cash, as those who have their Estates in their Hands?

Look. Really, Captain, this is new to me. ——— I could not have thought there had been so much Stupidity in this Age.

Capt. Why, is it not necessary it should be so? — Why, Estates would remain in Families from Generation to Generation were it otherwise. —— And then what would become of us that have none?

Look. That's true.

Capt. Sir, were Men to look to their Fortunes, and have an Eye upon their Families, in short, there would be no living. —— No Female of better Race would fall to our Shares: No first Fruits we then could ever expect. —— Really 'twould be a melancholy thing to think on it.

AIR X. To the Tune of the Jovial Beggars.

Capt. *But since it was decreed*
That we should be Help-mates,

And

And make all Fools to bleed,
And purge well their Estates;
Then let's glean 'em all from the high to the low,
For a gleaning we must go.
Look. *To Riches ev'ry one,*
We know was ne'er design'd,
But Money's the Loadstone,
That does attract Mankind,
And ne'er fails with 'em all, with both high and low;
'Tis their Passe-par-tout *we know.*
Capt. *Its Power is so great,*
That Men their Reason lose,
In Council ends Debate,
'Twill Church and State amuse;
For they are Gleaners all in their turns we know.
Capt. } Look. } *Then a Gleaning let us go.*

Look. Well, Captain, give me your Hand; for you're a Man of Sense, and judge Things right.—— I'll make it my Business to find out this Girl, and inform you of my Success.

Capt. Sir, lose no Time about it.——I'll to the 'Squire.——So your Servant. [*Exeunt.*

SCENE VI.

Changes to an Inn, and discovers Mrs. Haverly, *with five Country Girls, sitting round a Table; Bottles and Glasses.*

Mrs. *Haverly.* Come, Children, take another Glass of Sack; 'twill chear your Hearts after your Journey.

[*Fills out Wine, they all drink.*

So.—Now, my Girls, be frank. I am a Stranger to you all, but must tell ye, I have made the Fortune of some hundred Ladies in my Time, and came here

here purely out of Charity, (which I think the Duty of every good Christian) to assist, and to prevent your falling into bad Hands.——Therefore be free, and tell me what you propose to do.

[*Jenny Ogle gets up.*

Jen. Ogle. Madam, forsooth, Beggars mayn't be Chusers, as they say in our Country.—— But I shou'd be glad of a Chambermaid's Place, and you'd be so kind to help a Body. [*Sits down again.*

Mrs. *Hav.* What's your Name, Child?

Jen. Ogle. Jane Ogle, and please you.

Mrs. *Hav. Jenny Ogle.* — Look'ee, Child! — Service is no Inheritance, and if you'll follow my Advice, I'll take you all into such Business as will be profitable and pleasing. — You shall go home with me.— You shall live as I do, 'till such Time I can better provide for you.——— If you don't like your Entertainment, 'tis but going to Service afterwards.—— What say you?

Jen. Ogle. Forsooth, I can only speak for myself and *Mary Licklips*; for we have been Fellow-Servants together in the Country. —— And I believe she'll not scruple to go any where wi' me.

Mary Licklips. No, marry won't I.—— The Gentlewoman is very kind, I think; and I should count the other Lasses great Fools, an they refuse.

AIR XI. Ye Nymphs and Sylvan Groves.

Mary Lick. *In Mornings bleak and grey,*
By Dawning of the Day,
In Winds cold and raw,
In Frost and in Snow,
My Flocks they ne'er went astray;
But now I will try
Town Lasses t'out-vie,

And

And Preferment strive t'attain.
I'll not lose Time,
Whilst in my Prime;
But hence decline
To guard my Kine,
And think of nothing but Gain.

Har. Shuf. Why, as to my Peart, I'd go with a' my Heart; —— but *Sukey Slattern* has got a Promise to be a House-Mead to a Justice of the Peace; and her Friends wrote into the Country for her to come up to Town; and if I would come up with her, as being her Coosin, they would help me too.

Suk. Slat. Yes, forsooth, what *Harriette Shuffle* says is very true, and I am to have six Pounds a-Year.

Mrs. *Hav.* Six Pounds a Year to be a Slave!—— Why, if you go with me, you shall live better than the Wife of that Justice of the Peace, and get more Money in Presents, whilst under my Roof in one Day, than your Year's Wages will amount to. —— What say you to that?

Suk. Slat. Be Lady then I'll go with you, and Coosin will go too.

Har. Shuf. Nay, I'ze ne'er part for zure.

Diana Step. Then since my Fellow-Travellers are all determin'd, I shall put myself under your Direction, Madam.

Mary Licklips. Why then we are all agreed.

Mrs. *Hav.* That's well said. —— Come, take another Glass, and let's be merry.

[*Fills out Wine.*

AIR XII. Recruiting Officer.

Mrs. *Hav.* *Then ne'er refuse a good Offer,*
But look upon motherly Advice,
'Tis only Fools that will faulter,
Where Pleasure gets Money by Choice.

Since

Since Love is a Duty we owe,
And a Debt we with Pleasure can pay,
A Woman herself does not know
Who lets slip such a happy Essay.

Mary Licklips. Why, this is a merry Gentlewoman.—— Who wou'd have thought we shou'd ever have met with such good Fortune, *Jenny?*

Jenny Ogle. Not I truly.——Madam forsooth, and you please, my Service to you. [*Drinks.*

Mrs. *Haw.* Thank you, my Child.—— And now, my Girls, if you are for moving, I'll pay at the Bar, and attend you.

Omnes. We'll wait upon you, Madam.

AIR XIII. When my Love the other Day.

Farewell to my Kindred all,
Here's my Fortune, stand, or fall:
To my Churn and wooden Bowl,
I bid adieu, with all my Soul.
Now for Pleasure,
Woman's Treasure,
To my Senses yet unknown;
The Rose is nothing till 'tis blown.

[Exeunt.

SCENE VII.

Enter Sir Thomas Pairnails, *and Squire* Spendthrift.

Sir *Thomas.* Look ye, Sir, if you follow this Course of Life much longer, your Purse will be as empty as your Head; and all that you are to expect from me, is the Expence of your Transportation.— I'll pay that to get rid of you.—— What with Fidlers and Pipers, Dancing Masters and Whores, his

Levee has been as much crowded as a Prime Minister's. [*Aside.*

Spend. Sir, as you are my Relation, I am obliged to suffer your Correction; but were it otherwise, I wou'd not take that Speech from any Person living.

Sir *Thomas.* Od's bud! a pleasant Fellow, that has run out his Estate before he came to it, and, like all other fine Gentlemen, above Advice.

AIR IV. May Fair.

Sir Tho. *The Youths of this Age all alike are grown,*
And envy the greatest Rakes o'the Town.
To be a smart Fellow is now the Taste;
No Booby so great as he that's Chaste.
Borrow, Trick, Cheat, and Spend,
That's the Fashion they recommend.

Observe me, Sir, I was once as young as your self, but the Age I liv'd in was not so corrupt; or if it were, I had more Virtue, and cou'd withstand those Temptations which you daily fall into, and pride yourself in 'em, as Qualifications to make a Great Man.

Spend. Sir, what Indiscretions I have been guilty of, are no more than what all the World has done before me.

Sir *Thomas.* How, Sirrah! What! give me the Lie to my Face? — Out of my Sight, or I'll — Od! I could find in my Heart to lay my Cane over you.

Spend. Excuse me, Sir, I say what the indiscreet Part of the World have been guilty of before me.

Sir *Thomas.* Oh!———'Tis well you explain your self; and pray, Sir, if you please, no longer follow the Example of that indiscreet Part, but learn from the Sobriety and Chastity of an Uncle how to behave your self for the future, or you shall have Reason to repent it. [*Exit* Sir *Thomas.*

Spend. There goes my old Uncle, that for Women and Wine, with all the Appurtenances thereunto belonging,

longing, has been, in his Time, as keen as the best of us all;——but now, like all other old Fellows, exclaims at the Vice for want of the Power.

AIR XV.

Spend. *How easy 'tis to give Advice,*
When we've past a certain Age,
Forgetting what we made our Choice,
We grow of Course mighty Sage.
Since that's the Case, pray where's the Harm,
In loving a Girl or so?
A youthful Wench has such a Charm,
'Tis a Crime to let her go. [Exit.

End of the First Act.

ACT. II.

SCENE I. *Mrs.* Haverly's *House.*

Mrs. *Clarkwell*, Mrs. *Haverly*, and the *Country Girls* at Breakfast.

Mrs. *Haverly*.

LOok'ee, Mrs. *Clarkwell*, I'll have no underhand Dealings. You know the Conditions I took you in upon; therefore you must play above Board with me.

Mrs. *Clarkwell*. Madam, if you come to that, my Character is as fair as your's, I wou'd have you to know, and have always liv'd in as good a Reputation.

Mrs. *Haverly*. I don't Dispute how you have liv'd; but consider the Situation you was in when I took you.——Therefore, to avoid any more Words between us, I tell you plainly, I'll have no whispering.

Jenny Ogle. Madam forsooth, 'twas no harm; the Gentlewoman was only asking me how I lik'd 'Squire *Spendthrift* last Neight.

Mrs. *Haverly*. I was not angry with you, my Dear.——Harke'e, Mrs. *Clarkwell*, [*Aside.*] I have some Reason to believe you sunk upon me last Night, and did not divide the Money equal.

[*The Girls whispering together.*

Mrs.

Mrs. *Clarkwell.* Well then, I protest upon the Word of an honest Woman, that I had no more than twenty Guineas of the Squire, for procuring *Jenny.*— And you know I gave you ten of 'em immediately.

Mrs. *Hav.* Yes, but you know our Articles were two Shillings in the Pound, towards the Sinking-Fund; ——— for our Debts must be paid.

Mrs. *Clarkw.* To be sure, Madam.

Mrs. *Hav.* Well! but for the future, don't make such bad Bargains, for 'twas too little.——— Why, I could have had twice as much from an old Alderman of the City, and the Girl wou'd not have been the worse for the 'Squire afterwards.

[*Knocking at the Door.*

Mrs. *Clarkw.* Hark!

Mrs. *Hav.* 'Tis Sir *Francis*, I suppose.

Enter *Betty Drosslepate.*

B. Drossle. Here's Mr. *Xenodochy* desires to speak with you, Madam.

Mrs. *Hav.* Shew him into the Parlour.———

[*Exit the Maid.*

Miss *Ogle*, do you get your self dress'd, Child;— 'tis a Gentleman that is come to wait upon you.— Mrs. *Clarkwell*, do you go up Stairs with the rest of the Ladies.

Mrs. *Clarkw.* Yes, Madam.

Har. Shuf. I don't know why we are not to see the Gentleman, as well as *Jenny Ogle.*

[Exeunt *all but Mrs.* Haverly.

Mrs. *Hav.* Let me see! a new House that has had a Tenant is generally reckon'd the better for it, and my Friend the Merchant is able to pay a good Price.

AIR

AIR XVI. Butter'd Pease.

Mrs. Hav. *Sure Love can ne'er be bought too dear,*
By the impotent and old;
You must allow that Point is clear,
We adore but for their Gold.
Therefore, my Friend, you must come down,
With the Tribute that's our due,
Your sixty odd, it is well known,
Pay for what they cannot do.

SCENE II.

Enter Mr. *Xenodochy*, and Mrs. *Haverly*. They meet each other.

Mrs. *Hav*. Your Servant, sweet Sir.

Mr. *Xeno*. Dear Mrs. *Haverly*, your Servant.——Well! I hear you have laid a good Foundation for a flourishing Trade.

Mrs. *Hav*. Alack, Sir, these hard Times we must do as well as we can. ——— I do assure you, Sir, upon Honour, that upon an Avarage of last Year's Account, I did not get the Profit of Almond Powder for the Ladies Hands.

Mr. *Xeno*. Why, that was a bad Year with you then.

Mrs. *Hav*. O! very dead, Sir, ——— no Trade at all.

Mr. *Xeno*. Well! but now to Business.———I am imform'd you have fresh Country Goods come in;—if you can recommend an honest, innocent, sober Girl,———I'll take her to my self.

Mrs. *Hav*. Pray, Sir, where had you your Information?

Mr. *Xeno*. Why, to be plain with you, I promised *Betty* a Present, if she wou'd let me know; for I am am determined to run no more Hazards. And this Morning ſhe ſent me Word you had five Country Girls arrived.

Mrs. *Hav.* Sir, ſhe's an impudent Huſſey for her Pains, to impoſe upon a Gentleman of your Faſhion. —I have but one I proteſt, and I am to have a hundred Guineas for her from my Lord *Teazeall.* — But then ſhe's ſuch a one! O Sir! was you to ſee her Eyes,—Complexion,—Turn of the Face,—her Shape, ——her Make! in ſhort, ſhe's the compleateſt Girl I ever ſaw.

Mr. *Xeno.* But cou'd not you let me ſee this Beauty?

Mrs. *Hav.* No Sir.—— You know, was it your own Caſe, you wou'd not think it honourable.—— Then ſhe has ſuch a Look, that wou'd pierce you.— And ſo much Innocence and Good Nature.—Indeed, to ſay Truth, I never ſaw her Fellow.

AIR XVII. As *Jocky* and *Jenny.*

Mrs. Hav. *No Nymph of the Plain with her Charms can compare,*
Her Eyes are like Stars, that enlighten the Air;
Her Lips are like Rubies, her Breath is ſo ſweet,
No Balm goes beyond it, her Teeeh are ſo neat,
Her Shape it is neither too long, nor too ſhort,
She moves with ſuch Graces, you can ſee no Fault;
Her Skin's free from Freckles, her Hair 'tis dark-brown,
She'll appear like a Goddeſs, the Envy o'th Town.

Mr. *Xeno.* But Mrs. *Haverly,* ——ah! ——pray let me prevail upon you to ſee her.—— You know, I have not been the worſt of Cuſtomers

Mrs. *Hav.* Why Sir, I would do any Thing to oblige you, but I dare not venture it.

Mr. *Xeno.* But why, Mrs. *Haverly.*

Mrs. *Hav.* I'll tell you, I was once young myſelf;—and I judge of the World from what I have, and

and wou'd have done myſelf.——And had it been my Fortune to have had the Charms this dear innocent Creature has,—— I am ſure Mr. *Xenodochy*'s Generoſity, Addreſs, and Perſon, to be ſure, wou'd have been too much for me to have withſtood.

Mr. *Xeno.* O! dear Mrs. *Haverly*, you are a very well-bred Woman: But let me entreat you to give me a Sight of this Girl.

Mrs. *Hav.* Well Sir, if you'll promiſe to be contented with a Sight only, you ſhall.

Mr. *Xeno.* I give you my Word and Honour, you may command me.

Mrs. *Hav.* Well then,——ſhe's now dreſſing to go to my Lord, and ſhe ſhall come, and make her Obedience to you before ſhe goes.——[*aſide.*] Now for a good Market. ——If you pleaſe to ſit down, Sir, I'll go and inform her of it, leſt ſhe ſhould be ſent for in a Hurry.

Mr. *Xeno.* Pray do, Mrs. *Haverly.*——

[*Exit* Mrs, *Haverly.*

Come, if this Girl anſwers the Character ſhe gives of her, 'twill make me amends for the laſt unruly Jade.

AIR XVIII. To *Hanover* from *Edinbro'.*

Xeno. *Then now's the Time to bilk my Lord,*
And make the Girl my own:
Poſſeſſion's a Title on Record,
As good as any known.
As good, &c.

SCENE III.

Re-enter Mrs. Haverly.

Mrs. *Hav.* O! Sir, 'twas well I went to prevent her going; for there's my Lord's Gentleman has waited

waited with a Coach ever ſince you came to carry her away.

Mr. *Xeno.* But ſhe is not in ſuch a hurry, 'tis to be hop'd.

Mrs. *Hav.* Sir, ſhe was juſt ſtepping into it:—— But here ſhe comes.

SCENE IV.

Enter *Jenny Ogle.*

Mr. Xenodochy *goes and ſalutes her.*

Mr. *Xeno.* [*aſide*] Sweet Soul! what Bloom of Youth and Innocency does ſhe appear with.—— Mrs. *Haverly*, ———'tis to you I muſt make my Application, being a Stranger to the Lady.—— You have known me long, and therefore the moſt proper to recommend me to ſo deſerving a Perſon.

Mrs. *Hav.* [*aſide*] It works purely. ———But Sir; a Word with you, if you pleaſe. [*aſide*] Remember the Conditions.

Mr. *Xeno.* That's true.—[*Aſide.*] But what if I give you the ſame my Lord offer'd, will not that anſwer your Purpoſe as well?

Mrs. *Hav.* Not at all, Sir.———Conſider my Reputation and Honour lies at Stake. ——— Look'ee, Sir, as you have been my Friend and Cuſtomer, I'll give you the Preference.—Advance fifty more, and I'll come upon Oath to my Lord, that ſhe has run away from me.——And I'm ſure ſhe's worth your Money.—What's a hundred and fifty Pounds to you? —— Why, have you not your Penny-worth for your Penny?—I own to you the Diamond's rough and unpoliſh'd:—But ſtill it has its intrinſick Value, and when it comes to be ſet, you'll be a Judge of its Luſtre.

AIR XIX. Dame of Honour.

Mrs. *Hav.* *When you meet a Jewel that's good,*
'Twill always bear a great Price,
Like your Lands that are well manur'd,
Brings the Money in a Trice.
Then why should you thus make Delay?
Her Days are precious like mine;
Since Love is so apt to decay,
My Girl shall not lose her Time.

—Miss *Ogle.*—If you'll retire to your Apartment, I'll be with you in two Minutes.

[Mr. Xenodochy *offers to go up to* Jenny Ogle.

—Sir, I must beg you'll behave your self like a Man of Honour, and keep your Word with me.

Mr. *Xeno.* I think I have, Mrs. *Haverly.* — But give me leave to speak to the Lady.

[*Mrs.* Haverly *whispers Mr.* Xenodochy.

Jenny Ogle. [*Aside.*] I know not what to make of this.——— I was dress'd to see the Gentleman, and now he's not to speak to me.——— Not that I have any great Loss marry, for he has e'en a fowl Look with him.— I think I could never like him.

AIR XX. What Woman cou'd do.

Jenny Ogle. *Young Lasses, whenever to Love you're inclin'd,*
Make choice of your Man.
When the Object you like, your Desire's confin'd
Alone to your Man.
There's something so charming in youthful Toying,
The Bliss is Extatic, and never cloying,
When perfectly pleased with your Man,
Forbear if you can.

II.

II.

But when to a Man that is ugly and old,
A Girl's to be ty'd,
There's nothing can never tempt her but his Gold:
That's all of his Side.
Then why shou'd you chide for a Slip that she makes;
Consider the Task a poor Girl undertakes,
To love or to like such a Man,
'Tis not to be done.

[*Mrs.* Haverly *go's up to* Jenny Ogle, *and whispers.*

Mrs. *Hav.* You heard what I said to you, Miss.

Jenny Ogle. Yes Madam, I shall be sure to observe your Directions. [*Exit* Jenny Ogle.

Mrs. *Hav.* Well Sir, what say you?——You know I wou'd serve you, if 'twas in my Power; and I think I have made a very generous Offer.

Mr. *Xeno.* A generous Offer!———Why, a hundred and fifty Pounds would make some Men sell their King and Country.———'Tis too much, too much indeed. —— Besides, you ought to make an Abatement for the last Termagant.—After I had equipp'd her out in Cloaths and the Devil and all of Trinkets, she must keep Company with Lords, and upon that commenced a Woman of Quality, took her Title from the first Nobleman that tipp'd her the Favour, grew common in a Month, run away with my strong Box in six Weeks, and I have never heard of her from that Day to this.

Mrs. *Hav.* Why she was innocent when she left me, and I have heard by-the-by that it was entirely owing to your self.

Mr. *Xeno.* As how, pray?

Mrs. *Hav.* Why, Sir, to be plain with you, (asking your Pardon) I was inform'd you obliged her to change her Religion, and take up your's.— And take my Word for it. Sir, whenever a Lady changes her Religion, she loses her Morals.—Why, I'll tell you,

 Sir:

Sir: — There was a certain *Romish* Prieſt was us'd to come and drink a Diſh of Tea now and then with my Ladies, and as ſure as you are there, his Arguments were ſo ſtrong, that had I not forbidden him my Houſe, I ſhould have had my whole Family Prieſt-ridden. They began to have ſuch Notions! — O Lud, Sir! — Let me adviſe you never to pretend to alter a Woman's way of Thinking; — for when it comes to that, they don't think at all. — And that was the Caſe with Mrs. *Frisk*.

AIR XXI. The Spring's a coming.

Mrs. Hav. *If Girls give you Pleaſure,*
You find without Meaſure,
They then will contribute and add to Love's Treaſure;
But if they're neglected,
Or by you ſuſpected
To want either Judgment, Affection or Wit;
'Tis a Point they can't bear
As will plainly appear,
From the high to the low they'll all domineer.
You muſt not direct 'em,
They'll tell you it hurts 'em,
Wiſe Men to the Sex will at all Times ſubmit.

Mr. *Xeno.* Why truly, Mrs. *Haverly*, I was a little to blame; but ſhall learn better for the future. —— But now to the Point. — I muſt have this Girl.

Mrs. *Hav.* Well Sir, I will not diſoblige you; give me a hundred, and pay for her Rigging, and I'll ſtretch my Conſcience, and make her your's.

Mr. *Xeno.* Any thing in Reaſon, Mrs. *Haverly*. — But what may be the Demand of this laſt Article?

Mrs. *Hav.* Sir, here's the Bill.

[*Mrs.* Haverly *delivers a Paper to Mr.* Xenodochy, *and Mr.* Xenodochy *reads.*]

Xeno.

Mr. *Xeno.* What the Devil! —— for two Shifts, at twelve Shillings an Ell, — four Pounds. —— ha! ——For trimming of them, ten Pounds, —— mighty well! ——For a Suit of fine lac'd Night Cloaths, twenty Pounds. ——Modeſt enough! ——For a plain Luſtring Gown, ſeven Pounds. —— Very humble that! ——For a Pair of pink-colour'd Silk Stockings with Silver Clocks, ſix Pounds, ſix Shillings. —— That's neceſſary! ——For a Pair of Silver wrought Garters, one Pound. ——For a Pair of Shoes, five Pounds. — The Sum total, fifty three Pound ſix Shillings. —— A very decent Bill truly! Only fifty-three Pounds ſix Shillings for the Lady's Undreſs.

Mrs. *Hav.* Why, Sir, I never let my Ladies diſgrace any Gentlemen.

Mr. *Xeno.* But pray, Madam, give me Leave to ask you one Queſtion. —— My Lord, I think, was to give an hundred. ——— Was this Expence to be thrown in, Mrs. *Haverly?*

Mrs. *Hav.* Alack-a-Day! No, Sir. — This Bill was to be carried in afterwards.———Pleaſe to conſider that, Sir; and then you'll be a Judge of my friendly Diſpoſition to ſerve you. ——— You know, I offer'd her at an hundred and fifty. ——— And there, you ſee, I ſhould have been three Pounds ſix Shillings out of Pocket. ——— But I love to make Things clear to a Gentleman.

Mr. *Xeno.* Well! I find my Inclinations are bent upon the Girl; therefore I'll give you a hundred and fifty.

Mrs. *Hav.* Well, Sir, I don't love to diſoblige a Cuſtomer.——— She is yours; and I'll go put a Stop to her Viſit to my Lord, and diſmiſs his Servant.—— Come this is a good Nick to be made upon a profeſs'd Gameſter. [*Aſide.*] [*Exit Mrs.* Haverly.

Mr. *Xeno.* So —— Now ſhe's mine ——. Ha, ha, ha! I can't forbear laughing to think how my Lord is bit.

bit.——Methinks I cou'd wish to be present when he receives the Message.

AIR XXII. To the *French* Tune *Mirliton.*

Mr. *Xeno.* *My Lord, you are but a bad Schemer,*
To be absent at this Time,
The present Man will always win her,
Let him but produce his Coin.
That gains a Mirliton,
Mirliton, Mirlitain,
Commands a Mirliton, ton, ton, &c.

Few Girls were ever tempted alone
With Honour or with Beauty,
Give Gold enough, and it will attone
To make it then their Duty.
To sell a Mirliton,
Mirliton, Mirlitain,
To sell a Mirliton, ton, ton, &c.

And now for my Girl.

[*Exit Mr.* Xenodochy.

SCENE V.

Enter Sir Francis Firebriecks, *and Mrs.* Haverly.

Mrs. *Hav.* Ah! Sir *Francis,*——you see what Power you have over our Sex. ——Well! to be sure there are four of as pretty fashion'd Girls, as any Man would wish to be acquainted with.

Sir *Fran.* Well!——but have you talk'd to them upon the Affair.

Mrs. *Hav.* O, yes, Sir.——I've set your Honour's Character out in such a Light, that they are quite charm'd with their Preferment.

Sir

Sir *Franc.* But you did not ſay I would give each of 'em ten Pounds a-Year; but that they were to have it by Turns.——You underſtand me, Mrs. *Haverly.*

Mrs. *Hav.* O! very well, Sir.—But I think ten Pounds a Year a ſmall Matter for Girls that will have little or no Perquiſites.——Come, be rul'd, and take my Advice.——Sir *Francis,* you know by woful Experience, when the Ladies are pinch'd, it puts 'em upon mean Things; and 'tis ſo with all Mankind.

AIR XXIII. Joan's Placket.

Mrs. Hav. *A* Lawyer *his Fee but abate,*
Neglect but a Parſon *his Tithe,*
Or a Bribe miſplac'd by the State,
See, who will not take up the Scythe.

The Graſs they'll cut beneath your Feet,
And think 'tis their Part ſo to play;
Make their Court to the next they meet,
And tell you each Dog has his Day.

Then don't look upon Trifles.—Why, every Body muſt live.—I am not like a great many of my Profeſſion that are willing to get rid of their Ladies any how; but my Care is how to provide for them to their own Satisfaction, and to make it agreeable to myſelf.

Sir *Franc.* I believe ſo, indeed, Mrs. *Haverly.*

Mrs. *Hav.* Alack, Sir,—There's no Body knows the hard Task it is to have ſuch a Charge, but thoſe that feel the Weight of it.

AIR

AIR XXIV.

Mrs. *Hav.* *Pray how oft have I griev'd to see*
My Children bad Courses take?
You know what a Pain 'tis to me,
When good Council they forsake.

But Reproaches are all in vain,
Nature will have its Career;
So must suffer and not complain,
But in Advice persevere.

Sir *Franc.* 'Tis very true, and I know no one more capable of giving better Instructions than yourself. ——— But now inform me.——What's your Demand?

Mrs. *Hav.* O a small Matter will content me for the present, and you'll make it up to me another Time.

Sir *Franc.* Well, what is it?

Mrs. *Hav.* Why your Honour knows 'tis hard Times, and I think two hundred for the four Ladies is very moderate.

Sir *Franc.* Two hundred Pounds moderate!

Mrs. *Hav.* Was you to know all, you'd think so. [*Aside*]—Moderate—Yes, Sir, very moderate.

Sir *Franc.* Why, Madam, do you know what two hundred Pounds will do?

Mrs. *Hav.* Sir, I find you are not dispos'd to entertain my Ladies.—So, Sir, your Servant.

Sir *Franc.* Nay, hold!—don't be so pettish, Mrs. *Haverly.*——Why in such a Hurry?

Mrs. *Hav.* Sir, I have disobliged so many Noblemen and Gentlemen upon your Account, that I think 'tis Time to retrieve my Character with them, and trust to their Honour as I have done to your Word.

Sir *Franc.* Why, have I not always paid you well?

Mrs. *Hav.* Yes, as you have done your Ladies, with Statesmens Promises.——But for the future—

I am

I am not to be deceiv'd. You must come down with the Ready, or expect no Dealings with me.

Sir *Franc.* The Devil's in the Woman, and I thought myself a Match for her too.

AIR XXV.

Sir *Franc.* *In thy Youthful Days,* O Frank,
When Money was hard to get,
What Tricks hast thou play'd,
And never wast dismay'd?
Envy'd so much by the Great,
What Girls did I bilk?
From Stuff Gowns to Silk,
As the World can plainly prove;
But now Time's no more,
I must pay my Store,
And part with Siller *for Love.*

Well, come along, Mrs. *Haverly.*——I see you will get the better of me.

Mrs. *Hav.* Yes, Sir. — But I must have it in Hand, for too much Faith has been the Ruin of me.

Sir *Franc.* Well, well, you shall. [*Exeunt.*

SCENE VI. A Hall.

Table and Chairs, Pen, Ink, and Paper.

Enter Justice Touchmore, *Justice* Hamper, *and Justice* Bridleman.

J. Touch. Why, you have had a good Evening's Work, Brother *Bridleman.*

J. Bridle. Pretty well, Brother *Touchmore.*——But who expected to see you to Night?

J. Touch. Why, I was inform'd no Body was at the Office but Brother *Hamper*; and *Lookout* gave me to

 under-

understand there wou'd be Business: —— And you know how 'tis, Brother.

J. Bridle. Ay: ay, — ha! — Who comes here? [*Enter* Lookout.]

So, what's the Matter, *Lookout?*

Mr. *Look.* Nay, no great Matter. —— Only a Leash of fine Birds that want pluming, that's all.

J. Hamp. Where are they?

Mr. *Look.* Here comes one of them.

SCENE VII.

Enter Mrs. Feelmore, *Constables, Mob,* &c. *the Justices get seated.*

J. Bridle. Well, good Woman, what is this Affair?

Mrs. *Feel.* And please your Worships, nothing but Malice, — and to get Money from me.

Om. Just. How!

Look. Sir, if your Worships please to hear what is laid to her Charge, here comes two Gentlemen that will answer for what has been done.

SCENE VIII.

Enter Squire Spendthrift, *and Capt.* Wou'dbe.

J. Bridle. Pray, Sir, give me Leave to ask you one Question. Here's a Warrant granted by Justice *Touchmore* to take up this Woman upon your Account: — What is it that you lay to her Charge?

Spend. Sir, I suspect she has robb'd me. Therefore beg she may be confin'd till I can make some proper Discoveries.

J. Hamp. Why, the Woman looks like an arrant Jade. ——— Ay, ay, dispatch her.

Mrs. *Feel.* Dear Sir, be not so cruel, but save a wretched Creature. [*Kneeling to the Squire.*

AIR

AIR XXVI. T'amo tanto.

Mrs. *Feel. Oh! turn not from me,*
But shew your Mercy
To the Wretch that does your Pardon crave.
Hear me, Oh! hear me,
Thou dearest to me;
'Tis thy Betsey, *once thy faithful Slave.*
Oh! turn not from me,
But shew your Mercy
To the Wretch that does your Pardon crave.

[*The Squire in a melancholy Posture.*]

SCENE IX.

Enter Sir Thomas Pairnails, *and stands at the Back of the Squire.*

Sir *Tho.* Mighty fine, truly! —— But I must break the Neck of this, for the Boy melts already. [*Aside.*
[*Slaps him on the Back.*]
——Why, how now! what art struck dumb at the Caterwauling of a Syren? ——— ha!—you graceless Rogue, had your poor Father been alive, (as indulgent as he was to the Ladies) he would have play'd the Devil with you both. —— Come, Sir, I must trust you no longer. March, March.
[Sir *Thomas shoves him off.*]
——— So, now Gentlemen, you may take the Lady to her Country Seat.

AIR XXVII. There was a pretty Girl.

Sir Tho. *You there may learn a Trade, which will add your own,*
With a fal, lal, &c.

 Quit

Quite necessary for such Ladies of the Town,
With a fal, lal, *&c.*
The Work you'll there compleat, great Men will not refuse,
Let 'em have Preferment, 'tis what they all do chuse.
With a fal, lal, *&c.*

Mrs. *Feel.* Sir, have you no Bowels of Compassion?

Sir *Thomas.* No, Madam; no more than a piqu'd Minister of State, who no sooner gets in Power, but takes more Pride in Revenge, than a Priest in Charity. —Away with her, Gentlemen.

[Exit Mrs. *Feelmore, Constables,* &c.—*and Sir* Thomas *following.*

J. Hamp. Mr. *Lookout,* do you see the Constables do their Duty.———Harke'e.

[*Whispers* Lookout.

Mr. *Look.* Sir, I shall observe.

[Exit *Mr.* Lookout.

J. Bridle. Well, Brother *Touchmore,* what think you of that Girl?

J. Touch. Think!—— Why, I think she deserves to be punished. ——But how stands the Cole with her?

J. Bridle. I don't know.——But, to be sure, very strong; for you hear she has fleec'd the Squire.—— But come, Gentlemen, we are like to have more Business, therefore let's have some Wine.

J. Touch. } Ay, by all Means.—Here.—
J. Hamp. }

Enter a Servant.

Bring some red Port.

Servant. Yes, Sir. [Exit *the Servant.*

J. Touch.

J. Touch. Pray, Brother *Bridleman*, did you not obſerve Brother *Hamper*'s Eyes, how they were fix'd upon the Girl, when ſhe was upon her Knees?

J. Bridle. Hamper's a Wag Brother.

Enter a Servant with Wine.

J. Hamp. Come, come, Gentlemen, there's ne'er a one of you all that wou'd refuſe to releaſe ſuch a Girl as that for a Favour from her, if ye can find her again the next Day.

[*They ſit down.*

J. Touch. Why, that's true.

[*They fill out Wine.*

AIR XXVIII. In *Perſeus* and *Andromeda.*

J. Touch. *Come, fill, fill away,*
Trade to us all.
'Tis the Health of the Day,
That makes our Hearts gay,
Love pays for all.

Here's honeſt Drury,
Our chief Support,
All ſcorn Penury,
That there reſort.

SCENE X.

Re-enter Mr. *Lookout.*

J. Hamp. So, what's to be done next, *Lookout?*

Mr. *Look.* Sir, there are Conſtables with two more Ladies in Cuſtody.——Here they come.

SCENE

SCENE XI.

Enter Mrs. *Stroaker*, Mrs. *Frisk*, Constables, Mob, &c.

J. Touch. [*Aside.*] Business seems to encrease.—— Well, Friends! what have you to say?

1st Constable. An't please your Worships Right Honourable, the noble Captain *Wou'dbe* charg'd me with this Woman, upon Suspicion of Injuries done to the worthy Mr. *Xenodochy*.

2d Constable. And I, an't please your noble Majesties, am charg'd with this Woman for selling her self a Skreen to the other, I think the Captain says;— but here he comes, and can better inform your Honours.

SCENE XII.

Enter Captain *Woud'be*.

J. Hemp. Captain, your Servant.—Well, explain this Matter, and let us learn what these Women have been guilty of.

Capt. May it please your Worships, that Lady was entertained by Mr. *Xenodochy* for some Time, who will make Affidavit of her running away with his strong Box;——— and the other received a Silver-gilt Broadpiece to secrete her in her House.

Mrs. *Sroaker.* } But we'll come upon Oath there
Mrs. *Frisk.* } was nothing in the Box.

Omnes Justices. A plain Conviction.

J. Hamp. Where is Mr. *Xenodochy*?

Capt. Sir, the Gentleman is a very considerable Trader, and Ships coming in, oblig'd him to attend the Entry of his Goods, and therefore left the Affair to me,——so must beg you'll be pleas'd to send 'em

to

to the Houſe of Correction, 'till ſuch Time he appears againſt 'em.

Omnes Juſtices. It ſhall be done.

[*The Girls, in Confuſion, whiſper together.*

Mrs. *Stroaker.* Now I'm undone indeed.——Oh! *Friſk.*

Mrs. *Friſk.* Oh! *Stroaker*, who on Earth is there ſo wretched as my ſelf?

Mrs. *Stroaker.* Talk not of Wretchedneſs, but let us curſe our dull Stars, that have thus betray'd us.——Inſtead of a Continuation in the Delights of Love, a Bed of Straw, and our Keeper's Stripes is to be the Portion of our future State.

Mrs. *Friſk.* O wracking Thought!

AIR XXIX. De'el take the Wars.

Mrs. Fri. *Was e'er ſuch Fate as we've had together?*
Firſt to be routed by Sir Ralph;
Mrs. Str. *Had we remain'd ſep'rate from each other,*
We at this Time had been quite ſafe.
Mrs. Fri. *Curſe on ſuch pimping Juſtice,*
Mrs. Str. *That live upon their Practice,*
To perplex poor Women thus for Lucre of Gain.
Mrs. Fri. *To the great* Jove,
Mrs. Str. *The God of Love,*
Mrs. Fri. *Aſſiſt us now*
Mrs. Str. *In this our Vow,*
Mrs. Fri. *Mrs.* Str. } *T' impower us to give them Pain for Pain.*

Look. Ladies, if you'll give me Leave, I'll attend ye to your new Lodgings, that I may be aſſured Care is taken of you; for I always had a great regard for your Sex.

Capt. [*Aſide.*] *Lookout*, deal fair.

Look. [*Aſide.*] Diſtruſt not my Honour, and you ſhall find me a Gentleman.

Capt.

Capt. Pho!

J. Bridle. Mr. *Lookout,*——the Mittimus is made; therefore you may withdraw with the Ladies as soon as you please.

[*The Women put their Handkerchiefs up to their Faces.*

Look. Ladies, give me Leave.

[*Mr.* Lookout *takes one of each Side him, and they make their Exit with the Constables.*

The Justices rise.

Cap. Gentlemen, I've given Orders to Mr. *Lookout* to pay what Fees are due.

Omnes Justices. 'Tis well, Sir.

[Exeunt *the Justices.*

SCENE XIII.

Captain Solus.

Now, for the Soul of me, can I help being uneasy, lest this Dog *Lookout* should hold a Main, and I only stand Box.——Then again, I know he's a Woman's Man, which is the Devil.

AIR XXX. The White Joke.

Capt. *What Fears perplex the Gamester's Heart,*
Who trusts Mankind to play his Part?
Where Women have a powerful Sway,
That Man is ever sure to lose,
Who never can the Sex refuse,
But gives Consent to all they ask,
And tell you 'tis a pleasing Task;
Good Breeding will not say them Nay.

End of the Second Act.

ACT

ACT III.

SCENE I. *Sir* Francis Firebriecks' *House*.

Enter *Harriette Shufflle*, and *Sukey Slattern*.

Harriette Shuffle.

WELL, *Sukey !*——this will never do.— I almost wish my self in the Country again.

Suk. Slat. I can't say so much, but am far from being contented.

Har. Shuf. Where one's Interest is concern'd, there is something to be said for suffering the Caresses of an old Fellow ; —— but that being entirely out of the Question, ——'tis Folly all over.

AIR XXXI. Tweed Side.

Har. Shuf. *Oh ! then let me haste from this Place,*
My Heart is quite sunk in Despair ;
Since Beauty alone is the Case,
Alas ! 'tis well known I've no Share.
Then why should I range the World o'er,
My Fortune e'er strive for to make ?
To my Shepherd Love I'll restore
Nor Shepherd, nor Sheep, e'er forsake.

Suk. Slat. I own, my dear *Harriette*, we have both of us Reason to complain ; but the imaginary Pleasures of a Town Life, has given me an aversion to the Milking-pail.

Har. Shuf. I don't know what extensive Notions you may have of Pleasure; but the Prospect of it seems so wide to me, that I cannot perceive so much as a distant View of any thing that looks like it.

Suk. Slat. No.——Pray what think you of *Jenny Ogle?*——Does not she appear like a Lady?—Has not she a Watch by her Side, and dress'd as fine as a Queen? Oh! *Harriette*, thou know'st nothing of the World.—If one Man does not do, another may.

AIR XXXII. In vain dear *Chloe*.

Suk. Slat. *If so, no Girl should e'er despair,*
Her Shape, or Wit,
Something will hit,
To make her shine with Debonair.
Youth has its Charm,
Whilst kept from Harm,
And ever will excite.
Give one an Air,
Tho' she's not fair,
'Twill please, and give Delight:
'Twill please, and give Delight.

SCENE II.

Enter *Diana Stepwell*, and *Mary Licklips*.

D. Step. Why so melancholy, Ladies?

Suk. Slat. I don't know any one, excepting your self, and *Mary Licklips*, have any Reason to be joyful.

Mary Lick. Why, really was I to meet with no more Satisfaction than the Favours I received from Sir *Francis*, I should be pretty free from Envy.

AIR XXXIII.

How lasting is the Pleasure,
To those of rural Life!

What

What value is the Treasure,
That's free'd from anxious Strife.

Cou'd I once more obtain it,
How happy shou'd I be,
I'd leave the Town and submit,
In every Degree.

But hush, here he comes.

SCENE III.

Enter *Sir Francis.*

Sir *Fran.* So, Girls! —— Well, you must be all very clean and neat; I have Company coming, and I don't know but they may lie here. — If they do, you know your Lessons. — Pleasure is at all Times purchas'd, — and 'tis fitting the Promoter of it, when at any Expence, should be reimburs'd.

AIR XXXIV. To a *French* Tune.

Sir Fran. *You'll find it so with all Mankind,*
If you'll but consider,
T' Interest alone the World is blind,
Churchman and Lawgiver.

They each by turns will have their Share,
Yet preach up Doctrine to beware,
And tell you that their only Care,
Is Honesty for ever.

— *Harriette,* —— I believe I did not inform you how you were to behave. — You know your Wages are very handsome, and you have more Countenance shew'd to you all, than most Servants can boast of. — I expect you'll be well paid for secret Services to

Night: Therefore five *per Cent.* Vails is more than ought to be allow'd; but, however, I'll give you twelve Pence out of every Guinea you earn, towards buying you lac'd Shoes, — for I love to see Girls go neat about the Feet.

Har. Shuf. Was there ever such a Wretch?

AIR XXXV. As Love-sick *Damon.*

Har. Shuf.
How cursed is she,
In ev'ry Degree,
Whose Faith relies on Man!
There's nothing more sure,
Than she must endure
The Fate to be undone.

Suk. Slat. Don't take it to Heart. Consider, *Harriette,* Times may mend. — Hark'ee. [*Whispers.*

Enter a Servant.

Servant. Sir, here's Count *Bubble,* and Squire *Heartfree,* with two more Gentlemen, are come to wait upon your Honour.

Sir *Fran.* Shew 'em into the Parlour, and I'll be with 'em immediately.

[Exit *Servant.*

——— So! here are two of the four, as fine Chubs as ever were taken in a Net; and I believe there's no great Difficulty to guess at the others; — For a Man is generally known by his Company, but I'll to 'em, and *Reconnoitre* a little.

[Exit Sir *Francis.*

Har. Shuf. I own I did not expect we shou'd have met with such Usage.

Mary Lick. Why, 'tis provoking, and if you were all of my mind, you'd resent it.

Suk.

Suk. Slat. Resent it! —— Do you imagine there is one amongst us that wants Spirit? No, no, I hope no one here is of that Spaniel Nature.

Dia. Step. I advise you, Ladies, to be merry and wise, however.

Har. Shuf. Pray, Madam, how long is it since you have learnt so much Wisdom?

Suk. Slat. We all know how long. —— I suppose Mrs. *Diana* looks upon herself to be a Woman of Quality, from the Honours that are conferr'd upon her.

Dia. Step. I think you are all impertinent, and undeserving any Civilities from Sir *Francis*.

Mary Lick. Why, truly, Mrs. *Diana*, ——— I've known Sir *Francis* as well as your self; and for the future, will take Care (as to my own Part) never to rob you of any Civility he is willing to bestow upon you. Ha! ha! he!

Har. Shuf. Nor I, upon my Word, Madam.

Suk. Slat. Your Ladyship has him to your self for me, I assure you.

Omnes. Ha! ha! he!

Dia. Step. Vulgar Creatures! ——— Madam, notwithstanding these Airs, there is not one of you all but wou'd be glad to rival me, if it was in your Power.

Mary Lick. Indeed, and indeed, Mrs. *Diana*, I must beg Leave to tell you 'tis a Mistake; for as to my own Part, I am grown so nice, that nothing that is old or coarse will go down with me. — And I believe I can say as much for the rest of the Ladies.

Mrs. *Dia. Step.* Really, Madam, I can't pretend to answer for the Depravity of your Taste, or that of the other two Ladies; (for give me Leave to call it so, where Interest lies at Stake) I don't tell you, but I despise the Man; ——— but, then I like his Money; and if he is not so generous as he ought to be, a Woman must be contented 'till she can mend her self.

Har.

Har. Shuf. Come, come, this Dispute's ended.— I find Mrs. *Diana* is of our Opinion.

Mrs. *Dia. Step.* Of your Opinion! ——— Yes, Madam, let Fortune throw a young handsome Fellow in my Arms, with half the Views I have had from Sir *Francis*; ——— Then you shou'd see if my Constitution is not as warm as any of yours.

Suk. Slat. Why then, my dear *Diana*, thou art a Girl fit for the World, and to my Taste. ——— We now seem to know one another perfectly well; therefore let us fling off all Clouds of Despair, and make the best of our Market. ——— Come, let us Salute, and be Friends.

[Suk. Slat. *salutes Mrs.* Diana; *they all salute one another.*

Mrs. Diana. I am sure I never bore Ill-will towards any of my Companions.

Suk. Slat. I believe not, indeed, Child.

AIR XXXVI. Come, follow, follow me.

Suk. Slat. *Then Hand in Hand let's join,*
To Fends no more incline;
But let us all agree,
To live in Harmony.
Let Interest be our future Care,
And each, unenvy'd, have her Share.

Chorus. *Let Interest,* &c.

[*A Bell Rings.*

——— So there's the Bell, I suppose there will be Business for us all; therefore, Ladies, Adieu.

Omnes. Adieu. [*Exeunt.*

SCENE

SCENE IV.

Changes to Bridewell, *and discovers several People beating of Hemp; Mrs.* Stroaker, *and Mrs.* Frisk, *beating of Hemp; Mrs.* Feelmore *throws down her Instrument.*

Mrs. *Feel.* Now I am sacrific'd,— sold, — betray'd to Shame, and branded with Infamy. ——— Oh! that I had remain'd in some poor Cottage, free from aspiring Thoughts, I then, perhaps, had learnt to knit and spin.

Enter a Servant with a Letter.

Serv. Madam, is your Name *Feelmore?*

Mrs. *Feel.* Yes.

Serv. Then I have Orders to dischare you, and to deliver you this Letter.

[*Mrs.* Feelmore *takes it, and reads to herself.*

Mrs. *Feel.* Well! thank my Stars, I am once more at Liberty.

[*The other Girls lay down their Instruments.*

AIR XXXVII. Moggy Lauder.

Mrs. Feel. *My Heart with Transport now is full,*
Of Joy beyond Expression;
What Comfort 'twas to find a Cull,
When past Imagination!
In Time of Need,
They're Friends indeed;
No matter for the Reason;
Be't Charity,
Or Gallantry,
It comes in Time and Season.

Pray

Pray call me a Coach to the Door.

[Exit *the Servant.*

——Ladies, I wish you a good Deliverance.

Mrs. *Stroak.* From whence this speedy Change, pray?

Mrs. *Feel.* Ask no Qustions, Child; for I must be gone. —— So, your Servant.

[*Exit Mrs.* Feelmore; *they look after her.*

Mrs. *Frisk.* Well! we came together, and here must stay. —— Methinks the good Fortune of *Betty Feelmore* (as well as I wish her) gives me Pain.

Mrs. *Stroak.* Why, these unexpected Turns are too severe, I own; but 'tis ungenerous to repine at the good Fortune of a Friend, or grudge to others what was never allotted to ourselves.

[*Re-enter the Servant.*]

Ser. Hey Day! Don't you know the Wages of Idleness, Ladies? If you're above Work, you must pay for those that will do your Business for you; Or — come — how strong? [*They give him Money.*

—— This won't do, I must have a Twelver a-piece.

Mrs. *Frisk.* There. —— [*gives more Money.*

——— Sure, what a Brute this Fellow is, to use Women of our Rank, in such a Manner, when his Betters have given us the Preference to Women of the first Quality! [*Aside.*

AIR XXXVIII. O the Broom.

Mrs. Stroak. *Oh! why are we thus to be us'd?*
This Fellow's a Villain in Grain:
No Persons can be more abus'd,
I'th' Fleet by the Wardens again.
Mrs. Frisk. *Plunder is the Word from 'em all,*
Wherever 'tis in their Power:
Like Death, they seize both great and small,
And 'tis practis'd every Hour.

Mrs.

Mrs. *Stroak.* Why, 'tis true; and, till we're acquainted with ſome great Men, who have more Value for the Sex, than Regard to their own Intereſt, we muſt not expect Redreſs.——But come, Child, ſince we have paid our Money to be exempted from this ſort Work, we've no Buſineſs here.——Let's retire into another Room.

Mrs. *Frisk.* Ay, with all my Heart. [*Exeunt.*

SCENE V. Changes to the Street.

Enter Mr. Xenodochy. *To him Mr.* Lookout.

Mr. *Xeno. Lookout*, I am glad to ſee thee.

Look. I thank you, Sir; and, if you'll give me Leave, I can return the Complement, for more Reaſons than one;——for I am in Hopes to ſtrike your Honour for a Piece or two.

Mr. *Xeno.* Why, what's to be done now?

Look. Done! Why, the Birds are in the Cage.——Egad the Captain and I ſtood a dev'liſh Bruſh.——But he being a fighting Man (not that all Military Men are ſo) I put him at the Front of the Battle.

Mr. *Xeno.* And *Stroaker* is taken, you ſay?

Look. Ay, Sir, and her Companion Mrs. *Frisk.*—We ſeiz'd them both.——Indeed the Captain claims all the Merit;——and I am very certain there's a little of my Side;——for after I had them in my Poſſeſſion, they muſter'd up between 'em five Guineas, and gave it to me, to let 'em make their Eſcape.—I took the Money, indeed, but my Conſcience obliged me to bring 'em to Juſtice, becauſe I ſhould get more by it.

Mr. *Xeno.* I always ſaid thou wou'dſt turn out ſomething great.——There,——There's a Couple of Pieces for you.

Look. I thank your Honour.——Why 'Faith, when a Man has learnt the Art of Touching, there is some Hopes.——It helps him in his Schemes. [*Aside.*

AIR XXXIX. Maggy's Tocher.

Look. *'Tis Money that makes us great;*
We all do very well know,
This World it is all a Cheat,
No more than an outward Show.
To Knowledge some pretend,
Some of Family boast;
All Fools alike contend,
Who first shall stand the Roast,
But he's th' immortal Soul,
That Riches has in Store;
No Man will him controul;
'Tis Gold we all adore.

Mr. *Xeno.* Hark'ee, Mr. *Lookout.*
[*Mr.* Lookout *and Mr.* Xeno. *whisper.*

Look. Sir, I'll make it my Business to find it out.

Mr. *Xeno.* Prithee be diligent; for I would gladly know.

Look. Sir, you may depend upon me.
[*Exit* Mr. *Xenodochy.*

——Well! I am a lucky Dog, and my Godfather gave me an Estate in giving me my Name.——For when a Houshold Dove gets loose from her Pent,—no one so courted as *Lookout*,—to bring her to her Mate again.

SCENE VI.

Enter Captain Wou'dbe.

Capt. Well! *Lookout*,—What's the Dividend?

Mr.

Mr. *Look.* Ah! Captain, —— You know the old Proverb. —— You can have no more of a Cat than her Skin. —— I search'd their Pockets, one of 'em had a bent Six-pence, —— a King *Charles*'s Farthing, —— a piece of Sealing-Wax, and half a Nutmeg. —— The other had conceal'd a Golden Guinea in her privy Purse (which you know I had a Right to examine, as being an Usher of the Black Rod to the Noble Bench;) I therefore beg'd leave to be the Lady's Cashier.

Capt. And is that really all?

Mr. *Look.* Why, do you distrust me?

Capt. No; —— but from the Multiplicity of Business Men are apt to make Mistakes, and forget themselves.

Mr. *Look.* [*Aside.*] I wish the Devil has not help'd him to some Intelligence, but I'll brazen it out. —— Sir, you have had sufficient Proof of my Ability in Business, and my Fidelity in the Execution of it: — Therefore I take it unkind that you shou'd suspect my Honour or Honesty.

Capt. Nay, don't be captious. —— I meant no harm. ——

Mr. *Look.* [*Aside.*] Then, All is well again. —— Come Sir, you shall have no Reason to complain. I'll now let you into a Secret. — You are to know, I have just parted with Mr. *Xenodochy*; who informs me his last Girl is gone from him, and he has a Notion that she is at Mrs. *Haverly*'s with the young Squire. —— You know *Xenodochy* comes down handsomly; so that 'twill Answer our purpose if we can find her out.

Capt. How shall we manage it?

Mr. *Look.* Why, if Sir *Ralph* has but the Hint, 'twill be sufficient for him to make Search. —— And 'tis but making Tryal of it.

Capt. You are right. —— And he's fond of the Office.

Mr. *Look.* Then do you go directly to him, and give Information.

Capt. It shall be done.

AIR XL. Under the Greenwood Tree.

Capt. *To you, Sir* Ralph, *I make my Court,*
Reformer of the Age.
Look. *Since Love with you does not resort,*
We beg your Personage,
Capt. *To give us Aid,*
In this our Trade,
That we gain our End,
Look. *All Honours due*
We'll give to you,
Capt. }
Look. } *Nor for 'em e'er contend.*

Mr. *Look.* Come, *dear Captain,* we live but in this World to help one another. —— Honesty is the best Policy, and always a sure Game to play. —— Industry is to be commended in all Ages, and that Branch of it, that we concern our selves in, has more than singular Merit. — 'Tis our Country's Cause — a Cause that never dies.

Capt. Why Faith, our Business requires Men of Knowledge and Experience; and the detecting of others, is the only way to conceal our own Guilt. — That's all the *Patriotism* that I know of. —— But Mum!

SCENE VII.

Mr. Look. *And the Captain go to one Side of the Stage.*

Enter Sir *Tho. Pairnails.*

Sir *Tho. Pairnails.* What Difficulties, what Perplexities of Body, Mind and Estate, do the young Fellows of this Age bring themselves to, from their into-

intolerable Vanity. —— Half their Income goes to the Support of Fawning Flatterers, — Blood-Suckers, that never leave 'em till they have drain'd 'em to the lowest Ebb, —— and then appear the foremost in the Band to exclaim at their Follies, and expose their Weaknesses to the World. — Oh! this Boy, — this Nephew of mine! —— What a plentiful

[*Here the Captain and Mr.* Lookout *listen.*

Fortune has he thrown away, and made himself a Beggar! —— Yet wou'd he quit this last Woman, and pledge me his Honour to leave this Course of Life, —— I could shew the Affection of an Uncle in the strongest Light, and pride myself in the Act.

Capt. [*Aside*] Enough. — This must be *Jenny* the old Fellow means. —— Therefore go you upon the Scout, —— and I'll to his Worship.

[*Exeunt* Lookout *and the Captain.*

Sir *Tho. P.* — But then 'tis hard to trust him. — When Men are blind to their Passions, they are easily bore away: Infatuation leads 'em on, and all Advice give Pain.

Enter a Servant with a Letter and delivers it to Sir Thomas; *he opens it, and reads.*

Honour'd Sir,

After so many indiscreet Acts that I have been guilty of, 'tis a Presumption in me, to expect any Favours from you; but as you are my nearest Relation, and have at all times given me the best of Counsel, believe me, Sir, I never stood in more need of it than at present; therefore beg your Assistance to your affectionate

Kinsman, &c.

—— So, Limbo's the Word, I suppose. —— Where did you bring this Letter from?

Serv. The *Devil Tavern*, an't please your Honour.

Sir

Sir *Tho.* Ay, a proper Place enough.—— Well, you may go about your Business. I shall be there presently. [*Exit the Servant.*
—— 'Tis even so.—— His Spirit is too haughty to send to me, were it otherwise.—— But perhaps it may make him sensible of his Follies.—— However 'tis a proper Time to try him.

AIR XLI. In the merry Month of *June.*

How Traps are laid to ensnare! ——
To Mankind what is worse,
Than Passions that impair
Their Senses and their Purse! ——
The Fair she shews her Art
In making Man her Slave;
All Things combine,
And with her join:
He's Wretched to the Grave. [*Exit.*

SCENE VIII. Changes.

Enter *Sir Ralph Reformage*, Capt. *Wou'dbe, Constables*, &c.

Capt. Sir, this is the House, and if you'll stand at a little Distance, till I have made my Entrance, I shall quickly secure the good Woman, and give you an Opportunity to make your Search.

Sir *Ralph.* 'Tis very well.
[*Captain goes, and knocks at the Door.*

SCENE IX.

Enter Mrs. *Haverly.*

Mrs. *Hav.* Your Servant, Sir.—— Who shou'd have thought of seeing so great a Stranger as the Captain?

Capt.

Capt. 'Tis not my Fault indeed, Mrs. *Haverly.*——— But as I receive Pay for the Service of my Country, I must do my Duty, you know.

Mrs. *Haverly.* I did not know you were in the Army.—I thought 'twas only a Travelling Name to charm the Ladies: ——— For I never knew one that was not fond of a red Coat in all my Life.— And I take it, you have no Aversion to the Sex.

Capt. No, Faith. ——— And if you have any thing that is very cleaver, I shall esteem it as a great Favour to be entertain'd by a Lady of your Recommendation.

Mrs. *Hav.* You have tim'd it wrong, *Captain*; for I am quite out.

Capt. What! not one.

Mrs. *Hav.* I can't say that.—I have one Lady in the House; but to tell you Truth, she's engag'd for the present.

Capt. Hum!——— [*Signs to Sir Ralph.*

——— And pray, who may that Lady be?

Mrs. *Hav.* I must beg to be excus'd there.——— But if you'll walk in, or call some other Time, I'll endeavour to serve you, as far as my humble Capacity will admit of.

Capt. You're very good, Mrs. *Haverly.* ———I'll stay an Hour or two with you now, if you'll give me Leave, and we'll have a Sneaker of Punch together.

Mrs. *Hav.* With all my Heart, Captain.

AIR XLII. Soft Harmony dispenses.

Mrs. Hav. *Good Liqiuor always chears me.*
It gives new Life,
No Cares nor Strife
Do at that Time o'erwhelm me.
It is my Soul's Delihgt.

To

To the despairing Lover
Removes his Pain,
Let's loose his Chain,
He's for a Time a Rover.
Its Power is exquisite.

--Come, Sir, if you'll please to walk in, I'll follow you.

[Exeunt *the Captain and Mrs.* Haverly.

Sir *Ralph.* You must observe, when the Door opens, to be ready to enter.

Const. Yes, an't please your Worship.

[*A Noise within,* Help, help, help; Murder.

Enter the Captain.

Capt. Come, Gentlemen, you may advance; Iv'e secur'd my good Mother under Lock and Key.

[*They all enter the House.*

SCENE X.

Justice Hamper *runs out of the House upon the Stage, with a Flannel Night-cap upon his Head; his Coat and Waistcoat unbutton'd; his Sword, Cane, Hat, and Wig, in his Hand. The Constables after him, and seize him.*

J. Hamp. Stand off, Fellows.

Enter Sir Ralph *and the Captain, leading Mrs.* Feelmore.

Sir *Ralph.* Who's this? — What! my Brother Justice turn'd Sportsman!

Capt.

Capt. [*Aside.*] a Pox of my Mar-plotting Head,— I am all wrong. ——This is shooting at a Pidgeon and killing a Crow.

Sir *Ralph.* [*to the Constables.*] Retire, Friends, with this Woman, till I call for you.

[Exit *Mrs.* Feelmore, *Constables*, &c.

J. Hamp. Why, Look'ee, Sir *Ralph*, —— Nature will be Nature; —— the Girl took with me, and I releas'd her from the hard Labour I my self had sent her to, and appointed her to meet me here, that I might administer such Advice as wou'd learn her more prudent Behaviour for the future.

Sir *Ralph.* But this was not altogether a proper Place for Admonition, Brother *Hamper*.

J. Hamp. Not as it has turn'd out, Sir *Ralph*; but our Business is to overlook one another, and keep that Part of the World honest that is beneath us.

Sir *Ralph.* Those Fellows did not know you, I hope.

J. Hamp. Not one of them.

Sir *Ralph.* Why, then make your *Exit*; for I must go on with my Search, and send these wicked Women to the House of Correction.

J. Hamp. Spare the Girl, Sir *Ralph*, and do as you please.

Sir *Ralph.* Fie, Brother *Hamper*, —— have I taken all this Pains to gain a Reputation, in suppressing such disorderly Houses, and shall I forfeit it now? —— No! —— What wou'd the World say? —— he that has made it his Business to present all Houses under such Denomination, shall not only wink at the Fault of a Brother, but omit punishing those who were concern'd in the Offence. —— No, Brother *Hamper*, —— 'tis not to done. —— Therefore withdraw, and leave me to act as I think fit.

[Exit *Justice Hamper*.

I AIR

AIR XLIII. On a Bank of Flowers.

Sir Ralph. *'Tis manifest to all the World,*
Preferment I do seek,
My Character to young and old's
A Courtier very meek.

To Levees I have often been,
My Speeches there in Print are seen,
With a fal, lal, *&c.*
You know what I do mean.

Capt. You're right, Sir *Ralph*, and 'tis no new Thing for one great Man to make his Court to another.—Humility has its Merit, though at present somewhat out of Fashion.—— But to the Business:—Suppose I call in the Constables, and make a second Search. I am almost persuaded we shall find the Girl I am in quest of.

Sir *Ralph*, Do so, but let 'em take Care to secure the Girl they have already in their Possession.

Capt. Sir, that I have taken Care of.

Sir *Ralph*. Then call 'em in.

[*The Captain goes out, and re-enters with the Constables.*

Capt. Come, Gentlemen, I'll head ye.

[*They all enter the House, and bring Mrs.* Haverly *and Mrs.* Clarkwell *upon the Stage.*

SCENE XI.

Capt. [*Aside.*] I have fail'd of my Mark, that's certain.

Sir *Ralph*. Well, Women! — what have you to say for your selves? — Which Way can you answer for such abominable Proceedings, that encourage Fornication and Adultery, to draw in and ruin the Youth of of this Age? —— These are growing Evils; —— Evils of more mischievous Consequences to the Publick than can be well express'd.

Mrs. *Hav.* Sir, I can't pretend to give you an Answer suitable to your Question. — I have at all Times been desirous of getting an honest, genteel Employment, to support my self and Family, and if it has not turn'd out to your Worship's Taste, I am sorry for it.

Sir *Ralph.* What an execrable Wretch! — Here, Constables, —— see these Women convey'd to the House of Correction.—— Captain, as you are a Man that love to see Justice executed, I shall take it as a Favour if you'll see 'em taken Care of.

Capt. Sir *Ralph*, you may depend upon your humble Servant. [Exit *Sir* Ralph.

AIR XLIV. Ye Nymphs and ye Swains.

Mrs. Hav. *How cou'd you betray*
One that never said Nay,
To help you to a Girl that was kind and gay?
How often have you swore,
When at Tick *in Love you've run,*
No Friend e'er did for you more
Than I had truly done?

[Weeps.

Capt. Why, 'tis true.

Mrs. *Clarkw.* Then are not you an ungrateful Wretch? —— Is this the Return? ——This the Reward due for such Obligations?

AIR XLV. When the Kine had given a Pailfull.

Mrs. Clarkw. *Sure we shall in Time discover,*
Gratitude is but a Name.

Rich and Poor ape one another;
Dirty Work is done for Gain.
Perverse Creature,
Where's your Nature,
To Reward our Merit so?
We have you serv'd,
And ne'er deserv'd
To be thus treated by you now.
To be thus, &c.

Capt. Indeed it grieves me to see your Sex in Distress, and believe me, (Mrs. *Clarkwell*, and you Mrs. *Haverly*) 'twas a random Shot; I meant no harm; my Aim was at *Jenny Ogle*. I assure you 'tis not in my Power to prevent your going to *Bridewell*:—— but I love to be grateful, when you are there, I'll do what Services I can to get you a Release. [*Aside.*] That is, if you'll take my Word for it.

AIR XLVI. In the pleasant Month of May.

Capt. *Great Men they will condescend*
To cringe and bow to gain their Cause,
Promise what they ne'er intend:
Good Precept ne'er fails of Applause.
Since this is now the Rule,
I'll not be thought a Fool,
I need not go to School,
To read o'er Machiavell's *Works;*
But from my Betters learn,
And make it my Concern,
That I with Ease discern
The Art of all their Tricks and Quirks.

—And now, Ladies, I must beg Leave to attend you.

SCENE

SCENE XII. Changes.

Enter Sir Ralph Reformage, *and Sir* Francis Firebriecks.

Sir *Ralph.* So, you ſay your whole Family has deſerted you.

Sir *Fran.* Ay, Sir *Ralph*, they are all fled, and in good Time;———for had they ſtay'd much longer, I ſhou'd have had my Houſe about my Ears.

Sir *Ralph.* How ſo, pray?

Sir *Fran.* Why, Jealouſy rais'd Sedition amongſt 'em, that they were ſo curſed mutinous, my Houſe was at all Times ſurrounded with an inſolent Mob, that often kept me Priſoner in it for Hours.

Sir *Ralph.* Ah! Sir *Francis.*—'Tis Time you ſhou'd leave off converſing with ſuch Creatures.——— Conſider, you grow old, and you may be outwitted.— Read my laſt Speech to the Grand Aſſembly in *Petty France.*— Your Morals want improving.

Sir *Fran.* I know you're a good Speech-maker.— But, Sir *Ralph*,——why, you don't conſider the two chief Topicks the World is govern'd by;—— 'tis Self-intereſt and Pleaſure.—— Now my Scheme has been to Search out the Foible of all Mankind, and wherever I found a Man whoſe Wealth was burthenſome to him, I was always Maſter of ſome new Invention to go Snacks with him.

AIR XLVII. Cockamycari ſhe.

Sir Fran. *Some Men are taken like a Trout,*
Shew one a Fly;
He'll ſoar as high;
He'll play, he'll friſk, he'll jump about,
'Till by the Hook he's ta'en.

The

The greedy Bait he swallows down,
Like Children, pleas'd with Sugar-Plumbs,
Tempted alike he cannot shun,
Tho' it must prove his Bane.

Sir *Ralph.* But have not you fail'd in your Art lately?

Sir *Fran.* Why, the Age is somewhat improved, and not a little obliged to me for it. — But who have we got here? — Oh! I see 'tis an old Pidgeon, of mine, and his billing Dove. — Come, Sir *Ralph*, let us retire, for 'tis a Rule with me never to spoil Sport. [*Exeunt.*

SCENE XIII. Changes.

Enter Squire Spendthrift *and* Jenny Ogle.

Squire *Spend.* Well, *Jenny!* — This adverse Fate strikes deep to my Heart, that I must be deprived of one that is so dear to me.

Jenny Ogle. And is there no Hopes left?

Squire *Spend.* None in the World, my Dear. —— You're sensible, when I was taken into Custody, I must have gone to Goal, without my Uncle's Assistance.— My Estate is sold, — the Money spent, and I reduced to the last Extremity. — He therefore laid his Commands upon me, to part with you instantly, and he wou'd settle an Annuity for my Life, agreeable to my Wishes; — but expected to be obey'd, and insisted on the immediate Execution of it.

Jenny Ogle. Barbarous Man!

Squire *Spend.* He farther added, that upon Condition I wou'd renounce your Sex, excepting the Partner he shou'd give to me— I shou'd find him much my Friend. — I know it has been often talk'd, by Will he has made me his Heir; but my way of Life not concurring with his Morals, I am told he determin'd min'd to cut me off with a Shilling.—How far my Misfortunes may influence him to change his Way of thinking, I know not; but at present, Necessity, that brings all Mankind to Obedience, will oblige me to follow his Directions.

Jenny Ogle. And will you fly me?

AIR XLVIII. A Swain of Love.

Farewel to Joy and Pleasure,
No Peace my Soul can find;
To part with thee, my Treasure,
The Thought distracts my Mind.
O! why must Man for ever
Be made the Scoff of Fate!
Oh, Cupid! with thy Quiver,
Now end my wretched State,
Ungrateful Creature!

[Weeps.

Squire *Spend.* Not by my Choice you know;—— for I cou'd gaze on thy bewitching Eyes, grasp thee in those folding Arms, press thy panting Heart to mine, and waste my Life in Love.

Jenny Ogle. Then why will you go from me?

Squire *Spend.* What can I do? My Fortune's gone, even destitute of Bread;——'tis cruel Destiny, but we must submit.

[*Squire* Spendthrift *and* Jenny Ogle, *looking on each other.*

AIR XLIX. In *Perseus* and *Andromeda.*

S. Spend. *Must I then leave thee,*
My charming Jenny?
Oh! 'tis Death to me
That we must Part.
J. Ogle. *Oh! name it no more,*
Kind Death, I implore

My

My Peace you'll restore,
And strike the Dart.

S. Spend. *Oh! thy Words kill me.*
J. Ogle. *No more I beg thee.*
S. Spend. *Talk not so to me.*
J. Ogle. *My Heart will break.*
S. Spend. *Talk not so to me.*
J. Ogle. *No more I beg thee.*
S. Spend. *Oh! thy Words kill me.*
J. Ogle. }
S. Spend. } *My Heart will break.*

SCENE XIV.

Enter Captain Wou'dbe.

Capt. Joy, Joy, to my noble Friend; Health, Life, and Pleasure attend my worthy Patron, Sir *Trueman Spendthrift*.

Squire *Spend.* Whence this Banter, Captain? You did not use to joke thus with your Friends in Distress.

Capt. Sir, I acknowledge Truth is as great a Rarity from my Mouth, as Sincerity from a Hypocrite.— But this I think I can aver.

Squire *Spend.* What!

Capt. That you are Sir *Trueman Spendthrift*, Baronet, now in the Possession of five thousand Pounds *per Annum*, and twenty thousand Pounds Ready Cole;—— and here comes one that will attest it.

Enter Mr. Skinflint, *Steward to the late Sir* Thomas Pairnails.

Mr. *Skin.* Sir, I come to acquaint your Honour that Sir *Thomas*, your Uncle, departed this Life two Hours ago in an Apoplectick Fit. — By Will he has left you his whole Estate Real, and Personal ——

But

But it is upon Condition you marry Miſs *Arabella Lovely*: —— A young Lady of great Merit, but no Fortune. —— Her Father was a Sufferer in a late Scheme, and Sir *Thomas* was no ſmall Sharer of his Fortune. —— I often heard him ſay, Reſtitution was what every Man ſhould make, who in any Degree had partaken of the Plunder of his Country. —— And therefore had he liv'd he determin'd to givė this young Lady to you in Marriage, and made the ſame Proviſion in Caſe of Death, that if your Honoūr refuſes, —— the Eſtate goes to her and her Family.

Squire Spend. What a Change is here! 'twou'd have been more generous to have left it to my own Diſcretion; but I have ſeen enough of Miſery to learn more Conduct for the future. —— Therefore I ſhall execute my Uncle's Will in every Reſpect. —— As to you, Mr. *Skinflint*, I ſhall continue you in the ſame Office you were in. — You're now my Steward, and as Decency requires my Retirement, I expect you'll ſee the Funeral Rites due to my deceas'd Uncle faithfully executed. — My dear *Jenny*, you ſhall find me honourable, and tho' I am depriv'd of giving you my Perſon, you may be aſſur'd of my Friendſhip.

Capt. But, Sir. — I think your Honour ſhou'd ſend a general Releaſe to thoſe Cravat-makers; — Ladies that are forc'd to work *gratis* for their Country: — For this is a Day that will give Joy to all your old Acquaintance. — And if I miſtake not, you have a pretty many of 'em there.

Squire Spend. Well, well, let it be ſo. — It may be a means of making them as ſenſible of their Follies as I am of mine. — *Skinflint* ſhall furniſh you with what Money is neceſſary — and as you love to be employ'd, do you be the welcome Meſſenger.

Capt. Sir, with all my Heart. — My Friend *Look-out* knows how to draw a Releaſe, and we ſhall be all right again.

AIR L.

Capt. *My Credit I now ſhall retrieve;*
Sure no Man can do more:
An Act of Grace, as I conceive,
Was wanting heretofore.
Indulgence we give to the Fair,
And ſome Faux-Pas *excuſe;*
But ev'ry one is not to ſhare;
Some Folk we muſt refuſe.

The four laſt Lines to be ended with the firſt Part of the Tune.

—— Come, Mr. *Skinflint*, I muſt have a litttle of your Ready Rino — That's our *Primum Mobile.*

Mr. *Skin.* Sir, I will wait upon you.

[*Exit Mr.* Skinflint *and the Captain.*

Squire Spend. You muſt obey the Decree of Fate with Patience, Child; this is a turn that may be happy for us both.

Jenny Ogle. What Happineſs can I expect, if you forſake me.

Squire Spend. I ſhall not forſake you. — And to convince you of my Affection, I will make you a Settlement that ſhall maintain you like a Gentlewoman, and not in the Power of any Perſon to revoke but yourſelf. — But you muſt be deny'd to all Men that wou'd viſit you in a diſhonourable Way: — that's an Injunction I muſt lay upon you. — And tho' with great Reluctancy, —— I even debar my ſelf.

Jenny Ogle. That laſt Clauſe I beg may be left out. — Your Benevolence is great, and much beyond what I cou'd e'er expect — To be debarr'd from all the World is no hard Task for me, except your ſelf. But to be depriv'd of the Man I love, is worſe than Death. [*Weeps.*

Squire Spend. 'Tis in vain to think on't. — It must be so — And as the World approves of your Conduct, you shall find my Friendship increase. — This Embrace, and farewel. [*Exit the Squire.*

She looks after him.

AIR LI.

J. Ogle. *You cruel Powers! that leave me here,*
To sigh and make my moan,
Shew Pity, be not too severe!
Oh! hear my dying Groan,
No Passion sure can equal mine,
Were Men but half so true! —
Our Sex wou'd ne'er have cause to pine,
Nor bid to Love adieu.

Jenny Ogle. How foolish is fond Woman! — What is the World, that we shou'd covet it so much! — Pride and Ambition blows up one half of our Sex, the other falls a Sacrifice to Love and Inclination. — Yet when I reflect, and consider the wretched Fate of my Companions, and the miserable State of such who follow their Examples, I am happy. — My Eyes are now opened to that large Gulf of Misery, whose Precipice I was so near. — Then let me bless the Hand of Providence, that permitted me to escape.

And that my future Life I so may lead,
That in the Paths of Virtue I may tread,
Void of all Ills — I shall no Censure dread.

Exit Jenny Ogle.

SCENE

SCENE XV.

Changes to a Room in Bridewell, *and discovers Mrs.* Haverly, *Mrs.* Clarkwell, *Mrs.* Feelmoore, *Mrs.* Frisk, *Mrs.* Stroaker, *Capt.* Wou'dbe, *and Mr.* Lookout.

Capt. You're all free Ladies, every Mother's Child of you—— So if you have a mind to return to the old Trade of Basket-making, Why, very well: — And if 'tis possible for you to reclaim, so much the better; — But at present you have nothing to do but to sing and be merry.

AIR LII. Blowzabella.
CHORUS.

Capt. *My part I've Acted to please you all,*
No Statesmen e'er cou'd say so much:
I never did any one enthral,
Yet fail'd you not by Turns to touch.
Mr. Look. *Here's Freedom for you, to recompence*
Your Losses, were they e'er so great;
A Boon, that's of such Consequence
That Joy to all it must create.
Om. Wom. *Our Thanks you have with a loud Voice,*
That shall eccho thro' all the Town:
Mrs. Hav.
Mrs. Clark. } *From* Qual. *to the* Cit, *they'll rejoice;*
This Day they with Pleasure will crown.
Mrs. Feel. *Hence, Avaunt, my Fears are vanish'd,*
Mrs. Stroak. *Nor have I now ought to dread;*
Mrs. Frisk. *And as for me, my Cares are banish'd.*
Mrs. Feel.
Mrs. Stroak.
Mrs. Frisk. } *Sorrow now is from us fled.*
Gen. Cho. *'Tis so with Mankind the World o'er;*
When a Storm is blown over and gone,
They think of the Danger no more,
Nor imagine e'er to be undone.

FINIS.

1
Air I. (The Virgin Queen.)
Air II.
Air III. (In Perseus and Andromeda.)
Air IV.

2
Air V. (Moll Peatly.)
Air VI. (She would not die a Maid.)
Air VII. (What tho' I am a Country Lass.)
Air VIII.

Air IX.
Air X.
Air XI. (Ye Nymphs & Sylvian Gods.)

Air XII. (Recruiting Officer.)
Air XIII.
Air XIV. (May Fair.)

Air XV.
Air XVI. (Butter'd Pease.)
Air XVII (As Jockey and Jenny.)

6
Air XVIII. (To Hannover from Edinbro'.)
Air XIX. (Dame of Honour.)
Air XX. (What Woman cou'd do.)

Air XXI. (The Spring's a coming.)
Air XXII. (To y^e French Tune Mirliton.)
Air XXIII. (Joan's Placket.)

8
Air XXIV.
Air XXV
Air XXVI

Air XXVII. (*There was a Pretty Girl.*)

Air XXVIII. (*In Perseus and Andromeda*)

Air XXIX. (*Deel take the Wars.*)

Air XXX. (The White Joke.)
AirXXXI. (Tweed Side.)
Air XXXII (In vain dear Cloe.)

Air XXXIII.
Air XXXIV. (To a French Tune.)
Air XXXV (As Love sick Damon.)
Air XXXVI

Air XXXVII. (Moggy Lauder.)
Air XXXVIII. (O the Broom.)
Air XXXIX. (Maggie's Tocker.)

Air XL. (Under the Greenwood Tree.)
Air XLI. (In the Merry Month of June.)
Air XLII. (Soft Harmony dispences.)

14
Air XLIII. (On a Bank of Flowers.)
Air XLIV (Ye Nymphs and ye Swains.)
Air XLV. (When ye Kine had given.)

15
Air XLVI. (In ye pleasant Month of May.
Air XLVII (Cockamycary She.)
Air XLVIII. (In Perseus & Andromeda.

Air XLIX.
DC
Air L.
Air LI. (Blowzabella.)
Chorus

The Jew Decoy'd

Bibliographical note:
This facsimile has been made from a copy in the
Beinecke Library, Yale University

She is suppos'd Cashier'd her service i: then seen in grand keeping with a Iew and soon after turn'd upon the Common for misbehaviour

THE JEW Decoy'd; OR THE PROGRESS OF A HARLOT.

A New BALLAD OPERA of Three Acts.

The AIRS set to old Ballad Tunes.

LONDON:

Printed for E. RAYNER, *in* Marygold-Court, *over-against* Fountain-Court *in the* Strand; *and sold at the Pamphlet-Shop next Door to the* George Tavern, Charing-Crofs; E. NUTT, *at the* Royal-Exchange; A. DODD, *without* Temple-Bar; *and by the Bookfellers of* London *and* Weftminfter, 1733.

(Price One Shilling.)

A TABLE of the SONGS.

Dra-

Dramatis Personae.

MEN.

Col. *Goatish*,
'Squire *Spruce*,
Waggoner,
Ben Israel,
Julio,
Tom Pledge,
Mr. *Fingerfee*,
Justice *Mittimus*,
Rusty, Keeper of *Bridewell*,
Flogwell, his Man,
Constables,
Porter,
Pad, a Highwayman,
Dr. *Nostrum*,
Dr. *Meagre*.
Mr. *Smellcorps*, an Undertaker,
Parson *Smirk*,
Time-teller.

WOMEN.

Mother *Lurewell*,
Moll Hackabout,
Alice, her Maid,
1st. Woman, } in *Bridewell*.
2d. Woman, } in *Bridewell*.
3d Woman, } in *Bridewell*.
Mrs. *Pimpley*,
Three more Women attending on *Moll* in the Salivation,
Three Women Mourners at the Burial.

INTRODUCTION.

PLAYER. AUTHOR.

Player. THE *Harlot's Progress*! o' my word a fit title for a —— taking performance.

Author. And let me tell you, a title now-a-days is half the work; I have known many a book sold by it, and many a play damn'd thro' the want on't.

Pl. Well but, good Sir, let me propose an objection or two to you concerning your performance. You must know I act in quality of a critic to this company of Comedians, and as I'm paid for't, you must not take it amiss that I find faults.

Au. I'm sensible there are enough; but pray, Sir, go on.

Pl. Why then in the first place, Mr. *Marscene*, give me leave to say, that bawds, whores, pimps, bullies, constables, and parsons, are an odd mixture of people to be seen on a stage: I don't think there's any such thing to be met with in any of the plays of *Congreve*, *Wicherly*, or *Steele*; and therefore, Sir, d'ye see.

Au. Do I see? Yes, Sir, I a'n't blind either to your faults or my own, and if you possessed the qualifications necessary even to a *Bartholomew* fair critic, you'd never have made such an objection as this. Comedy, Sir, must always be drawn from the life; fops, rakes, and coquets were the weeds grubbed up by those excellent authors you have named: Our's is a ranker age, and if we did not lash the gross medley of characters you have run over, we should have no chance for applause, because our performances would be out of nature and fashion; S'death, Sir, a fool of the last age would be a man of wit in this.

Pl. I stand convinced as to this point, but there is another, which if you can get over I'll have done.

Au. 'Pr'ythee let's hear it then.

Pl. Why, I don't conceive in such a representation as this, how the unities can be at all preserved.

Au. Why, look ye, I thought you had stole your system of criticism from some *French* author, made sillier yet by his translator —— why, in few words, Sir, rules are out of fashion, method is a jest, and order in this age is taken for want of spirit; the stage is quite altered, ballad opera's are an invention of our own times, and as they are compounded of comedy and farce, I have to solve this difficulty made free with the chorus of the ancient tragedy, and introduced something like it between the scenes, in order to acquaint the audience with what length of time is supposed to be taken up, while they are shifting them.

Pl. But is not this a little improbable, Sir?

Au. Ay, and unnatural too, or I should have very small hopes of success; Sir, I tell you the age is out of humour with nature, she has done them a capital injury, and they'll never forgive her.

Pl. Well, well, waste no more time, but see how it will look upon the stage.

Au. Bid the time-teller mind the tone I gave him. [*Curtain draws.*

THE PROGRESS OF A HARLOT.

ACT I. SCENE I.

Enter the Time-teller *solus*.

WELL met, good folks, —— our author bid me say,
To-night we'll ſhew you ſomething —— like a play.
He frankly owns 'tis wrote againſt all rule,
Yet hopes that this conceſſion will not cool
That paſſion which ye ſhew for all things new,
And which with eager fondneſs ye perſue.
Truſting to this firſt made him write—let then
Your love for novelty protect his pen:

As from your praise the Ballad Opera rose,
A motly drama patch'd of verse and prose,
So here to-night —— let your applause maintain
Our new invention added on that plan.
Since quickly it occur'd unto our bard,
That neither time nor place could he preserv'd,
He pitch'd on me —— and to fill up the space,
Has rais'd me to a new-invented place,
Call'd Time-teller —— my office is to shew
What has been done, the manner, when, and how,
Between the scenes of the ensuing piece,
Farce, Opera, Comedy, or what you please.
Perhaps you'll say 'tis an odd whim--that's true;
But pray consider, Sirs —— 'tis also new.
That for your sakes we quit the common road,
And therefore 'tis but grateful to applaud.

So much for Prologue —— I am next to say
On what Foundation we have built our play;
From the keen satyr in sly *Hogarth*'s prints,
We own we took for most that follows — hints.
The Harlot's Progress —— Not a face I spy,
But knows the subject full as well as I.
Why then ------ e'en let the actors now begin,
I'll to your understandings —— trust this scene.

Scene draws, and discovers Col. Goatish, *'Squire* Spruce, *and Mother* Lurewell; *a table before them with bottles and glasses.*

Col. Weel, ye say there wul be brau borny sound lasses i'th' this same *York* waggon, whan it comes.

M. L. In all the time I have dealt in woman's flesh, I have always made it my observation, that your *Northern* Lasses come up the fittest for trade to town: Colonel, you know the *North*, and will bear me witness, that the Assemblies

ſemblies at *York* are compoſed of as well-bred people as any that come to the Drawing-room; and for *Scarborough*, it's become ſo noted, and ſo much frequented, that agad the people come to town from it as polite and as wicked, as if they had been bred all their life-time at St. *James's*.

Col. Deel a bit do I like them the better for that —— waunds wife, have ye ken'd me ſo long, and fancy I ſhould like a laſs the better for her geud manners; na, na, give me a bouncing, ſtrapping, ſonſy looking girl, wha'll ſcratch, and fight like auld Nick himſel, afore ſhe'll loſe her maidenhead.

S. Sp. Nay, nay, I'll anſwer for Mrs. *Lurewell*; if you tell her your taſte, ſhe'll ſoon give the Girl her cue; and for a maidenhead, the ſecret of making it is no ſecret to her.

M. L. Sir, I ſcorn your words —— the Col. knows me to be a woman of honour: I'm none of your *Needham's* nor your *Thomas's*; if I aſſiſt a young ſpark, like you, with my endeavours to prevent your dying of the green-ſickneſs, or have good-nature enough to help an old Gentleman, like the Colonel, to a ſoft warm hand to chafe him when in pain, I value my reputation, and would not make any uſe of your mean bawdy artifices for the world.

AIR I. An old Woman cloathed in grey.

Through folly fops all things miſcall,
Hence you my profeſſion deſpiſe;
Yet liſt to my ſong, and it ſhall,
If that's to be done —— make you wiſe.

To riches the merchant lays claim,
Ambition doth title embrace;
The soldier's persuing of fame,
And courtiers still cringe for a place.

Yet let but bright beauty appear,
The merchant grows lavish and gay;
It strikes both the courtier and peer,
And heroes are proud to obey.
Since beauty's a thing thus divine,
Superior to ev'ry degree,
And while the disposal is mine,
Who is it shall take place of me?

Col. Ha, ha, ha! I hope you're answer'd, Sir.

S. Sp. Split me, Mrs. *Lurewell*, I never dreamt you were a wit before; come, you and I'll be friends; I set a great value on wit.

M. L. How comes it you never bought any then?

Col. Nae, for that matter, *Jammey* is nae fool; come gae us a merry sang, lad, and put the auld wife in a geud humour again.

M. L. Ay, let's hear it —— there's two of the fellows that belong to the waggon, it will be here presently.

S. Sp. Well, upon condition all quarrels are made up, I'll try what I can do.

M. L. Try what you can do! Ha, ha, ha, [illegible]'s the out-side of a modern beau's perform-ance. Pray, Sir, come to action.

S. Sp. (Sings.)

AIR

AIR II. Young Philoret, &c.

Love is alone
To me the sun,
That warms my am'rous soul;
My Celia's *eyes*
Dart endless joys,
And all my cares controll.

To me she's bright
As Phoebus' *light,*
Where Eastern *spices blow;*
But if she fly,
Unhappy I
Feel Greenland's *night and snow.*

M. L. Well, we are friends 'till next time we fall out; come, Colonel, I hear the waggon wheels; have you any instructions to give me?

Col. Troth, I'm sae weel pleased with this morning's work, that I'll gae ye my directions, as our auld lards gae their charters, in rhime.

(Colonel sings.)

AIR III. Cold and raw the wind did blow.

What though it be true I grow something auld,
My passion I yet can discover,
And tho' through time my head may be bald,
I'll still prove a lusty lover.
Sae gang i' th' yard and pull up a leek,
Nae snaw than its head looks whiter;
Yet downwards if to the tail ye seek,
Nae green i' th' warld shines brighter.

Sine

Sine look me a lass that's blith and young,
Wha'll struggle and fight i' th' storming;
My passion will make me bath stout and strong,
Then never fear ye my performing;
For beauty resisting still makes a man bauld,
Such vigour its rays are still flashing;
As tho' bath the flint and the steel be cauld,
Yet fire is soon struck by their clashing.

S. Sp. Bravely performed! Colonel.

M. *L.* [*sighing.*] Ay, would his back were half as strong as his lungs!

Col. Nae mair dauffing, woman, I'se hear the folk i'th' yard, we'll sit here, and observe your management.

M. *L.* Let's do nothing too hastily. [*fills a glass of brandy.*] Here's to your honour's better health, [*turning to 'Squire* Spruce] and to your having more money, Sir; and then I shall be sure of two good customers. [*Exit.*

SCENE III.

[*To Mother* Lurewell *enter* Moll Hackabout. *The* Colonel *and* Spruce *are seen at a window.*

M. *L.* On my faith a pretty country wench! what a pity it is she's come up to this lewd town! —— [*chucks her under the chin.*] how old are you, child?

Moll. About nineteen, Madam.

M. *L.* What, I warrant you are come up to service; have you any relations in town, child?

Moll. Yes, an't please you, I have an aunt and two cousins —— odds me! what's become

of

of my cousin *Sweetapple*'s goose? it has the direction on its head, and if it is lost, I sha'n't knaw where to find her, nor myself neather.

Enter Waggoner. Moll *runs to him.*

Moll. Tummus, Tummus, do'st knau what's become of my goose and my box too? if any rogue should steal it, as they say there's a mort of such kind of things done in *London*, I should be undone: there's two stuff-gowns, nine round ear'd caps, three new suits of pinners, 23 *s.* in money, five silver groats, and half a piece of gold, that our *John* the gardener and I broke, when I left 'Squire *Booby*'s.——

Wag. By lady! I believe the girl has a mind to be robb'd, what dost give us such an innumtery of your things for? I'se take care enough on 'em, on you don a make such a din about 'em, I'se warrant ye.

M. *L.* Art provided of any place, my dear?

Moll. No, forsooth; I'se trust to my cousin *Sweet Apple* to get me a place, she promised mother to seek out for one last *Lammus*-tide, and I hope she has found it by this.

M. *L.* Why, if I knew any body who could give thee a character, I should be glad to take thee myself; I want an innocent girl, of sober conversation, that may tend me a-days, and read me to sleep a-nights out of the *Practice of Piety*.

Wag. By the mass then she'll fit ye! she's as honest a girl as e'er come out of *Yorkshire*; I strained my ancle on the road, and got up into the waggon, and there she sung *Chevy-Chace*, *Robin Hood*, *Patient Grizzel*, and read the Histories of the *seven Champions*, and the *wise Men of Goatum*; before *George*! I went to sleep in spite

of

of my pain. By Lady! ſhe's as good a ſcholard as the clerk of our pariſh, and the volks go to him to read the Letters when they come from town.

M. *L.* Thou ſeemeſt to be a good honeſt fellow, there's a ſhilling for thee to drink, be ſure you take care of the Maid's things; come, my dear, you ſhall go with me.

(*Moll* ſings.)

To London *fair town I am come for a place,*
I now ſhall grow rich in a very ſhort ſpace;
My fortune I'll make, and get a ſilk gown,
And then I'll deſpiſe all the youths of our town.
There is Molly *and* Kate *were backward to come;*
Such fearful young huſſeys may ſtay ſtill at home,
While I to the full do enjoy what I pleaſe:
Who would not leave milking to drink of fine Teas.

Moll. But what mun I do with my Couſin's gooſe?

M. *L.* Oh! I'll take care to ſend it.

[*Exit* Waggoner *ſinging.*

AIR IV. Bonny *Dundee.*

My waggon before, and I in the rear,
Thro' wind and thro' weather together we go:
Sometimes the road's ev'n, and ſky too is clear,
And ſometimes 'tis deep, and cover'd with ſnow.

In paſſing thro' life like fate we abide,
O'er hills and thro' vales we continually ride,
In joy it runs ſwift, in trouble moves ſlow;
And now we riſe high, anon we ſink low.

SCENE

SCENE draws, and discovers a room, in which are the Colonel *and* Spruce. *To them enter Mother* Lurewell *and* Moll.

Col. S'bread, ſhe's a bonny laſs, of a brau height, geud features, and twa pawky een; there's nair a luckie in au *Edinburgh* could a helped me to ſic a laſs.

S. *Sp.* Egad, ſhe's as fair as the light, and as freſh as the day, ſweet as the flowers in *June*, and bright as a ſummer's morning.

M. *L.* Nephew, and brother, I have juſt been hiring a young country-maid; for in troth I am quite wearied out with the vices of thoſe who have lived in town: I have not been able to get a ſervant theſe three months, that could forbear talking to the fellows, or had learnt ſo much as their catechiſm by heart. Well, 'tis a ſad age we live in; [*ſighs.*] would I were in heaven!

S. *Sp.* [*aſide.*] A very modeſt wiſh for a bawd truly! but I find ſhe has dubb'd me her nephew; gad, I like her procuring mightily, this is a ſweet pretty girl.

Col. As ye ſay, Madam, it's a ſad age this we live in, there's hardly an honeſt man to be found in a hundred; and for the women, Deel a me gin I believe one o' them honeſt but your ladiſhip.——Wull you ſit down, ſweet-heart?

M. *L.* Ay, ay, ſit down by the gentleman, child, he's my brother, and a very good, modeſt old man, he'll do you no hurt, I'll warrant you; come, your countryman the waggoner told me you could ſing prettily, let us hear now: tho'

I

I hate all indecency, yet I confess harmless mirth was ever agreeable to me. —— don't be ashamed, child. [*chucks her under the chin.*

Moll. Indeed, Madam, I never sung before any gentleman in all my days.

Col. Out, fie, lassy, I'm thy countryman, or at least not far fra it; there's a crown-piece for thee: now let me hear a *Scotch* song.

S. *Sp.* But lay by your hat first, child.

Moll. [*as in confusion.*] By mass I am so asham'd I can hardly speak; but, since your worship will have it so, and my mistress bids me, I'll try.

AIR V. *Bessy Bell* and *Mary Grey.*

As I gid down by yon brook-side,
I spy'd a maiden weeping,
Her lilly hand held up her head,
Her flocks as she was keeping:
At length to sooth her throbbing heart,
Her song she thus beginning;
Such sweetness did her voice impart,
I listen'd to her singing.

Fra' me, ye maids, said she, be wise,
Ah! let my ruin warn ye;
Fly from the flatt'ring lover's lies,
E'er the deceiver harm ye:
False Strephon *swore eternal truth,*
And tender inclination;
E're I believ'd the perjur'd youth,
Or yielded to his passion.

But when he had thro' language fair
Of chastity bereft me;
With cold neglect to wild despair,
The faithless shepherd left me:
Thus roves thro' fields the gaudy bee,
In restless mischief toiling;

With

With humming joy and loaded thigh,
Each flow'r of sweets despoiling.

Coll. That's my brau lass, geud faith, I ne'er heard any thing sweeter in my life, unless it were the rattling of the dice at hazard.

S. *Sp.* Her throat's more melodious than a nightingal: would I had her on condition the Devil had them both. [*aside.*

M. *L.* Well, brother, shall we be going?

Coll. Ay, as soon as ye like; gang ye your ways with that pretty lass in a coach, and wese come after ye in the chariot. [*they rise.*

M. *L.* Sha'n't we call for the reckoning?

Coll. Na, na, wese pay that at the bar.

[*Exeunt omnes. The Colonel hopping upon a stick,* Spruce *making mouths behind him.*

SCENE V.

The Time-teller *comes forwards.*

In hands like these you'll easily believe
Moll quickly learnt each method to deceive;
With each alluring, each seducing grace,
Her innocence quite lost——but in her face,
There still with study'd care its look she wore
But with a purpose to deceive the more.
Numbers the lightnings of her eyes subdue,
But more her art to love and ruin drew.
At last, of *Israel*'s scatter'd race there came
A wealthy lover, welcome to the dame.
Gold soon prevail'd—Vain was old *Lurewell*'s weeping,
The *Jew* she hated—but was fond of keeping;
Manasseh had her——at a price how dear!
Will quickly from the following Scene appear.

SCENE VI. *A handsome Bed-Chamber.*

Moll *in a rich un-dress,* Spruce *near her, both sitting by the bed-side.*

S. *Sp.* And so, dear, this rascally old *Jew* allows you no money.

Moll. No, love; he says I have every thing about me that I can wish, and what need have I of money?

S. *Sp.* A covetous old hunks; but let me see, can't you let me take the diamond out of one of your rings, and tell him you lost it? money I must have, for since I have lost my support from the Colonel, I ha'nt a farthing but what I earn as a Puff at a *Pharo*-table.

Moll. O la! a Puff! what's that? I protest all my adventures have not brought me to the knowledge of that term; tho' old *Manasseh Ben Israel* has been at the expence of a master to teach me *English*, a master to teach me *French*, a master to teach me writing, a master to teach me dancing, a master to teach me musick; and in short, so many masters, that I am scarce mistress of two hours in the four and twenty, unless when the old fool's at *Richmond* with his daughter.

S. *Sp.* What a deal of pains the simpleton takes to make himself hated; I wonder how these out of the way fellows comes to fancy it's possible for a woman to like them?

Moll. Oh! I find you're a novice in some things as well as I —— come, tell me what you mean by being a Puff, and I'll explain to you the arts I make use of as a Mistress.

S. *Sp.*

S. *Sp*. Why, a Puff, child, is one who, thro' want of wit, has lost his own money at play; and when he comes to have a little better sense, he trepans others into the same snare, in order to share the booty: in a word, he's a decoy-duck to all those dangerous pools, called hazard-tables, billiards, publick rooms, and private places for play at taverns.——Now satisfy me a little, as to the mystery of wheedling; for I suppose that's the way you manage your old son of circumcision.

Moll. No, no; my art lies quite another way; I put on my bent brows as soon as he comes into the room, hardly ever speak to him but in an angry tone; and whatever it is I have a mind to I have it e're he has a pleasant look; but here, take the stone out of the ring: now, ten to one but he'll be inquisitive about how, and when, and where, it was lost. Some sneaking silly jades would be immediately coining a hundred plausible lies and stories to make the matter pass off; instead of which I shall only tell him, that I have lost it, and expect another before to-morrow-night, on pain of his never touching so much as my hand till it is produced.

S. *Sp*. Well, a wench with beauty is a more arbitrary tyrant than the Grand Signior with all his power.

AIR VI. The bonny bush aboon Traquair.

Ye swains whose hearts from love are free,
Ah! shun its fatal anguish;
Seek not the blooming maid to see,
Lest for her sake ye languish:

Just fears should kindling passion cool,
While thus with ruin toying;
Like Eastern tyrants beauties rule,
And triumph in destroying.

Moll. But hark ye, Mr. *Spruce*, I hear you are very great with *Betty Peel*, the orange-wench at the new play-house: you had best take care that your assignations be very private; if I should catch you, it might cost you your life.

S. *Sp.* Puh, puh, such a pretty sweet creature as thou art could not be guilty of any cruelty, upon any provocation whatsoever.

Moll. Don't you trust too much to that; gaming, drinking, and the rest of your genteel vices, I can bear with well enough: but egad, if a woman should be in the way, I should be a very fury. A man who had insulted a *Spaniard*, lain with an *Italian*'s wife, or had been trusted with a secret by a minister of state, would be safer by half than you; they might all use caution in their revenge for their own sakes; but I should never think of self-preservation, till I saw you dead at my feet. Remember that of all fiends the most mischievous is a jealous woman.

AIR VII. Man in Imagination.

Of tender inclinations,
And of soft swelling passions,
Our sex's to fondness prone;
While love with love ye pay:
But in affection zealous,
When once with cause we're jealous,
Nought can the fault atone;
Nought can our rage allay.

Enter

Enter Alice *in a great hurry.*

Alice. O la, Madam! here's Mr. *Ben Iſrael* entering the very paſſage; I'd compound for a leg or an arm of Mr. *Spruce*, that his body was ſafe out: you know he always carries a ſtilletto about him, and darted it thro' the hangings when the wind blew, when he fancied a man behind them; for heaven's ſake, Madam, make haſte!

(*She takes up* Spruce's *hat and ſhoes, throws his coat over her arm, and claps the ſcreen within half a foot of the door.*

Enter Mr. Ben Iſrael *haſtily.*

He runs to the bedſide to Moll, *whilſt* Spruce *and* Alice *ſlip from behind the ſcreen out at the door.*

(Moll *ſtarts from the bed.*)

Moll. I wonder what you mean, Sir, by coming into the room ſo haſtily; you know I can't bear a ſurpriſe: I proteſt the next time you ſerve me ſo, I'll throw the tongs at your head.

Ben. Pray you, my dear, no be in a paſſion; I thought I heard a buſtle in your ſhamber, and that make a me come up ſo haſtily to ſee what was de mater.

Moll. What, at your naſty ſuſpicions again; I thought I had ſchool'd you ſufficiently for your impertinences of this ſort before: let me hear any more of this language, and you ſhall never ſee my face again; you ſha'n't, villain, (*puſhes him from her*) as you are.

Ben. No paſſion, *Molly*, no paſſion; I come a from *Richmond* dis morning by ſix o' clock, I want a my breakfaſt very much: let us drink a de tea, and be friends.

Moll. You may do as you pleaſe; but I won't bear theſe ſort of ſuſpicions, I tell ye, I won't.

Ben. Here! *Julio!*

Enter a black boy.

Julio. Sire.

Ben. Bid a *Alice* bring de kettle and de tea-things.

Julio. Yes, Sire. (*Exit.*

Ben. Come a my dear, be in one good humour.

Moll. Not till you ſubmit, and make me a preſent of a purſe of moidores; I like that coin becauſe it is your country.

Ben. Here a den there is nine of them, dey are all I have about me; but what a you do wid money? have you not all things? ſpeak a what you want.

Moll. No matter what I want, give me the money.

Ben. Give me a kiſs den.

Enter Alice *with a tea-table and things,* Julio *following her with a kettle and a lamp.*

Ben. Here a Mrs. *Alice*, your lady and I quarrel, and wid much ado I bring her to be good friends; come a you know I love de lute, it be de favourite inſtrument in *Portugal*, your lady will give me a leſſon on it. (Alice *going.*

Moll. Stay! I won't play.

Ben.

Ben. Den you ſhall ſing me a ſong, (*pulls out his watch*) come a 'tis paſt eleven; ſing a de ſong, and I will drink one diſh of tea, and ſo to *Shange.*

Moll. Will ye, *Naſſy*? come then, I'll be good. (*ſings.*)

AIR VIII.

What ſhall I do to ſhew how much I love her?

Beauty was form'd to give joy in poſſeſſing,
Not by dull coyneſs our pleaſures to ſowre;
Pride turns to a curſe even this high bleſſing,
When the fair's cruel becauſe ſhe has power.
Kings themſelves, hateful grown by long oppreſſing,
Often in exile lament their hard fate;
Beauties too after much coldneſs expreſſing,
Fain would be kind when, alas! 'tis too late.

Ben. Der is my ſherubim, (*chucks her under the chin.*) now why cannot you be always ſo good?

Alice. Oh! dear Sir, my miſtreſs takes it ſo ill that you ſhould have a ſuſpicion of her honour, that ſhe neither eats nor ſleeps for it, though ſhe won't tell you ſo much; (*Ben Iſrael looks kindly on* Moll.) but you can't imagine, Sir, how *Julio* improves both in ſinging and playing on the violin: I proteſt I believe his muſic is as harmonious as the ſpheres; ſhall he bring his fiddle, Sir, and let you hear him?

Moll. Piſh, the devil I think's in the wench; I'll have no ſcraping here.

Ben. Come a den, ſweet one, let a him ſhew me his voice in an air or ſo, and den I muſt be going.

Moll.

Moll. Well then, *Julio*, ſing the laſt new ſong Mr. *Gamut* taught you.

Julio. So me will as well as me can.
(*Bows and ſings.*)

AIR IX. The laſs of *Paty*'s mill.

If in ſoft bliſsful eaſe,
Thro' life's ſhort courſe you'd move,
To be the lord of peace,
A ſubject be to love:
For love it is alone
Can laſting joys unfold;
'Tis love's the wond'rous ſtone
That all things turns to gold.

Ben. (*pulling out his watch, and laying it on the table.*) 'Tis a widin five minutes of my time, and I have appointed to meet Deputy *Treacle* the ſugarbaker, about a concern of ſome touſand pound; I am obliged to go to *Richmond* in the evening, but I ſhall be to town again to-morrow, and ſhall ſtay here de reſt of de week —— ha! what is dis?

(*takes up a ſnuff-box off the bed.*

Julio. O la! 'tis Mr. *Spruce*'s ſnuff-box.

Ben. O you ſtrumpet, you cockatrice, I will turn you out of doors this minute, you grand-daughter of de devil; (*goes to draw his ſtilletto.*) no, I will act like a true *Portugueſe.*

Moll. And I like a true *fille de joie.* (*knocks him backwards, ſnatches the watch off the table, throws the tea-kettle at the black boy, and kicks the things into the middle of the room.*) (*Exit* Julio *crying* me a ſcalled, me a ſcalled.) Ben Iſrael *ſtrives to get up,* Moll *keeps her hand upon his throat, till* Alice *takes a bundle out of a drawer; then*

Moll

Moll *and* Alice *run out, and seem to lock the do after them.*

Scene shuts; Ben Israel *is heard within, crying Murder, Thieves, Whores, Devils, Witches, Murder, Thieves, &c.*

End of the first Act.

ACT II. SCENE I.

TIME-TELLER.

LOve, mighty love can wond'rous matters do,
Maids are soon smitten when spruce lovers woo;
Pleas'd with the face and figure of the man,
His fortune or his worth they never scan,
But take a coxcomb, tho' not worth a groat,
If smartly powder'd in a tawdry coat.
Nay, widows too, who've broke the marriage chain,
Are often mad to have it on again:
If wealthy left by some departed fool,
Until again she's coupled never cool:
On lusty youths she looks with longing eyes,
And chuses, like a butcher —— by his size.
At last once more the wedding yoke's put on,
And by the help of money ——— she's undone.
But stranger still! even damse's o'th' common
Are still in this respect like better women;
And tho' with all the other sex they rove,
Yet on some bully fix peculiar love;
And for his sake with unrelenting mind
Jilt, cozen, cheat, and ruin all mankind;

While

While he perhaps, to her own maxims true,
Strips her —— and has another girl in view.
So *Molly* from her *Hebrew* keeper fled,
To take beau *Spruce* the easier to her bed;
By whom she's treated -- much at the same rate,
Beguil'd and bubbled to a wretched state;
Falshood on falshood waits -- in each degree,
And vice will still its own chastiser be,
As in the coming scene you'll quickly see.

SCENE II.

An ordinary room all over litter'd, Moll *sitting in dishabilee.*

Moll. My head akes. —— I am so dry I don't know what to do. —— This is a cursed life. — After venturing soul and body for a couple of guineas, to let *Spruce* wheedle me out of them! —— I deserve to be hang'd to be sure; but what signifies thinking? —— If I muse much longer, I shall do it in earnest. —— Here, *Alice*!

Alice. [from within.] Coming, coming, madam.

Moll. La! this wench, though she has lived with me so long, answers for all the world as if she'd never been out of an alehouse.

Enter Alice.

Moll. Do, *Alice*, get me a farthing's worth of small Beer.

Alice. As I hope to live! we ha'n't a farthing in the world.

Moll. La! what shall we do for breakfast?

Alice. Indeed I can't tell, and I'm sure I'd do any-thing to get a dish of tea.

Moll. [takes a little bottle from under the bed, holds it up.] What, the dram out too! [sighs.]

[ſighs.] then I'm quite undone. —— Dear *Alice*, think how we ſhall get ſome tea and a half-pint.

Alice. Why, may I be a maid again, if I know how that's to be done!

Moll. What! have you quite loſt your credit at Mrs. *Doubleſcore* the chandler's?

Alice. You know as well as I we owe the woman ten ſhillings, and that for theſe three weeks we have fetched all our things from Mr. *Shortweight*'s, in the next court.

Moll. Why can't you have a breakfaſt of him then?

Alice. Ods-fiſh! we are in his debt above two ſhillings, and he has made a ſolemn oath never to truſt any-body to the extent of half-a-crown.

Moll. La! I ſhall go mad; I muſt have a breakfaſt, ſo I muſt, if I turn out naked at night.

[Alice *goes near her, and pulls down her ſhift ſleeves.*

Alice. Why, theſe are pretty clean, you may go out well enough without ruffles; I'll carry them to mine aunt's over the way, and get eighteen pence.

Moll. Do, do then; —— and d'ye hear, bring in a pint of citron. [*Exit* Alice.

Moll. What ſhall I do 'till ſhe comes again? if I think, I ſhall run diſtracted. —— I'll ſing *Jenny Tattle*'s ſong, that Lord *Littlewit* admires ſo much. (ſings.)

AIR

AIR X. The bonny grey-ey'd morn.

In Autumn, *when the clouds are moist with rain,*
The gaudy glitt'ring bow aloft is seen;
Its varied hue delights the gazing swain,
Where purple's mix'd with red, and that with green.
With it in lustre bright may woman vie,
In all the pomp of youth and beauty gay;
A while the lovely form attracts each eye,
Then like the painted cloud it fades away.

[*Re-enter* Alice *with a pat of butter upon a piece of paper, a roll, a broken sugar-dish with sugar, and a little paper of tea in it.*

Moll. O la! *Alice*, where's the bottle, where's the bottle?

Alice. Never fear my forgetting that (pulls it out of her pocket) I went to Mr. *Limbeck*'s for this, and you know it was proper to hide it, for fear the chandler-woman shou'd make a noise.

Moll. Well, good now give me a dram, I'm restless when I'm sober. [*Alice* looks about.]

Alice. La! I can't find the dram-cup, madam.

Moll. Here! here! take any-thing [gives her a water-glass without a foot, *Alice* fills a little in it] a drop or two more —— a little higher; —— nay, *Alice*, don't grudge it me. [she fills it almost up to the top.]

Alice. I am deadly afraid it will do you hurt, you know *Sukey Skuttle* killed herself with it.

Moll. [taking it from her] Prithee don't tell me melancholy tales [drinks it off] —— So! I hope this will give me ease.

Alice. Why, if you had told me you had the belly-ach, I would have fetched cholic water.

Moll. The belly-ach, fool! no, but I had the heart-ach,

heart-ach, and that is ten times worſe.

Alice. Now you talk of the heart ach, I'll tell you what paſſed here yeſterday morning. —— You know you lay out becauſe it was the day you appointed ſome duns to come.

Moll. Alack-a-day! poor *Alice!* well, and what did they ſay?

Alice. Why, it was about nine a-clock, and I was juſt up, when d'ye ſee, up comes a man, and thunders at the door as if he'd knock it down; who ſhould it be but Mr. *Skinflint*, the tallyman. What, is not your miſtreſs at home? [ſays he] No [ſays I] I did not think ſhe would have uſed me at this rate [ſays he again] but tell her from me, that if I don't hear from her next *Monday* to ſome purpoſe, I will ſpeak to Mr. *Courthand*, the attorney of the *Pou'trey*, to get her nap'd, for I hear ſhe plies in the city lately. So down ſtairs he went, muttering and curſing all the way.

Moll. Well, we are rid of him 'till *Monday* then.

Alice. Ay, but he was ſcarce gone down ſtairs, before comes *Tom Pledge*, the pawn-broker's man, to tell you that Mr. *Ben Iſrael* had been with a warrant to ſearch their houſe for two diamond rings and a gold ſnuff-box, and ſaid as how his maſter would tell him where you lodged, if you did not come down a guinea, and conſent to let him ſell the things.

Moll. Well, I hope you were at quiet all the reſt of the day.

Alice. No but I wa'n't; in half an hour's time who ſhould knock at the door but Mrs. *Tawdry*, that ſells the ſecond-hand cloaths; ſhe ſwore you ſhould not trick her, as you did Mrs. *Bobbin*, the lace-woman; if you had quitted your lodgings, she'd send *Tom Warrant*, the Marshal's-court officer, after ye. *Moll Hackabout* should get nothing by tricking of her.

Moll. A saucy jade —— *Moll Hackabout!* marry come up, how great we are grown since Mrs. *Flimsy*, my lady duchess's woman, has trusted us to sell her cast-off cloaths. —— Well, but did there come any more?

Alice. More! no, there had not need; by this time I had hustled on my cloaths, and away I popped to *Jenny Gigget's*; there we had three salt herrings between us, and two quarts of small beer; so I sat there 'till it was near dark, and then I came home and went to bed, because I had neither fire nor candle to sit up by.

Moll. Good wench, put on the water; we'll have a week's good living, I am resolved on't.

Alice. I am glad to hear that, but how shall we come by it?

Moll. Why, we'll melt *Ben Israel's* watch; the gold on't will sell, I warrant you, for four or five pounds —— where did you hide it, *Alice*?

Alice. Why you know I put it into the hole in the bedstead. (Moll *goes to the bed, and pulls it out; hangs it upon her finger, and looks at it.*)

Moll. Well, I protest it is a wondrous pretty thing; I can hardly find in my heart to part with it.

Alice. Can you find stomach good enough to eat it, or is it grown so bad that you can live by looking at it?

Moll. Neither, but we'll lay it down till after breakfast, and then ——

A noise without; Tom Pledge, *is this the door? ay, ay, break it open, break it open.*

SCENE

SCENE III.

The door flies into the room, enter Tom Pledge, *two constables, three or four assistants, followed by Justice* Mittimus, *Mr.* Ben Israel, *and Mr.* Fingerfee, *the justice's clerk.*

Pledge. There *(pointing to* Moll) that's *Moll Hackabout*, and this is her maid *Alice.*

Ben. Dis is my watch; I vil swear dat, Mr. Justice, before the whole bench *(takes up the watch.)*

Justice Mittimus *sits down in a chair, the constables bring* Moll *and* Alice *before him, the clerk takes his book out, pulls a pen out of his hatband, and dips it into the thumb bottle of ink that hangs at his button.*

Fing. Sir, Sir, shall their commitment be to *Newgate* or *New-Prison?*

Just. To neither till I hear the charge —— where is Mr. *Ben Israel?* [*They look ab ut.*

Fin. I suppose he is gone home with his watch.

Just. If he is, I suppose these women won't charge him with stealing it, and if there is no oath against them, I can only send them to *Bridewell*, as persons of ill fame—— so do you hear? *(to the constables)* take them away.

Moll. Good your worship, consider I am a very young woman; have pity on me.

Just. If I were sure you deserved it I would, but the character I have heard of you is such, that I take a month's confinement to hard labour to be a reprieve for so long a time from the gallows. You are a young woman it is very true, but an old offender, and therefore in pity to honest people, it is my duty to bind up

 your

your hands from hurting them further, at least for some time ——— take her away.

[*they carry her off.*

Justice. (*sighing.*) She's a very pretty girl; I had much ado to maintain my magisterial gravity in committing her. (*Exit.*

Mr. Fingerfee *solus.*

La! if it had been but my good luck to have lived with what the folks call a trading justice, of but half the business of my master, what a rare time I had had on't; but here, where I am allowed to take nothing but my due, I have much ado to live, at least in a manner I call living. This honour is a damn'd qualification in a master, would mine were rid on't!

(*Exit singing.*

AIR XI. Old Sir *Simon* the king.

The trickster who deals still in law
Looks well both in person and face,
And the parson's as smart as a beau,
Who picks up his living by grace.

'Spite of honour that makes such a rout,
The soldier's both ragged and thin;
His silver's all tarnish'd without,
And the devil a penny's within.

SCENE IV.

TIME-TELLER.

Alas, poor *Molly!* is it come to this!
How fleeting is the course of lawless bliss!
But twice twelve months have flown since you became
The common mistress of each roving flame.

At

At first your charms endear'd you to the sight,
Then were your days of unrestrain'd delight:
Now by misconduct comes a fatal turn,
Expos'd to labour, infamy, and scorn!
The sequent scene will shew what jailors are,
And how the wretches fare beneath their care;
How they contrive to pass th' uneasy time,
And curse the punishment, but not the crime.

SCENE V.

An outward room of the lodge in Bridewell.

Rusty *and his Man* Flogwell.

Rus. I never knew times so bad, since I have had to do with the prison; people are so bare, that they have nothing to be wronged of. —— Most of the poor devils that come here have scarce rags to their backs, and though I think I know the art of squeezing as well as most of my brethren, yet I have much ado to keep my chaise and pair out of the profits. ——— 'Gad I wish the great folk would do something to make times mend, o' my conscience I believe most of my customers will grow honest by force, for want of having something to lay their hands on.

Flog. Ay, as you say, Sir, these are sad days; time was when *Jenny Filch* has brought me home half a dozen silver snuff-boxes of a morning, but now 'tis odds if she get any thing better than horn or japan'd iron; a tortoise-shell with a silver rim is a kind of a miracle; and then for the criminals, I ha'n't had three for these six weeks, who have given me a penny to be favoured in their lashing, and yet I am obliged to use them very gently, for fear of wearing my whip out.

Rus.

Ruf. Well, comfort thyfelf, dear *Bob*, there's to be a great meeting next week, of the chiefs of our fraternity, to confult ways and means for promoting imprifonment, and raifing double fees, without falling foul on the letter of the law.

Flog. Ay! that's a fine project indeed; I know a 'fquire in the *Temple*, will tell you how near you may tread with fafety in an inftant.

Ruf. I'll juft ftep as far as Juftice *Bindover's*, and be here again in an inftant; be fure you take care of the gate, and fee that *Moll Termagant's* fpark don't get in here again. (*Exit.*

Flog. So, till he comes back again, I'm fole monarch of thefe regions: I'll go in prefently, and chufe me a doxy; if fhe isn't as willing as I, I'll ravifh her; and if any words fhould be made of that, fwear I only knock'd her down as fhe was attempting to make her efcape, and there's an end of the matter: ——'tis here as 'tis all the world over, power does any thing.

AIR XII. The Abbot of *Canterbury.*

Since the laws come from power, then grant it we muft
Whatever power does is lawful and juft:
For juftice to it muft owe its free courfe,
And ftatutes are trifles, if not back'd by force.

Derry down.

So monarchs, if once we difpute their defire,
Strait argue with cannon, and anfwer in fire:
Hence I with my whip make my fubjects be ftill,
And govern by law——that is, by my will.

Derry down.

A

(*A loud knocking at the gate.*)

Flog. S' fish! what have we here?

(*Opens the gate.*)

Enter the Constables and their Assistants with Moll *and her Maid.*

Con. Here we have brought you a first rate madam; 'gad, she'll be a sweet penny to you, I warrant.

Flog. Not a penny the better for her fine cloaths: we had a sharper brought in last night dizen'd out in a blue silk coat, black velvet waistcoat and breeches, with a pair of faded scarlet stockings on with silver clocks, which he was forc'd to pawn to the woman at our tap to pay his garnish.

Moll. (*aside to* Alice.) Oh, what a new misfortune's this! by his dress and his poverty, I dare say it's Captain *Spruce.*

Alice. Nothing more likely; I wish old *Nick* had had him when I first saw him: we might have liv'd still in the old *Jew*'s lodgings, and roll'd in money, if you had not been such a foolish creature as to be fond of that incorrigible rascal, the cast-off pimp of Col. *Goatish*, and the new-receiv'd puff to the gaming-house by *Covent-garden.*

Moll. How now! who is it you talk to in such terms? insult me in my misfortunes, hussey, and I'll fell you to the ground.

Flog. (*takes her by the arm.*) Come, woman, none of your sawcy airs here; commitments make all equal, and if that wench was your maid

maid elsewhere, she may be strong enough to be your mistress here: let's see, can you tip us an ounce now for civility? come down, Madam, come down.

Moll. As I hope to live I have nothing about me! but I have sent to Mrs. *Lurewell*, as we came along; and I'm sure she'll be so good as to relieve me.

Flog. Well, Mr. Constable, if this affair turns out any thing handsome, we'll not forget you.

(*Exit* Constable.

And so you are one of Mother *Lurewell*'s children, hey! (*chucks her under the chin.*) this night-gown of yours will fetch money, (*taking it up, and looking at it.*) has it ever been scower'd, *Moll*?

(*turning to* Alice.

Alice. Her name's *Moll* indeed, but my name's *Alice*: you had best take the gown for your garnish, for I don't think she has any thing else about her that will yield it.

Moll. O you traiterous slut! —— I shall find a time to be revenged on you, —— I shall, you Minx you.

Alice. Why you talk the language of *Billingsgate* as well as if you had been got in an oyster boat, born in a night-cellar, and been bred up at a fish-stall. I warrant you expected I should have treated you with ceremony for bringing me to *Bridewell*, did ye? but you're mistaken; confinement, as my master says, makes us all equal; egad, I'll make you know it.

AIR

AIR XIII. Ye Commons and Peers.

It's needless to flout,
And make such a rout,
As if you were somebody now;
You're sure grown a fool,
Or confoundedly dull,
To hope for respect now you're low.
Fa, la, la.

There was time I allow't ye,
I thought it my duty,
To shew you submission profound;
But fortune that jade
Us equal has made,
By throwing us both on the ground.
Fa, la, la.

Flog. I fancy you'll change your tone, good woman, bye and bye —— come, get you in to the rest to work; I'll fit you with a block presently.

SCENE VI. *draws and discovers several Malefactors beating hemp, amongst whom 'Squire* Spruce *in a very dejected condition; as soon as* Moll *enters, the rest fall to whooping and hallooing.*

1st Wo. Hy! you *Doll Diver!* can you tell who this fine Madam is, that's come to work hard at her last necklace here?

2d. Wo. Not I truly; I suppose she's some whore of quality or other.

3d. Wo. O la! it's the famous *Moll Hackabout*, that robb'd the old *Jew*, and her maid *Alice*, one

one of the ſurviving concubines of *Jonathan Wild*.

1ſt. Wo. Do, Mr. *Flogwell*, let's huſtle her; I long to ſtrip one of theſe fine fowls of their feathers.

Flog. Mind your work, you toad, do.

(*gives her a ſtrap croſs the ſhoulders.* (*turning to* Moll.) Come, come, miſtreſs, you muſt not ſtand idle; (*places a block next to* Spruce, *lays hemp on't, and gives her a hammer; ſhe ſeems to weep.*) nay, blubbering ſignifies nothing: let's ſee how you can thump, if not, I muſt lay on you. (*lifts up his rattan, ſhe beats aukwardly*; Alice *laughs.*) I fancy I ſhall ſpoil your mirth. (*gives her two or three ſmart blows on the ſhoulders, then ſets a block before her.*) let's ſee now whether you can do it any thing handier, Mrs. *Malapert*, or I ſhall let you blood in the back. (*ſhe thumps ſturdily.*)

1ſt. Wo. I hope, Mr. *Flogwell*, you have got money for the garniſh.

Flog. Not I, ſhe ſays ſhe has not a penny.

2d. Wo. Hang her, let's take her gown then.

Moll. Pray, good women, have pity on me, I never ſaw ſuch a place before: I have ſent to an acquaintance, who I'm ſure will ſend me money.

3d. Wo. Hang your ſendings; we'll have it now, or ſtrip you to the ſkin.

Omnes. Strip her! ſtrip her!

Enter a Porter.

Porter. Is one Mrs. *Hackabout* here, pray?

Flog. Yes, what do you want with her?

Porter. I come from a gentlewoman in the New-buildings, ſhe has ſent her this parcel, and

and desires she won't be cast down; for she'll get her out by to-morrow-night.

(Moll *takes the parcel.*)

Moll. Tell her I send her ten thousand thanks; I'm sure it's more than I deserve of her.

(*Exit* Porter.

1st. Wo. I hope the gentlewoman has sent you some money, Madam.

2d. Wo. I can assure you the folks here are very reasonable; you need not beat hemp, if you can afford but a trifle to pay them for your time.

Alice. Heavens send she has sent something, my poor mistress would have broke her heart in this dreadful place.

Flog. I'll make you howl for something, you dissembling toad, I will.

(*gives her half a dozen strokes over the back.*

Moll. O! pray, Sir, don t beat her so hard; if you please to tell me what it comes to, I'll pay both for her and myself.

Flog. Then you must give me half a guinea for your fees, and a crown to excuse you from working, as you are to stay but a night.

1st. Wo. Do, Madam; make it up an even guinea, and Mr. *Flogwell* will let us all play the rest of the day to bear you company.

S. *Sp.* (*hanging down his head.*) Ay, do, good Madam; for my arms are so sore, I can hardly lift them to my head.

Moll. I never was ungenerous when I had it: there, Mr. *Flogwell*, is a guinea; pray let us have a dozen or two of drink to comfort these poor souls.

Alice. Ay, my mistress is all goodness.

1st. Wo. Heavens bless your ladyship!

2d.

2*d. Wo.* Do, Mr. *Flogwell*, let Mr. *Pad* the Highway-man down to ſing the priſon-ſong, we'll bear a chorus; mayhap it may divert the gentlewoman.

Flog. With all my heart——here, *Skip!*

Enter Skip.

Skip. Go tell Mr. *Pad* here's a gentlewoman would be glad to hear his voice; but be ſure take *Surly* with you when you let him down.

3*d. Wo.* Come, Madam, will you do as we do? (*throws down her block, and ſits upon it, the reſt do ſo too.*

Flog. I'll order a chair to be brought you preſently.

Alice. Pray order another for me.

Flog. Yes, to be ſure, Mrs. Impudence.

(*Enter* Skip *and* Surly *leading in* Pad, *a fellow following 'em with two great flaggons of drink.*)

Skip! fetch a chair for the gentlewoman out of the parlour, and another for me; —— the folks here, I think, Mr. *Pad*, want you to ſing the priſon-ſong; and becauſe I have a reſpect for gentlemen of the road, I order'd you to be let down.

Moll. I fancy you had beſt drink firſt, Sir.

Pad. I thank you, Madam —— (*drinks.*

1*ſt. Wo.* Now the ſong!

2*d. Wo.* Ay, ay, the ſong.

Pad. Well, have patience a little, good folks; hem! hem!

AIR

AIR XIV.

Ye ladies of Drury *attend,*
And listen a-while to my song;
For when all our money we spend,
A padding you send us along.

If money we meet with you're kind,
If not you deny us your charms:
'Tis poverty, thus we all find,
You fling with disdain from your arms.

This age, sure, is ripe for each vice;
We study new evils each day:
And now we with women and dice
Consume all our life-time away.

Dear Moll, *I must ask this of you;*
What made you go out of your trade?
You might have been kept by the Jew,
And not have turn'd thief, silly jade.

Altho' you're so fine, master Spruce,
Believe me, you will not live long;
The county will find you a noose,
And Holbourn *afford you a throng.*

But as long as we can let's drink,
And merrily drive away care;
For when we are drunk we can't think
At all of approaching despair.

End of the second Act.

ACT III. SCENE I.

TIME-TELLER.

YOU'VE heard how *Lurewell*'s charity was shewn
In freeing *Molly*, —— next it must be known,
How after this she far'd; — to tell you truth,
The Beldam made the most of *Molly*'s youth:
Expos'd her to each rake who had but wealth,
Until infections vile destroy'd her health;
Then, after twenty quacks had try'd in vain,
By wild receipts, to ease her horrid pain;
At length, as the last point in rotation,
The languid wretch is put in salivation.
Meagre and *Nostrum* both on her attend,
'Tho' fate had certain been from either hand.
Bullets have sometimes miss'd their aim to kill,
But none e'er 'scap'd, if hit by *Meagre*'s pill.
Where *Nostrum* comes, expect expiring breath;
Th' approach of *Nostrum* is th' approach of Death.

SCENE II.

Mrs. Lurewell *and Mrs.* Pimpley *sitting together.*

M. L. Well, to be sure, no woman in *England* ever had such hard luck as I have: it is not above three months ago since I took her out of *Bridewell*, paid all her charges, took her home to my own house, took her up good cloaths, and made her fit company for the best man of quality in *England*; and here she is now in in a ſalivation, ſo bad that there's no expecta-tion of her life: I'm the verieſt toad alive, if I believe ſhe has earn'd me forty guineas ſince ſhe has been in my houſe; and what with the expence of Dr. *Meagre* and Dr. *Noſtrum*, to be ſure, I'm threeſcore pounds out of pocket: beſides, I don't know how many half crowns, crowns, and half guineas, laid out in admirable pills, wonderful bolus's, and never-failing elixirs; which, from the characters I ſaw of them in *Fog's* journal, made me imagine they'd do the work at once. ——— I vow I'm almoſt mad; if I had but five hundred pounds in the world, I'd retire to ſome country ſolitude or other, and give over all thoughts of this world.

Mrs. *Pimp.* (*aſide.*) What would ſhe think on next? ſure ſhe has not the impudence to expect any thing in the world to come.——(*aloud.*) it is but the courſe of things here, Madam; good-natur'd, charitable people are ſure to meet with loſers; I vow, if I did not keep up my ſpirits, (*pulls a dram bottle out of her pocket.*) I believe, as you ſay, I ſhould run diſtracted at the times. (*drinks.*

If, Madam, your ſpirits are failing,
There's nothing, I think, is more handy,
Or any thing ſure more prevailing,
Than drinking a glaſs of good brandy.

M. L. (*taking the bottle.*) Ay, as you ſay, one muſt comfort one's ſelf ——(*drinks.*) but what a ſad thing this is, that this girl ſhould drop off before Ld. *Snuffle* comes to town: his breath ſtinks ſo, and his voice is ſo diſagreeable, that the ladies won't bear him near them; I could have had a couple of guineas a night, for his only talking to *Molly*; his lordſhip being now ſo bad, that he's incapable of doing any thing elſe. And then there was Alderman *Fribble* was ſo taken with her, that I might have had what I would of him: nay, Dr. *Seemboly* would truſt himſelf with no-body but her, for fear of loſing his character. Well, I ſhall be a hundred pounds at leaſt out of pocket by her death.——— (*weeps.*

Mrs. *Pimp.* Good Madam, moderate your paſſion, you ſuffer no more than many other good people do; there's no diſputing with the diſpoſition of things, as father *Scapula* my confeſſor told us, at his laſt lecture; or, as the old ſong ſays.

AIR XV. To all the ladies now at land.

Dame Fortune with unſteady hand,
Doth worldly matters guide;
Her wheel, you know, muſt never ſtand,
But round for ever ride:
Then let not your brave courage die,
One turn from low may raiſe you high.

Fa, la, fa, la, la.

M. *L.* I'm much obliged to you, Mrs. *Pimpley*, for your kind endeavours to divert me; for that matter, I don't want a taſte: when I was a young woman, about ten or a dozen years after the Reſtoration; though I ſay it, there was not a lady of quality in *England* had a better voice, or was more admired for it than I.

Mrs. *P.* I dare ſay you had, Madam, your voice has a peculiar ſweetneſs ſtill; I am prodigious admirer of the tunes made in the days of of King *Charles* II. won't you oblige me with an air? come, it will divert your melancholy.

M. *L.* That's impoſſible; beſides, the loſs of teeth will not permit me.

M. *P.* I warrant you, good madam, try, we are alone, and out of hearing; beſides, I have heard ſome people of faſhion ſay very lately, that you ſung with great judgment.

M. *L.* They did me too much honour, I aſſure you; but however, I'll try. (*ſings.*)

AIR XVI.

Gather your roſe-buds whilſt you may,
For time is ſtill a flying,
And that ſame flower which grows to-day
To-morrow will be dying.

The glorious lamp of heaven, the ſun,
The higher he is getting,
The ſooner will his race be run,
And nearer is to ſetting.

That age is bleſt that is the firſt,
Whilſt youth and blood are warmer,
But being fled, grows worſe and worſe,
And ill ſucceeds the former.

Then be not coy, but ſpend your time,
And whilſt you may, go marry,
For having once but loſt your prime,
You may for ever tarry.

[*While ſhe ſings,* Pimpley *turns the ſtone of a ring outwards, and plays it ſo as to make her obſerve it.*

M. *P*. Well, I proteſt 'tis very fine, the moral is exceeding good.

M. *L*. You're very obliging, madam, —— pray let me ſee that ring, it's a mighty handſome one.

M. *P*. Ay, it is ſo; I had it of a nobleman's caſt-off miſtreſs; I'm to borrow five guineas on't in the afternoon; the fool won't take more, though ſhe wants it; yet I dare ſay ſhe'll let it be ſold, for the want of paying the intereſt.—— But, good madam, how does your niece do? I hope my lord duke's as fond of her as ever.

M. *L*. I can't ſay truly but he is. I have very little money, heaven knows! but if you pleaſe, I'll venture the money you talk of on the ring, and if ſhe does not redeem it, I'll make you a preſent of a guinea for the bargain; I dare ſay it's worth thirty pounds.

M. *P*. Alack-a-day! how your ladyſhip wrongs your judgment! a diamond of that bigneſs worth but thirty pounds? I dare ſay I could ſell it for fourſcore.

M. *L*. Hardly for ſo much, —— but I'll go fetch you the gold. [*Exit*.

Pimpley *ſola*.

Well, I ha'n't loſt my labour I find; the ring conſidering the extraordinary niceneſs in its ſetting, coſt me thirty ſhillings; and to ſay truth, the middle one is the fineſt *Briſtol* ſtone I ever ſaw; I dare ſay it will never ſee the ſun again, 'till the old carrion dies herſelf: Well, flattery is a fine thing, it will ſooner help one to five guineas than charity to five farthings.

AIR XVII. Dame of Honour.

In these blest days, through stronger wit,
Our fathers ways despising,
To virtue all pretence we quit,
For easier arts of rising.
A smooth address we only prize,
'Tis this gains on ev'ry donor,
And he who enjoys it is sure to rise,
Tho' void both of worth and honour.

Re-enter Lurewell.

M. *L.* Well, you're of a happy temper (*gives her the money.*) a twelvemonth is the time I'll keep it; if I have not the money before, it's mine.

M. *P.* Yes, madam, I dare say no-body will take it from you.

M. *L.* But won't you walk to t'other end of the house, and see poor *Molly*; I know you're a judge of such matters, perhaps she may not be in altogether as much danger as we think her.

M. *P.* I'll attend you, madam.

M. *L.* Come this way then.

They go as it were backwards, the Scene draws and discovers Moll's *room; she sits covered from sight by a screen, three women attending her;* Alice *leaning over the screen, and Dr.* Nostrum *writing upon a little stool.*

M. *L.* Is there any hopes, Doctor? (*he does not seem to mind her.*) d'ye think it's possible for her to do well, Sir?

Doct. If she does it's a miracle; I never knew any-body hardly do well, after *Meagre* set his foot within the room.

M. *P.*

M. *P.* La! I thought he had been a great physician. (Nostrum *smiles disdainfully.*

1st Wo. But, Doctor, is there no hopes?

Nost. Am I any judge of your hopes? you may hope or not hope, just as you please.

2d Wo. But we mean, is there any room to hope?

Nost. I have sent for another Pot of my Elixir; if that does not do, nothing will; I will venture to assert she is past curing by physick, and incapable of relief, though attended by the whole college.

3d Wo. Ah! poor soul! she's in sad agonies; well, this chawing flannen is the devil of a remedy; I'd go to the grave rotten, before I'd take a grain of this same Marcry; I have known at least half a dozen of our profession die on't.

1st Wo. Ay, they may say what they will, but Doctor *Anodyne* for my money; 'gad he's the cheapest physician in town: I bought but six pennyworth of his purging sugar-plumbs, and they scower'd me so effectually, that I was hardly able to walk about house for two or three days.

Nost. Heaven help the ignorance of these poor creatures! how should a graduate physician like me get into practice, when such illiterate quacks as she speaks of, and that outlandish emperick *Meagre* run away with every-thing.

2d Wo. Why, for all you, Sir, I have known Doctor *Meagre* do great cures; he freed a gentleman's son in our neighbourhood of this distemper in three week's time; 'tis true he died four months after that of a consumption, but what was that to the Doctor?

Nost. Nay, as you say, nothing at-all, if he was but paid.

M. *P.*

M. *P.* Methinks it would be more proper for us to remove into another room; we certainly disturb this unhappy woman, and she does not seem to be in a condition very capable to bear it. (*Dr.* Nostrum *rises to go away.*

M. *L.* Nay, good Doctor, go with me into the next room; I want to consult you a little.

The Scene shuts, the Doctor, Mrs. Pimpley, *and Mrs.* Lurewell *come forward.*

M. *P.* Perhaps you did not think it convenient to say so much before the poor woman; be so good as to tell us true, Doctor, what you think of her case.

Nost. Truly I think she will not get over it; there's no disease in the world so fatal as *Meagre's* pills: I wonder some method is not taken to prevent credulous people from being poisoned with impunity.

Enter Meagre.

M. *L.* Oh! here is the Doctor.

Mea. Vel, how do de young gentilvoman?

M. *P.* In troth, Doctor, we all think as bad as can be.

Mea. Halas, poor voman! I feared so much; vel, heaven deliver us from the pox and from pockey doctors.

Nost. A very good prayer truly, since she was poisoned by your pills.

Mea. Morbleu, poisoned by my pills! Sacrament! murdered by your Electuare.

Nost. I despise your insinuations, I can have numbers of substantial citizens round *Bow-church* to testify the efficacy of my medicine.

Mea. Begar, me have cura half de quality of t'oder end of de town.

Nost. But they wo'nt come to your reputation.

Mea. Assurement but dey vill——why not?

Nost.

Nost. Becauſe two thirds of them are dead of your cure.

M. *P.* O fie, gentlemen, do not fall into a paſſion; conſider how much your quarrel will affect the credit of the faculty in general.

Mea. Begar, me value no the faculty one ſtraw; I have one ſon at home, a littel boy, who know more *Greek* and *Latin* than half of them, tho' he was taught it by one who remarkable at de Univerſity for not underſtanding it himſelf.

Nost. Your ſon and yourſelf are impoſtors alike, and he knows as little of the languages as you do of phyſick.

Mea. Begar you are one lying *Engliſh* quack.

Nost. You're an impudent, ignorant, pretending, foreign ſcoundrel.

Mea. You lie, you lie, you lie. (*offers to draw.*

Noſtrum *takes out his ſnuff-box, goes cloſe up to him, and throws it all in his eyes.*

Nost. I believe I have diſarmed you.

Meagre *ſtamps with his feet, roars, and endeavours to pull out his ſword;* Pimpley *and Mrs.* Lurewell *hold him.*

Mea. Let a me go, let a me go, I am enrage; morbleu! I will put a de medicaſtor to death.

Nost. That you can't do, while I avoid your phyſick. (*Exit.*

Meagre *breaks from them, and they all run out.*

SCENE III.

TIME-TELLER.

Poor *Molly* having now giv'n way to fate,
The Bawd reſolves to bury her in ſtate:
Prodigious kindneſs this —— perhaps you'll ſay;
But mark who 'tis muſt the expences pay.

A

A contribution of the ſiſterhood
Is rais'd on a deſign ſo wond'rous good.
'Tis done. - Each damſel with a good-will gave it,
For wh—— are mighty generous when they have it.
Diſtreſs'd and poor ſhe yeilded her laſt breath,
But pomp attends her now ev'n aft r death.
Strange friendſhip this--or rather a ſtrange claim
Of ſelfiſh vanity to friendſhip's name.

SCENE IV.

Draws, and diſcovers a large room, in which Mrs. Lurewell, *Mrs.* Pimpley, *and three or four other women are ſitting, dreſſed in mourning, and handkerchiefs at their eyes; a parſon at one corner of the ſtage ſitting by a plump well-looking girl of the town; an undertaker paſſing to and fro fitting their gloves, while* Alice *ſtands weeping behind, with a bottle and glaſs in her hand.*

M. *P.* Well, ſince we ſhall never ſee poor *Molly* again, why ſhould we ſuffer ſorrow ſo much to affect our hearts? poor girl! ſhe was of a merry diſpoſition, and I'm ſure, if ſhe knows any-thing in t'other world, would be ſatisfied with the care that's taken to bury her ſo handſomely, without the addition of ſuch a vain and extravagant ſadneſs.

[*Turns to Mrs.* Lurewell.

Come, chear up, madam.

M. *L.* It is true, I am under the heavieſt affliction imaginable for the loſs of the poor young creature; I proteſt I thought I ſhould have died this morning, for not being able to reſiſt my curioſity, I got Mr. *Smallcorps* to unſcrew the

the coffin, that I might have a last view of her before ſhe was put into the ground; and believe me, her complexion was ſo fine, and the air of her features ſo little alter'd, that if ſhe had recover'd, I'm perſuaded ſhe would have been worth five hundred pound a year to me, and the very thought of her untimely death had almoſt ſent me to the ſame place with her.

[*1ſt Woman whiſpering one of her companions.*

1ſt Wo. What a ſad old beaſt this is; why ſhe is worſe, *Sukey*, than Mother *Cartiey*, that put Colonel *Hackum* when he was drunk to bed to a dead woman, and reckoned him two guineas the next morning for his night's lodging.

2d Wo. Really, Mrs. *Lurewell*, you had great occaſion to grieve for the loſs you have had; — for my part, I am ready to break my heart for poor *Molly*, though I never ſaw her but twice in my life, once at a play with an *Iriſh* lord, and another time at the Baronet's near *Bloomsbury-ſquare*, who, though near ſeventy, has always a company of pretty girls to divert him after ſupper.—— So that my ſorrow is perfectly diſ-intereſted, for you know we may all come to the ſame fate, and it's fit we ſhould do as we would be done by; 'gad I'd have gone without a dram for a week, but I'd have ſaved half-a-guinea towards burying her handſomely.

3d Wo. Well, this is a melancholy ſcene! — my ſiſter *Slylook's* died but a quarter of a year ago —— and ſince then I was at Mother *Burley's* funeral, who broke her heart on her ſtanding in the pillory for keeping a diſorderly houſe. — I am ſure I had ſorrows enough to have kept me away, but as *Jenny Jilflirt* ſays, no-body knows whoſe turn's next. (*ſighs.*)

[Mr. Smellcorps, *the undertaker, comes up to her.*

Mr. *Smell.*

Mr. *Smell.* Madam, will you give me leave to try on your glove?

[*She ſtretches out her arm, and while he is pulling on the glove, ſhe ſinks down in the chair as if in a fit;* Smellcorps *lifts her up in his arms.*

She's a ſweet pretty creature, and wondrous good-natured I perceive; 'gad I fancy one of my ten ſhilling mourning-rings would tempt her; la! how ſhe pants.

[*The reſt of the company croud round them, ſhe takes the opportunity to pick* Smell-corps's *pocket of his watch, and with much difficulty is brought to herſelf.*

M. *L.* Here, *Alice!* bring the poor gentlewoman a glaſs; a drop or two of ſpirit of clary will revive her —— how is it, ſweet one? (*aſide.*) 'gad if I could get her, ſhe'd make me amends for the loſs of *Molly*; it run in my head I ſhould make ſomething of this burial.

[*The woman ſlides the watch to* Alice.

3*d Wo.* (*aſide.*) Be ſure you lay that by ſafe.-- So! I am pretty well come to myſelf now; I'm ſorry I have given you all this trouble.——

(*The women compliment her in dumb ſhew, and then go to their ſeats.*

M. *Smell.* Come, ladies, I think 'tis time to be going; I'll ſtep in, and put things in order, and then bid my men light away. (*Exit.*

(*The parſon having been all this while whiſpering to the woman next him, now riſes and addreſſes himſelf to the company.*

Parſon. Sweet ſiſters, why ſhould ye ſuffer the moth of ſorrow to prey on the lovely contexture of your delicate complexions? or why ſhould ye be overwhelmed with trouble at the ſight of what all your care could not prevent, nor even those precious tears recall! beauty, charming as it is, like all worldly things is frail, and quickly fades away. 'Tis true that the crimson of the rose, and the milky whiteness of the lilly adorned the countenance of our deceased sister; but alas! do not roses and lillies themselves shrink and die away? why then should we wonder that they no longer bloom on her face? let not then superfluous grief needlessly distract your heaving bosoms, but let this example of that suddenness, with which female charms pass away, excite ye to make a due use of yours, while ye are yet in your prime.

[*Leers upon the woman by whom he had been sitting,*

1st Wo. (*aside, to her companion,*) who is this hypocrite in a gown?

2d Wo. (*aside.*) why 'tis one Dr. *Smirk*, who was originally toad-eater to a famous mountebank, became next holder-forth in an Anabaptist meeting, fells afterwards to the Muggletonians, and as he is an acquaintance of Mrs. *Pimpley*, is now shrewdly suspected to be a Jesuit, tho' he plays the parson on these occasions.

Enter Smellcorps.

Smell. Come ladies, 'tis time to go.

[*They rise, clap their handkerchiefs to their eyes, and go out in order, sighing, and shewing the utmost marks of sorrow.*

Manet Alice.

Alice. So —— there's an end of my poor mistress: now if I had but a thorough stock of hypocrisy, I should blubber as heartily as the rest. —— Why that I could do upon occasion, but to what purpose should I do it here?

[*takes up a bundle.*

I have

I have made bold with what little my miſtreſs left worth taking, which with Mr. *Smellcorps*'s watch, the woman was ſo good as to ſteal for me, will ſerve to ſet me up in a brandy-ſhop, in *Wapping* ; ſo I'll e'en rub off, while they are all out at the burial.—— I ca'n't ſay 'tis mighty grateful to my deceaſed miſtreſs, or my living benefactreſs ; but 'tis as all the reſt of the world do.

Since honeſty now and compaſſion
Are laugh'd at amongſt the polite,
Why ſhould I maintain an old faſhion,
Or ſet up myſelf for a ſight ?

FINIS.